LOCKED INSIDE

A Fast-Paced Psychological Thriller

MARILYN BENNER SOWYAK

This is a work of fiction. Names, characters, places, and incidents either are the product of the author's imagination or are used fictitiously. Except as listed in the acknowledgments, any resemblance to actual persons, living or dead, events,or locales is entirely incidental.

 Published and printed in the United States of America by Kindle Direct Publishing and IngramSparks Books.

If you have comments or questions, please feel free to e-mail me
@ MarilynBennerSowyak@gmail.com

Please Feel free to visit my website:

Crematorium | Marilyn Benner (marilynbennersowyak.com)

Also By Marilyn Benner Sowyak

Crematorium

Available through Amazon.com and Ingram Sparks Publishing

Carolina's Journey

Available Through Vella Books Online

Coming Soon

Missing Girls

Table of Contents

Chapter 1

Hell Pays a Visit

December 25, 2022—Christmas Day Night

Saint Vincent's Medical Center was the largest hospital in Charlotte, North Carolina, with over eighteen hundred hospital beds. It was the only Level One Trauma Center for over one hundred and fifty miles, serving most of North and South Carolina. Helicopters frequently landed, delivering the most critical patients in the surrounding area. The patients they received were acute, with many lives simply hanging by a thread. Failure to keep patients moving through the system led to chaos. And once it started, it was hard to reign things back in.

Maggie Lee Bennett reported to the Nurse Supervisor's office in the Emergency Department and took a report from the off-going supervisor. She sighed. Three sick calls would make for a stressful night.

After Maggie doctored the assignment sheet, she brushed lint from her black scrubs, noting how much her baby bump seemed to have grown overnight. She was twenty-two weeks pregnant and almost at a safe stage. Maggie was shocked when she found out she was having a baby because she'd been on the birth control pill, taking it diligently, cautiously waiting to have a little one until the threat of the Covid pandemic had subsided. Maggie smiled, kissed her fingertips, and patted her belly.

Maggie would name him after her husband, Kerrington Blanchard, her beautiful, handsome business guru husband. He always looked like he stepped straight off the cover of GQ magazine with his sophisticated high fashion suits and premature silver hair. He was a man who powered over a board room as if he owned it. And, usually, he did. Maggie smiled. She was one incredibly rich and lucky woman. Unfortunately, his fame and massive fortune had led Maggie not to change her name. Her attorneys declared the name Blanchard might set her up for bogus malpractice lawsuits as nurses were being sued more frequently these days.

She scrubbed her hands, loaded them with hospital-grade hand foam, cleaned her stethoscope, and donned a fresh pair of goggles with a new NIOSH mask. It hurt to wear the mask some days as the constant friction of the material against her skin twelve hours a day caused skin irritations. She sighed with great relief. The end of Covid felt so close. So close.

Even though Maggie was fully vaccinated and had high antibodies per lab tests, the hospital barred her from patient contact due to her pregnancy. So, Maggie was confined to the glassed-in part of the nurse's station until she went out on family leave which started after tonight's shift.

As Maggie left the office, she was blindsided by a sudden uncomfortable feeling. A sickening sense of doom she could not shake—like something was going to go seriously wrong. She didn't get the feeling often anymore, but as a child, this type of anxiety was a living, breathing monster. Why would it appear after such a long time? Maggie was living a beautiful happy life.

When Maggie entered the break room, she quickly smiled at her good friends, Benny and Willow Maxwell. Benny was the Chief Tech for the E.R. and was close to college graduation, which would grant him a Registered Professional Nurse license. Willow was already a Registered Nurse, and they made a great couple. Both were of mixed ethnicity—Asian, white, and black. Benny was trimmed from demanding work and donned a braided black ponytail and glasses. He was a star in the E.R. because he was intelligent and reliable, and the nurses and doctors depended on him to get things done—the things others didn't know how to do. Having worked for the hospital since high school, Benny had developed friendships in high places over the years—and as a result, he held tight to his chest some of the hospital's biggest secrets.

Maggie and Benny were close friends and had been so for over a decade. Willow became one of Maggie's best friends two years ago. Benny's cheerful personality, sense of humor, and benevolent strength went well with Willow's intense drive, brilliant clinical skills, and beautiful nature that matched her kind heart.

The two of them had spent the Christmas holidays at Maggie's house—having become tight friends during the serial murder debacle two years earlier. Maggie took a deep breath, glad the memories of the horror she suffered back then were finally fading away. She took a quick look back at the schedule to make sure she had assigned Benny and Willow to different areas due to their relationship. It was a Human Resources policy that they could not work in the same area because they were married. Willow was being forced to transfer from the E.R. soon.

Maggie couldn't help but grin as she looked around the break room. The staff was in full Christmas party mode. The wobbly break room tables were covered with boxes of pizza and homemade desserts and casseroles. Staff had pulled a stretcher into the room and decorated it with party favors. It was tradition. The staff believed if they had to work Christmas night, then they would feast all night long. History proved that every minute they had free tonight, they would be in the break room getting their plates loaded with goodies and eating them in the open-air park just outside the back door. Even the doctors would slip in and out, sometimes lingering to talk, sometimes carrying heaping plates of delicious food.

Betsy Lee, one of the secretaries, wore her famous Santa hat that looked as old and worn as the forty years she had worked in the department. Nurse Eric wore his annual outfit of elf pants with candy cane-colored stockings attached to green curled elf shoes—shoes with small bells that lightly jingled with his every step. Topping his head was a green elf hat. The rest of the staff wore holiday dress-up comprised of decorative tee-shirts, Santa vests, and ugly sweaters. Were they violating the dress code? Clearly, but it was Christmas. She was not going to be a Grinch. They'd been through enough over the past two years with Covid. It was essential for the staff to get happiness in any way they could to heal from the emotional roller coaster ride of so much tragedy they had watched daily throughout their job. After Maggie gave out the assignments, they slipped on their goggles and headed out the door, ready for a long night's work.

At the nurse's station, Maggie smiled as she recalled tidbits of her Christmas morning. Kerrington had given her a hybrid Tesla along with some lovely earrings. Annella Wryn, Kerrington's sister, a hot A-List movie actress, had given Maggie a case of Lamborghini wine before flying out on the studio's private jet to finish her recent film in South Hampton, New York. "We'll drink this together when I return," Annella promised. "Tomorrow, just the two of us will sit around and catch up on our lives. I have so much to tell you." They'd laughed, hugged, and said goodbye, promising to have a wonderful time together when she returned.

Maggie met with Doctor Glenn Sloan; the attending physician assigned to the Critical Bay. She was delighted he was working tonight because Glenn was intelligent and swift and knew how to keep patients moving. Time was always of the essence as the E.R. was constantly overcrowded. Glenn and Maggie had been close friends since the start of his residency almost fifteen years ago. He was now the Medical Director of the Emergency Department. He was a good man, a brilliant doctor, and the patients loved him. The doctors held him in high esteem. Glenn had been to dinner at her house a lot lately. He was a close friend of both Maggie and Kerrington, the latter of whom served on the Board of Directors at the hospital.

Wearing dark blue scrubs with his name initialed in white over the pen pocket, Glenn made his way over to join her in front of the large, brightly colored computer screen hanging on the wall above the main desk. His blond hair, sprinkled with grey, made him look like a leader, which, with his position, was important. Glenn's handsome face held a strong jawline, and the bright lighting in the E.R. showed off his flawless complexion.

They stood at the Census Grid and reviewed all the active E.R. patients. The two of them went over each patient and reviewed the care plan for them—admission, discharge, or observation. She updated him on the hospital bed availability. Maggie was relieved to see there were only nineteen patients left to be treated versus a usual volume of over fifty at this time of night. She hoped the night remained on its smooth sailing course.

Maggie noted Glenn looked super cheerful tonight, and she was happy for him. She smiled at her good friend. The riptide of gossip on the E.R. street was that Glenn had a new love. No one knew who it was, which was odd because everybody in the E.R. was always in everybody's business. But Glenn was super tight-lipped as always when it came to his personal life. Glenn caught her looking at him, and their eyes held for a moment—as if he wanted to tell her something—but he paused, smiled, and returned to the board rounds.

Maggie studied him and whispered. "You're in love." Glenn grinned with a smile. "Shhh."

"Shhh, nothing," she responded in a whispered voice. "Your face is glowing. You've changed like—overnight." Maggie caught his eyes and gasped. "Oh, my gosh! You <u>are</u> in love. And it's serious. It's about time!" Maggie quietly squealed, squeezing his hand.

"Okay." Sloan admitted, grinning. "You got me. We'll talk later. But, not one word, pal."

"I promise," Maggie said. "I'm so happy for you."

IT WAS A HECTIC SHIFT with several gunshot victims. However, by eleven p.m., it was settling down—until Maggie heard a scream coming from the main entrance to the E.R. The sound of the familiar voice brought such intense fear that it caused the hair on the back of her neck to rise. Nausea and the urge to vomit violently swept through her as she looked down the long corridor and wanted to run the other way.

"Maggie, my little tater. It's Mommy. Merry Christmas, baby!" Darlene Sutton, her mother, yelled from across the unit, her arms held out wide in the air, her speech slurred. Her coat was tattered and dirty.

Horror raced through her mind as her safe world shattered before her eyes. Instantly, Maggie's mind catapulted back to childhood, experiencing agonizing emotions as if they were fresh. She felt like a toy top spinning around the floor out of control. Fear tightened her throat as intense shame swept through her. Maggie glanced at the shocked staff staring at her—for good reason.

Her mother's hair was ratted and frizzled, and her exposed skin was filthy, covered with dirty stains over her face, arms, and legs. Maggie was sure her mother stank severely, enough to make staff gag.

Pretending to be in complete control of her senses, she took the report from the medic, whom she also knew well. She was grateful for his kindness and for keeping a professional manner about him—as if they were talking about a stranger. "No ID on her. She looks to be in her 60's. Reportedly hit by a car. The vehicle stopped at a red light. The driver denied hitting her, and witnesses confirmed his story. No visible injuries. She has no complaints other than she's intoxicated and claims she wants to kill herself. She refused vital signs."

Maggie could hear her mother's screams coming from the psychiatric room. "I want to see my daughter," Darlene demanded. When Maggie entered the doorway, Darlene began crying, "My baby. Come here, baby. You're so beautiful. Hug me. It's Christmas." Her mother cried out, reaching for Maggie with her arms outstretched with black filth caked under her fingernails. Nicotine stained the skin of two fingers on her right hand.

"I don't hug you when you're drunk. Did you try to kill yourself?" Maggie asked dryly, arms folded defensively across her chest, her voice stoic and professional, considering her current internal state of emotional disarray.

"I will tell you when you give me a hug."

"That's not happening," Maggie said. She gave the technician orders to put her mother in a gown and place a HUGS bracelet on her. The HUGS bracelet would warn staff if her mother, now considered to be a suicidal psychiatric HOLD patient got too close to a door. Finally, she assigned a sitter to keep her from escaping.

Maggie shook her head in dismay as she left the room, whispering to remind herself. "*Same game, different day. Do not fall into her trap. Don't do it,*" She went straight to her office, locked the door, sat at her desk, buried her face in her hands, and cried her eyes out, hating her mother but loving her simultaneously. It took all she had not to hug her mother because she'd missed her severely. Memories engulfed her heart, some were loving, but most were dreadful and filled her with extreme shame and heartbreak. She vowed never to allow the staff to see her private disgrace. As it was, they would talk about Maggie's mother for weeks or until something new came along to fill the gossip topic. But, if she let them see her emotions, it would take forever to die down. It was one of those things that could quickly kill a manager's career.

After Maggie pulled herself together, she was about to return to the main E.R. when a "Code Elopement" was called over the E.R. speakers. Maggie burst into the Critical Bay to find frenzied staff checking the bathroom, exits, and patient rooms. The Team Leader explained in a frantic voice. "It's your mother. She eloped before we could get the HUGS bracelet on her. She kicked the sitter to the floor and bolted."

Maggie called security to inform them to secure the campus, which was probably too late. He reported they'd do their best, but they were severely short-staffed campus-wide with officers out with Covid.

Finally, when all was said and done, Darlene's elopement from the E.R. was successful, forcing Maggie to notify the police so they could issue BOLO (be on the lookout) announcement over the radios. Last but not least, Maggie filed an Incident Report which would end up before a committee for review. The report would be taken seriously by the upper administration.

BY MIDNIGHT, THE TENSION the E.R. was easing, with most of the patients trying to sleep or begging for discharge. The staff was all relaxing and joking about how it would be peaceful as usual until the bars closed and drunk drivers rolled in, causing chaos until five. Many headed to the break room to binge on the food layout while they could.

When her Charge Phone went off, it was Kerrington; his voice panicked, which was rare. "Annella was severely injured on the movie set. They stabilized her and transferred her here to Doctor Richardson's care. Close to home. The medical jet just landed at the airport, and she is leaving by helicopter now. She'll be coming in through the E.R. I'll be right there."

Maggie notified Glenn about the incoming trauma just as he hung up the medic phone after getting the report. "Let's go. It's a head injury," he said. "Seen at a New York Hospital and transferred here. Must be a local VIP or something."

"It's my sister-in-law, Annella Wryn."

"Annella?" Glenn barely whispered. Maggie watched as the color drained from his face. She knew instantly that Annella was his new love.

"Yes," she confirmed. "It's Annella."

Maggie broke the rules of staying six feet away from patients and stepped into the far corner of the room, away from others but close enough to supervise Annella's nursing care. Glenn, dressed in trauma gear, stood waiting beside Maggie when she received news that there were two choppers on the roof. One was Kerrington's, and the other held Annella's injured body. Since Kerrington was on the Board of Directors for the hospital, he was allowed landing pad privileges.

When Annella arrived in the trauma room on a stretcher, everyone briefly froze, taking in her breathtaking beauty. Her elegant movie wedding gown flowed over the side rails of the stretcher. The sheet under Annella's head and her long beautiful blonde hair were blood-stained. The respiratory therapist disconnected the ambu bag from the endotracheal tube coming from Annella Wryn's mouth and quickly reconnected it to a ventilator.

"Do we cut the dress?" One of the new techs asked, eyes widened with fear, looking at Benny for instructions.

Benny looked astounded. "Do we look like wardrobe folks working on a movie set? Of course, we cut the dress!" Benny pulled out his trauma shears. "She's critical," Benny spouted, directing the rookie techs working under his supervision.

Glenn did his initial assessment and looked over at Maggie. "Get a repeat head CT. I want our own images. She's stable, but I don't like how things look neurologically. There's a brain injury. No other injuries."

Surprising everyone present, Chase Hayworth, Annella Wryn's costar, burst into the room, dressed in a tuxedo. The hot A-list actor was still wearing movie make-up and was undoubtedly the most beautiful man Maggie had ever seen, and it was hard to top Kerrington. Chase's blazing blue eyes shot around the room with such intensity that it looked like he might be able to **fry** people on the spot. His appearance was captivating, and quickly made up for his disrespect.

Chase's bodyguard/handler and personal assistant, Tony Jackson, stood directly behind him, seemingly uncomfortable with Chase's presence in the room. Tony was solid muscle, with blond hair and blue eyes, and had massive shoulders, much like a football player. Maggie read his facial expression, which hinted that Chase's behavior needed handling and that the most significant part of Tony's job—was keeping his inappropriate behavior in line. Annella had spoken about it.

Kerrington entered right behind Chase with Titus Wilkes from Security

"Sir, you can't be in here," Titus ordered. Titus made for an impressive security guard. The big, brawny, black man was a former Green Beret and made for a formidable sight with his solid muscled body, braced and ready to back up his staff, one hundred percent. But Chase didn't flinch. "Don't tell me I can't be in here!" Chase touted loudly. "Annella's my wife! I demand to know what's going on."

All eyes shot at Annella's ring finger, graced with a giant diamond ring. Maggie did a double take, then looked at Kerrington, who held a non-plussed horrified stare. Glenn wore a catastrophic look of shock, clearly cut to the bone by the news.

"How bad is she, doctor?" Chase demanded.

"She has a head injury. We won't know the extent of the damage until she wakes up," Glenn stammered, still in a state of disbelief.

"I thought she was dead," Chase said quietly before leaving the room. "How could she not be dead?"

"What an arrogant ass," Benny touted as he released the brake on the stretcher and pushed the bed out of the room. "He acts like he owns the room and everyone in it."

"Excuse me?" Chase shot back.

"You heard me," Benny replied, glad no one else had caught his rude remark.

Kerrington followed Benny and Annella out into the hall as Maggie and Glenn stayed behind in the trauma room, leaning against the counter, arms folded across their chests. Maggie shook her head sadly. "I'm so sorry, Glenn. Talk about being blindsided. Annella has never mentioned having a relationship with Chase. Again, I'm so sorry."

"Hopefully, her CT will tell us what's going on," Glenn said, trying to act indifferent. "Kerrington is getting her a VIP suite in the ICU. He said he's staying with her whenever possible."

"Sure. Please keep me posted about her results."

"You bet," Glenn replied and walked off. He paused and turned back. "Thank you, Maggie."

Maggie paused, looking at his face. It held such melancholy. "Is there something you need to talk about here? About Annella?"

"Yes," Glenn said, walking back towards Maggie. "She wouldn't have married him. I will stake my life on it. We were getting married. But it was confidential due to some publicity clause in her contract. You catch my drift?" Glenn said, anger flickering across his face.

"I don't think Chase is telling the truth, quite frankly," Maggie said. "A publicity contract would not have kept Annella from telling her brother Kerrington about her wedding plans—better yet, she would have told you. She's that kind of person."

"We had a lot of plans. Things we were going to do when she got home." Glenn said, shrugging his shoulders and lowering his head.

The constant ringing of Maggie's Charge Phone interrupted their private moment. Maggie waved goodbye before returning to her glass-enclosed desk to answer her call.

Moments later, Maggie, careful to follow the rules of no contact with patients, stood at the door entrance where Glenn was putting on his gloves to suture a large knife wound. The patient was wearing prison garb and had a sheriff at the door. "I hate to interrupt you," Maggie announced. "We need you. I have a resident to take over."

Glenn took off his gloves and exited the room bypassing the replacement resident. "The media have arrived in droves," Maggie announced quietly, "And they're waiting outside and asking for a press release. Our Public Relations department requests you deliver it."

"Give me a minute to gather my thoughts and I'll be right out. Come with me?"

"Sure," Maggie replied. As soon as Maggie stepped away from Glenn, Kerrington headed straight for her, wrapping her in his arms. They stood for the longest time, each trying to comprehend how such a beautiful day had turned out so awful.

As Kerrington left to wait for Annella Wryn in the ICU, Maggie struggled to pull herself together. Benny and Willow tried to console her over Annella but failed at their attempt. She sent them both to eat before returning to her supervisor duties.

Not a minute later, as Glenn and Maggie were heading outside to meet with the press, a nurse entered the front door, returning from their meal break. "You guys better get out there. The movie star is a jerk. He's holding a news conference—telling a pack of lies and giving out all the actress's private healthcare information."

Maggie and Glenn rushed outside and interrupted Chase's glorious moment. Bit by bit, the reporters blindsided them with unbelievable questions, and it became clear that Chase had done the unthinkable. He had embellished the story for reporters, telling them Annella was not only in a coma but also suffered from a punctured lung, a liver laceration, and a spinal cord injury that most likely would leave her paralyzed—"if she survives the night."

After displaying a tear-jerking moment of grief, Chase announced their secret wedding had taken place earlier in the day in the same dress she'd worn in their movie. He added that the hospital destroyed the dress and all the precious memories. "Annella loved the gown and wanted our daughter to wear it when she walked down the aisle." Chase was a pretty persuasive actor and had the press eating out of his hand. There was no undoing the falsehoods. After all, when a movie star speaks, the media treats it like God Himself had spoken. Glenn was made to look like an idiot as he tried to undo the movie star's report.

The media was long gone an hour later, following Chase to his hotel. At the nursing station, Maggie muttered *Merry Christmas* to herself as she completed her second Incident Report regarding the inappropriate disclosure of protected health information regarding Annella Wryn.

ALL THE PATIENTS had been transferred to their beds upstairs, and an unusual calm hovered in the air. Maggie looked around and saw Glenn. He was the only person present except for Betsy, the secretary, who was busy tossing clipboards into slots and entering orders into the computer. Maggie looked up at the board census and smiled, happy to see it blank, devoid of patients—noting how rare it was to see an empty critical area. It felt quiet and eerie. Odd. Usually, the area hummed with people, even when they were empty of patients. She assumed the staff was in the breakroom feasting while they could.

Far down the corridor, she saw Willow returning to Critical Bay. Maggie headed over to Glenn. Now was the perfect time to talk with him about Annella.

Everything moved so fast that Maggie could barely comprehend what was happening. A masked man stepped out from a side room directly behind Willow and put a gun to her head. The steel doors closed behind her with a loud resounding lock.

Titus called out on the overhead speakers, "Critical Bay is on **Lockdown**. I repeat Critical Bay is on Lockdown."

Maggie saw Glenn moving her way with an ominous warning on his face just as she felt a cold gun barrel meet her temple, knocking her goggles to the floor.

"Don't move!" A man's voice resounded in her ear. Out of the corner of her eye, she saw Willow being dragged into the medication room at gunpoint. Willow opened the narcotic cabinet and loaded the drugs into a sizeable beige cloth bag held by the robber. Maggie tried to memorize his description, but he was so generic-looking. He was dressed in black with a hoodie covering a fully masked face. Average height. Taller than Willow. Average weight. Bigger than Willow, who was tiny.

Maggie's concentration broke when out of the corner of her eye, she saw Betsy, the secretary, surreptitiously move to push the *secret panic button* that sent a silent call to security for help.

The sound of gunfire exploded in Maggie's ear as Betsy's head spun sideways, spewing blood splatter across the desk. Her Santa hat flew into the air as her body slumped sideways off the chair to the floor. When Glenn reached for the phone, the gun fired again, hitting Glenn in the center of his forehead. His body bounced violently backward as a look of disbelieving shock registered on his face. For what felt like a segment of suspended time, Glenn stood frozen in place before finally collapsing to the ground.

"Give me your phone," the man ordered. His voice was one she would never forget. It was husky with a thick country accent. She could smell the stale odor of cigarettes on his breath. As she turned her head to hand him the phone, his image reflected off the glass wall of room two. He was thin, dressed all in black, including a hoodie and mask. Just like the other man—except he was slim.

Maggie's neck cracked hard as the shooter grabbed her by her ponytail and dragged her down the corridor. She saw Willow being pushed to the Trauma Bay medication room. "If you make even the tiniest wrong move," the man's husky voice warned, "I will shoot you just like I did the old woman."

Tears rolled uncontrollably down Maggie's cheeks when she saw Betsy's face with her eyes holding a dead stare. The large circle of blood on the floor surrounding Betsy's head glistened with the reflection of the Christmas tree lights flickering in the background. Glenn lay breathing with his eyes open, repeatedly blinking, glaring at the ceiling.

The robber who had Willow—dragged her kicking and screaming out of the main E.R. doors. "I have a child," Willow begged. "Please, please let me go. She needs me." Willow reached her hand out to Maggie, flapping it wildly through the air before disappearing around the corner.

The gunman yanked Maggie to the desk and shoved her hard against the floor next to Glenn. "We have control of all the cameras in the E.R. We can see and hear everything you do. You can help the doc, but that's all," the husky voice ordered. "If you try to call for help, we will know it, and we will kill the nurse. Do you understand?"

"Yes. Yes," Maggie promised, bobbing her head up and down in an animated manner that matched the terror she felt inside. She begged. "Please don't hurt her. Please. Please."

"See the clock?" Again, Maggie vigorously shook her head, acknowledging. "In thirty minutes, you can call for help. No sooner."

The man threw Maggie's phone on the counter and backed out of the E.R. with his gun held straight at Maggie until the doors closed behind him. She sat horrified in place, shuddering with terror and unable to move out of fear. Finally, she looked at the clock and turned towards Glenn.

Maggie was shocked. Glenn was conscious and capable of following simple instructions, but he couldn't form words when he opened his mouth and attempted to speak. He looked stunned, like he was struggling to keep his brain functioning. While cleaning and examining Glenn's wounds, Maggie carefully explained what she was doing. Yes, he was a physician, and as such, he certainly knew what she was doing and why—but since the bullet had gone straight through his brain, Maggie wasn't confident that he fully understood.

Several phone calls rang out simultaneously, demanding to be answered. The Medic radio kept going off as multiple medics attempted to give a report and establish their ETA.

"We're at your door and can't get in," one reported. "The door won't open. Is everything all right inside? We've even tried calling on the hard line." Maggie stared at the radio and felt like she was in a suspended state of confused shock—wondering and not knowing—what to do. It was so unlike her. Maggie always knew what action to take. Patients were waiting in the ambulances, but the whole place was a crime scene. And Willow's life was hanging in the balance.

Maggie felt glued to the floor as if her body had grown roots into it. Her heart thudded in her chest as she stared down at Glenn and listened as more phones rang out—sounding like a strange orchestra of harmony playing in the background of a horror movie. Maggie wanted to scream. Glenn looked up at her. His beautiful eyes held hers as if he were saying, *keep it together, girl.*

And she did. The price for answering the radio or phone would be Willow's life. So, she sat listening to the non-stop noise, determined to wait out the ten minutes left to go. Her shaking converted into vibrations running deep through all her muscles. Maggie stared at Betsy—her dead eyes seemed focused on Maggie—making her feel spooked for a split second.

Again, she feared losing her mind. *Get a grip girl*, a voice from inside her demanded. So, Maggie moved her gaze to the clock and concentrated on watching the time pass.

Glenn held his eyes tightly closed as if trying to shut out all the day's memory or possibly the light. Maggie's eyes trailed to the white embroidery on his dark blue scrub. His name was covered in blood.

Chapter 2

The Fallout

Precisely ten minutes later, Maggie dialed 911 from the desk. When the responder came on the line, he asked, "Do you need police, fire, or medic?"

"I believe I might need them all, sir," Maggie replied, thinking about the rest of the E.R. With the doors bolted shut, she had no idea whether there were more victims on the other side or not.

"Can you give me your phone number in case we get disconnected?"

Maggie complied with their order, noting her shaking was returning. She suddenly felt cold.

Her legs became weak, like Raggedy Ann's legs.

"Tell me the reason for your call, ma'am," the responder demanded. Maggie heard a couple of clicks on the line and knew supervisors from all departments were listening.

Maggie could hardly talk as she looked around the E.R., trying to decide where to start. "I'm the Clinical Supervisor for Saint Vincent's E.R. We had a robbery with a shooting. And they took a nurse hostage. One person is dead, and our doctor has a gunshot wound to the head."

"Medic is on the premises," the 911 operator declared. "Medic reports the entrance is locked. Is there an **active shooter** in the E.R.?"

"They left my area. I'm not sure about the other departments. "

"Police and fire are on the way. Is the doctor breathing?"

"Yes. And the doctor has a pulse. He is alert. There may be more victims as we are locked in the main E.R. I don't know what else may have happened beyond the critical area. Other E.R. departments may have been robbed." Maggie's tears flowed silently down her face as she struggled to keep her voice professional. "We are currently a crime scene, so I'm giving formal notice we are closed and request complete diversion of all ambulances until the police give clearance to re-open."

Many more questions came, and Maggie answered them. The responder reported he would stay on the phone with Maggie until she saw the Fire Department—they were on the property. At that moment, Maggie heard the Fire Department calling out, warning that they were breaking the door down.

The smashing against the door was deafening as the heavy steel doors gave in to police and fire assault. Within seconds the E.R. was flooded with police and the SWAT team, holding their weapons out and searching the place like bees buzzing over flowers hunting for pollen. Maggie cried without shame as she yelled out excitedly. "I see them! There are a lot of them. God, thank you." Several officers encircled her for protection as the rest of the E.R. was searched.

"You can hang up now, Ma'am."

"Thank you," Maggie said, weeping with relief as she hung up the phone. The constant police chatter over the rescue radios comforted her as she sank into the closest chair before her legs collapsed beneath her.

"They're gone," Maggie said, watching. "They took one of our nurses. Please hurry. They might kill her," Maggie said as medics approached her. "I'm okay. The doctor is in the room behind me with a gunshot wound to the head." Both paramedics were gone before she could say another word.

Maggie watched, calmer, as the first on-arrival officer ordered the crime scene area to be blocked off around Betsy and the floor surrounding where Glenn was shot. Maggie, feeling dazed, repeated her story to two officers as the rest of the E.R. was blocked off with additional crime scene tape.

When Maggie's phone rang, she heard Greta Jenkins, the Nursing Supervisor, on the other end, huffing and puffing as if she were running. "Is there a disaster going on? I didn't get a call. The entire hospital driveway and surrounding streets are filled with police cars, lights flashing, and at least ten fire engines. Do we have a fire? The alarm didn't go off! Why are so many ambulances here?"

Maggie re-told the story once again. "We need neurosurgery stat for Doctor Sloan. The police will have to unlock the elevator to give them access. Call me when they're ready. Oh, and they'll want a CT of his head. Can you arrange it?" Then she hung up and protectively rubbed her pregnant belly, which ached from the hard fall to the floor. She prayed her baby was okay.

Detective Mark Hanes from Homicide rounded the corner, his eyes immediately surveying the crime scene. Despite the hour, he looked as fresh as he did on any given day. His light brown slacks and the crisp, white, long-sleeved shirt was pressed neatly without a wrinkle, making a great impression. His polished, black leather belt shined in contrast to the gold badge, and his black gun clipped to his trim waist. He smiled at Maggie on his way to examine the scene. After his initial business was taken care of, he went over to Maggie and gave her a big hug of support, having heard what she'd been through. He'd once been her adversary during the serial killer investigation two years earlier when Maggie was initially his suspect. But they were friends now that she was cleared of any wrongdoing. He was a frequent visitor to the E.R.—sometimes, daily, and they often worked together on cases as Maggie was a certified forensic nurse. She looked up at him, unable to respond—her raw emotions close to breaking into sobs again—her sanity barely tethered to a fragile string ready to snap.

"Are you okay?" Hanes asked with genuine sincerity.

"Not really," Maggie replied. "Willow is missing. We have to find her. We didn't give them a reason to kill her. I did everything they told me to do. Exactly like they said. I did!"

"Of course, you did, Maggie. You're that kind of nurse. We will find her."

Maggie heard the loud metal clicking sound at the far end of the main E.R. as the doors unlocked and opened. The staff, wanting to talk with her, was stopped by the police as they rolled crime scene tape from wall-to-wall preventing their entry.

Hanes saw Benny and pointed at him, waving his hand and signaling permission for the officer to let Benny and enter.

"What's happened?" Benny asked, giving the area a quick scan. "Oh, my God! Betsy. What the hell happened? We were locked in the break room. The police just got us out." Benny looked around again. "Where's Willow? She wasn't with us." Maggie looked at Hanes. Hanes stepped over to Benny. Benny moved around him. "Maggie!!! Where's Willow?" Benny raged, his voice all but screaming. The look on his face was one of sheer panic.

"They took her," Maggie stumbled, getting the words out.

"Willow?"

"We were robbed."

"They took her—as in hostage?" Benny asked, practically screaming. "She's been kidnapped? Tell me you're lying—please, Maggie. No. No. Oh my God. No!!!!!" Benny cried, ripping his mask and goggles off, throwing them to the floor. He covered his face with his hands and openly sobbed without shame.

Hanes took over. "Benny. We have every cop in the city on the lookout for her as we speak." Hanes motioned to the chaplain to help him. "I have someone to speak with you and help you deal with what's happened. Unfortunately, this is also a homicide investigation, and I must interview Maggie as soon as possible while things are still fresh in her mind. She's the only witness. I'd rather she not say anything to anyone until I've officially gotten her story."

"Sure. Sure. I apologize. I just can't believe this," Benny said, turning towards Sister Marguerite, who led him away. According to Maggie, the chief nun for the E.R. was one of the most compassionate people on the planet. The Sister had comforted her many times over the years. Maggie wanted to cry for him and hug him as she watched Benny's face wrinkle up with fresh tears. "They took my wife. Lord have Mercy."

Hanes's interrogation held similar undertones to his first investigation of Maggie two years earlier. This time, it was hard to focus because her ears were ringing from the gun firing so close to her ear. She shivered hard as she described it to Hanes because, at first, Maggie thought they had shot her in the head—for a split second, Maggie recalled thinking she was dead. She'd felt relief to discover it was Betsy who had been shot.

The questions felt mundane after a while. Maggie felt like her mind was skillfully and carefully being peeled open to reveal deep memories like one might peel away the layer on an onion to get to the juicy inside.

"Where were you standing?" Hanes asked. "Where was the shooter? Did you get a description? Did you notice the time? What about a description of the person who took the nurse?"

Times seemed to crawl as she answered Hanes' questions. Minutes turned into an hour.

"Did the secretary push the panic button?" Hanes asked, his face curious as he reread his scribed notes from his overly-used leather note pad.

Maggie didn't like the way her friend looked at her. So rigid. Harsh. Severe. It was like she didn't know him. Yet he was her friend.

"I don't know," Maggie said, staring at the small bunion on his third finger from writing so many notes over the years. Maggie ran her thumb over her own bunion as she looked up at Hanes, noting Hanes was staring at her, waiting for an answer. "The panic button doesn't make a sound when you push it." Maggie felt inept. She was the only witness and felt inept—unable to give them any helpful information. Her descriptions were alike and vague. She thought about Willow, and tears formed in her eyes again. She wanted to crawl into bed in a dark room and never get up.

Another detective entered the room, pulled Hanes aside, and whispered in his ear. Hanes turned his face away as they continued to talk back and forth.

When Hanes turned back to face her, his face was grim—hard—cop face—definitely not the face of a friend. Whatever he'd been told, it wasn't good. She wondered what could have turned him against her?

"Was your mother in the E.R. tonight?" Hanes asked, hard-eying her without letting up. His questions came hard and fast. They were harsh, hammering, and accusatory, causing a sour queasiness to fill her stomach. "Is it true your mother is a drug addict? Is it possible she was part of the robbery? Checking out the E.R. before the strike? I hear she suddenly disappeared; is that correct? You let her escape not long before the attackers arrived. Was she part of a diversion? Where would she have gone? What were you doing at the time of her escape?"

Maggie would never tell him she was crying in her office. Hiding. Ashamed. She felt smothered with shame in front of Hanes and answered his questions as best as she could, sometimes stammering. Maggie was stunned at the direction Hanes seemed to be going with his line of questioning. Anything related to her mother had always made her feel off-guard, uncomfortable, and guilty because her mother usually was guilty of something. "I have no idea where my mother might have gone. We don't have contact. I haven't seen her in over a decade."

"You don't have contact? And yet, she chose tonight to show up in your E.R. to say *Merry Christmas, baby*? The detectives over there are wondering if you were possibly part of a plan?" Hanes added, pointing the end of his pen toward the other detectives. One of which was glaring directly at Maggie. "They think it's convenient that you're the only witness."

Maggie looked back at Hanes, stunned, shaking her head back and forth, staring at him in disbelief. Finally, she spoke. "I can't do this anymore tonight, Detective Hanes. I'm pregnant. I was pushed to the ground, and I hurt too much to go on. I'm not answering any more questions for now. Besides, you sound ridiculous. I would never put my baby in harm's way. Seriously?"

Hanes closed his notepad with a harsh thud. "So that's how this is going to be? Off the record, Maggie. This situation does not look good."

"No, Mark. It's your line of questioning that does not look good. I had nothing to do with my friends being shot, kidnapped, and killed," Maggie said, her lips quivering, betraying her attempt to look like she was entirely in control. "And I cannot for the life of me see how you can possibly think that. I am done for tonight, and I'm going home to go to bed to rest—for my baby's sake. You were my friend, and I feel betrayed. No more questions."

"My job doesn't allow me to have friends under these circumstances, Maggie. The facts are what they are. I have to ask questions, and we can't get around that."

"Then. It's a sure thing. We are not friends."

AS THEY PUSHED GLENN on a stretcher past Maggie, to the O.R.—Maggie phoned Greta to tell her she was going home and to give her the off-going report.

"We were granted total diversion by EMS until further notice," Maggie reported. "And I filed an injury report. I was pushed to the floor, and I'm pregnant."

"Were you injured?"

"No. I hope my baby wasn't. But my body is fine, thankfully. It's just required paperwork," Maggie reported.

"I didn't know you were pregnant. Oh, honey. I'm so happy for you. I'll pray for your baby."

"I can't wait. It's a boy," Maggie said with a subdued happiness.

"Go get some rest and be well, girl," Greta replied. "I'm so sorry you had to go through this, Maggie. Call me for anything. You hear?"

Maggie hung up the phone and headed out the door, officially on maternity leave.

And for the first time in history, Saint Vincent's Emergency Department closed.

AS MAGGIE RODE HOME WITH BENNY, she wondered how they would deliver such tragic news to Willow's daughter, Dorrie. A thousand questions rolled through her mind. She wanted to talk about it with Benny, her dearest friend, but he was in no shape to speak, much less plan.

Benny was like the brother she'd never had. Maggie's friendship with him dated back to her first day of employment as a nurse at Vinnie's Place, a nickname for the E.R. Maggie had felt apprehensive and out of sorts from the moment her foot crossed the threshold of the hospital. Benny noticed her fear and encouraged her, helping her thrive in the wild, chaotic E.R. environment.

As the Lead Tech in the E.R.—Benny carried an air of confidence and immediately took Maggie under his wing, teaching her all his secrets and the ins and outs of people who worked there. "Never let them see your fear," Benny had strongly warned. "They'll eat you alive. Head up. Back straight. And never tell your personal business to anyone."

They developed a devoted friendship that became even tighter as the years went on—especially when they got wrapped up in trying to unravel the mystery of the serial killer two years earlier.

Thanks to Benny, Maggie quickly grew out of the underdog feeling. Her thoughts lingered back to her good friend Willow. She was one of her absolute best friends. Willow had pointed out Maggie's scaredy-cat thinking and helped her learn to let go of her fears. And love sparked the minute Maggie introduced Willow to Benny. They became such an adorable couple. Willow inspired him to attend nursing school, and Benny would soon graduate.

One couldn't have a better-adopted family than Willow and Benny. She fought tears as she drove up to the mansion. Maggie had every luxurious resource behind those walls—except for the wisdom of knowing how to care for a child whose mother was kidnapped. She felt so inept.

Chapter 3

The Ride

Willow's ride in the trunk was rugged, despite the smooth roads. She fought the urge to vomit as the car shifted violently right, then left, speeding, and swerving over the streets. It felt like the car was weaving in and out of traffic, which was probably heavy due to the holidays. Many people like to drive at night to avoid traffic. She tried to focus on listening to sounds outside the car that might give her a clue about where she was headed. She estimated she'd been in the car for about two hours.

Willow noticed when the car seemed to turn; the tires sounded like they were grinding against gravel on bumpy roads, which caused the gasoline can to bounce about her head. She felt nervous about the gas sloshing around, releasing vapors that smelled strong. Whoever had put the gas cap on had not placed it securely. She pulled her jacket about her face to protect her lungs from the toxic air.

She estimated the vehicle had traveled about a mile when the car came to a stop. Willow heard doors opening and closing and rustling sounds in the car seat. Then there was silence. Willow assumed the driver had gone inside a house when she heard a door close far away.

As Willow listened hard, straining to hear the sounds around her, she couldn't help but wonder what they would do with her. Vivid thoughts of how she might die blended with the sounds of cats fighting and dogs barking not too far away. Willow felt calmed by the presence of a radio playing country music in the distance. She hoped it meant they were in a happy mood rather than a killing one. Soon, her body began to ache from lying in the same spot.

Willow wondered if the police were looking for her. It had been pitch dark when they dragged her from the hospital. All the exterior hospital lights were out, so it had been hard to tell where she was going despite her familiarity with the campus. They pushed her hard and quickly down the sidewalk, then crossed the street, and eventually, they shoved her into the trunk of a dark car that was not only filled with a bunch of junk—but it also stunk to high heavens of filth. Everything happened so quickly that she'd felt disoriented, not to speak of the horrifying thoughts running through her head. Would they just abandon her somewhere and leave her in the trunk? Or take her somewhere and kill her? Hopefully, they would ask the hospital for ransom and let her go.

It was getting colder by the minute during her ride. She was glad she'd worn her E.R. warm-up jacket. It kept her torso warm, but she began shivering from the cold. The local meteorologist on NBC television, **Brad Panovich**, had predicted an overnight low of thirty degrees, but it felt well below that now. Were they headed toward the mountains?

The driver got back into the car, and not soon after, Willow noted the car was tilting higher, and gravity shifted her closer to the tail end of the vehicle. Soon her ears popped. Willow didn't cry over stressful events, but this situation was terrifying. The details of the robbery swirled through her mind while bullying winds pushed the car to sway uncomfortably at times. Whoever was driving was having difficulty controlling the automobile. Every time she tried to move to a position of comfort, the car swerved, forcing her back to the same spot, rolling about over the filth in the vehicle.

It wasn't easy to hear at best due to the gasoline sloshing around in the can beside her head. The queasy feeling in her stomach and the roaring noise in her head was most certainly related to the inhalation of gasoline fumes. She was getting high, and her head was beginning to spin.

At long last, the tires screeched against what sounded like another bumpy gravel dirt road. Finally, the car abruptly stopped. Willow was ready to vomit from the lengthy exposure to fumes mixed with all the tossing and turning. The driver got out and slammed the door hard against the door frame. Footsteps faded away. A door squeaked, then closed. Willow's heart thumped hard against her chest from intense fear. Her chest felt like a tornado was inside, twisting around and suffocating her, causing her heart to race faster and faster. Her head started pounding, and soon, her body began to feel weaker with each moment. So, this was how she was going to die? Gasoline inhalation poisoning out in the freezing cold.

To Willow's surprise, the heavy footsteps returned, and suddenly she could see the night sky. The masked man, dressed in black—threw a blanket over her and harshly pulled her from the trunk. His hands felt different from the ones that had forced her into the car. They were stronger. Meaner. That was not a good sign. Willow struggled to free her face from the blanket to breathe as she gasped for fresh air. She staggered as she tried to walk uphill on an uneven gravel path. Willow strained to get air as her kidnapper pulled her up some stairs into a musty-smelling place that was warm. She wanted to cry with relief. The man's hands dragged her across what sounded like a wooden floor and shoved her onto a bed.

The door slammed, and a key turned in the lock, echoing across the room. Then it was quiet. Willow shoved her face from beneath the blanket and gulped in several gasps of fresh air, but it wasn't fast enough. The dizziness and weakness took a solid grip, and she passed out.

IT WAS STILL DARK when Willow finally awakened with a fierce headache. She didn't move for the longest time. The ringing in her ears and nausea slowly subsided, but the fear did not—as memory after memory of Christmas night in the E.R. returned. She wondered if Maggie had died. And Benny. She had no idea what had gone on in the other part of the E.R. Most certainly, the other areas were also robbed. The robbery was well coordinated. Had they killed other staff members in the different areas?

About an hour later, her kidnapper opened her door. Willow lay mortified, wondering what he may do to her as she listened to the shuffling sounds and watched the figure dressed in the black hoodie move about the room, scraping furniture against the floor. She ducked her head under the blanket as if it might afford her protection; then, she curled herself into a ball. There was a clanging of silverware, then the door closed again, and the lock clicked.

It was quite a while before Willow dared to lift the blanket off her face. The moon shining through the window above her bed dimly highlighted the small, wood-paneled room. A nightstand with an old, worn lamp sat on the table beside her bed. She turned it on.

On a small wooden chair in front of her, the kidnapper had placed a bologna and cheese sandwich and a cold diet coke—her favorite drink. She stared, stunned at the meal, as if it were a blast from the past. She had made this same meal many times before in her life. She loved bologna and cheese sandwiches. How odd.

Her stomach settled after her meal, and she sat waiting for disaster to strike. But it didn't. After a few hours of anticipation, she finally settled down enough to fall asleep. Not a restful sleep—but a light sleep, a state where she was still aware of things around her.

WILLOW AWAKED TO THE SOUND of footsteps approaching her door. She bolted straight up, pulled the blanket tightly around her, and stared at the door as the sound of a metal key turned in the lock. Willow shut out the light. Through the darkness, she saw the handle turn. A figure dressed in dark clothing and wearing a full-face black mask placed a meal tray on the chair beside the door and, without speaking, closed the door and turned the key in the lock. She sucked in her breath, afraid to move or breathe, fearing he might return.

A good five minutes went by before Willow dared to move. When she could no longer bear the smell of hot fresh bacon and coffee, she shimmied out of bed, grabbed the food tray, and hustled back to bed. Willow still felt drugged and weak. As she ate breakfast, Willow wondered where she was and what time it was.

Sated with a full stomach, Willow laid back and fought the urge to go back to sleep. As soon as she closed her eyes, memories of the chaos in the E.R. came flooding back—a hand tightly grabbing her throat—fingers digging deep into her neck. Then, Maggie's frightened look.

Instinctively, Willow rubbed her neck, noting it was still painful. As all the other events flooded back to her, her breathing increased. In her mind's eye, she saw her hand enter her password into the medication system. She'd frantically removed all the narcotics and put them into a bag as instructed. The man behind her had seemed well-versed in the number of narcotics stocked in the system. And it was a lot—as the E.R. was a busy place filled with a constant flow of critically injured patients who required heavy doses of narcotics to ease their pain.

Willow recalled the image of the gun being held to Maggie's head—and the sound of the gunshots as the noise bounced off the walls and stainless-steel cabinets. She remembered how Betsy looked, lying dead on the floor in a pool of blood at Doctor Sloan's feet. Betsy had been planning on retiring this year. Willow's final recollection was looking into Maggie's frightened eyes as they dragged her out of the E.R.

Filled with panic, Willow jumped up and ran to the small window. It was snowing outside, and the snowcapped mountains nearby were barely visible. She tried to open the window, but it was firmly in place. The windowpanes didn't look or sound like glass when she knocked her knuckles against them. The panes felt like plexiglass.

She jumped at the sound of a slamming door. A car engine started, and tires scraped against gravel and snow as it exited the drive. Willow held her breath as she tiptoed across the cool floor to the door and held her ear against it. The house was silent. It sounded like she was alone, so she twisted the cold doorknob to no avail.

Willow explored her room, seeking any means of escape. The house felt like a cabin with its wood-paneled walls and the fact that it appeared to be in an isolated area. On the far wall was a small television with rabbit ears. Radiators lined the edge of the wall behind her, hissing occasionally. An old metal fireplace in the far corner looked like it hadn't been used in decades. In another corner of the clean room was a rustic-looking rocking chair.

A simple five-drawer dresser made of old wood was against the wall at the foot of the bed. Willow hesitated before opening the top drawer. Inside, there were two books. One was a medical-surgical nursing book. The other was a Mandala coloring book with a box of coloring pens. A slow chill edged up her spine. Her captor knew her.

In a frenzy, she opened the rest of the drawers breathing heavier with each discovery. Bras and panties, her size. Pajamas, her size. Every item filled her with a sickening feeling. She sat on the chair by the door, facing the dresser, her eyes widening in terror.

Willow bolted to the bathroom through the narrow door. The linoleum tile floor was clean, as was the tub, except for a spot or two of mildew in a corner. A small cabinet with a sink looked like a cheap hotel room. A threadbare towel was folded neatly in the corner with small, dollar-store samples of body soap, shampoo, lotion, a packaged toothbrush, and toothpaste—all her favorite brands.

She backed out of the room with her hand covering her mouth. Her kidnapping was personal.

They didn't intend to kill her, which was a relief. But why? Who?

Chapter 4

Dorrie

The wind whipped wildly as the black chauffeur-driven limousine approached Blanchard House. Ronald Willis, the elderly butler whose employment with the Blanchard family went back generations, waited at the top of the stairs. His face registered sympathy as he bowed to acknowledge Willow's kidnapping. Kerrington took Maggie's hand as they silently climbed the bold stone steps leading to the two-story magnificent double doors decorated with sizable fierce panther statues on either side of the entrance.

Blanchard House belonged equally to Kerrington and Annella. The magnificent four-story Gilded Era mansion had been handed down to them through their inheritance. It was built to house several Blanchard families at once, as it was the family tradition for them to live together. Kerrington led Maggie by the hand and put his other arm around Benny as they walked silently to the dining hall.

Kerrington, as usual, had taken care of everything as he always did. When he didn't know how to respond to tragedy, he threw lavish items at you to distract you from his uncomfortable state. She appreciated his generosity and could tell Benny was equally as thankful as he stared at the table covered with an enormous array of food. Maggie was starving.

The chef hovered briefly, looking over their needs as she and Benny scoured their favorite breakfast of omelets and French toast. Kerrington chose salmon and bagels to go with his orange juice. To Maggie's relief, a simple nod of his head dismissed the chef. She still wasn't used to the frills of luxury Kerrington took for granted, having grown up in a lavish lifestyle his entire life. Of course, Benny loved the excessively expensive lifestyle when he visited. Today, he was different. Usually jovial over meals, now he ate in silence. They all did.

Maggie found it odd that Kerrington, who was always sharp-witted and well-spoken, now lacked the words to provide comfort. But then again, his mind was probably dwelling on his sister Annella.

Benny broke the silence as his fork hit hard against his plate. He buried his face in his hands with his elbows on the table and bawled. “I don’t know how to do this. How the hell do I take care of a child by myself? And what about her father, Jack Webster? He’s the meanest son-of-a-bitch on this planet. He could easily get control of Dorrie—and he’s a monster. Willow would be horrified,” Benny sobbed, wiping his face with his napkin. “In my heart, Dorrie’s my child, and I can’t let her go to him. She’s a teenager—going through tough times. And now this.” Benny let out another cry.

Maggie spoke in a calming voice. “No one has seen or heard from Jack in the longest time.”

“That’s only because a restraining order mandates that Jack stays away from Willow. After completing his anger management classes, the judge restored his visitation rights with Dorrie. So, he can take her. He is her father,” Benny argued.

“We will fight him in court,” Kerrington said quietly but firmly. “Our lawyers will handle it. Our security team is already in place to help the police find Willow.”

“I don’t think Jack is interested in getting Dorrie, quite frankly, Benny,” Maggie said, trying to lift his spirit.

“But I don’t have the resources. Who is going to take care of Dorrie while I work?” Benny asked, his voice escalating. “I want to take care of her, but I’m not equipped to handle her alone.” Maggie looked down at her plate, deep in thought. She hadn’t given the idea any consideration. Benny was in their house simply because she invited them for Christmas. The plan had been for them to return home after breakfast. The reality was that Benny worked four twelve-hour shifts to help cover all the vacant shifts due to Covid. Who would take care of Dorrie?

Maggie looked at Kerrington and asked, “Can they live here temporarily until Willow is found?”

“Absolutely. If Benny agrees—we’re like family anyway. We’ll hire an Au Pair to care for Dorrie and manage her schedule to ensure she gets where she needs to be and is kept safe.” Kerrington offered. “It’s the least we can do.” Maggie smiled at him, sending a quiet thank you.

"Thank you both," Benny said. "Willow would be so grateful, as well."

Dorrie Webster interrupted the conversation from the doorway, where she was standing with a smiling face, happy, and carrying her new IPAD. "May I have pancakes?"

"Sure," Maggie replied as she took Dorrie's plate, loaded it with pancakes and whipped cream and placed it back on the table. She bit her lip and fought tears when she looked at Dorrie's innocent face as Dorrie delightedly dipped her finger through the middle of the whipped cream and stuck it in her mouth, delivering Maggie a big, satisfied grin.

They were silent as each occasionally looked at Dorrie when she wasn't looking. The small framed pre-teen sat beside her mother's empty chair. Maggie watched as Dorrie's eyes curiously observed her mother's vacant seat. She looked like she might say something for a split second, but then she became distracted by the food.

Dorrie was a beautiful child and the spitting image of her mother, Willow. Her petite frame offset her wide, kind-looking chocolate brown, mildly shaped Asian eyes. Her scrubbed face was free of pimples, and her long, curly black hair was pulled back and tied in a blue ribbon—her favorite color. Maggie's heart sank as emotions swirled inside. She was forced to look away, thinking about how the tragic news would blast Dorrie's naïve lovely world into shattered remnants she could never repair.

And that was how they handled it. Dorrie ate and enjoyed what little time she had left as an average child, talking excitedly about her new IPAD all through breakfast. When her plate was removed, she finally asked the dreaded question. "Where's Mommy? Is she sleeping late? Or did she stay over at work?"

They all cleared their throat—ready for the moment—yet clearly unprepared. They'd failed to decide who was the best one to tell Dorrie. Benny and Kerrington both looked at Maggie.

Thoughts raced through Maggie's head. How much truth could a twelve-year-old child take? As a nurse, she'd told many children about sad things that happened to their parents. She reminded herself—*take the middle road until you know how much she can handle. Make the news brief. Let her ask the questions.*

"There was an incident at work last night. The hospital was robbed, and they took your Mommy. The police are working hard to find her."

Dorrie's eyes shot wide open with fear and terror, acknowledging she had absorbed the news. Her face scrunched slowly, and tears fell streaming down her cheeks. Maggie handed her a table napkin. "Is Mommy alive?" Before anyone could answer, she broke down in a heart-breaking sob that only a child could let out. So innocent. So helpless.

Maggie took her into her arms and led her to the sofa. Dorrie asked many questions, and Maggie answered them as truthfully as possible without getting into the gritty details of the bloody night.

"Why did they take Mommy? Why didn't they take someone else?"

"I don't know, Dorrie," Maggie said, barely able to answer the question, wishing hard that they had taken her instead of Willow.

"Honey, nothing makes sense about the whole situation," Benny said.

Dorrie then asked Benny if he was still going to be her father.

"Of course, Baby. I will always be here for you. Always." His lips quivered as he bravely fought tears.

"What's going to happen to me? You're not my birth father. Will they take me away from you? Where will I live? Oh my God," Dorrie cried out, a prolonged sobbing followed.

Kerrington stepped in immediately and assured Dorrie she would always have a home in this house. Kerrington leaned in and hugged her. She returned his hug and finally stopped crying.

Benny sat opposite Maggie, holding Dorrie's hand until he could no longer stand the pain in his heart. Finally, he retired to his room to cry his tears privately. Eventually, Dorrie fell asleep in Maggie's arms, exhausted from the news. Maggie held Dorrie until her arms ached so much, she couldn't hold her anymore. Kerrington helped Maggie settle Dorrie on the sofa and covered her with her blanket. They lay down on the opposite couch facing Dorrie. As she watched Dorrie's innocent sleeping face, Maggie felt safe as she nested in Kerrington's loving, strong arms, eventually drifting off to sleep.

BENNY WAS WHISPERING to Dorrie when Maggie awakened. Dorrie seemed calmer. More like she was in a solid state of shock, Maggie thought. Benny got her busy, moving their stuff from the guest rooms to the suite of rooms on the third floor which would be theirs. It had its own living room, den, eight giant bedrooms, eight baths, and a balcony overlooking the grounds. No, they wouldn't use it all, but it would provide them with privacy. Maggie felt happy—like they were a family—at least for now.

Later in the evening, Maggie entered the nursery next to hers and Kerrington's Master Suite. Formerly it had been Kerrington's *Thinking Room,* where he was known to sit for hours. The room previously held the manly appearance of a desk and elegant leather chairs. Lush carpeting. A fireplace. Kerrington had stripped the place of all electronic devices except his cell phone, which he rarely took inside the room. The suite had been designed simply for thinking. It was where Kerrington made significant business decisions for his companies or solved problems.

The space looked different now. Kerrington's *Thinking Room* was moved to the far side of the house, and the most elegant baby furnishings replaced his furniture. Maggie brought in a decorator at the Housekeeper's request but the struggle over little Kerrington's crib turned into a nerve-wracking fiasco as Maggie was not a big spender of money. The designer insisted a child of his breeding should have a walnut crib with gold detailing at the cost of almost fifteen thousand dollars.

"He's a baby, and he doesn't need gold," Maggie argued. When the designer lost patience with her, Maggie went digging in the attic and had Kerrington's crib pulled from storage. And that ended the debacle. Yes. It probably had cost more initially than the designer's crib choice, but Maggie loved the idea that Kerrington had slept in it. It was so sentimental. And made the nursery majestic looking.

The walls were painted a soft light gray, and Maggie had hired an artist to paint a mural of colorful animals on a wall. She wanted the room to be happy looking, soothing, and serene. Maggie smiled as she looked around. When closed, the long, heavy, silk-lined drapes would darken the room for naps. It was perfect. And ready for her little boy.

Kerrington was delighted with the nursery and sat with Maggie in the baby's room almost every night, planning the future and talking excitedly about how he couldn't wait to see the little bugger. Maggie chuckled at the term he had for his little one. Kerrington wondered aloud if his boy would play softball or want to take over his business dealings one day. If not, maybe they'd have a little girl later on who would. "I want our children to be what they dream of being," he said as he hugged her tightly, telling her how much he loved her. And he did. She could feel it. Always. Warming her like a summer sun. Maggie was delighted how Kerrington was so engaged with the future of his unborn son.

When Kerrington climbed into bed, he ran his fingers through Maggie's hair and kissed her lightly on the forehead before telling her how grateful he was that she was okay and unharmed.

No sooner had he spoken the words when a long-lasting cramp encircled Maggie's pregnant belly—so fierce it momentarily took her breath away. Maggie placed her hand over her baby.

Dover, her precious half-breed blond dog, sat up on his bed watching her, seeming to feel her distress. He quietly stepped over to Maggie and nuzzled his nose against her arm as she grimaced and buried her face in her pillow.

Maggie tried to appear stoic on the drive to the hospital, not wanting to alarm Kerrington any further than he already was. The E.R. put her in a wheelchair and took her straight to Labor and Delivery.

Chapter 5

The Awards

The flashing cameras practically blinded Annella as she climbed the long red carpet leading to the coveted film awards. She felt beautiful as she lifted the luxurious black silk of her **Oscar De La Renta** gown, covered with a heavily beaded top. It felt delightful between her fingertips, and she chuckled at how sore she would be after wearing such an incredible but heavy gown. The dress fit her like a glove which gave her confidence.

While standing at the top of the stairs, waving at her fans, Annella recalled her joy at learning that she had been nominated for the Best Actress award. She'd jumped all over the furniture with delight. Annella had worked many long and hard days learning her craft. Starting straight out of high school, from daylight until dusk, she was in classes studying acting, drama, theater, movement, and private tutoring classes in New York City. Nights and weekends were filled with practicing her art. She played many distinct roles, learning to stretch her acting ability. Harsh reality followed her dedication as audition rejections followed one after another. Then, finally, she landed her first decent role in a soap opera. Later, she moved on to films. It was a burdensome, nerve-wracking, and frightening process when she first started. And she was incredibly grateful she had the money to do nothing but study and audition to be successful, unlike many of her acting friends who waited tables or hustled as a bartender to survive.

Annella looked down at the faces of the screaming fans and winced. The world beneath her spun in a swirling circle as a sharp bolt of bright light shot painfully through her brain.

THE FIRST SIGN OF LIFE RETURNING to Annella Wryn ripped her from her pleasant dream. *Where am I?* she wondered as she tried to open her eyes but couldn't. It felt like a jelly-type substance was coating them. Her eyelids felt like they were taped shut. *Am I making a movie? That wasn't supposed to happen!* A frightful hot feeling shot through her as she tried to recall whether she'd signed a contract to star in another feature film. According to her agent, Annella was supposed to have a year off to marry Glenn. And after a honeymoon to Greece, they planned to go on a two-week Mediterranean cruise with her brother Kerrington and his sweet and caring wife, Maggie, who had become her best friend—the sister she'd always wanted.

The sound of footsteps approaching from her right side made her want to turn her head to talk, but her body refused to follow her brain's commands. She couldn't move. Repeatedly, she commanded her brain to move her arm and then her leg, but her body wouldn't respond. She couldn't even move her finger. She panicked and tried to talk. A tube was in her throat but still, her mouth wouldn't move. A frightening thought raced through her mind. *Am I paralyzed?*

A southern woman's friendly voice spoke, but it sounded distant and muffled. "I'm Doctor Sunday Richardson," she said, introducing herself. Then, she addressed the nurse, "I've ordered additional brain imaging."

Annella felt the doctor's experienced but gentle hands examining her and was delighted she could feel them. Annella recalled the Covid pandemic. It explained the doctor's distant voice. On the news, she'd seen nurses and doctors wearing alien-looking high-tech respiratory devices while treating patients in intensive care units. Annella wondered to herself. *Is that where I am? Do I have Covid? Why can't I move? Yet—I can feel. Doctor, please speak to me,* Annella said to herself as she tried to reach for Dr. Richardson's hand, only to be reminded that her brain was defying her orders. A hideous fear set off a chain reaction of adrenalin. Her heart pounded in her chest, feeling much like stage fright. The medical alarms resounded, signaling a racing heart, the noise scared Annella even more. Dark utter horror set in.

"Let's get the tape off her eyes so light can get in," the doctor directed as she removed the tape and wiped the goo from her eyes. Annella was delighted—she could see. The doctor was female with chestnut brown hair. Her eyes were mahogany brown, and she was wearing a thick mask.

Annella felt a wisp gently flick over each eyelid. “This is interesting. She has a blink reflex,” the doctor noted. “Stunning. She’s paralyzed and can’t breathe but has a blink reflex. Hmm.”

“Her vital signs have been stable,” Annella heard the nurse say. Annella figured she was a nurse because her badge read Bonnie RN-MSN, CCRN. She looked to be in her mid-twenties, with curly light brown hair, cute but not beautiful. She sounded like she knew her stuff, and Annella was glad. “Could it be Guillian Barre Syndrome?” Bonnie asked.

“Possibly,” the doctor responded. “But she does have a head injury. The question is which came first. Did she strike her head after becoming paralyzed? It could be a plethora of other things, too,” Doctor Richardson continued as she wrote notes in her Gucci notebook. “There’s akinetic mutism, myasthenia gravis, poliomyelitis, or polyneuritis. It’s not likely a brain tumor; CT ruled that out, but let’s get an MRI/MRA of her brain and take a closer look at everything,” the doctor said in a manner that seemed like she was thinking aloud. “I’m also ordering an EEG and EMG nerve conduction study. Until then, we watch and observe until we really know what’s going on.”

“There’s good news,” Bonnie announced. “Her Covid test just came back from the lab. It’s officially negative.”

“That’s good. But let’s keep her negative. Limit visitors to immediate family—and only if they’ve tested negative. Also, limit their time in case they’re false negative. She’s too high risk. How were her point-of-care labs?” the doctor asked.

“Within normal limits,” Bonnie replied.

“Well, she takes diligent care of her body. That’s a plus,” Richardson said. “I heard she’s an actress.”

“Doctor Sunday Richardson!” Bonnie admonished, shocked. “You don’t know her? She’s an award-winning actress, one of the most famous actresses in the world. Her movies are beyond awesome, especially the last three, where she played Ursula. She has all these special powers. And she can read people’s minds. Be careful what you think.”

Annella laughed on the inside. Bonnie was a delightful soul—a genuine, down-to-earth person. Annella listened to them chatter.

“I’m glad I don’t know her, Bonnie. Makes my job easier when I don’t see her as a movie star. Not that I have time to watch TV or movies,” Sunday said, breaking her first smile. “I’ll have to watch my mind. Ya think? I wouldn’t want her to read it.” She let out a light laugh.

"Yeah. She might steal your talents with her mind and become your competition. You know, doctor, we all work a lot. Today makes my fifth twelve-hour shift in a row, so you're not the only one living in the hospital. But that's no excuse for not having a social life. It wouldn't kill you to watch a movie. I bet your kids know her."

Sunday rolled her eyes and looked at Bonnie. "I have four surgical cases today, Bonnie Lulu. And—I have three daughters and a husband. Plus, a Covid pandemic which, thank God, seems to be winding down. Finally, but I still make it to the tennis courts for exercise. That's about all the life I can handle for now," she added before leaving. "Please stay on top of things in here. I know you will. You always do. But she has very unusual findings—and I don't quite know what to make of them yet."

Bonnie looked down and smiled as Sunday walked away. Sunday's fancy and expensive Golden Goose tennis shoes were beautiful and came at a hefty cost of well over five hundred dollars a pair. And she was wearing them straight into a bloody O.R. Shoe covers didn't always protect shoes. But Bonnie had heard the shoes were real comfortable, which would help Sunday make it through standing still for twelve hours operating on a patient. Bonnie was amazed. She'd never seen Sunday wear the same shoes twice. *When did she get time to shop when she couldn't even make time for a movie?*

A few minutes later, Bonnie returned. Annella loved her voice and her caring tone. "Annella," Bonnie said softly. "I mean, Kathryn—I know Kathryn is your real name. Let me introduce myself. They like us to do that. My name is Bonnie Holiday, and I'm your nurse. I know you're not awake, but they always say it's good for nurses to talk to patients as if they're awake. Patients have been reported hearing things we say while in a coma. So, I will go with that thought and assume you can hear me. And, if you can. I also assume you know the treatment plan. You have a great doctor. If you want your life saved, Doctor Sunday Richardson is the woman to do it. She has special powers too. People come from all around to have her operate on them. She studied at Johns Hopkins. I heard she was in the O.R. one day for over thirty hours, trying to save a child's life. And he's still alive and doing well, five years later," Bonnie added as she washed Annella's mouth with a small sponge on a stick. "I'm so proud of her. A woman neurosurgeon. You can see her smartness in her eyes, which look fierce if things aren't going her way. Yeah. She has special powers in real life. If Doctor Richardson watched your movies, she would love them."

Annella could slightly taste the delightful sweetness of the toothpaste-laced swab, and the tiny bit of water eased her drenched, dry throat that was sore from the tube in her mouth that went to her lungs. Annella was grateful for the breathing tube and the machine that breathed for her, or else she'd die. She felt Bonnie place a stethoscope over her lungs. "Excellent breath sounds. Strong heartbeat. It's a good thing you keep yourself fit and healthy. I believe we'll have you off that ventilator real soon."

Annella was never so happy to have a Chatty Cathy nurse. It helped her feel secure. And alive. Bonnie kept her mind from wandering off onto horrifying thoughts. "I can't wait until your next movie comes out. The numbers are dropping with Covid. And the movie theaters are opening back up. I love going to the movies. It's better when you can watch them on the big screens. You must fight to get well, Kathryn—I want to see Ursula again. If you made twenty more Ursula movies, I'd watch every single one.

And, of course, Chase needs to be in them. Honey. He is one Hottie if I ever saw one. You two make such a cute couple. And now that you're married in real life, it's just so cool. You two will make the most beautiful babies," Bonnie sighed, tapping Annella's hand with the kindest, most genuine pat. "Well. I have to go. I'll be back as soon as possible."

As Bonnie exited the room, heavy tears formed in Annella's eyes. *I'm married*? she said to herself, hanging onto the word itself, stunned. It was true—Chase had asked her to marry him, but she'd flat-out declined. That would never happen. Over the years, he'd gotten so hyped up with his stardom that he became challenging to work with, and frankly, she could hardly bear to be in the same room with him, much less kiss him anymore.

Doctor Glenn Sloan was the true love of her life. And as soon as the mandated movie publicity ended, they planned to marry. The studio wanted her and Chase to act like they were in love off- screen because it would sell more tickets. And it would. The agreement was that the minute the film left the big screen, she could publicly end her supposed love affair with Chase. She couldn't wait for the moment to come.

The thought of Glenn being her husband warmed her heart. He was a good man who talked about and cared about his patients with genuine reverence. Glenn was attractive with thick, slightly curly hair. His green eyes sparkled with intensity when he was excited. And his personality drew her to him like a magnetic force. He was charming, brilliant, and driven—like she was. They fit together like hand-in-glove. It was hard for her to find a man she could talk to all night about any subject. And their sex life. Well. That was way over the top.

What would Glenn do if he heard the rumors that she was married to Chase? It would hurt him terribly. She had to tell him it wasn't true. Annella desperately tried to move to get out of bed but was reminded she couldn't. It was like her brain was locked inside, unable to transmit any commands. Her mind churned.

Memories were hard to come by. Annella concentrated and finally recalled filming her last scene on the beach in a wedding dress. *It was cold. A snowflake caught on my fake eyelash. The wardrobe lady covered me with a fur coat. I hugged her goodbye. I was drinking the last of my champagne toast for the movie being wrapped.*

After less than an hour, Annella was emotionally and mentally exhausted from trying to force herself to recall more memories. She prayed for healing to come and trusted God would bring it to her. She had to trust. It was all she could do. Slowly, she drifted off into a sound sleep.

LATER, BONNIE ENTERED THE ROOM carrying Annella's exquisite body care products. "Your brother Kerrington brought you a gift. I sanitized them all really well on the outside for safety." Bonnie set the items on the counter and prepared Annella for her morning bath. "So, this is how movie stars keep up their good looks? I have the inside scoop." Bonnie chuckled, talking to Annella as she checked out the elaborate basket the products came in. "They're from France. And the basket. It's so professionally done. No wonder your skin looks so perfect. I'm not asking you what you paid for this, girl. I'm afraid to."

Annella chuckled inside and felt like she'd just stepped into a spa as Bonnie gave her a bed bath, washed her hair for the first time, and massaged her hands and feet. The smell of her beauty products sent Annella into a beautiful world of calm. She also enjoyed the company of the other nurses who had entered *oohing* and *ahhing* at the wonderful, delicious fragrances, chatting amongst themselves, Googling the **Clé de Peau Beauté** products from her basket. One of them gasped at the staggering seven hundred and seventy dollars cost for fifty ounces of one of the cremes. Annella smiled inside. They were genuinely enjoying themselves, and she loved the attention. Little did they know the products had been free, given to her by the manufacturer every month.

Chase abruptly interrupted her beautiful morning. The moment he entered the room, she could feel the hostility of the nurses as they quickly fled.

Annella tried to keep her eyes on Chase, though it was hard to follow the movement with her eyes. He wore a shifty look and had an uneasy feeling about him. She felt a funny feeling along her arms and wondered if she had goosebumps. Unable to look down, she assumed she did.

After being his co-star for so long, she knew him like a book. Something was up, and it wasn't good. He lifted the sheets over her right foot, moving her great toe sideways. Annella could hear her heart rate climbing on the monitor as Chase pulled a syringe from his pocket, aimed the needle at her foot, and delivered a painful injection between her toes with an evil smile. The sting was so hot and fierce it felt like he'd put a match to her foot. Chase pressed his thumb against the inside of her toe and massaged it, making it throb more. Then, he replaced the blanket over her feet just as Tony Jackson, his personal secretary, entered the room and handed him a cup of coffee.

Terrified, Annella wanted to cry out to Tony to help her just as Bonnie burst into the room to investigate. "Her heart rate is up. What's going on?"

"I have that effect on her. Let's go, Tony," Chase ordered. "I've told her hello."

She wanted her heart rate to stay up so Bonnie would investigate a little more, but the drugs made the world spin in circles above her as she wondered in terror. *What did he give me? What did he do? Why?????*

Chapter 6

The Final Loss

Maggie could tell by how the nurses treated her that they knew about the shooting in the E.R. last night and that she was the nurse involved. As gossip vines went, the nurses most likely heard the repeated retelling of the story in its entirety. She could read the pity on their faces. Their intense feelings hovered in the air as they worked diligently and quickly—determined to help her baby live—to try and prevent another tragedy in her life so soon.

But as the hours passed, she saw facial expressions change to manifestations of defeat. There were other tell-tale signs that only a nurse could read. Their voices became softer as her room transformed into a tomb. The thickness of sad reality lingered in the air with the faces that held gentler expressions. Their hands became over-kind in their touch as they tried to ease her emotional pain. Nurses did that for their own. And how many times had she done the same for them? Many. Knowing they were here for her was comforting, but it wouldn't stop the inevitable.

The pain soon progressed to regular waves, and when Maggie placed her fingertips on her abdomen over her uterus, she felt it become firm and then relax with undeniable contractions. She didn't need a doctor to tell her she was in pre-term labor. She didn't need anyone to spell it out for her. Things did not look good. She prayed hard for her baby that it would be strong enough to live. All the treatments to stop her labor had failed. And little Kerrington hadn't moved inside for over an hour. The fetal monitor was unable to register a heartbeat. When they tried to deliver ANY unwelcome news, she wouldn't let them. She argued, "He has not been born." She knew in her heart he was most likely dead. Yet, she didn't want him to be born. Because to be born would be an actual pronunciation of death.

The pain was unbearable, both emotionally and physically. Maggie fought the fast labor process trying hard to hold it back, wanting to keep her beloved baby inside of her for as long as she could. The heartbreak was indescribable. Such hope for a life with her little one diminished with each wave of pain. The more she looked at Kerrington, the more her heart ached. She'd wanted more than anything to give him a child. Maggie didn't want to fail him. She didn't want to add to his pain over Annella.

With every contraction, she felt rage building inside. A profound hate ballooning towards the man who had pushed her onto the floor with such harshness. Her child's killer. And she promised herself that one day, she would find him and make him pay and suffer as she was suffering. She would hunt him down with her last dying breath if that's what it took. Maggie had never felt the urge to kill. But it was undeniable now. She wanted to commit murder. At the same time, she prayed it would dissipate because she didn't want to be that kind of person.

As she rocked back and forth from side to side, she saw six nurses dressed all in blue gowns, caps, face shields, and masks, standing in a circle, in the hallway, their arms around each other. They were praying for her and her little baby. How kind, she thought to herself, grateful to have some goodness surrounding her at such a horrible time.

She turned away as visions of Christmas night intruded into her thoughts, choking her with misery. The memories were fresh. So malevolent. Betsy's blood splattering. The sound of gunfire. The smell of stale cigarettes in a killer's breath. And Glenn. His happiness earlier in the shift— then the look of horror as he realized his life as a respected physician was gone.

The final excruciating labor pain left her breathless as her body did what it was supposed to do—push her baby out into a living world—a world he would never get to experience. Her cries were those of a grieving mother, filled with anguish and love.

Maggie felt little Kerrington emerge from her body and strained to see him. She howled like a mad woman as she stared at her precious tiny baby boy, making no effort to breathe. She placed her finger over his fragile chest. His heart wasn't beating. The doctor grimly nodded and hung her head in defeat, acknowledging that efforts to resuscitate her little one would be cruel and useless. Baby Kerrington was too small to survive. Kerrington's sobs echoed behind her as she lifted her precious infant and placed his wet body against her breast. He wasn't warm anymore. Frantically, she aggressively rubbed his back, knowing her efforts to warm him were useless.

She held him for the longest time, staring at his beautiful, handsome face. She put her finger into his tiny hand, longing to feel his fingers grasp hers. She smiled at his eyelashes—so little, yet perfect. His delicate skin was so thin she could see his blood vessels through it. Time seemed to stop as if she willingly made it so—to soak it all in and hold the memory forever. Maggie didn't know how to let go.

Eventually, she gave baby Kerrington to his father, noting their child was so small he easily fit into one of his father's hands. The moment was too much to bear. She covered her eyes and sobbed like she'd never sobbed before.

When they carried little Kerrington out of the room, Kerrington held Maggie in his arms for the longest time. Just the two of them left in the world to comfort each other. God how she loved him. She would give Kerrington another child. Someday. It would happen.

Maggie and Kerrington left the hospital as soon as possible, carrying the small white memory box the nurses put together for them—containing little Kerrington's footprint card and a mold of his hand.

After they returned home, Maggie went to bed. Benny briefly came in, hugged her, and told her he was sorry for her loss. Later, she heard Kerrington and Benny taking the baby crib apart and restoring the nursery back to Kerrington's *Thinking Room.*

They worked in silence. Maggie wanted to stop them but didn't. It was probably for the best—for Kerrington—to help him move past their baby's death.

Chapter 7

Titus

Maggie felt strange when she returned to work. Being home alone after the loss of her baby was unbearable. It gave her too much time to think and dwell on what might have been. She was intensely angry with the robber who had pushed her to the floor and murdered her baby, and without any avenue for her anger, her boredom kept her spinning in one big black dark circle.

Work would be a relief.

When her pager had gone off with a call for help for nurses and techs, Maggie talked Benny into going in with her. It was his day off, and Dorrie was in school.

The utilitarian-style break room had been given a complete facelift since the robbery. It was the administration's attempt to show the staff they cared. A used blue-black sofa replaced the ugly green one. The walls were freshly painted beige, covering the yucky green sick room color from the sixties. And the old ratty-looking lockers were now brand new, as was the refrigerator.

Maggie felt eyes watching her and Benny—probably because the staff expected them to be close to a nervous breakdown state—which they were—but they promised each other they would not let it show. They were a team, and they'd get through this together.

She studied the staff roster and pretended to look at it harder than needed. Maggie took a deep breath. She had no idea what to say even though she'd gone over it many times in her head. She could tell they were waiting for her to talk, but she was caught for words. Her mind felt frozen.

Cora, her friend, came over, gently laid her hand on her shoulder, and whispered in her ear. "Just give out the assignments, Maggie. Save the announcements for later."

Maggie fought tears and finally strummed up the courage to stand.

"I know all of you have questions about Willow and what happened. As for the events that night, I am not allowed to speak about them, per the police request. Please be kind and do not ask." Maggie gripped the edges of the roster assignment as she spoke and noted her body tremors were visible to others through the moving edges of the paper. "I only know what you know through the television reports. If you need to talk about the situation, I can arrange for the chaplain to hold a group session later today. Just let me know." And with that, Maggie regained her professionalism and gave out the assignments. She was not about to talk about her lost baby with any of them, as she knew she couldn't hold it all together in their presence. Maggie posted the sad news on Facebook and received over several hundred responses. She asked for privacy and explained as best as she could that she needed time.

DESPITE THE E.R. BEING BUSY, Maggie sensed a high level of tension all day. She noticed staff members secretly gathering behind closed curtains to talk. It was something they always did when they were struggling emotionally. They would deny the chaplain the privilege of comforting them as only they knew what each other felt. They might, however, seek out Sister Margarita for a hug, Covid or not. Maggie sighed. Day after day, each of them would begin to mend. Slowly. But not if Willow remained missing.

Maggie closed her eyes briefly, trying to imagine how healing might come. With Willow still missing, no one knew what to say. They were all walking on eggshells, watching the main entrance door, wondering if someone else might step through it with a loaded gun and shoot them dead where they stood.

She missed seeing Betsy at the desk, along with Glenn—as most of the staff did. One of the nurses had told Maggie earlier in the day that she was transferring to the Trauma ICU. "Raleigh had a shooting in their E.R. That's two North Carolina E.R. shootings in less than a year. I don't feel safe here anymore." Maggie hated to lose her as she was a strong, dedicated nurse.

Benny kept hanging around her as the day wore on. She could tell the recent tragedy was prickling his nerves, too, and he held an anxious look that she wanted to fix. Clearly, they both missed Willow not being there. Finally, he spoke. “Is Titus from security here?”

“I didn’t see him on rounds.”

“I find that peculiar,” Benny spouted. “He’s supposed to be here today. And the staff say he’s been out since the shooting. It’s a long time to be out of work. You think maybe he caught Covid?”

“I hope not,” Maggie replied. “But I don’t have any way of knowing. The security department manages its own sick calls, and Employee Health and Infectious Diseases handles staff Covid. What’s got you so worked up? You look angry, buddy.”

“I am. Something’s not right about it. Titus works the night of the robbery, and no one has seen him since. He normally doesn’t work at nights. Why was he working that night? And then he disappears into thin air.”

“I would say… it’s a bit odd.” Maggie felt like an egg was stuck in her throat and wouldn’t move. “Are you thinking he might have been involved? But—Titus was a Green Beret.”

“A very unhappy Green Beret lately,” Benny countered. “He didn’t get the big promotion. Maybe they kidnapped him too!”

The medic radio went off, loudly announcing CPR in progress. “Overdose.” Sirens blared in the background, confirming the significance of the call. “ETA two minutes.”

“We’ll talk later. At home,” Maggie called out as she got ready to receive the patient. Her ***no patient contact*** was over now that she was no longer pregnant.

“You bet,” Benny called back as he rolled a fresh gurney into room one and called for other techs to help him get ready to do chest compressions.

It was dramatic when medics rolled in. Everyone was soaking wet from the heavy rain at the scene. The medics’ feet were covered in mud, and a leaf or two clung to their jackets. They looked cold, their cheeks were slightly flushed from demanding work yet pale from winter wind. Benny took over compressions as Medic gave a report. “Found down in Tent City covered in a high pile of blankets. Not breathing on arrival. No pulse. Started CPR. Has a known drug problem. Little or no response to Narcan. Probably too late for that to work. Police found several syringes at the scene. Some full. They recovered a vial of Fentanyl. They think it came from here during the robbery.”

As they continued CPR, Maggie and Benny caught each other’s eyes. The woman was dead; it was just a matter of the senior resident declaring the time of death. Maggie stared at the patient as her mind spun back to the robbery as if not a second had passed. She felt smothered. Hot. Dizzy.

Her ringing phone saved her, allowing her to escape. She rushed through the medic doors into the cold, rainy air. "This is Maggie. How can I help you?"

LATER, AT THE MANSION, Maggie put Dorrie to bed, grabbed two cold Miller Lites, a bag of plain Ruffles potato chips, and a cup of Onion Dip, and made her way to the solarium. The warm moist air hugged her like a soft, cozy blanket, instantly relaxing her. The gentle trickling of the waterfall and the constant heavy raindrops hitting against the solarium ceiling made for an inviting atmosphere. Benny lay in the far back corner on the other side of the giant oak tree, waiting on her with his eyes closed. She sat in the lounge chair beside him and handed him a beer.

"So. Let's finish the Titus discussion," Maggie asked.

"I'm thinking either he was kidnapped, or he was involved. And, for the likes of me, I can't imagine anyone being able to kidnap Titus. As big as he is and a Green Beret at that, he'd kick their ass all over the place before they even knew what hit them."

"Seriously."

"Yes. And that's just the beginning of what I've been stewing about all day. It had to have been an inside job, Maggie. You said the guy holding the gun to your head told you the place was wired—meaning they hacked into our security system and hijacked the cameras for their use." Benny explained, sitting straight up at attention, staring at Maggie. "Titus was heavily trained in all that high-tech stuff. It was his specialty."

"This whole ordeal has all of us spinning in circles, wondering who was behind it. Hanes even accused my mother of being involved. And somehow, I looked suspicious because of her."

"Holy shit, Maggie."

"Yeah. But Hanes will soon discover that I don't have a relationship with my mother. And, haven't had one with her for over a decade or more."

"I heard about her coming in. Man. That had to be hard."

"It was. I was humiliated. Are people talking about it?"

"Oh, hell no," Benny said with a light laugh. "No worry about that. They moved past gossiping about your mother the minute the robbery happened.

Some are really worried it might happen again. Several say they're looking for another job—outside the E.R.—sorry to say."

"That's even more reason we need to find out who it was or wasn't," Maggie insisted.

"I have a lot of questions to ask Titus," Benny said. "He applied for a promotion he rightly should have gotten but didn't get, and he was pissed off with the hospital and his whole department because of it. That would be a strong motive if you asked me. I'm gonna do some more digging around and find out what the word is on the street."

"Well. I hate to think Titus might have been behind the overdose death today. It's too much for my mind. I'm getting ready to turn in."

KERRINGTON CAME HOME LATER that night looking like the world's weight was on his shoulders. He was reticent and avoided Ronnie, refusing to let him take his coat.

Kerrington gave Maggie a peck on the forehead, forgoing the usual hug, and fled to his *Thinking Room,* where he said he needed to be alone for a bit. When he closed the door to his lavish mahogany wood-paneled room, it was always a signal that he needed to be left alone. It didn't happen often, but when it did, Maggie learned something serious was going on. When they first got married, Maggie used to worry about it but didn't anymore because when Kerrington came out of his secluded area, he was always in a better mood, and he gave Maggie lots of love and attention. He was a good man, through and through, and made for a great husband.

Maggie took a hot steaming bath with lavender balm, hoping it would calm her down from such a frenetic day. Her mother invaded her thoughts, despite Maggie trying to push the memories away. *What in God's name made her pretend to be suicidal and come to her hospital on Christmas night?* She could ponder it all night and never have the answer. Her mother had traded their life together for drugs. And for that, Maggie would never forgive her. She forced herself to think of Willow and wondered where she could be—and if she were alive or dead. And if Willow was dead, how had they killed her? She prayed that someone would find new evidence soon.

Chapter 8

New Year's Eve

The day was busy with a variety of critically ill patients. Four nurses called in sick—some related to Covid, some not. Some probably had New Year's Eve plans. It was a holiday, meaning they would get written up but not fired for calling out. That made five nurses down if she included Willow, who hadn't been replaced on the schedule.

So, Maggie closed the Boo-Boo Room aka the minor treatment area and moved Benny to Trauma. She then asked the physician assigned to the minor area if he could go to Triage and discharge as many non-emergent patients as possible straight from there. Maggie put out an emergency call to all nurses offering a twenty dollar an hour incentive to come in. The twenty dollars extra was in additional hourly rate plus overtime, meaning senior nurses, already making high hourly wages, could make a thousand dollars for the day. By noon, she still hadn't received any response for help, so she placed another one offering twenty-five dollars.

Several nurses asked if there was news about Willow, but all Maggie could say was no because there hadn't been. Hanes had his lips sealed. He was only working peripherally on Willow's case. Primarily his responsibility was for Betsy's death which Maggie gathered had come to a complete halt.

Benny caught Maggie in the Trauma Room after the case ended. The blood-covered room was awaiting a thorough scrubbing by Environmental Services. Benny cleared the bloody instruments from the sterile instrument tray, then wiped it down with a cleaning solution. "Three guesses what I know!" he said.

"Benny. C'mon. I'm not up for guessing games."

"Okay, then. I confirmed my suspicions. All the security cameras were definitely hijacked the night of the robbery. No recordings exist from

Willow's kidnapping, and that really pisses me off. How can that happen?" Benny touted, noisily placing the oxygen tank into the heavy steel cylinder holder.

"Where did you hear that?"

"How do you think I hear most things about this place?" Benny replied, his eyes displaying amazement. "I have over fifty extended family members plus some very tight friends that work throughout this god-forsaken place that let me down by letting Willow disappear without one shred of video evidence. Do you know that one of my friends even works in the Ivory Tower—for the President of the hospital? Idle talk has turned into a riptide of gossip upstairs. Everybody is blaming everybody, and someone's going down over the failed cameras."

"They should," Maggie agreed, replacing blood vials on the counter.

"I'm going to Titus's place as soon as I get a day off," Benny announced, his voice low as he wiped the monitor cables down and snapped clean electrodes in place. "I'm going to look around. If he's there, we'll have a chat. If he's not, then we'll know something is up. All the cops, homicide detectives, and crime scene peeps are so busy with all the killings going on in this crazy city. Let's say—I'm gonna help them out."

"You got shot the last time you tried to play detective. Remember?"

"Maggie. You're not stopping me. Time is running out for clues. Titus worked in security. The cameras got hacked. A major heist occurred worth lots of money. And he's trained in Special Ops."

"You're making a mountain out of a molehill, Benny. So, Titus was a Green Beret. He's one of the greatest security guards we've ever had. He's probably got Covid."

"So. Why, out of nowhere, did they decide Titus could no longer carry a gun?"

"That was a system-wide decision."

"Not true. The guards up on Hell Ward carry guns."

"That's because it's a hospital prison ward, Benny. You need to think twice and give your plan more thought. I know it's been hard on you. But this—is not a promising idea."

"You are wrong, my friend. I'm doing it. Now. Are you in? Or are you out? I could use some help." Benny said, folding his arms across his chest and cocking his head sideways, his eyes sending an *I dare you* message.

The loudspeaker in the E.R. blared above. "Pediatric M.R. with CPR in progress. ETA five."

They both moved into action without another word. Maggie pulled the pediatric crash cart into place as Benny flattened the bed and tossed the Broselow board on it for measuring height and estimating doses of emergency drugs and sizes of resuscitation equipment. Maggie pulled a Peds *Medical Resuscitation* (M.R.) packet from the file cabinet and laid all the papers out on the counter. All the required paperwork was ready to go with the alias name M.R. PEDS ALASKA stamped on all the pages with an ID bracelet to match.

Maggie heard Medic voices before she saw the victim. "Thirteen-year-old female found down in the school bathroom. CPR was in progress by the school nurse on our arrival." Maggie took in the color of the girl's feet, which were a mottled purple and pale, with toenails painted a bright, sparkling pink. Maggie hit the big red button on the wall to start the clock, which would time the resuscitation.

Fifteen minutes later, the small-framed girl was pronounced dead. The tentative cause of death was presumed to be an overdose of opiates per drug screen results. According to the police who escorted the ambulance to the E.R., a substance found at the scene had been positive for opiates, believed to be fentanyl. The school nurse thought the girl was already dead when she was found.

Benny pushed the crash cart back into the corner. Rage owned his eyes when he turned to face Maggie. "That little girl looks just like Dorrie. And the drugs that killed her most likely came from here. I'm going to see Titus, Maggie. No one is going to stop me. Not even you."

"I'm in. I'll go with you. But not tonight. Day after tomorrow. We're off. We can take our time talking to him," Maggie quietly replied. "Besides, we'll probably both end up working overtime tonight. Sick calls have already started. I'll call Kerrington and let him know we're working over."

Benny smiled and pumped a fist in the air. Maggie shook her head, wondering if she'd lost her mind. No. They had to do something to find Willow, even if it was wrong. She looked back at the dead girl. Her heart ached, and she felt profound guilt. She agreed with Benny. The drugs had most probably come from this very E.R.

MAGGIE STOOD AT THE nursing station completing the death paperwork when Hanes startled her. "How's your mother doing?" His intention to make her nervous was effective.

Hanes responded to the overdose, hoping to link it to the robbery and homicide of Betsy. He'd used this same method before—coming up behind her back and startling her while she was concentrating on work. Maggie immediately started shaking inside. She wasn't falling for his interrogation methods this time. She turned, walked into the closest patient's room, and pulled the curtain.

She turned to find an elderly man removing his glasses to wipe his tears. His frail, thin hand trembled, pulling at her heartstrings. Without even thinking, Maggie instinctively reached out and took his hand in hers to comfort him.

"Please pray for me, nurse. I can't take anymore."

With her other hand, Maggie reached up and stroked his face while looking into his green cataract-laden eyes and began to pray out loud, asking God to send him peace and calm. As he closed his eyes in prayer, Maggie's mind swirled with emotions, and she noted her prayers brought calm to his soul as well as her own as she bonded with him during his time of spiritual need. A smile crept over her face as she kept praying and noticed his rhythmic trembling ease. His breathing slowed as he fell off to sleep. When Maggie exited his room, she felt transformed—strong and powerful enough to face Hanes again. But Hanes was gone.

In a whiff, the peace dissipated as medics burst through the door with a woman who looked like Darlene, her mother. Her heart flipped in the worst way until she knew for sure it wasn't her. They treated her aggressively, believing she'd had a massive stroke. No reflexes. Incapable of breathing on her own. The woman's presentation began to remind her of Annella's case.

Maggie pushed her rapidly to a CT scan and then transferred her to Neuro ICU, where she reported to the nurse that the head CT scan was negative. Maggie's report was interrupted by nurses shouting and running toward the patient. The patient had successfully sat up and pulled out her breathing tube.

The supposedly brain-dead woman exclaimed, "Wow! Man! That was definitely the best high ever." She looked at Maggie. "Nurse, I could hear everything that everybody said. And I felt everything you all did. I was alive—listening to you when the doctor said he thought I was brain dead. What a beautiful thing feeling the tube sliding down my throat and the machine breathing for me!"

Maggie stood dumbfounded, staring at the woman. “What happened to you?”

The woman laughed. “I took a lot of GHB. And a wee tiny bit of vodka,” she claimed— showing her two fingers measuring the size of the liquor in her drink.

“Do you know how close you came to dying?” Maggie asked, her voice holding a disbelieving tone.

“That’s what made it so cool. I was really, truly dead but alive. You ought to try it sometime. I couldn’t move. I couldn’t talk. But I felt everything. And now I want to leave. Bring me my papers. I’m signing out.”

Maggie let out a litany of warnings as to why she should never attempt something so foolish again. After losing the battle to convince her to stay, Maggie finished her papers and exited the unit pushing the empty stretcher. A second-year resident physician passed her and retorted that Maggie shouldn’t have been so harsh with the patient.

Maggie stood aghast as anger erupted from deep inside like hot lava spewing from a volcano.

It was the last straw of the day. “Did you tell her that?”

“I did. You were a bit harsh with the girl, don’t you think?”

“Not at all. She stopped breathing. We intubated her. The only reason my patient is still alive is that someone found her in time. We have a five-minute window of opportunity to re-educate her before she walks out of here—with your approval that it’s okay to do it again. You weren’t in the E.R., and you didn’t examine her. But an attending physician, who is much smarter than you are, **did** examine her. She needed education and I just happened to get the opportunity.”

“I’m her doctor, now.”

“Even more reason for you to humble yourself and go back and re-educate her. The last thing she needs to hear is that what she did isn’t dangerous.”

The patient walked out, crossing between them wearing paper scrubs. “Thanks, guys,” she said, waving her fingers goodbye.

“Catch her before she’s gone. Your time is running out,” Maggie warned, waiting. A look of disbelief crossed her face as she watched the doctor walk in the opposite direction of the patient.

MAGGIE FUMED FOR HOURS, knowing her deep-seated fury towards the doctor was misdirected and way over the top. And her rage was directly related to her feeling guilty about the dead teenager's overdose earlier in the day. She replayed the robbery repeatedly in her head, wondering how she could have stopped it and prevented the drugs from being stolen. PTSD and Survivor's Guilt raged inside. Owning her. Stealing her dignity and pride. The remorseful thoughts raging through her head made her lips tremble, and tears stung her eyes. *Two patients died from the overdoses. My baby died. Betsy died. Glenn lost his career and still might die. And yet, here I am, full of life. I should have tried to get the gun. I should have fought. I could have saved them all.* Maggie shivered inside at the memory of her feeling paralyzed with the cold gun to her head. Even though she knew common sense would dictate she wasn't responsible for the deaths, she still lay victim to Survivor's Guilt which robbed her of the truth, leaving her with severe feelings of inadequacy, guilt, and helplessness. Maggie had felt powerless to do her job—powerless to act—a scaredy cat to move—to protect the staff. She'd been a failure. And worst of all, she felt like a child again, plunging back into her nightmare childhood, trapped in the horrid world of her mother's making. A world of drug addiction.

Work was her only answer. She should get busy. Take her mind off her problems. Maggie thought about Annella Wryn. The things she'd witnessed in the treatment of the woman with the GHB overdose seemed oddly like how Annella presented in the E.R. when she was admitted.

MAGGIE MENTALLY REVIEWED what she knew about **GHB (gamma-hydroxybutyrate)**. Classified by the DEA as a Schedule I controlled substance—GHB is mainly used illicitly—at rave or club drug parties because of its ecstasy-type effect of aphrodisiac euphoria and sociability effect. Legally it is used to treat narcolepsy. Maggie pondered over the illicit use. Predators used GHB quite often as a date rape drug because of its ability to render unconsciousness and memory loss when given to unsuspecting individuals.

Maggie headed straight for Annella's room in time to catch Bonnie before she went on dinner break. "Was Annella tested for GHB?" Maggie asked. She shared her experience with the earlier GHB overdose with Bonnie.

Bonnie looked alarmed as she listened to Maggie's presentation, yet Maggie could see a look of hesitation cross her face.

"I know it's a HIPAA thing, Bonnie. But I also need to know if someone may have harmed Annella. Her presentation was similar but not as severe as my patient's. If you don't feel comfortable, I'll look it up myself."

"That would cause trouble for you, especially since you're a family member. I'll look it up."

"Thank you, Bonnie. I know we sent blood from the E.R. The lab got the tubes, but I need to know if Dr. Richardson ordered that specific test and if it was done. It's urgent."

"Promise me you will tell no one I told you."

"Of course, Bonnie."

Bonnie's eyes rapidly scanned the computer screen as she scrolled through several documents. Maggie watched the screen surreptitiously, taking in what knowledge she didn't already have from the night Annella was admitted.

When Bonnie finally paused, she blew out a breath. "Well, I'll be dog gone. She was positive."

In deep thought, Maggie folded her arms across her chest and put her hand up to her face. "It's probable that a good amount of the GHB metabolized from her blood during transport. The drug certainly could have influenced her unusual neurological picture on arrival. I know Annella did not do drugs. And she did not have narcolepsy. Yet, the illegal substance was in her blood, meaning someone drugged her."

"Something is not right about this picture. I'll tell Dr. Richardson when she makes rounds and emphasize Annella did not use drugs," Bonnie offered, a frown burrowing on her forehead. She hesitated before speaking again. "I know I shouldn't tell you this, and you must swear to God you'll never tell anyone what I'm about to show you. Do you swear?"

"Yes! What?" Maggie cried impatiently.

"Come with me," Bonnie said, leading Maggie into Annella's room, where she gently undid the bedsheets at the foot of the bed and lifted them gently to expose the feet. Bonnie tenderly pried Annella's toes open at the great toe. "Take a look at this and tell me what you think."

"Oh my, Lord," Maggie gasped as she leaned in and took a closer look. "What in the world?"

"I think it's a needle puncture, Maggie. Look close there, in the center of all the bruising—see the tiny mark and the small clear center around the injured site? Everywhere else is bruised."

Maggie pulled back, letting out a light gasp of shock as her mind raced a mile a minute. "Annella did not have that injury in the E.R. I'm sure of it. It's very noticeable. Glenn does a thorough head-to-toe assessment. I watched him. That injury was not there," Maggie stressed her point.

"But, then again, if it was a fresh injury maybe it wouldn't have shown bruising yet," Bonnie surmised. "Thinking back, I gave her a foot massage the other day. And it wasn't there. I'm positive," Bonnie emphatically stated, pointing at the injury. "I plan to show it to Doctor Richardson when she makes rounds."

"What are you thinking, Bonnie?"

"I'm thinking it may have happened here in this hospital room. I'm gonna keep my eyes peeled wide open when a certain person visits. And we're gonna check her for drugs," Bonnie replied. "I have to get an order for it, and that might be hard convincing Doctor Richardson."

"Have you checked her for more needle marks?" Maggie queried.

"I did a full body check. No more marks. At least not ones visible to the naked eye."

"Unfortunately, not every injection leaves a mark. Can you keep me posted? Please?"

"You got it. I'm going to check on my other friend," Maggie said, sighing.

"I'll go with you. I need to change his dressing."

ANNELLA WATCHED THEM WALK AWAY, so proud of her friend nurses. Maggie and Bonnie were thorough nurses, and she prayed they would discover what Chase was doing to her.

Annella thought about the GHB conversation and was relieved that Bonnie had shown Maggie her foot injury. Maggie didn't let sleeping dogs lie when she became suspicious about things. Annella smiled in her heart. Maybe there was a rainbow out there for her. A miracle.

Chapter 9

The Surprise Visitor

The following morning Maggie entered the family dining room, smiling at the beauty of the sunlight filtering through the tall window creating images of the tree shadows against the polished dining table. Kerrington, Benny, and Dorrie were already seated and talkative. Everyone's mood seemed lifted for the first time since the robbery.

Dorrie's excitement was palpable as she spoke about her previous night's adventures. "Maggie! Mr. Blanchard took me out in the helicopter last night to see the fireworks. They were everywhere! All around the city, no matter where you looked. It was beautiful. So magnificent, as Mama would say. I've never seen anything but small fireworks before." Her beaming face turned towards Kerrington. "Thank you, Mr. Blanchard," she exclaimed. "That was the best night ever!"

Kerrington smiled back. "Anytime, Dorrie. I had a wonderful time, too. And you can call me Kerrington."

Maggie took a sip of coffee, then loaded a biscuit with soft butter and a heaping spoon of strawberry jam. When she looked up, she dropped her knife with a loud clatter and sat with her jaw dropped, frozen in place, holding her biscuit in mid-air.

"Good morning, everyone," Darleen said, taking a seat beside Kerrington at the head of the table. She was dressed in Maggie's clothes, including her pearls. Obviously, she'd spent the night in Maggie's former suite, the one she'd used during the harshest times of Covid before Maggie became vaccinated.

Silence swept the room as Maggie looked back and forth between Kerrington and her mother.

"What are you doing here, mother?" Maggie demanded.

"I was invited."

"By whom?"

"Your husband."

Maggie turned to face Kerrington, shooting him an astonishing look of disbelief. "You invited her?"

"I did," Kerrington replied calmly. "She's your mother. I thought you would like to see her."

"Well. You were wrong!" Maggie declared, standing up and tossing her napkin in her chair.

"We're undoing this right now. Let me help you to the door, Mother." That said, Maggie escorted her mother by her elbow to the sidewalk and ordered Ronnie never to allow her back in the house again. Then, she asked for privacy, and Ronnie shut the door.

"Maggie," Darlene called back. "I don't understand."

"You are a drug addict, Mother! What is there to understand about that?" Maggie walked back up the steps, ignoring her mother's protests.

"Not anymore. I'm clean. Three days now."

Maggie turned on the stairs and stood between the two black panthers, arms folded. "Three days is nothing, Mother. I spent almost a decade in the hell hole you created for us. And I fell for your same song and dance about being clean too many times. And I always believed you. What a fool I was. You left me waiting at my sixteenth birthday party at Pizza Hut. Alone. A party you were throwing for just the two of us. I was so happy. I believed in you again. I felt whole again. And you left me. If it hadn't been for the police coming to get me, I'd still be sitting there waiting for you to come to my party. Every Mother's Day, I prayed you would come to see me."

Maggie shook her head sadly. "I don't have a mother. Three days clean means nothing." Maggie walked up to Darlene, her voice quiet and calm. "I'm grown up now, Mama. I see things clearly, now. I can't help you. I want to. I've always wanted to. But you must do this alone. Not for me. For you. You must choose a clean life over drugs. And I can't be around you anymore. The police think you might have been part of the hospital robbery that happened not long after you eloped. Did you know about that? A woman was murdered. A good woman. And a mighty fine doctor was shot in the head." Maggie paused, looking at the shocked look on her mother's face. "And now, the police question my involvement because I have connections to you. No more, mother. We are—no more."

After stopping at the front door to gather her feelings, Maggie returned to the dining room. She refused to allow herself to cry. Not over her mother. Never again. Maggie entered the dining room with a smile and took her seat, ever so neatly replacing her linen napkin in her lap as if nothing had happened.

"I apologize, Maggie," Kerrington said. "She came to the door and said she was your mother, and I told Ronnie to let her in. She didn't have a place to stay, so naturally, I offered her one."

"Everything is okay, honey," Maggie said with a smile. "It's over. Let's not talk about it anymore," Maggie added, looking toward Dorrie. Maggie gave Dorrie a comforting smile and went on about breakfast as if all were well. All the while, her head was spinning and wondering. *How can I explain this to Hanes? To Kerrington? Why is she trying to return to my life after all these years? What if mother really was part of the robbery?* She trembled inside, nauseated by the event.

Maggie hugged Dorrie goodbye at the front door and held her longer than usual. She had learned to love Willow's child as her own over the years, watching her grow up. Maggie knew Dorrie's deep pain personally and wanted more than anything to help ease her anguish over her mother's disappearance by dishing out as much love as possible. She kissed Dorrie goodbye and told her she'd see her when she got home. She promised Dorrie a game of Fortnite and was delighted to see a big smile come across her face.

Dover jumped in between them, demanding a goodbye hug, which Maggie delivered, along with a kiss to the bridge of his nose. She ran her hand through his golden fur and gave him a final pat. It was their love language. Every morning and every night.

Chapter 10

Hospital Chaos

It was chilly outside, despite the bright sun, and the air felt fresh. The minute Maggie and Benny got in the car, dressed in their black scrubs, and headed off to work, Benny couldn't wait another minute.

"That was your mother, I presume? The woman they suspect was part of the robbery—who made you look guilty?"

"Yep. The living, breathing version of my mother."

"She doesn't look like she's living on the street."

"That's because she was wearing my clothes and probably took a nice long bath upstairs, in my old room, or wherever Ronnie put her."

"Jeez. What a mess. The police are investigating your mother being tied to you, and she spends the night in your house. Not good."

"Yep. Can't get any worse than that."

"Yes, it can," Benny replied in a low voice, staring out the window with a look of loneliness.

The air was quiet and still as Maggie watched Benny sort through his private thoughts. She knew he was thinking about Willow. Poor Willow. *Where is she?*

FOUR HOURS LATER, Kerrington appeared in the E.R. Clinical Supervisor's office looking incredibly handsome and proper in his smashing suit and luxurious long black winter coat. His premature silver hair glistened in the light from the ceiling. Maggie assumed he'd just visited Annella. Surprising her, he closed her office door for privacy.

"How's our movie star? I haven't been up there this morning."

"She's asleep," he answered, then paused, placing his hands in his pockets, and looking at the floor for a moment, very unlike himself. "We need to talk."

"Yeah. I figured you'd say that. I'm sorry. I went a little over the edge this morning," Maggie said, pulling a wisp of hair off her face.

"Do you want to tell me what's going on? You don't have to. Just know I'm here if you want to talk about it."

Maggie hesitated, searching for what to say. "I wanted to tell you before now, but I didn't know how. My younger life was painful," Maggie paused. "My mother is a drug addict. And as a result, my life wasn't pretty. I've been in and out of the orphanage because of my age and lack of appropriate foster homes. When I did get into a foster home, I became the maid for the whole house. But I had a great counselor who helped me make my way through it. I can't let her back in, Kerrington. I won't let her in because I've learned my lesson. I trust. And love. And then she crushes me. And it hurts so bad when she does." Maggie felt tears forming on the edges of her eyes.

Kerrington handed her his handkerchief. "I'm not going to push you if you don't want to talk about it now. But I'm here when you do," Kerrington whispered, taking her into his arms. "I love you. Are you okay?"

"I am," she lied, knowing her emotions were all over the place from having lost the baby and her unstable hormones. "Once I get busy here, it'll all wash away. I'm good."

"That's a relief because I have something to tell you."

Maggie felt him stiffen and pull away. She looked directly into his beautiful crystal blue eyes. "I have to go to Ukraine."

"**Seriously?**" Maggie looked at him with stunned amazement. "The President just asked all Americans to leave, Kerrington. You can't go there! Russia is going to war with Ukraine. Please don't. Please."

"I have no other choice, Maggie. I own businesses in Ukraine. I must get my employees out safely. They are Americans, and I can't leave them trapped. Our plan is solid. Get in—and get out. Won't take more than a day or two."

"Can't you send someone else?"

"No. I can't. It's a new drug that's ready for clinical trials. And I need it in my hands and out of a potential war zone that could destroy it—and all we've worked for. My signatures are required to move the product internationally. It's something only I can handle. Plus, I have almost a dozen hotels that need to be evacuated. Please look after Annella. I'll only be gone a couple of days."

Maggie knew there was no use fighting it once Kerrington made up his mind to do something, albeit dangerous. "When do you leave?"

"In one hour." He hugged her tight for a long time, then kissed her sweetly before turning around at the door. "When I get back, I want to talk about Dorrie. If, by some sad chance, we don't find Willow, I'd like us to consider adopting her. She's a great kid and I'd like to be her father. Benny can still live with us, and we can all raise Dorrie together and give her a nice home. Think about it."

"I'd love that. But I do hope Willow comes home."

"We all do," Kerrington said, smiling and waving a small goodbye before walking out the door. "I love you."

Maggie wanted to run after him, but the overhead speaker went off, "**Trauma Code One**. Five minutes out by air. Trauma Code One. Five minutes out by air."

THE DAY WAS WICKED and it quickly helped Maggie get her mother and Kerrington off her mind. It was hard not to be mad at him. Indeed, he had worked on the cancer drug for such a long time and was devastated when it failed the first go around. Maggie wanted him to be successful with this clinical trial.

All of Kerrington's other companies worldwide ran like silk, with great Chief Executive Officers making him lots of money. GlixMorganthal was different, though. Kerrington felt passionate about the company and was a very hands-on person. Drive—would be the right word. He was well-known on Wall Street for being a man who ruled his companies with a tight fist. And reporters called him cunning and even ruthless when he was in a battle for business. Known as a *Corporate Raider* and even a *White Knight* at times, he pretty much got what he wanted.

Maggie didn't understand his world, but she was trying—just like Kerrington was working to understand her wild life in the hospital. Kerrington served on the hospital board of directors and tried hard to keep personal issues out of the hospital business. He didn't always win his battles there because the hospital was so politically driven—and it frustrated him a lot.

She briefly wondered what was happening in Ukraine. Maggie had heard the news about impending war but hadn't paid it too much attention because of her distractions about Willow.

GANG WARFARE ERUPTED in two different parts of the city. Eight dead in total, and six died in the E.R. The paperwork was brutal and never-ending, plus dealing with the medical examiner, homicide, and crime scene so many times in a day made her feel like she was a cop and not a nurse. Gathering forensic evidence was a significant task and required a certified forensic nurse to complete the job, so the evidence could be held up in court. The specialty work left her down one nurse for most of the shift.

As if that wasn't enough, her boss, the Executive Director of the E.R., called and wanted to meet with her at four p.m.—the worst time of the day.

MAGGIE ARRIVED FOR HER MANDATED MEETING five minutes late. She felt anxious, her nerves fried, and her legs felt weak with fear like she had the legs of an octopus. Having no idea what the meeting was about, Maggie was trembling because she rarely ever got called by the director. Usually, her nurse manager took care of organizational issues.

As she entered the director's office, Maggie was caught off guard by the presence of a Human Resources representative. H.R.'s presence labeled the meeting severe, and it was not good news.

Maggie's mouth immediately went dry. Her lips were already chapped from the constant flow of adrenalin throughout the day, which made her lick her lips often. She sat in the only chair left in the room and wondered if the meeting was over accessing the information on Annella's labs. The H.R. representative got up and closed the door.

Jeff Evans, the new E.R. Director, was a pencil pusher that was hell-bent on cutting the cost of nurses, starting with senior staff because they made the most money. His plan was to bring in new grads who started at low pay grades. He didn't care about Covid or the danger of bringing in rookie nurses that didn't know how to save mangled bodies. The more he saved. The more he made in his bonus check. His greed made Maggie's job challenging. Even her Clinical Supervisor partner, David Pullman, disliked him. So did the staff. Usually, Maggie avoided him as much as possible, knowing E.R. Directors came and went, usually not lasting but a couple of years. Maggie's plan was to steer clear of him until he got canned.

Maggie greeted the thin-framed, forty-year-old director with a smile, but her friendly greeting was squashed by unfriendly eyes aimed directly at her. Tiny, piercing dark eyes. Stern. Harsh. He held his hands firmly clasped on the desk like what he was about to say was well-rehearsed. Maggie felt sweat dripping under her scrub top. The hair on her arms stood on end, and her mouth felt sticky. She craved water.

"I received your incident report regarding the elopement of a psychiatric patient," Evans explained. "It's a Sentinel Event, and as such, it goes to a hospital committee for further investigation since the police were notified and the patient wasn't recovered. Let's hope to God she doesn't kill someone and make the front page of the Charlotte Observer. I can see it now, St. Vincent's escaped psychiatric patient commits murder. Frankly, I'm concerned it might trigger an inspection investigation by the Joint Commission or the Centers for Medicare and Medicaid Services. Things like that can affect us financially." Evans handed her a form to fill out. "I need an in-depth detailed report by morning. Now. What complicates this situation significantly is our surprise visit this morning from homicide Detective Hanes."

Maggie's stomach lurched. A nauseous feeling swept through the middle of her abdomen as hot acid rose in her throat. A cold feeling swept through her as she began to feel even weaker.

"The missing patient is your mother, I understand, who has an addiction problem."

"Detective Hanes questioned me at length about her," Maggie said, jumping in to defend herself. "I am not involved." Maggie went on trying to explain her situation.

"Well. This is where we stand," Evans retorted, dismissing Maggie's comment as if it was of no concern to him. "We will be doing our own investigation as we prepare to respond. Your job is on the line. Any confirmation that what you have told us is false will result in severe consequences. We'll leave it there. Let's see. Yes. Another issue," Evans said, his voice firm as he glanced at his notes. "I was not happy to discover you closed an area of the E.R. That's not good for business. We want to keep our numbers up."

"I didn't have enough staff to keep it open safely," Maggie explained, her voice cracking due to her thirst. "And we managed the flow by utilizing the physician at Triage, which was quite successful. I think it is something we should consider for the future. Patients were happy to see a doctor right off and not have to go through the E.R. No patients *Left Without Being Seen*. I checked the numbers as I do at the end of every shift."

"It takes money to hire another physician. Have you considered that consequence? No. Because you aren't responsible for the financial operations of this emergency department. You overstepped your duties. You should have called me first."

"And finally, we get to your latest complaint with a doctor upstairs. He reported you as rude, disrespectful, and out of line. After reading his complaint, I have found that your behavior is not in keeping with the Customer Service Values our organization supports."

A deep, hot flush of humiliation swept across Maggie's face betraying her desire to appear confident. It was clear Evans was out for blood. At that moment, Maggie understood why so many people hated the man. The room fell silent as Evans signaled the Human Resources person to take over. "We need you to sign this," he said, nodding to the H.R. person.

Human Resources handed Maggie a document. It was a *Final Written Warning*. Any further incidences of unacceptable behavior or mismanagement would result in immediate termination. They had skipped the Verbal and Written warning and had chosen to take a hard line seeking to fire her. Maggie signed the form and sat very still, unable to move from fear itself.

"The nurse manager will tie things up here," HR announced curtly. "And you will be asked to participate in random drug screens."

"I'm telling you—I don't use drugs!" Maggie replied defensively.

"We'll find out, won't we? We need you to submit one before you leave," Evans said with a smug look. "And you will not be allowed to work until we get a negative report."

She stood, made her way to the door, and took the urine cup. A female employee health nurse followed Maggie to the bathroom and observed her give a sample. She handed the cup to the nurse, washed her hands, foamed them, and left the room with her head hung low, filled with complete total humiliation.

Maggie went back to the E.R. and fought embarrassment as she gave her report and turned over her keys, phone, and pager to the Nurse Manager. It was apparent the manager knew what had happened.

ON HER WAY TO THE PARKING GARAGE, Maggie got a call from Bonnie. "Doctor Richardson is making rounds if you can come."

Maggie raced to the ICU and arrived in time to greet Doctor Richardson at the bedside.

Maggie was less than happy to see Chase present. Tony nodded a friendly greeting.

"I have a few questions, doctor," Bonnie plunged forward. "I noticed in the labs that our patient had an elevated GHB level on arrival. And possibly it could have played a part in her mixed neurological picture in her presentation to the E.R. Could that be playing a role in how she is now?"

"Not this far out. Did Annella have a history of substance abuse?" Richardson asked, looking at Chase.

"What can I tell you?" Chase replied with a smug smile. "We're Hollywood."

"What exactly does that mean?" Doctor Richardson asked, annoyed.

"We use—substances—from time to time."

"That is not true," Maggie retorted, "Annella did not do drugs. I'd stake my life on it."

"Well, you might very well die from that bet," Chase said, giving Maggie a hard stare before lifting the sheets and exposing Annella's feet, pulling her toes apart. "This is the last place she used, doctor."

Richardson looked at the bruising and appeared surprised.

"People don't usually inject GHB. They drink it. With alcohol," Maggie said.

"Well—you know my Annella. She's different. Like they say, different strokes for different folks. It was probably some other drug."

Doctor Richardson looked around the room. "Hmm. The rest of her drug screen panel came back negative. I guess we'll have to wait until she wakes up to find out. At any rate, I don't believe that's currently her problem. Call me if you have any issues, Bonnie."

After Richardson left, Chase sharply announced he would like private time with his wife. "That is my right. Right?"

Maggie and Bonnie gathered across the hall and out of earshot of Chase but close enough for Bonnie to keep her eyes on him.

"Well. At least Chase didn't kill Annella," Bonnie said, leaning against the wall. "Thank God for that," Maggie said, deflated, crossing her arms.

"Something funny about it, though," Bonnie added. "His private assistant Tony looked uncomfortable through the whole thing, like he thought Chase was lying. Lately, he always seems awkward when he's around Chase. It's weird. At first, he didn't stay all the time, but now it seems he tries to be here, in the room with Chase, every time Chase visits her. As I said, it's weird, like he doesn't trust Chase."

"We should be talking to him. See what he thinks. Furtively. Without him knowing what we're up to."

"Oh, honey, I can handle anything with that man. He is such a cutie pie. I can hardly take my eyes off him. When he looks into my eyes—I just want to melt to the floor as the bad witch did in *The Wizard of Oz*," Bonnie said, patting her heart for dramatic effect.

Maggie laughed out loud. "If I didn't know any better, I'd say you have a mighty crush on Tony."

"Can you think of anyone better? I mean, really, Maggie. Have you ever taken a good look at him? Talk about eye candy. My. Oh. My. They don't come any better looking than that. Tony's the one who should be on the screen. Not Chase."

"Girl. You are on fire," Maggie said, fanning her face as she walked off, thinking to herself what a peach of a girl Bonnie was. She deserved a good love life. Maggie just hoped she didn't get her heart crushed.

Maggie stopped by Glenn's room to say hello, but he was in a deep sleep.

On her way home, Maggie recalled the meeting with the Executive Director and cried all the way to Blanchard House. It was like Déjà vu from two years ago. She shuddered at the thought of him finding out her mother had spent the night at her house. When that happened, it indeed would be all over but the crying. She would again experience the dramatic moment of being escorted off hospital property by security. It was humiliating enough to have that happen once in her life, but twice—Maggie began to cry.

When Maggie got to the house, she couldn't go in and drove all around town, not fazed by the heavy traffic and the honking horns. She wanted to be alone in her humiliation with her puffed-up face from all the tears. Maggie pulled into an Arby's and ordered comfy food—a giant diet coke, a big-sized curly fries, and a turkey, bacon, and cheese sandwich. Then she sat in her car and tried to think of a way out of her troubles, realizing in the end, there was none.

Chapter 11

The Conference

Retired homicide detective Lamar Floyd tried to loosen his rigid body posture as he entered the Homicide BullPen where he used to work. The bullpen held an unusual eerie silence and the smell of stale coffee. Usually, it was like a beehive with detectives humming about, talking on the phone, eyes buried deep into death charts, or feet propped up, hands behind the head, eyes closed, or deep in thought. He assumed everyone was in the meeting in the conference room.

Lamar felt tense for a good reason. He was head of security for Kerrington Blanchard, and everything in the Blanchard household had gone to hell in a handbasket in a short amount of time. And Kerrington had made no beans about his unhappiness with Lamar. Kerrington was usually a man in charge and wore that image well. People listened when he spoke up at meetings—because he only spoke when he wanted something done. Lamar was proud to work for him. And it was an immense amount of pressure—making sure the security departments of his companies, scattered all over the world, ran smoothly.

Kerrington didn't blame Lamar. They usually got along quite well. Friends almost. He simply wanted Lamar to fix everything. He wanted the missing girl, Maggie's friend, Willow, found—or it was the end of his job. That was the last thing Kerrington said to him before hopping on his helicopter to the airport, which housed his private plane, where Kerrington then flew off to Ukraine. He hoped Kerrington didn't mean it—only that he was letting off steam.

Lamar rubbed his fingers along his forehead, checking to make sure it wasn't covered with beads of sweat. He straightened his cufflinks, tie, and silk suit jacket, having ditched the cowboy look long ago for a proper appearance as Chief of Blanchard Security.

Several years ago, luck changed his life when Maggie walked through his door and hired him as a private detective to investigate her deceased husband's activities before his death. As a result, he'd landed his golden employment with Blanchard as a reward for helping solve the serial murders. He'd grown considerable gray hair along his previously black-haired temples. Convinced it came with the job. Today's meeting would probably bring more silver locks. He looked at his image in the reflection of the glass door window. He was handsome and healthy looking. Not bad for a fifty-five-year-old man and a longtime smoker. It was a habit he intended to break. He'd stopped ten days ago, of all times, and was now in desperate need of a hit off a butt.

THE CONFEREENCE ROOM was packed. Lamar searched for familiar faces. As always, his best friend Hanes sat to the side, writing notes. They'd worked twenty years together, side-by-side as partners in the homicide unit. Since Lamar was retired, it had taken many persuasions to get Hanes to allow him into today's briefing. The fact that he still held a private detective license probably helped. Hanes's rule was clear—no talking. No notes.

Detective Smart spoke as he paced back and forth with his protruding beer and donut belly sticking out over his low-waisted belt. Occasionally, he'd pull out his handkerchief and wipe the building sweat off his face and neck. His tone was laced with exasperation, probably because he was tired of delivering the same briefing daily and, thus, knew it by heart. Lamar was quite familiar with the feeling. It had been his job for decades.

Lamar felt the heightened pressure in the room. It was thick as ice. Stiff. He knew the politics circling the department, having been a homicide cop for so long. The hospital and the city managers from the mayor's office on down held a sickening, choking, and enormously stressful political grip over the police department. During high-profile cases, they made it their daily task to pester the hell out of homicide and every higher-up authority they could connect with, sending a clear message to get things done. Today. Lamar could feel the pressure on Hanes—the constant unhappiness emanating from the members of the mayor's office and the legal eagles from the hospital. Today's meeting involved a complete update on all aspects of the crime. Homicide. Missing Persons. And so forth.

"Descriptions of the perpetrators lack useful information at best," Smart said. "They were dressed in black. Hoodies, masks, generic-looking shoes. All were the same size. The shooter had a thick southern accent and smelled heavily of cigarette smoke."

"It's still not clear how they entered the hospital. The areas robbed of narcotics were Day Surgery and the east wing of the O.R., which was closed for the holidays. Homicide wasn't notified about the O.R. at the time of the E.R. investigation. It wasn't until the day shift came in that they discovered the missing narcotics. Gathering the forensics and sorting things out, like the E.R., was complex due to the high volume of nurse, doctor, patient, and visitor traffic through each area. The perpetrators were clever. They knew what they were doing and coordinated the robbery down to every tiny detail."

"The drugs are potent," Detective Smart went forward. "Sky high street value due to its quality and variety. Many of the vials contain extremely high doses of narcotics used to make I.V. drips. So far, the city has experienced six overdose deaths related to the robbery. Talk to your street contacts. Let's do a deeper dive into social media related to the kidnapped victim."

The meeting went on with details of the doctor who was shot and the deceased secretary. Neither victim was linked to the crime other than they just happened to be at the wrong place at the wrong time.

"In closing, the nurse, Maggie Bennett, aka Blanchard, may or may not be involved. That is an ongoing part of the investigation. She's linked to an elopement of a psychiatric drug-addict patient just before the robbery. The patient just happens to be her mother. It may go nowhere. Or somewhere. We think the mother was there to scope the place out."

Lamar nervously moved to the edge of his seat, hoping Darlene's visit to Blanchard House would stay hidden.

"The eloped patient is Darlene Sutton. Arrested many times for possession. Rehab 4 times. She lived at a Charlotte Homeless Shelter until Christmas Eve—when she was kicked out for intoxication. This is her picture," he added, pointing to the enlarged photo on the big screen. "Keep your eyes open. She might be the key."

A female blond cop's hand shot wildly into the air.

"Yes?"

"I saw the woman exiting the entrance to Blanchard property on Sharon Road."

Lamar closed his eyes. *Damn. Damn. Damn*, he muttered in his head. His hands folded into fists, his forehead digging into them as the briefing continued. He wanted to leave but didn't dare draw attention to himself. Hanes turned his head and shot Lamar a pissed-off look before returning his attention to the conference.

A thin, beautiful brunette female detective stood to speak and looked like she was straight out of a television cop show. She said with a southern voice, "The kidnapped individual has been identified as Willow Maxwell, a 34-year-old registered nurse who works full time in the E.R. Her husband, Benny Maxwell, works in the same department as a technician. During the robbery, he was locked up with many other staff members in the break room.

Willow has a daughter from a previous marriage to Jack Webster. There were domestic violence issues in the home. Due to domestic violence, the victim issued a restraining order against Mr. Webster. It is still in enforcement, and the ex-hasn't violated it. Reportedly, he got a gig on an oil rig and moved to Alabama two years ago. Not likely he's involved, but we'll keep digging."

Hanes looked at Lamar and shook his head in dismay as more updates came fast and furious from various task members.

"One witness was sitting on her front porch smoking during the robbery and shooting. She saw a vehicle but couldn't identify anything about it, saying the streetlights were out all around the hospital. So far, no one else living in the immediate area was awake. Both outside and interior hospital cameras were non-functional. We're pursuing security footage from nearby businesses and homes, hoping we might prove helpful in getting a fix on the car."

Hanes stood up and pushed his chair aside. "Meeting adjourned." Lamar watched as the non-police visitors left the meeting. Hanes avoided looking at him.

"How can everything come to a dead end?" the Chief asked, his voice filled with loud annoyance. "We'll meet again in the morning. Meanwhile, we need every single security employee of that hospital interviewed. And stop the whining about being overworked. I want the O.R. crime scene report on my desk by the end of the day."

"And don't forget, the officials are being freakin' crybabies about us not doing our job fast enough," Hanes added, avoiding looking at Lamar before leaving through a side door.

Lamar bolted out the back, deliberately side-stepping the bullpen, afraid someone might ask about Darlene being on Blanchard's property. Talking about Blanchard's business with anyone would definitely be a termination. He was crest-fallen and nervous the rest of the day, having no idea where to turn or what to do next. He couldn't go to Hanes and confide. He felt like he'd betrayed his former partner of twenty years by withholding information, which is precisely what he did. His situation caused severe anxiety and burning in his gut twenty-four hours a day. He needed answers about Willow. Today.

AN HOUR LATER, Hanes sat at his desk, livid. The notes he'd taken were few, which was the cause of his infuriation. This case was, without a doubt, the worst homicide case he'd ever been assigned. The investigation had gone south from the very beginning. Forty-eight hours into the inquiry, they'd uncovered such little evidence that he'd started getting the dreaded **loser looks** from his superiors in passing through the building. And Hanes always took considerable pride in his work. This time he couldn't. The political pressure was unbearable. Every day the questions were the same—and he had no answers. His mind felt heavy. Burdened. Hanes grabbed his jacket and headed for the Wicked Wolf, a local bar, to get a stiff drink.

Chapter 12

Movement

It was morning, Annella was so happy to get another bed bath, and Bonnie gave her a good one. Lying in bed twenty-four hours a day made her feel dirty, and even though she knew she wasn't, It still felt that way. Bonnie was fast, and the water was always pleasant and warm. All the while Bonnie worked, she talked, which was great because it made Annella feel like she was still part of the living.

"Well, on this fine day, there's so much stuff going on. Colorado is on fire, and over a thousand homes are gone near Denver. A snowstorm moving in from the west has travelers stranded on the roads all over the country. And **Bennifer** may become real, but I bet you already knew that being you're in show business," Bonnie said, covering Annella with a warm blanket. "I'm going to get some help. We're moving you into a fancy new bed that automatically turns you side-to-side slowly to prevent bed sores and pneumonia. I think you'll like it."

Annella felt her body float into the air—then, a few minutes later, she was lowered onto another bed. Then, she felt Bonnie's gentle touch on her arm as she left to tend to other patients. "I'll turn on the news so you can hear what's happening. Your brother Kerrington said you like the news. We'll start with CNN. I'll change it when I get back to give you more variety of news. I'll be back very soon to check on you."

Annella was grateful for the news distraction, and Bonnie was right; between Covid, Ukraine with war threats, and all the snowstorms, there was little room for anything else. She wanted to smile. She felt better today, like her strength was returning—emotional power, not muscular.

Eventually, she drifted off again and had a disturbing dream. She was with Chase, drinking champagne in her dressing room on the movie set and still in her wedding gown from the film's final scene. They'd given out champagne. She didn't like the taste, but Chase kept urging her to drink it.

"I need to go home, Chase. I have a plane to catch," she'd said, trying to get him to leave her dressing room, glad her working relationship with him was finally over. When she stood up, she stumbled backward and spilled her champagne.

Chase laughed and handed her the glass. "Champagne is made for drinking and enjoyment. Take a drink. Sit down for a minute, and let's enjoy having made such a fine movie. It's a good one, don't you think?"

Annella sat down lest she fall again. She was tired. Over tired. Annella briefly wondered if she had Covid—though that was nearly impossible as she'd only been exposed to the people on the movie set. The set nurse performed Covid tests daily to ensure everyone was as safe as possible. Nevertheless, she felt her head, and the temperature of her skin felt normal. No fever. She swallowed. It didn't hurt. She took another sip of the champagne.

"That's a good girl," Chase said, encouraging her. "Enjoy this expensive stuff. Drink the champagne. We have a lot to celebrate."

ANNELLA AWAKENED, FRIGHTENED. She wanted to scream, get out of bed, and run as far away as possible. But her inability to get help pushed her deeper into the ravines of desperation. *What did Chase do to me?*

She felt her blanket move. A cold hand lifted her nightgown. Through her peripheral vision, Annella saw Chase's face draw close to hers. She felt his warm breath on her cheek as he kissed her. At the same time, she felt a stinging sensation on the left side of her thigh, followed by a dull ache. "Sleep tight, my love."

Annella thought she might be dreaming but realized she wasn't.

"What are you doing there, pal?" Tony said, his voice incredulously angry. "You're supposed to stay six feet away from her."

"I'm kissing my wife. Is that okay with you? I don't have Covid. Let's go get coffee. Then, I'll sign some autographs. You like that? I'll work a little bit."

Annella watched the men walk away as a thick translucent gray veil swept over her eyes. Her lids became heavier by the minute until she could no longer hold them open, and she plunged into a deep sleep.

THAT EVENING, Maggie visited Annella and sat silently in the visitor's chair, studying her, motionless and unconscious, appearing like an angel asleep in her perfect white bed. Annella's freshly combed locks of her long, shimmering blond hair trailed lifelessly over the edges of her shining white silk pillowcase, undoubtedly, brought from home by Kerrington. Annella always carried silk pillowcases with her everywhere she traveled.

Maggie admired the diligent work of Annella's nurse Bonnie. She had tilted a single lamp towards the ceiling giving the room an ethereal effect. Annella looked angelic in her appearance—like a sleeping princess.

The low humming sound of the beeping monitors and pumps of various tones and qualities sounded like a small orchestra playing music. Maggie took in the sights of the complicated intravenous lines that carried vital and intricate medications into Annella's body—the delivery rates titrated ever so carefully by complex pumps. The iridescent-appearing tubing looked like twisting vines intertwining around each other like a well-tended garden. Bonnie's attention to detail was evident in how she carefully color-coded each I.V. line with small labels so she could quickly tell them apart during an emergency.

Maggie took Annella's limp hand in hers. How had everything gone so wrong so fast? So far, no one could explain what happened to Annella Wryn—whose real name was Anna Ella Kathryn Blanchard. Kerrington called her Wryn and, on some occasions, laughingly called her Bossy Britches. Maggie smiled. They always laughed about the nickname. Maggie called her Annie, and she'd occasionally call her **Star**. The rest of the world called her Annella Wryn.

Maggie sighed. Kerrington was busy trying to get to the bottom of what happened to Annella. Her huge VIP hospital suite revealed proof of his devotion to Annella. It had a private living room in the back for the family to stay during non-Covid times. It overlooked the river, which gave the room a peaceful feeling. The hospital built the unique large room as a haven for the rich and famous. Occasionally, it housed maniacal patients with a wicked history of crimes that reporters wanted to capture pictures of for a story. In those situations, the patient was moved closer to the river, and police occupied the entry space. Occasionally, less critical patients were allowed river views. Still, Bonnie wanted Annella close to the wall of windows on the hospital corridor side because Annella was on a ventilator and her condition was critical. She wanted her close to the front, where the nurses could see Annella easily.

The room was situated at the far end of the unit. Visitors had to pass the security guard to access the only two VIP suites. Glenn was in the other one. She could see him from where she sat. She softly smiled. Since Glenn was a physician, he was given star treatment as well.

Maggie stared lovingly at her sister-in-law, the sister she'd never had. Maggie didn't see her as a movie star because they'd become so close. Annella was simply a person who had an exciting job that she loved and was good at. The only times Maggie appreciated Annella's fame was when they slipped out to go shopping—with security details following their every move. During these special trips, Maggie discovered how Kerrington got his **GQ** look. Annella did all his shopping in New York City at upscale stores, buying clothes she wanted him to wear. Her favorite designer was **Ralph Lauren**, a good friend of hers.

Annella got a lot of attention during their shopping sprees. Crowds always gathered, but Blanchard Security kept the curiosity seekers at bay. Maggie began to understand why Annella stayed at home most of the time. On many occasions, some stores, especially the up-scale boutiques, would close the store to give her privacy.

Annella gave up a lot to be an actress. And that's how she saw herself. She was an actress. Not a movie star. And she was humble about it all despite her skyrocketing celebrity status over the past five years—to the point that she was often on the cover of at least three to four magazines a month—many of them with Chase.

Annie's purported relationship with Chase, the co-star of her last four films, was the talk of Tinseltown and the world. They were another ***Bennifer***. But Annella had told her not to believe what she read in the smut magazines as it was merely a part of the movie-making business. Maggie believed Annella because she never talked about Chase except for the one time when she'd claimed he was a terrible kisser. Until yesterday, Maggie hadn't even met him.

So, what was the marriage bit all about? Maggie wondered as she looked at Annella. *Why would Annella marry a man who was a terrible kisser? And what was the deal with Glenn*? With Annella in a coma from a brain injury and Glenn unable to speak, she could not figure out the truth. Simply put, she could not believe Annella would have married Chase. Period.

Tears formed in Maggie's eyes as she recalled their fun times lying around Annella's bedroom, reading the piles of scripts. "You need to get better, Annie," Maggie cried. "So, we can vote on which script is the best for you to do next. We never got to vote. And we still have Lamborghini wine to drink. So, wake up! And make it quick."

Annella was already awake and laughed inside at the *make it quick* comment. It was so like Maggie to demand it. Annella noticed she felt more awake than ever. The last dose of medication wasn't the same. It wore off early.

Maggie looked back at her best friend and wondered what her future held. The longer she remained in a coma, the worse the odds of a full recovery became. The vision of Annella being confined to a bed or wheelchair for life without the ability to communicate was an unbearable thought. Before leaving, Maggie kissed Annella's small, frail hand, noting her need for a manicure as she gently placed it on the bed.

At first, Maggie thought she imagined things when she saw Annella's little finger move. "Annella! Did you move your finger? Move it again. Move it again." Then Maggie stared in disbelief as Annella moved her finger.

Maggie jumped to the door and called Bonnie into the room. "She moved a finger. Watch! Annella. Move your finger again." They both watched, waiting with eyes widened. "Annie, move your finger. Bonnie wants to see." When nothing happened, Maggie continued begging for some time. "I'm not losing my mind, Bonnie. She moved it when I kissed her hand. And then, she moved it on command. I know what I saw."

Finally, Bonnie suggested they give it a break, and she promised to check Annella for movement every hour with her neuro exam. After Bonnie left, Maggie held for the most prolonged moment, overwhelmed with disappointment. It was such good news. She sank into the chair, recalling some paralyzed patients' meaningless movements. Maggie chose to believe it was otherwise.

Maggie's mind eventually moved onto other thoughts as she wondered if she should tell Annella about Glenn, then decided not to. It might be too much for her in an injured state.

She kissed Annella's hand again, waiting for a movement that never came, and left to visit Glenn across the hall.

Maggie felt the most profound sadness when she stepped into Glenn's room. At first, she thought he was asleep. He had two very black eyes from his injury, and his forehead was swollen. He held a pen on top of a clipboard with blank paper and chicken scratch markings in his hand. Maggie's throat felt thick as she fought tears. He couldn't write. But he had tried. That was Glenn. He was one determined man.

Maggie stepped up to the bedside and took a seat in the chair. When she looked at Glenn's eyes, they were open, and tears traced down his face. Maggie could tell he had so much to say. She could see it in his bloodshot green eyes. For the first time in a long time, Maggie felt caught for words wondering what she should say. His days as an emergency physician and medical director were over. And she knew in her heart he didn't want to live this way. Glenn looked hard at Maggie, and when he knew he had her attention, his eyes darted across the hall, and he stared at Annella. Glenn's eyes went back and forth from Maggie to Annella until Maggie got his message. "Annella?" Maggie asked. "She's alive. And stable. But paralyzed. Unable to communicate."

AFTER MAGGIE LEFT, Glenn lay patiently in his bed waiting. That was his life nowadays. Waiting on the nurse or the doctor or another health care worker. Bonnie was the best. She was his nurse, and someday he hoped he'd get to tell her she was a great nurse.

And Maggie, God bless her for her patience. She figured out he wanted to watch the news. It kept him from dwelling on his life as it now was —without the ability to speak and a fuzzy brain that struggled to think.

Glenn was angry. Angry at the world. Enraged with his shooter. And furious with Annella Wryn, who lay within his view across the hall. He wanted to scream at her. Ask her why she betrayed him. And Chase, there weren't enough words to describe his hate for the arrogant ass who paced back and forth outside Annella's room when Bonnie was taking care of Annella's personal needs. Glenn wanted to strangle him. Hurt him. Get even. Although he would never truly harm anyone, Glenn still thought about it, and the thoughts helped him deal with his disability.

Where do I go from here? Glenn wondered. He'd recently bought the most expensive diamond for Annella. He could not work for the foreseeable future—maybe never again. His soon-to-be- published book now lay unedited on his desk. His credentials—all but in the trash.

Glenn's life as a physician, the enthusiasm for his life, was gone, destroyed by the flash of a single bullet.

On television, he listened to broadcasters arguing about gun control. Their passion to change things was too late for him.

At least he could look at Annella. At least he had that left. It didn't bother him that she was always on television with Chase. In Glenn's heart, he knew Annella Wryn loved only him and wanted to marry him. Something had drastically gone wrong. But what did it matter now? He could never ask for her hand in marriage in his condition. She was such a majestic creature on every level. He would never put her through such a thing—being married to a man who can't even say *I love you* anymore.

Right at that moment, Annella's bed rotated mechanically to face him. He stared at her for the longest time, his heart soaring by leaps and bounds. She was looking at him! Annella could see him. He smiled. She didn't smile back. *I know she sees me! I know it. Maybe she doesn't love me after all.* Tears rolled down his face. Glenn closed his eyes. And then, he opened them again. He couldn't help not looking at her. She owned his soul—lock, stock, and barrel.

ANNELLA STRAINED TO LOOK at the man across the hall. *Poor fellow. He looks like he was injured badly.* She studied him. Why was he staring at her so intensely? He looked like he wanted to talk to her. Maybe he recognized her. *But he looks so familiar. Really familiar*. Even with his black eyes and swollen face. Struck by surprise, Annella suddenly recognized him. *It's Glenn. It's Glenn.* She tried to talk back with her eyes.

Chapter 13

The Secret Code

Hanes opened the newly delivered crime scene analysis report three days late. And he studied it until his eyes became weary. To say he was disappointed was an understatement. The new evidence collected from the crime scene was so small in proportion to what he hoped—three simple items.

A speck of dirt.

A fiber from worn-out blue jeans. A partial boot footprint.

A short strand of straight black hair.

Analysis was still pending on all items to determine their relevance to the crime and its potential source.

A review of the traffic control was even less helpful.

Traffic flow. In any given twenty-four hours, an estimated one hundred or more employees are in and out of the Day Surgery med/supply room because the space doubles as both a supply station and the medication room. Hanes knew with such a high traffic flow—it would be difficult to determine who may have been involved in the incident with employees coming and going. High-traffic areas can also contaminate evidence, making it more challenging to decide on what evidence is relevant and what is not. Hanes's mind raced. The evidence could have come from anyone, including repair people from different departments.

He looked at the evidence list again and excluded the Emergency Department from his mind. All the evidence came from Day Surgery. That fact alone made it more relevant. Evidence would be easier to pin down due to the requirement of shoe covers and caps, and they would be wearing scrubs, not jeans and boots.

He tossed the report aside and moved on to the next piece. Upon reading the new information, Hanes jerked straight up in his chair, filled with newfound energy. Willow Maxwell's secret, *or not-so-secret code*, was used to gain access to the **Pyxis** drug supply system in the O.R. precisely two minutes before her entry code was used to access the Pyxis system in the E.R. The same code number. Two minutes apart. Four stories apart. E.R. elevators were on Lockdown.

Hanes rubbed his jaw, deep in thought. *It's not possible. Willow didn't open the O.R.* Pyxis *because timing placed her in the E.R. Someone had access to her secret code. How did they get it? More importantly, who entered it? It seems logical that Benny might have had access to her code. They were married. And Benny was on a meal break at the same time as Willow, per Maggie's statement. Did he rob the Pyxis in the O.R. while she robbed the one in the E.R.? Had he really been locked up with the others in the break room?* Hanes looked at the foot-high paperwork on both edges of his desk. Had Benny been interviewed? Who interviewed the people in the break room? He looked back at the stacks of papers, overwhelmed by the work on his desk. The piles had never gotten this high before. His computer mailbox was filled to the brim as well.

Where did Darlene go when she eloped? Did she meet Benny? Did he give her Willow's code? Did Darlene rob the Pyxis and take the goods out of the hospital? Did Maggie know the code as her supervisor and provide it to her mother? He needed a list of people who accessed the floor with an ID badge, or had the ID scanners even been working at the time? Hanes looked back at his stack of papers and wondered—while Maggie played the *Sunshine Goody Two Shoes Hero* downstairs, acting all scared while they put a gun to her head—she was possibly the orchestrator from behind the scenes. Why would she have her employees shot? Maybe the shooting wasn't a part of the plan. Perhaps the gunman went rogue and started doing his own thing. It was hard to imagine Maggie would do such a thing, but Hanes had shot himself in the foot a time or two in the early days by dismissing suspects early on because they didn't fit the profile. He'd been blindsided by several killers who had taught him a lesson once or twice.

It was a monster of a case all by itself. Hanes would need to work many overtime shifts to sift through all the information coming his way.

MAGGIE ENTERED THE POLICE STATION with Benny, afraid to go alone. Since Benny was also called in, they decided to go together.

The room was small, hot, smelly, felt grungy, and gave Maggie an uncomfortable feeling of claustrophobia. Hanes was already seated in the chair across from her. Another detective stood, leaning against the wall.

The moment Maggie sat, Hanes jumped right in with his questions, holding his pen eagerly to his sacred notebook, ready to write her every word.

"Have you seen your mother since we last talked?" Hanes asked eagerly. Maggie sat very still, terrified to answer the question, wondering what to say. "Maggie?"

"Yes," Maggie mumbled as she felt sweat breaking out in her armpits. "She came to my house."

"I thought you no longer had contact," Hanes replied, his tone accusing.

"We didn't. I'm telling you the truth. Other than Christmas night, I hadn't seen my mother since I was a teenager, and then she just showed up at my house uninvited. My husband Kerrington invited her in. He didn't know about our relationship. He invited her to spend the night. I didn't see her until the morning."

"I'm glad you didn't lie about it. Tell me about your relationship."

And so, Maggie dragged Hanes through the memories of her life—living with her mother, then living in an orphanage. And how she went back and forth repeatedly as her mother was carted off to jail or the hospital for overdoses. "The last time I saw my mother before the robbery was my sixteenth birthday. I sat up all night in the hospital, watching her sleep off her drugs, snoring, and slobbering everywhere. It left quite a vivid image for me to savor. And then, out of nowhere, she showed up in the E.R. as a patient at Christmas." Maggie intentionally made the story as ugly and hideous as possible, so maybe, just maybe, Hanes might get it. "And that is the truth," Maggie said, sighing. "When I found her in my house, I kicked her out and told her never to return."

Hanes went forward without even acknowledging her pain. Maggie surmised he'd probably heard the same type of story repeatedly. "Do you now, or have you ever had access to any employee's private and secret Pyxis code?"

"I do not. I don't know of anyone who does. The pharmacy would be able to answer that question."

"Have you ever watched Willow enter her code?"

"I have not. I would not."

"So," Hanes said, pushing harder, "If I pulled the security videos from the med room on the days you worked together, would I find footage of the two of you talking over the Pyxis machine? I've noticed this is common. Nurses talking while they are in the Pyxis."

Again, Maggie hesitated as she thought about the question. "Not that I recall."

"So, you're saying it is possible."

Maggie paused, her stomach growling loud enough for Hanes to hear. "What I'm saying is—I don't know. But, in answer to your real underlying question, detective, I do not know Willow's password and would never have watched her enter it. If I had accidentally come across Willow's or anyone's code, for that matter, I would insist they change it immediately, as is the policy. Does that answer your question better? I was in no way a part of the robbery."

"Why would Willow's code work in another area?"

"The emergency department nurses have system-wide access because we respond to Code Blue events and often work overtime in other areas, since the outbreak of Covid," Maggie explained.

"Was Benny Maxwell in the E.R. at the time of the robbery?"

"You know he was," Maggie replied, becoming annoyed. "You were there when he learned about Willow. Yes. I saw him in the back of the E.R. with her when they returned from break. They went their separate ways."

"So, you can't tell me where Benny went? For all you know, he could have gone up to Day Surgery."

"He wouldn't have a reason to go there. They were closed."

"Do you know for sure if Benny stayed in his area?"

Maggie caught for words, sat stoically, struggling, then finally said, "I do not."

The questioning went on for at least another thirty minutes—monotonous questions, at least from her point of view. Eventually, Hanes brought the inquiry to a close and brought Benny in.

Maggie waited until he was done, and they went home together. "That was bad," Benny declared. "I felt like a criminal."

"Yep. That was bad."

"You think we're suspects?"

"Yep. And I think we need to do what we have to do to protect ourselves and find Willow."

They're wasting valuable time barking up the wrong tree. I say it's time to go to Titus."

Chapter 14

Covert Operations

Titus's house was tucked back in the woods off an unpaved country road. As Maggie surveyed the charming little white house, complete with a delightful front porch and a swing, she couldn't help but notice the surrounding white wooden fence that desperately needed a fresh coat of paint. It appeared that a woman had carefully selected the house as her dream home many years ago.

Unfortunately, the front flower beds were now overgrown with drooping flowers that had been choked by the frosty winter weather, leaving brown sticks and stiff, dry petals. The bird feeders, which hung empty, looked dirty and neglected. The once-lush hanging ferns were dying, having been left outside throughout the harsh, freezing nights. Maggie couldn't shake the feeling of sadness that overcame her as she wondered why such a charming home appeared so neglected, as though something terrible had occurred within its walls. As they drove around to the back of the house, she didn't share her private thoughts out of sensitivity to Benny and his suffering over Willow.

They parked in the back and stepped up to the house. Piles of dead leaves covered the back porch, topping the lids of an old washer and dryer. In the distance, Maggie could see dark clouds heading their way. She even thought she saw a streak of lightning. It was an unseasonably warm day, with temperatures in the low eighties, for it to be wintertime. But odd weather was a worldwide event nowadays.

Maggie heard the click as Benny picked the lock and opened the back door. The den was dark- paneled and furnished with the country-styled decor of rooster pictures, rocking chairs, and an old antique-looking fireplace. In the corner was an old antique desk with a framed family photograph of Titus, his wife, and two children.

"Let's start here at the desk. We need to work fast. Try to put everything back in its original place." Benny ordered, looking overwhelmed at his task.

After a few minutes of pillaging through the papers cluttering the desk, Maggie held up a white business card. "Looks like Hanes visited him. Wonder how that went?" Maggie said, moving the card back to where it had been prominently displayed.

Benny picked up some papers and looked through them. "No wonder Titus is so angry. Look at these," Benny remarked, handing the documents to Maggie.

"Oh my Gosh," Maggie gasped as she flipped through the documents. "Overwhelming hospital bills from a Burn Center. Three patients. His two children and his wife. They were underinsured on their auto insurance. What the heck?"

"It gets worse," Benny added. "The car that hit his wife and children didn't have insurance. Plus, he was missing her salary which helped pay normal bills. Titus can't possibly pay off this debt."

Maggie picked up the checkbook and thumbed through the register. Her eyes widened. "Titus made a hundred and fifty-thousand-dollar cash deposit and sent checks out totaling the same amount. Where'd he get that kind of money?"

Benny leveled his eyes with Maggie's. They had the answers they came to find and got a glimpse into the tragic life of Titus. Three funeral bills. And sadly, last, of all, a suicide note from his wife stating she couldn't live without her children and didn't want to be a burden. Maggie sank into the chair, wanting to cry her heart out.

Benny wiped his face. "Titus lost everything. House. Family. No wonder he's been so angry. And on top of it all, he didn't get the higher paying promotion he obviously needed and deserved." Neither of them moved for a long moment as they digested what had happened to their co-worker.

They quickly checked the rest of the house and found evidence that Titus was still living there. A load of laundry smelled freshly washed and needed to go into the dryer. Empty suitcases lined the bottom of the closet, still full of hanging clothes. His chest of drawers was full as well.

"I'm starting to feel creepy, like we're wallowing around in things Titus is desperate to keep secret. It's not right. Us being here," Benny said quietly.

"I agree," Maggie replied quietly, walking lightly across the floor. "We know he did it. Let's go before we get caught."

They searched the garage and found his car. "Gawd, Maggie. Smell that stink?"

"A dead body? I'd know that smell anywhere." Maggie whispered.

"A good and dead body," Benny replied.

They both moved slowly toward the smell coming from the hen house. They slowed when they spotted a man's legs poking out the door.

"We need to go, Benny. Now!" Maggie said, popping Benny's arm to get his attention. "I ain't going anywhere, girl."

"I can't do this," Maggie said. "No more murders. Dead bodies. I think I'm going to throw up."

"So am I." Benny retorted, pinching his nose shut and holding his hand over his mouth as he stepped into the hen house. "It's Titus," Benny cried out. "They shot a hole in his back. Probably used a shotgun."

Maggie couldn't help but look. Titus was cold and dead. Bloated. Eyes frozen open. Mouth gaped. "Please, let's leave, Benny. Please," Maggie begged.

"Maggie," Benny said, his voice low as he looked around. "We can't walk away from a murder scene. Our DNA is everywhere," Benny warned, stepping out of the hen house, hurling vomit in the high grass. The wind whipped through the yard just as a fierce downfall of rain pelted heavily from the sky. They stared helplessly at each other, not moving as the rain drenched them. Maggie finally spoke, holding her hands above her eyes to shield them from the raindrops. "I'm leaving, Benny. Even if I'm forced to walk fifteen miles home in this downpour, I can't be caught here."

They escaped to the car and sat quietly, pondering the situation, staring out at Titus. Finally, Benny spoke, his voice low, stripped of energy. "He was the perfect guy for the crime. Green Beret. Trained in Special Ops. High-tech computer operations. Hacking into the hospital security system was easy for a man like him." Benny deeply sighed.

"You're right. And as I said, we can't be here. Let's go. We'll tell Lamar. Nothing's going to change in the next few hours. The one man who could tell us where Willow is or if she's alive or dead—is dead. And we've confirmed the people we are dealing with are deadly, brutal people. Let the police come to us—<u>if</u> they find our DNA here."

THEY DROVE STRAIGHT to Lamar's office and shared their adventure, seeking his advice. After calmly listening to their excited voices as they cut each other off and often interrupted the conversation. Benny's eyes blazed with worry and Maggie's flamed with paranoia. Lamar wanted to laugh at the two of them—always biting off more than they can chew. He probably would have laughed had there not been such a critical issue at stake. They had to report it in some shape or form. The question was how?

Lamar sent them on their way, suggesting they both go have a drink. Lamar headed out to take a look at Titus with his own eyes. He also called Hanes to meet him for a beer in an hour.

Chapter 15

The Wicked Wolf

An hour later, Hanes showed up at the Wicked Wolf bar, their favorite hangout, often frequented by cops, doctors, and nurses, as it wasn't far from the medical center. The quaint, warm, and cozy bar exuded an ambiance of comfort and calming charm inviting customers to take a break and unwind, which was precisely what Hanes needed—a break from the hustle. The soft, warm lighting cast a gentle glow over the room bringing an instantaneous feeling of an intimate and inviting place. Hanes especially liked the eclectic décor of college pennants lining the top of the walls and mismatched wooden tables and chairs—covered with red and white checkered tablecloths.

When Lamar arrived, he took in Hanes's impressive detective look, appearing quite intimidating, causing the people at the bar to look his way, some with alarmed glances, taking in the gun clipped to his waist beside his shining golden badge. Lamar took off his jacket before sitting down. His weapon also stood out like a sore thumb strapped to the side of his chest. He'd dressed down for the occasion, feeling dumpy in his jeans next to Hanes. He envied Hanes's badge, longing for the days when they worked side by side.

They settled in their usual chairs at the back of the bar where they could talk privately. Their beers were delivered promptly, in frosted mugs, without a word being exchanged with their bartender friend. It's how it always went. The bartender left without a word, knowing that when the two men sat in the back, they weren't interested in social babble. When they sat near the front, they ate peanuts, watched sports, and participated in lively conversation.

"So. What's up?" Hanes asked, taking a long drink from his mug before letting out a sigh of pleasure at the taste.

"I need a deal."

"What's in it for me?" Hanes asked before letting out a crooked smile.

"A tip," Lamar replied, edgy, knowing he was not going to share anything about the drugs, and he hoped Hanes didn't bring the subject up. Hanes was good at reading him. After all, they'd been partners for over twenty years and shared the worst of the worst.

"Coin flip. Who goes first?" Hanes queried.

Lamar flipped a quarter and called heads before it landed on tails. "There's a dead body." Lamar blurted out, observing Hanes's face. "Wow. How do you know?" Hanes asked, eyebrows raised.

"I saw it with my own eyes," Lamar spouted before going forward. "What I can tell you is where the victim is and that he was shot in the back."

"You've been to the scene?" Hanes asked, his eyes narrowing. "Yeah," Lamar replied. "Just left. Pretty gruesome."

"You have an I.D.?"

"Titus Wilkes. Worked at the hospital."

"I paid him a visit," Hanes said. "Not long ago. He wasn't home and there definitely wasn't a dead body on the property. I looked all around and left my calling card tucked in the crack of the front door. Did you call it in?" Hanes asked, business-like, before sucking down more beer.

"No. I wanted you to get the credit. Titus has been dead a bit. Didn't see the sense of hurrying up when I could help my partner out. So now, out with any news, you have regarding the girl, Willow. You know, her husband Benny lives at the mansion now. With Willow's daughter. I've been charged with finding *Missing Mommy* per Blanchard's personal order or I'm quite possibly out of there."

"Ouch!"

"That about spells it out."

"This is top secret," Hanes said, firmly. "I don't want to hear it on our street. Capiche?"

"Spill it. My lips are sealed," Lamar replied, waiting intently for the news spill.

"We may have gotten lucky in the O.R. It was closed for the holidays. Foot covers are required in the area. And we found a speck of dirt we're still analyzing."

"My hat's off to you for finding something with all the people going in and out of the O.R. no less." Lamar was quiet for a minute as he digested

Hanes news. Lamar felt anxious but tried to cover it as he continued to drink and laugh.

"You know, Maggie is a good girl," Lamar said. "She's not in on this. Neither is Benny. They are working too hard to solve the kidnapping. All that boy wants is his wife. All Maggie wants is her best friend safe. Plus…she doesn't need money. Not by a long shot."

"But her friends do. Like I always said, you never know about people."

"Her friends are not into making money, same as Maggie. They're into saving lives and working hard. It's their life. They're good peeps, Bro."

"Well, that's your tip. Hanes said, setting his drink on his napkin. "We're chasing a speck of dirt. It's all about the dirt. And some other minor stuff."

They both laughed. "Dirty business," Lamar replied. They chuckled again and continued to drink for an hour as Lamar wrote the address on a napkin where the body could be found. He smiled. That would be a nice big fruitful tip for his friend, pushing his investigation forward on high speed.

"There's more," Lamar said, hoping Hanes didn't catch on to the nervousness in his voice. "You'll find prints and DNA from Maggie and Benny at the scene. We all went together to talk to Titus. They were suspicious of him."

"What in the hell did you do that for? I'll be damned, Lamar. You didn't."

"I did. Maggie and Benny were hell-bent on going to Titus' house, and I wasn't about to let them go there alone," Lamar lied. "You might want to go through his desk. We did. Might be helpful. But again, you'll find all our prints there. It's the old homicide cop still alive inside me. I loved it! The whole adventure. Finding a body. Makes me want to come back home. I miss you guys."

"I miss you too, old friend. But you don't want to come back, it's too dangerous nowadays," Hanes looked at Lamar hard before finally breaking out in a smile. "You know I'd love to have the old days back but you're getting lame as a detective Lamar, going and screwing up my scene with visitors." Hanes let out a healthy laugh.

"Makes me a witness, I guess. A strong one. They didn't kill Titus." Lamar got up, flipped some money on the table before walking away. "Next week?"

"Sure. Same spot. Same time."

Chapter 16

The Transfer

Chase entered the massive, elegant lobby of Baderman Bank, one of Charlotte's most prestigious banks based in one of the city's tallest skyscrapers. Today, Chase's entourage was comprised of three bodyguards as he wanted to make the impression, he was a man to be reckoned with.

Despite the line of people waiting to be seen, Chase was greeted immediately and taken to a private office. He hadn't called ahead, nor did he have an appointment. He never had to—no matter where he went, people recognized him and immediately saw to his needs.

"Mr. Hayworth. I'm Gordon Owens," he said, holding out a firm hand which Chase begrudgingly shook—surprised that the banker offered a handshake with Covid still hanging around. But then again, Chase was a movie star. Everyone wanted his hand. "Congratulations on your marriage," the young banker said, straightening the cuffs of his shirt, revealing a large Rolex watch and a **NASCAR** ring. "That was exciting news to hear. What can I help you with today?"

"I need to transfer some funds related to Annella, my wife. Before we married, we took care of legal things." Chase waved to Tony, who stood outside the door holding a briefcase. Tony quickly stepped into the room, opened the leather case, and left the room, closing the door behind him. "I have documents here related to my wife's financial holdings. I don't know if you're aware, sir, but she's in critical condition, specifically a coma, and I have duties to take care of for her until she recovers, which I pray she does."

"Oh, we all do, sir. What a tragedy," Owens remarked.

"Yes. Indeed, it is," Chase said, pouring on the act of heartbreak the way a good actor would. "We've always been so close, working together all these years, it was natural we would marry. So, the point is, I need to move her money to our joint bank account and empty her safety deposit box. Managing our finances scattered over so many banks is too difficult for me. And under such tragic circumstances."

Chase got the look he expected from Owens, one of shock and awe. "We'll need proper documentation."

"It's all here—a power of attorney and so forth. You'll find it perfectly executed the way Annella likes it. We planned exactly what to do if this type of circumstance occurred. It's all part of our rather extensive prenuptial agreement. The papers were signed and executed by two well-known attorneys representing each of us. I never expected we would have to execute it, but it seems Annella isn't coming out of her coma. We have a new financial adviser who will care for us. I need to tidy things up quickly as I have a film project due to start shooting any day in Australia. I could be away for up to a year." Chase stopped talking. It was a lie, and he figured he better stop while he was ahead.

"I'll have our legal department review these, and pending approval, we will be happy to move the assets for you," Owens said, standing. This time he didn't offer his hand.

"But you'll take care of it today. Correct?"

"By the end of the day, sir."

"Thank you, Gordon. Hopefully, Annella will recover. And when she does, we'll move things back to how they were. So, with that in mind. Would you kindly leave a small sum—a million dollars, in the account to keep it active? And give me a call when the transfer has taken place."

With the peacekeeping statement being said, Chase smiled and told Owens he'd see himself out. After securing Annella's money in a joint account, Chase's next move would be to remove her name, making the funds his—and his alone.

CHASE CROSSED THE STREET, walked half a block, and entered the Bank of America Building. He entered a posh-looking real estate attorney's office on the twentieth floor, smiling to himself. *Ah. The surprises coming Blanchard and Annella's way.* He chewed his bottom lip in anticipation. Talk about a blindside! He so wished he could see Maggie's face when she got home and saw the gift, he had waiting for her. Chase envisioned hundreds of millions more. Step by step.

An hour later, Chase left the building and dismissed the bodyguards. He looked at his watch and picked up his pace. He was late and needed to get to Annella soon. It was time for her next dose.

Chase entered his hotel suite and opened the room safe, pulling out a syringe and a vial of clear medication. Carefully he withdrew enough medication from the vial to fill the syringe. After gently returning the vial to the safe, Chase placed the capped needle and syringe in his pocket, washed his hands, and headed to the hospital. He wanted to catch the doctor on rounds, then slip the medication to Annella. Chase shook his head and made a grimacing frown. He was tired of all the hassle. Sick to death of trying to keep Annella looking like she was in a coma. So far, he'd been successful in his endeavors, but each day brought a higher level of anxiety. He longed to take some of the drugs himself.

He only needed a few days, tops, then Chase would never have money problems again. This time he wouldn't be foolish. He would never gamble again. Another long stint in Rehab would work for him this time. And it would probably get the production studios to insure him again, minus his babysitter, Tony. He would kick back. Get his act together. And after Annella's funeral, all would be well again, and he could even tell the studio to kiss his royal ass. He'd have enough money to finance his own film.

Chapter 17

Diagnosis

When Chase entered Annella's room, Doctor Richardson was present with Maggie and Bonnie. Annella's eyes were open, looking directly at the doctor. "Can you blink for me?" Doctor Richardson asked. Annella blinked. Then, with her limited eye movement, she gave Chase a hard look—a stare-down glare. His heart began to beat hard. There was no mistaking the meaning. Annella knew what he was up to.

Chase waited impatiently as Doctor Richardson swiftly completed a thorough assessment. "Blink once if you can clearly hear me." Annella blinked once. "Blink twice if you are in pain." Annella didn't blink. "Blink once if you are free of pain." Annella blinked once. The doctor said, "Hmmm," before crossing her arms in front of herself, appearing deep in thought. "I'm ordering more tests, Bonnie. Please make sure they get done STAT. Stay on top of them."

"I will. I'll call you in the O.R. with the results." Bonnie watched closely as the physician leaned in toward Annella. The doctor deliberately softened her gaze and made her voice gentle.

Bonnie's lips quivered. The news was going to be bad. Really bad. She'd previously watched the doctor deliver tragic news, and this is how she did it. Every time. Gentle. As humanely as possible. Fully aware that the impact of her words would be equivalent to plunging a knife into her patient's heart. When it was done, Sunday would leave the room and cry behind a palm tree in the hall. Bonnie could hardly control herself as she listened.

Sunday's voice was kind and soft-hearted. "I'll tell you what I'm thinking, Annella. I believe you may have what we call *Locked-In Syndrome.* It's extremely complicated and difficult to diagnose."

“I’ve never heard of it,” Bonnie said, her eyes filling with tears.

“It’s exceptionally rare. I’ve only seen one case myself. Basically, it occurs when there’s damage to the pons part of the brain, and since we’re dealing with a known head injury, it’s possibly the cause. The tip-off is that you can blink your eyes and respond to questions, indicating that your brain can think but not transmit signals properly to the rest of your body. You are very fortunate to have limited eye movement. But now that you can blink, we can communicate with you through your blinking, and maybe we can find out how you were injured and what all happened the night you were admitted. There are other causes of Locked-In Syndrome often referred to as L.I.S. It’s quite complicated.”

“What other things?” Bonnie asked.

“For starters, sometimes it’s confused with Guillain Barre, a viral infection. I’ve ruled that out. Then there are drugs like Curare, GHB, and others that can mimic L.I.S. Also, poliomyelitis and Krite fish poisoning can mimic a vegetative state.”

“Will she breathe again? Or talk? Or move?” Bonnie asked.

Doctor Richardson was careful to make sure she addressed Annella with her answers. Maggie stepped in on the other side of the bed and took Annella’s hand in hers.

“Very few patients have gotten off the ventilator. And it really is a blessing you can communicate with eye-blinking. Some patients have been trained to communicate using sophisticated equipment. But will you be able to talk normally? Probably not. Will you be able to move? Probably not. I’ve discussed your case with many colleagues of mine, and as I said, it’s a difficult diagnosis to make. We are all searching for the causes of your L.I.S., and if we can discover the cause, we might be able to treat it. We’re also searching for clinical trials. We’re doing everything we can to make this a better situation for you. I’m so sorry to give you this news, Annella.”

Annella wanted to scream, die, or do anything to change what she had just heard. She wanted everyone to leave and never return, and she desperately tried to communicate her message by looking at each person and then looking at the door. They all continued to stare at her in shock as if they, too, were paralyzed and couldn’t move.

Chase digested the news quickly and stepped outside, where he immediately placed a call to South America. He had to act fast. Chase hadn’t planned on Annella being able to communicate. He had to pick it up a notch. Fast.

Annella closed her eyes and refused to open them. Everyone soon got the message and left, except for Chase. She waited for the needle, wanting to laugh at the irony of it all. For the first time, she craved the drugs, hoping it would put her into a happy deep sleep. She heard his footsteps as he walked out the door.

The deep, welcoming haze melted her into a place where she didn't care about being *Locked Inside* her body. She was grateful to be floating in a place where nothing mattered. It was a different haze this time.

MAGGIE RETURNED TO WORK, feeling brokenhearted for her friend. She didn't even know how to begin to break the news to Kerrington. Not that she could get a hold of him. He wasn't answering his phone.

She thought about Annella, remembering their fun times reading scripts together and Annella running her lines, jumping around on the furniture like she was on a movie set. She wanted to cry at the memories as a lump built in her throat. Those happy days were gone forever. She could remain Locked Inside for life.

Maggie was on her way out of the hospital when a strange man approached her. "Are you Maggie Blanchard?"

"I am," Maggie answered with a quizzical look on her face. "You've been served," he said before quickly walking off.

Maggie stood stunned before opening the papers. It was a Search Warrant to search her house on Park Road. *Why?* she wondered to herself and headed home to Blanchard House.

Chapter 18

The Nightmare Begins

When Benny and Maggie left the E.R.; they were too tired to speak. Silence owned the car the entire trip home. Maggie slammed on the brakes when she got to Blanchard House. A large wooden expensive ***For Sale*** sign was posted at the gate.

"What the hell?" Maggie exclaimed before making her way through the winding, heavily wooded, private drive. "Kerrington wouldn't put the house up for sale without telling me! That's totally weird."

As they pulled up to the mansion, a bigger surprise brought a loud gasp from both Benny and Maggie as her hand flew up to her mouth.

"What the hell?" Benny asked.

They stared in disbelief at the homicide detectives and the dozen or so police officers swarming the property. Other officials in suits were also present. The front door was propped wide open as officials entered and left carrying boxes.

Lamar, having spotted Maggie, bolted out the front door before she could even get her car parked. For the first time ever, Maggie saw a surprising look of panic spread over Lamar's usually tightly controlled face. Lamar practically pulled Maggie from the car and motioned for Benny to follow him. They rushed across the lawn to his private office and closed the door. All of them were out of breath from running and feeling panicked from the situation.

"They found your mother living in your house, Maggie," Lamar started in. "They also found Willow's scrubs and her hospital ID, which they believe she wore the night of the robbery. It's enough evidence to make them believe your mother, Willow, Benny, and you engaged in the robbery. Also, they know about Titus. I told Hanes. Had to. Hanes served a search warrant for our property, looking for Willow and anything else that can help them."

Maggie and Benny stood horrified, watching the residence. Maggie's eyes grew weary from staring so hard, straining to see what she could through the windows. She finally surmised it would take the search team forever because of the size of their house. "Is there anything I need to do here, officially?" Maggie asked Lamar. He shook his head negatively. "What do you know about the *For Sale* sign out front?"

"That was today's <u>first</u> surprise," Lamar replied, clearly annoyed. Chase claims Annella owns half the house, which is accurate, and therefore he says he's selling her half of the property as her Power of Attorney, and they're buying a new home in Los Angeles. Chase said that as the co-owner, you have what's called a **Right of First Refusal**, which means, unfortunately, you have the option to buy him out before it's sold to someone else. I wrote it all down to make sure I got it exactly as he said. He also added that if you do decide to exercise your right, he wants five million for Annella's half, which he declared was a cheap bargain, and that if you don't act fast, he has a buyer, and you can take it up with the new owner."

"He's insane! Who tries to sell half a house that's occupied?" Maggie declared. "He's trying to force us to pay for her half. Can you reach Kerrington?"

"No," Lamar answered quietly.

"Do you have contact with his lawyers?"

"I do. Yes."

"Here's the plan, Lamar. First, have your people remove that ridiculous *For Sale* sign as soon as possible. And then call the lawyers and set things up for me to purchase Annella's share of the house."

"That's a lot of money," Lamar replied, doubtful of the plan. "Millions. Well over five."

"I have the money. It's my money. I want Chase out of our lives."

"I'm not sure, Mr. Blanchard..."

Maggie cut him off. "Does Kerrington look like he's here, Lamar? We can't wait for what- ifs. I'm done with this. All of it." She waved her arm towards the house.

Lamar calmed her down and directed her into a discussion about account numbers and in- depth information regarding the transaction.

Benny called the Au Pair and instructed her to take Dorrie to a South Park hotel for the night. "Take her shopping. Tell her we had to work overtime. Get her a nice meal. Buy her anything she wants. And make it exciting enough that she doesn't want to come home. Let her call me if she wants," Benny instructed.

Lamar suggested Benny look at his and Willow's house in case they might have plans to search it too someday. He advised them to stay out of the line of fire until the search unit left. "Unless you like answering questions. And, at this point, I strongly suggest you don't talk to them without a lawyer being present. Seriously."

Benny suggested they hide out of sight at the lanai, where they turned on the television, poured themselves a stiff screwdriver, and phoned the chef to bring diet cokes on ice, cheeseburgers, and fries.

"We're deliberately being set up, Magdalene. Why? What a conundrum. It never ends."

"Exactly," Maggie muttered quietly, burying her face in her hands. "I can't even fathom what they're thinking. They're a bunch of lunatics. And my mother—so help me when I get my hands on her."

"I can understand her part of it. She's homeless and knows you aren't staying there. See? I told you. You should have sold your house."

"Don't defend that mad woman, Benny. She's constantly crossing boundaries in my life. And it's freaking me out. You have no idea how horrible my childhood was—if you can even call it a childhood."

"I'm sorry, Maggie. I was inappropriate. But I don't know what else to say. My mind is spinning with questions and innuendos. It's too much." Benny shook his head as angry tears formed in his eyes. "We don't deserve this. We are two of the finest people in this world—putting it out there every day, bringing home things in our minds that would drive the normal person bat-shit crazy. And look at us. First, the serial killer taunts you and then tries to kill us not even two years ago. We've barely gotten over it—and now this. How do such things happen to us? And now they tell us Willow was living in your house on Park Road—with your mother. I want it to be true, but on the other hand—it's preposterous! Willow would never hide from me. She was kidnapped. You saw it with your own eyes."

They poured more vodka. When the cheeseburgers and French fries came, the chef brought a tray of petit fours, Maggie's favorite dessert. They decided not to talk anymore about the crisis and flipped the television on, turning to the series **Yellowstone**. Neither one of them had to work the next day. And neither one of them dared to go inside. So, they called for blankets and spent the night in front of the television and the fireplace.

The last thing Maggie mumbled before she went to sleep was, "By the way, Benny—so help me if you call me Magdalene again, I will start calling you Benjamin."

RONALD WOKE THEM UP the following day and told them the house was in order. "You'll never know they were here. I promise. They left a list of what they took. I looked it over, and it wasn't much. It won't be long before they return it. Lamar turned everything over to the lawyers to handle. And he told me to tell you the sign was taken care of."

Later that afternoon, they went to Maggie's little blue house on Park Road to see what damage may have been left behind by the search team. Maggie loved the modest home she'd purchased with her own money, all on her own, before marrying Kerrington. It was like a trophy. Proof she'd been financially independent without Kale's insurance money and evidence she could survive happily on her own without Kerrington. That was important for her to achieve, so when she added Kerrington to her life, she added him as a partner.

After turning it over to her financial advisor, Maggie left her inheritance alone, and it multiplied. Thank goodness. She didn't have to bat an eye when she told Lamar she would purchase Annella's half of the mansion.

She looked around her homey, cozy-feeling house and took in the joy her small home brought—total privacy. No servants. No maids. No butler. No security. It had taken a lot of deep thought to finally say yes to Kerrington's marriage proposal because that's what she traded—her privacy. And Maggie had always been a private person.

Kerrington, Annella, and Benny suggested she sell it since the market was so hot. But Maggie didn't have the heart to do it. Many dreams went into buying this place, and she wasn't ready to let it go. She was considering turning it into a travel nurse residency. The rent would pay the mortgage as the house accrued value over time.

Benny entered Maggie's little blue house before she did. The two stood still in the living room, looking about. It wasn't too messed up. Papers from her desk were disorganized. She had no idea what they had taken. What clothes Maggie had left behind were removed, probably to see if they belonged to Willow.

They straightened up the house in no time. Maggie made them iced tea since there weren't any beers in the fridge. She missed not having fresh mint and lemon for her glass. They had pretzels with the tea. Simple, cheap, ordinary snacks. Something that rarely ever made an appearance at Blanchard House.

"There's too much we still don't know about Titus. Who are his friends? We know he didn't plan this on his own. Someone helped him do it." Benny stated. "If we can find one connection, they might lead us to Willow," he said as he propped his feet up on the well-worn coffee table. "We're not moving fast enough."

"It's hard moving faster with all that's happening. Chase is up to no good with Annella, but I can't prove it. And finding Titus dead. Then, the police raid. And to top the list, Kerrington is gone and not answering his phone. It's a bit much to handle at once."

"What's it about? Kerrington being in Ukraine?" Benny asked.

"I have no freaking idea," Maggie replied, irritated with his question. What bothered her most was that she couldn't answer his question, even if she wanted. "How have you been handling Willow's absence?" she asked, skillfully changing the subject, and turning to look at him. "We haven't talked about her. You keep hiding out in your room."

"That's because sometimes, I think I might go crazy. I mean, I try to keep it together for Dorrie's sake, but man, it hurts something awful. Thank God, I have work to keep my mind busy for most of the day. Otherwise, I'd go nuts," Benny said. "What we need is a lawyer. That's a bad idea. I certainly can't pay for one. We could just let Hanes sort out all this robbery stuff."

"They searched my home. We need a lawyer." Maggie quipped back. "Kerrington needs to come home. Actually, he should be home any day. I say we let him handle it."

"Great idea," Benny spouted. "This is right down his alley." Silence permeated the room as they sat side by side, thinking about the day's events. Benny frowned. Maggie held firm. Finally, Benny stood up.

"Don't go. Not yet," Maggie begged. "I'd like to talk about hospital gossip and pretend all is well."

"Well, it's not all well, Maggie. And this little fellow here has got to go home and get some sleep. Something we both need. And, I have a paper to write."

"Yeah," Maggie agreed. "Me too,"

"In the meantime, I'll take out the trash. I assume you won't be coming back here soon," Benny offered.

Maggie sat looking around her pretty house, waiting on Benny to return—when suddenly, he burst through the back door, carrying a black trash bag, which was odd because Maggie used white trash bags. Benny urgently shut the door, locked it, and pulled the drapes shut before placing the big black plastic bag on the table. "You're going to need that lawyer, Maggie. You're in deep shit trouble."

"What do you mean?" Maggie said, pulling her feet out from under her. "Take a look," Benny demanded, opening the top of the bag.

Maggie peered inside and gasped before sticking her hand inside and pulling out an empty hospital narcotic vial. Instantly, she dropped it like a lump of hot coal, then threw her hand over her mouth. "What do I do? What do I do?"

"Jeepers creepers, girl. Please don't ask me. I have no idea."

"They're from the robbery. They're all empty vials of hospital-grade narcotics," Benny added, sinking onto the sofa.

Again, they sat in silence, neither one of them able to come up with an action plan. Maggie felt cold. Her whole body shook from fear.

Finally, Benny spoke. "It was beside the trash can—not <u>in</u> it—which meant whoever left it wanted to ensure we found it. Interestingly, the bag is still warm, like it was just placed there."

"You mean—they know we're in here? Holy cow," Maggie cried, touching the bag to feel its warmth. The contents felt like they might have been sitting under the heater vent of a car.

"It couldn't have been here during the police search. It was planted while we were sitting here. Which means the robbers are trying to set us up and are probably calling the police as we speak, to catch us with the goods. What do we do?" Benny asked, his voice cracking.

"<u>We</u> do nothing. You go home and stay there. I'll hide it."

Maggie replied firmly. "No, you're not. Let's think a minute," Benny said, his voice laced with panic, setting Maggie even further into an alarm state. "Where will you take them? Our prints are on the bag. And your prints are on the vial. We could burn the house down."

"Benny! They'd still find the drugs. You're talking nonsense."

"I'm a desperate man," The two of them stared at each other in silence before Benny suggested they leave immediately.

"How?" Maggie pondered. "We take the drugs? Then, what?"

"We go to Lamar," Benny suggested. "It's his job to protect you. I'm sure he's got a safe he can lock them in."

Benny scurried out to the car first, watching for suspicious persons along the way, then Maggie hastened behind him, carrying the bag. Benny nervously drove the eighteen blocks to Blanchard House, terrified the police might stop him.

Maggie sat trembling in shock and staring with disbelief at the garbage bag. She was mortified. Maybe her mother was involved, which solidly linked her to the load of evidence at her feet. That would bring charges of armed robbery, kidnapping, and even murder. Maggie wondered all the way home if she should tell Kerrington and decided not to because he had enough on his mind with Annella being in a coma and his businesses in Ukraine up in arms over an impending risk of war.

RONALD GREETED BENNY at the front door and Benny began his chore of diverting Ronald's attention while Maggie entered the side of the mansion and made her way to Lamar's suite. She knocked on the heavy wooden door.

Lamar answered her knock, dressed in a cobalt-colored silk robe and leather slippers, both hand-me-downs from Kerrington. "Maggie. What's wrong? Come in."

"You need to come with me. Now."

"Let me change."

"No. Hurry. It's an emergency."

Lamar followed her back through the corridors and out of the house. Maggie could hear Benny at the front entrance talking about the two bronze panthers that decorated the door. "Kerrington has a box at the Panther's stadium?" Benny asked, stalling for more time to keep Ronald distracted.

"He does," Ronnie replied. "He doesn't go often but lets the employees use it. I get to go every now and then. It's rather exciting."

Maggie tiptoed around the car to the trunk and opened it quietly, checking to see if Ronnie heard her. Confirming he hadn't, she nodded, and

Lamar joined her in the shadows as she opened the bag and watched his reaction. To say it was a jaw-dropping moment was an understatement. Lamar's eyes popped open so wide it was easy to see the whites of them, even in the dark shadows.

"Is this what I think it is?" Lamar gasped in a faint voice—still staring at the narcotics. "Yes," Maggie confirmed, whispering back. "We need a safe—or something—somewhere private, or I'm going to jail."

"Tell me you weren't a part of this, Maggie."

"Of course, I wasn't," she whispered louder. "Someone planted them at my house in the back garbage. They were still warm when we found them, which means someone knew Benny and I were there."

"Benny is involved?" Maggie nodded. "He is."

Lamar stood silent with a shocked, frightened look on his face. Finally, he spoke. "I can't get involved in this, Maggie. I'll end up in jail beside you for aiding and abetting. I'll be charged with accessory to the fact after a crime, along with Benny."

"I'm innocent, Lamar. I swear. And should I remind you that you were hired to protect me from harm?"

"From a serial killer that is now dead."

"That was not Kerrington's agreement. My safety is your job. And every minute we stand here arguing about the details, the police could drive up. And you are right. We'd both be in a big peck of trouble. Now, is it possible you have a safe?"

"I do," he said, hesitating. "We have several of them. We can put them in the panic room. No one ever goes there. Not even homicide could find the room. I'll hide them and get dressed and meet you in the solarium. You keep everyone busy, so they don't see me. Everyone has gone to bed except for the chef. Follow me and divert him."

So that's what they did. Maggie took a detour into the kitchen and asked for dessert and red wine to be served in the solarium.

When all was clear, Maggie, Benny, and Lamar gathered over wine and had a long talk where every single detail was pondered over.

Lamar retired to bed, claiming to have an intense case of indigestion and fear he'd never experienced. "I've never been on this side of the law before. It's quite frightening."

Chapter 19

The Hidden Truth

Maggie awakened to a glistening ray of sunshine trailing across the threads of her gold silk duvet. She pressed the button beside her bed to close the drapes. She smiled with relief as the sparkling sun glaring at her through the tall bedroom windows began to fade. Maggie turned on her back and spread her arms out, enjoying the first moments of her day. When she didn't feel Kerrington next to her, the rush of reality felt fresh and hit her hard.

She slipped on her heavy robe and stepped onto the veranda, taking a deep breath of the refreshingly crisp air, appreciating how deliciously clean it smelled after a fresh rain. Ronnie brought her a hot cup of coffee and lingered a bit before getting the hint that she wanted to be alone. He missed Kerrington almost as much as she did, but graciously, he didn't ask questions.

It had been days since she'd heard from Kerrington. Lamar denied reports of speaking with him and even shared his concern that Kerrington had missed two board meetings. His private secretary was becoming alarmed. So was she. Maggie rocked aimlessly in her chair, worrying as she stared at the fountain. She felt incapable of appreciating the sun cascading beautiful rainbows off the sprinkling water, which generally made her happy.

Kerrington was due to leave Ukraine yesterday, but she hadn't heard from him in two days. And that was unusual. He generally called her several times a day just to check in. Maggie figured poor reception was why he didn't answer his phone. She couldn't wait to see him. But fear still lingered inside. He always called her. Always. It plucked at old memories of Kale, her deceased husband—who had disappeared without warning or explanation several months before he died.

He'd held deep dark secrets from her. And she couldn't help but wonder if Kerrington was keeping something from her as well.

Maggie had worried endlessly about Kerrington since he left. That misery gave her a tremendous appreciation of how horrible Benny must be feeling with his constant fret over Willow. Maggie had gained a clear insight into how Willow's long absence could affect Benny's work. He'd become moody and had difficulty concentrating at times. Maggie promised herself, whenever possible, she would assign him to a less stressful area for the duration—until Willow returned. She didn't want him on the radar of her boss.

Kerrington's absence caused her mind to spin to a point where she felt like she might go crazy as her vivid imagination brought visions of everything that could go wrong in a war-torn country that Kerrington was trying to escape. Reportedly, hundreds of thousands were trying to escape along with him, which could make his plans complicated at best.

Dover strolled out of the bedroom, sensitive to her worried state, and lay at her feet. His devoted love brought her security; thus, tears finally dropped that she'd been struggling to hold back. Kerrington's absence hurt her more than she'd been willing to admit.

Maggie turned on the balcony television and surfed news channels. Kerrington told her not to watch the news while he was gone, and she had done as he asked, but now, he was tardy, and therefore she felt she could violate his request.

She felt antsy as she clicked through channel after channel until she finally gave up and resorted to her iPad. Within less than a minute of searching, Maggie's breath caught in her throat, thick, as if she'd sucked in a deep breath from a sandstorm. Per the newscaster, ***Russian hybrid forces launched an attack in eastern Ukraine on January 3, 2022. The onslaught of automatic easel grenade launchers occurred near Svitlodarsk.***

Maggie stared at the television screen, stunned. Horrible flashes of war images went through her mind until she couldn't bear it any longer. Maggie returned to her room and crawled back into bed. Her strength and resolve—eroded and gone. How could so much happen so quickly? Her chest heaved heavily with sobs as she let her pent-up worry out.

Dover crawled onto the bed and cuddled close, licking her tears and running his wet nose over her cheek. Eventually, he snuggled beside her until she finally fell asleep.

MAGGIE, HAVING SLEPT HARD, could barely get up hours later when she dragged herself to the kitchen and opened the refrigerator doors.

"May I help you, madam?" The chef stood nearby, his arms folded across his chest, looking annoyed that Maggie was in his kitchen. Maggie paused, irritated, holding her hand on the refrigerator door—wanting to scream—*Can I not raid my own refrigerator in my own house?* But instead, Maggie bit her tongue and replied, "I don't know what I want. I'm hungry."

"Leave it to me, madam. I'll make you something nice."

"Whatever," Maggie muttered under her breath and wandered back into the corridor. "I'll be in the office."

But Maggie didn't feel like studying. Instead, Maggie found herself stepping into the elevator. Things weren't sitting well with her over the GHB thing and Chase declaring Annella used drugs. Maggie stepped out of the elevator on Annella's floor and entered her room. Beautiful, elegant, delicious aromas immediately put her at peace, which intensified as she wandered around aimlessly before stopping in front of Annella's long, sleek dresser. Maggie opened the drawer and searched for anything to take to Annie's room to heighten her sense of memory or something that might bring her peace. She chose the silk blanket Annella favored and picked out three lipstick colors. After pillaging through all the dresser drawers and finding no evidence of drugs, Maggie went over to the nightstand and found Annella's diary in the top drawer. She held for a moment, unsure if she should invade Annella's private thoughts. Maggie finally decided that if the roles were reversed, Maggie would want Annella to read hers. So, she opened the book to the last entry, marked by a long golden bookmark ribbon. The entry was written on Christmas Eve.

Dear Diary:

I will be thrilled when this film is wrapped. It's time for me to say goodbye to Ursula. I love her character, and the director is incredible, always stretching me to my limits. But it's time for a baby, and I can't wait to marry Glenn. Imagine both Maggie and me being pregnant—at the same time. What a joy that would be! I want to spend the rest of my life being a mother and a wife to Glenn. I wish I were marrying Glenn tomorrow, in real life, instead of Chase, on a movie set. Merry Christmas.

Maggie sat on the edge of the bed, holding the closed diary in her hands. Her suspicions were spot on. Annella would never have married Chase, and now she had proof. How to handle it was the problem. Chase was in charge. And he had legal documents to prove it. Not even Kerrington could make a move.

Sunday was a close friend. They played tennis at Quail Hollow Country Club. Should she get her involved? Or Bonnie. Maybe both.

MAGGIE STARED OUT THE WINDOW, deep in thought, when she saw what looked like a giant bird flying by repeatedly. She went to the window to get a better look when she found Lamar, Benny, and three other men standing in the grassed area of the great lawn. Their laughter held an exciting, boisterous sound—like children playing and having fun. Then they became quiet as their heads came together with intensity, talking, and planning. Dover was jumping around, barking, and hopping like she'd gone mad, not knowing what the objects were in the sky.

Maggie slipped the diary back into the drawer, took the elevator to the first level, and ran outside. The chef was hot on her heels, carrying her food. She lifted her head and looked up to see not one or two but four large drones flying over the property in the clear blue skies.

"What's happening?" Maggie asked, out of breath.

"We have drones, Maggie!" Benny announced. "Lots of them. **Parrot Anafi USA** drones, used by our army and who knows who else."

"Why do we have drones?" Immediately, she surmised it was due to the drugs they kept on the property. Lamar was going to make sure no one got close to the house without being stopped.

Lamar introduced Landon Sykes, a tall man with curly brown hair and a friendly smile. He owned a drone business in Hickory, and Lamar hired him for his filmmaking and surveillance ability. "Call him Sykes. It's what he prefers." Lamar explained that hiring someone from out of town made secrecy easier, and Sykes had a good reputation for keeping his mouth shut, having worked for many private detective friends of Lamar. The plan was to film the property twenty- four hours daily for Blanchard security officers to review via live feed. "I gave him a guest room until we get fully operational."

"You've got about thirty-two minutes of battery life in each one," Sykes explained. "It does an excellent job with thermal imaging and is frequently used to find missing persons. The **Pix4Dreacy** software that comes with it allows for 3D mapping and swift data processing. The army appreciates that aspect. Lamar mentioned possibly using it to search for your friend."

"I like the plan, especially the part about using it to find Willow," Maggie exclaimed, hopeful for the first time since Christmas.

"Take a look at that, Maggie," Benny replied, watching the graceful drones dancing through the air. "Can you imagine what we can get from these things?"

Maggie chuckled at Benny. She knew him well. By tomorrow Benny would be flying one around the property. Yes, he'd get the entire operations drill from Sykes, and that would be that. He was like a starving child let loose in a candy store. Maggie had to admit she was intrigued as well.

Chapter 20

Rosie's Bar

Maggie and Benny shared after-work martinis in the solarium. Several of Dorrie's friends were over for a spend-the-night party, joyfully splashing around in the indoor heated pool. Dorrie, acting every bit like a teenager, asked them not to stifle her newfound fun. "Don't act like parents. The Au Pair is all I need." The Au Pair was glad to have the extra overtime income.

Benny wore a Hawaiian bowling shirt like *Charlie Sheen* wore on ***Two and a Half Men***, his favorite television show. Maggie wore casual, soft, hang-out clothes. And they drank the hard stuff. The day called for it. It had been wicked and sad with non-stop brutal stress. So, they were going to de-stress. Nature music played gently over the hidden sound system hidden in the gardens. "Ya know, Maggie, I keep thinking about Titus and wondering who his pool-playing friends are. Even more, I wonder if they work for the hospital. It seems freaky to me to think that we might be walking around in our *Holy Place* amongst people who might have been involved in shooting us. We know Titus was in on it. But who else was in on it with him? I keep coming back to his pool-playing buddies. They hang out at the Rose's Bar on South Boulevard."

"I think I know where you're going with this, Benny. And I do not like it."

"We should go, Maggie, and try to find out who was Titus' friend."

Maggie's eyebrows shot up at the thought of going to the pool hall. "There is no way on God's green earth I'm going to that Honkytonk joint, Benny. Don't even ask me to. They are not my kind of people. Do you catch my drift? They have a lot of fights there."

"Hell, they're not my kind of social crowd either. But if we want information we need to go there. We'll get a group from the E.R."

"No one will go."

"Wanna place a bet on that?"

"No. But you can go by yourself. I'm not supposed to party with people I supervise. It's one of our boss's unwritten rules, and I'm in enough trouble with that jerk as it is. He'd probably terminate me for it."

"You don't know what you'll be missing," Benny sang. "You're a coward. The two of us can go alone then. What you're forgetting is that this is about Willow. Not you."

Maggie stared stone-faced at Benny before doing an about-face on the issue. "You win. One hour. No less. No drinking. In. And out."

"Thank you, Maggie. You're such a swell ole gal," Benny replied, holding his drink up in a toast to her.

"I'm not old."

"Sorry."

About Annella, Maggie said, changing the subject, "Getting a divorce from Chase would be a piece of cake," Maggie said. "Tomorrow, we'll get her to tell us through blinking that she wants a lawyer and a divorce. And we're filming it. Make it quick and fast. So, we can ensure everyone knows she doesn't want Chase near her anymore."

"It's against the law to film a patient in the hospital without signed consent," Benny warned. "We don't have time for that, Benny. I really, deep in my heart, think Annella is in danger. Nothing makes sense, either. I'm doing it and don't care if I get fired and lose my job defending her. Are you in or not?"

"How about I do the questioning, and you do the filming?" Benny asked. "Agreed."

"Let's go. Get ready."

"Ready for what?" Maggie asked, confused by the question.

"Rosie's. You said you don't care if you get fired. Get ready. The timing is perfect. The au pair is in charge. Hurry."

IN PREPARATION FOR THE TRIP to Rosie's, Maggie dressed in old loose jeans, beat-up cowgirl boots, and an old frumpy flannel shirt over a tee shirt. She didn't put on a shred of make- up and let her long hair hang loose beneath her old cowgirl hat. Benny looked about the same, except he wore a baseball cap and stuck a toothpick in his mouth. Maggie wanted to laugh aloud at Benny getting into his character.

The left side of the room held four pool tables, all busy with guys and gals drinking beer. The faint odor of marijuana lingered in the atmosphere as happy laughter circled the air, blending in with the sounds of pool sticks hitting balls. The brown walls were decorated with faded cigarette posters, a giant Pepsi bottle top, and several neon beer signs. Maggie raised her eyebrows at an old, weathered bat that stood upright in the corner near the register beside rows of liquor bottles and glasses. The battered bat looked like it had seen a lot of fights.

Benny headed for the pool table and started buddying up with people as Maggie moved over to the dining booths beside a small deli counter. It was close to the exit, which Maggie liked. The booth held an unobstructed view of Benny. After she ordered a pitcher of water, she used her time to read e-mail and browse ads that came her way over the phone. She watched Benny out of the corner of her eye. He'd figured out a way to blend right in with the rough-looking group, the likes of which she'd seen more than she wanted in the E.R. post-brawl fights that resulted in broken jaws, hands, etc. It was the last thing she wanted to see tonight.

She groaned when she saw Benny pick up the pool stick. It meant he'd gotten in good with someone interesting, and they would be much longer than an hour. So, Maggie leaned back in the corner, propped her feet up on the old cheap plastic-covered seat of the booth, and settled in for a long night of browsing the Internet.

After an hour or so, Maggie was itching to call it a night when a voice suddenly shot her deep into a pit of ferocious fear.

"Hey, baby. How ya been?" The voice sent an ice-cold chill through Maggie's body, catapulting her into what felt like a house of horrors. It was him. His voice. None other than the **killer** who had murdered Betsy and shot Glenn. "Let me buy you a drink. You look hot tonight. Really hot."

The shooter was in the booth beside her. Maggie heard a woman's sexy voice reply. "Hmm. Talk about hot."

The killer's husky voice held a thick country accent, and it was easily recognizable—one Maggie would remember for the rest of her life. Maggie sank into her booth and covered her face with her cowboy hat, scooting lower and lower in the seat, grateful he hadn't spoken to her.

At the same time, Benny decided it was time to leave, declaring the crowd was getting drunk. As she got up, Benny whispered, "Look back at the guy I was playing with. Remember his face," he said as they approached the door. Maggie checked the pool player out. He was guzzling beer before letting out a huge burp giving her plenty of time to memorize his features. He looked oddly familiar. Maggie quickly looked over to get a look at the face behind the shooter's voice. The booth was empty.

On the way home, Benny talked about the pool player. "So, the dude I pointed out to you played with Titus every Wednesday night. He said his name was Franklin Wilkes. The stepbrother of none other than Titus."

"Titus? For real?"

"Guess where he worked. At Vinnie's—in the pharmacy. He retired a year ago. That was how I got him to talk to me. I told him I was thinking of transferring to security. I got lots of reasons why I shouldn't do such a foolish thing. Titus had told him all about how the bosses are hard to get along with."

"I heard the shooter's voice," Maggie said quietly as she pulled the car to a stop in the driveway. "He was there—in the booth next to me. It was him. No doubt in my mind, Benny."

"What did he look like?"

"I don't know. I was too afraid to look, fearful that the shooter might recognize me. I don't think he saw me. He was too busy flirting with a girl."

When they reached the door, Maggie quickly looked back, but he was gone.

Chapter 21

Memories

Maggie rushed to Annella's room in time for Doctor Richardson's rounds, hoping she had good news. The doctor was just starting her physical examination on Annella. Maggie, Bonnie, and Chase looked on.

Maggie noted the doctor seemed to linger when she listened to lung sounds. Then she stood erect and spoke to Annella, whose eyes were open and observing the doctor. "We're up against a timeline ventilator-wise, Annella. If we can't get you off the breathing machine soon—we'll have to do a tracheotomy to prevent permanent damage to your voice from the endotracheal tube. It will require an incision in your neck, leaving permanent scarring. So, our immediate goal is to try and wean you from the ventilator. And the good news is that Bonnie reports you are trying to breathe on your own, which is amazing. So, today, I was hoping you could focus on breathing whenever you think about it. Do you understand?"

Annella blinked once, her eyes sluggish. Then she took a breath.

"That's a girl. That's what I want to see." Doctor Richardson went forward and shared, "There's more uplifting news. My colleagues and I have done a great deal of research, and we found documentation where a few patients have fully recovered from LIS. It's very rare. But it shows there's room for hope. Moving on. I want us to look forward with the hope of full recovery until all possibility is gone. And, with that in mind, I'm going to order intense physical therapy for you. Something else I'd like to explore is the use of infrared eye-tracking devices that might allow you to communicate with others by using a computer. You can surf the Internet and send e-mails. But it takes time."

Maggie looked at Chase, whose body shifted from one foot to another, his hands shoved into his pants pockets, appearing alarmed by the news.

When the doctor left, Maggie asked for a few moments with Annella. She wanted to tell her she had read the diary and knew the scoop. But Chase refused her visit. "My time is limited today, Maggie. You can come back later."

Maggie stepped across the hall and checked in on Glenn. She deliberately did not update him about Annella because he had taken a turn for the worse. Glenn's fever was one hundred and three, which was both high and dangerous. His lips were parched despite the fluids running wide open into his vein. The last thing he needed was to go into septic shock or develop a brain abscess.

Glenn could barely open his eyes when Maggie covered Glenn's hand with hers. "Hey, Buddy," she whispered, trying to appear bright to cheer him up. And then it came out of her mouth. "I read Annie's diary. I know how much she loved you. I know everything. She was planning on marrying you. She said so. She would retire from acting, marry you and have your children. That was her plan. I wanted you to know."

Bonnie gasped, having entered the room unnoticed, carrying bags of I.V. antibiotics. She'd heard it all. "Oh, my goodness. What a beautiful, sweet love story. Then—why?" Bonnie asked as she set one of the antibiotic bags up on the I.V. pump and punched buttons on the number panel.

"That's the question of the year. And you're sworn to secrecy. As a nurse." Bonnie stared back and forth from Glenn to Maggie and back to Glenn.

"How long has he had such a high fever?" Maggie asked, changing the subject.

"Since early this morning. It spiked fast. Doctor Sloan doesn't have Covid, thank God. We tested him first thing. He is negative. We consulted Infectious Diseases and did the whole sepsis work-up, including cultures of his wound. And, as you see, we've already started antibiotic treatment."

Maggie motioned for Bonnie to step outside to talk and told Glenn she would check back on him later.

They leaned against the wall. "I'm so worried about Glenn's fever. And he seems very depressed."

"Doctor Sloan has a good reason to be," Bonnie shared. "He's a doctor and knows the seriousness of everything you just said and ten times more. He understands what the fever means and realizes it can be lethal. But I think the news about the diary will help lift his sad mood. And now that I know about the diary, his behavior makes sense. All he does all day is stare across the hall at her, waiting for her bed to turn so he can see her. It's so sad."

They both looked across the hall at Annella. Chase was standing at the head of the bed, leaning in towards Annella. "That little brat," Bonnie quipped, marching across the hall towards Chase.

Maggie returned to the E.R., grateful Bonnie was Glenn's and Annella's nurse.

WHEN ANNELLA AWAKENED LATER, she was facing the window. It was dark outside. She watched the helicopter land on the roof across from her and heard a second one land simultaneously on the adjacent pad. She had to admit, this place was busy, and she was grateful for the entertainment, though hopefully, she would never have to fly in one again. Not that she remembered any of it. She'd tried. But it wasn't in her mind.

Annella was glad Chase wasn't present. He hadn't given her a shot today because Bonnie threw him out again. She felt better. More vibrant.

Chase had changed. In the beginning, it had been fun working with him. They laughed and joked a lot, both on and off the set. He was a serious actor, as was she, and together magic happened, and fans loved them together.

The publicity team and producers met with them right after their first film exploded at the box office. They said they wanted to take advantage of their *special magic* and signed them to three more films. The agreement had a specific publicity clause. They had to pretend to be a couple in real life to ensure increased ticket sales. They agreed.

Box office sales soared the day the paparazzi caught them supposedly 'secretly' vacationing in Venice, then in Greece—both of which had been arranged by the publicity team.

By the time they got halfway through the last film, Annella had realized Chase had developed a severe drug problem during their Covid hiatus and thus had undergone extreme personality changes. He was sarcastic, moody, undependable, and hard to work with. He often showed up unprepared for work. Chase couldn't remember his lines which caused expensive re-shooting. He was the cause of them having to re-shoot the wedding scenes after Christmas, and he'd ruined her holiday because of it.

Worst of all, Chase wasn't in character most of the time, which made Annella work harder to make Ursula believable. And the onus was all on her to create the chemistry the audience loved during their love scenes.

Annella closed her eyes. She could still feel the tension Chase created on set. She refused when the studio asked for another two-sequel contract promising to get Chase into drug rehab between films. Chase was headed down a self-destructive path, and she certainly wasn't letting him take her with him. Chase made twenty million per film after taxes and had blown through all his money.

Most importantly, she'd met Glenn. Kerrington and Maggie had often invited him to charitable parties and dinners. They quickly fell in love when they met and planned to marry and start a family. Her heart was sad. Glenn was the first and only love of her life. She longed for her hospital bed to turn back his way.

MAGGIE RETURNED TO VISIT Annella with Benny at the end of their shift. Annella was awake and eager to see them both. She started blinking and looking side to side excitedly. Maggie and Benny kept guessing, struggling to help her talk. Benny was the first to get it by naming the alphabet and telling her to open her eyes when the letter was correct. Slowly the name formed. Glenn.

"I read your diary, Annie," Maggie confessed. "And I know everything. I found it while I was looking for things to bring you. Once I saw it, I had to read it. I'm glad I did." Maggie and Benny exchanged glances. Maggie filled Annella in on the full story of the shooting in the E.R. and was careful to emphasize that Glenn was still alive. Annella's eyes shot across the hall. Glenn was staring at her. He smiled. She wanted to smile back but couldn't make it happen.

"I have to ask you a question because things don't make sense. Did you really marry Chase?"

"Stop!" Benny warned, bumping Maggie hard with his elbow to get her attention. "Look," he whispered quickly, leaning in towards Maggie.

"What are you doing, Maggie?" Chase's loud voice blared from the doorway. "Trying to stir up trouble? Of course, she married me. I think it's time for you to run along now. It's my time."

"We'll see you tomorrow, Annie," Maggie said, tagging behind Benny as she left the room.

Annella stared at Glenn until she fell asleep as Chase surfed the Internet on his iPad. She was still sleeping when she felt a hot breath on her cheek and heard Chase whisper in her ear. "Hello, Wife." She refused to open her eyes. "You can be such a difficult woman. I know you can **hear** me. Your eyelashes are quivering," Chase went on, his voice louder and bitter as he walked around the bed. "It was such a simple thing. Get married. Let the world enjoy our fun." Chase leaned in and stroked his index finger across her face. "But you had to go and be such a bitch about it. And, you had to go and keep a diary. You damned fool." With that, Chase pinched her arm hard. "You ruined my career by refusing to work with me. So, now you will pay. Here you are. Helpless. And what an ugly mess you are, too, I might add. No make-up. Unable to move. Unable to do anything, including marrying Glenn. You would not make for good wife material to him now. But you're where you deserve to be. You deserve it. And my problems have disappeared."

He leaned in and whispered again when he got to the other side of the bed. "The GHB worked—seems it made you marry me. I gave you a new scene and told you the director needed to add it. The scene called for you to sign paper after paper. And you performed the scene brilliantly, I might add. You signed a will, a Power of Attorney, and a Marriage License. Then you said your vows like a good little girl. Thinking we were re-shooting the wedding scene. My friend played the pastor and filmed the whole thing for legal purposes. Now you're my wife. And I have your money."

Annella's eyes popped open just in time to see him pull a syringe from his pocket and shove the needle deep into the side of her leg. "I wanted you to die. But being in a coma—that works just as well. Soon, I'll be signing you out of this dump and taking you to our new home, where you will have a private-duty nurse. If you're smart, you won't answer anybody's questions. And I'll let you live."

Chase capped the syringe and placed it in his pocket. Her mind drifted into a lovely place.

She had to admit that it made dealing with her current state more manageable. "What are you doing?" Annella heard Nurse Bonnie's harsh, demanding voice. "I'm giving her a kiss goodbye," Chase replied.

"Not during Covid, you're not!"

"I'm wearing my mask," Chase said, shooting her a look of pretend shock.

"This is your last chance, mister. You will lose your visitation privileges if you break the six-foot Covid rule again." Bonnie quipped, reprimanding him. "Visiting hours are over. Goodbye."

"I'm leaving," Chase added, his voice fading as he exited. "Keep a good eye on her, Nurse Bonnie."

DRUGGED ANNELLA FLOATED from her bed into the air and landed on the South Hampton Beach movie set. She was running. Afraid. She staggered. The blow to the back of her head stunned her for a moment. The silky soft wedding gown wrapped around her, softening her fall. She saw the ocean waves not far away pushing cold, gentle sea foam onto her face. Through blurred eyes, she saw Chase holding a rock high above. Her body felt heavy as she turned her face to the sand. The rock hit the back of her head again. The realization came. *He tried to kill me. That's why I'm in the hospital. Maybe I can't move because he's drugging me.* Blackness enveloped her, and she faded away.

Annella floated deep into another world where walls were made of shimmering gold, and rich, bright red blood ran in huge waves down giant crevices of shining silver rocks into a sea of molten lava where giant black snakes with neon green eyes licked at her feet. She tried to scream, but nothing came out as she fell into a different world—the land of OZ with fields of the most colorful, beautiful flowers.

Chapter 22

The Evil Deed

Chase cautiously looked out the window before closing the heavy drapes of his luxurious hotel suite overlooking the cityscape. Then, he dimmed the lights on the far side of the room and made his way over to the desk where he turned the three-way light on bright, donned a NIOSH high-quality mask, a hospital protective gown, two pairs of heavy gloves and a thick pair of goggles and sat down. Chase slowly and carefully opened the package he'd picked up from the post office.

On the table before him was a tightly sealed container of Curare. Chase learned about the paste while filming on location in Central America with Annella Wryn. While sitting around the campfire with local men, he learned how they used the paste on the tips of their arrows to paralyze animals. Chase tantalized the hunters by telling them he was writing a new screenplay and wanted to use the poison in the movie—using a syringe. They helped him devise a way to convert the paste into an injection so he might kill the bad man in his movie. They chortled excitedly and told him exactly how he might accomplish the murder. It came together perfectly. He had watched Annella while listening to the men. She was across the campfire in the distance, dancing with the camp's women. Chase wickedly smiled as the plan to kill Annella viciously formed in his head.

Last month, he'd paid money to one of the men to cook up the dark heavy paste and turn it into an injectable liquid. **Chondrodendron tomentosum** bark derived from the moon-seed family of **Menispermaceae** was perfect. He probably could have gotten his hands on a hospital vial of curare, but he lacked access, and if he had purchased it, the paralytic drug could be traced back to him as evidence. As it was, no one would suspect. When he injected the liquid into Annella, it would completely paralyze her, causing respiratory arrest. He would inject it as soon as they took her off the ventilator, and she would stop breathing—and die. It would all be over. She would be dead. The money would be legally his.

It had been a difficult journey for Chase. What had seemed like a solid plan had gone awry. The hard whack to Annella's head had not been part of the original plan. The GHB he'd given at the movie-wrap celebration had worn off too soon, and she'd fled, still in her wedding gown. Luckily, he'd been able to catch her, knocked her on the head, and as she woke up, he'd dosed her with more of the drug.

If it hadn't been for the unexpected visit from the wardrobe people to retrieve the wedding gown, all would have gone well. But, the head of the wardrobe department called the ambulance and complicated everything, infuriating Chase, and sending his mind in a whirl as to what to do next. He had to keep her from talking. At least they'd gotten married; that was the critical part.

Annella's complex diagnosis of Locked-In Syndrome was a splendid and unexpected outcome. He believed the GHB he'd given her had led to the diagnosis. No one suspected him of sedating her to keep her quiet. The other sedatives and mind-altering drugs mixed in different combos had accomplished his immediate need to keep Annella quiet.

But now Annella's rapid improvement required immediate action—or else, his plans were foiled. Soon, she'd be spilling the beans with her damn blinking eyes. Hell, she'd probably start moving soon as well. The problem was that he could not continue giving her GHB and alcohol. He couldn't slip it into her I.V. or deliver it by injection. There were so many complications—and it pissed him off. If only Annella had cooperated. They would have made the perfect couple. He loved her. If she'd just agreed to marry him, all would have headed in a different, happier direction. He would have made her happy. But Doctor Sloan had walked in the door, enticing her. Pulling her out of Chase's plans with a resounding thud.

Chase blamed his failures on Annella's decision to take a long hiatus from films. According to his agent, studios were reluctant to send scripts his way. Turns out Annella was the one the fans loved. Not so much him. Reluctantly, Chase finally got the message. His career was shot. He'd managed to get himself blacklisted, and no amount of begging would bring scripts his way. Yes. Maybe he did a little too much partying and drugs. And yes, perhaps he'd suffered some bad late-night bar partying publicity. But

Annella, being seen with him side-by-side in a great true-to-life love story had made up for his bad boy routine. His last film would pay off his creditors, but then poof, he would be stone-cold broke!

Chase stared at the syringe. It wouldn't take much. After a deep injection into a muscle, the Curare would take approximately twenty-five to forty-five minutes to reach full effect, meaning he would have to distract Bonnie. And that would be harder than catching a fly in a wide-open room.

After completing his task, Chase meticulously stored the rest of the Curare in his room safe. After scrubbing the desk and kitchen thoroughly, he retired for the evening. He had an early rise.

Chapter 23

Code Triage

On rounds the following day, Doctor Richardson approved the plan to remove Annella from the ventilator and extubate her if indicated. Annella blinked her beautiful blue eyes to indicate she greatly favored having the tube removed from her mouth. Chase watched anxiously from the foot of the bed, waiting for his time to make his move.

SIX HOURS LATER, Bonnie had finally gotten Annella up in a chair and off the ventilator, breathing without assistance. Bonnie's other patient had been discharged, so she had nothing else to do until her next patient arrived from the O.R. later in the day. Bonnie was proud of Annella's success. Coming off the ventilator was a big deal, as patients often developed complications from being on a respirator for an extended time.

Chase looked at Bonnie, smiling down on Annella as she puffed the pillow behind her head and made her chair more comfortable, adjusting it here and there. It made him sick as he waited impatiently, finishing off his hospital coffee which tasted bitter and stale, so much so that he wanted to throw it on Bonnie.

"Why don't we let her rest today? Let her get used to breathing on her own." Bonnie suggested—her tone more than suggestive.

"What are you? My boss? Why don't you get out of here and give me peace." Chase snarled, becoming more irritated as each hour passed.

"Please keep the curtains wide open, so I can always see her." Bonnie coldly ordered before departing. "She just came off the ventilator. Please. Kind sir." Bonnie said with a tone that belied respect as she leveled her eyes directly with his, challenging his next move.

Tony walked up in time to hear Chase's rant. "Chill, man. You're walking on thin ice with the hospital."

"Is that what they told you in your high-level meeting?" Chase sneered.

"That. And other things." It was all Tony could do to not to walk out on Chase. But that would be leaving Annella to Chase's wicked whims. Tony secretly believed Chase had a reporter in his pocket that he was personally feeding false news. It kept Chase powerful over his victim.

"Go get me another coffee. And a roll," Chase demanded, so full of himself it was sickening. Tony didn't respond, knowing it was wiser not to say anything anymore. Not that Chase listened anyway.

Bonnie's ears perked up when the overhead speaker went off—the voice much louder than normal. "Attention, Please. Code Triage. Attention, Please. Code Triage. Attention, Please. Code Triage."

In healthcare, Code Triage is a severe and rare event that is only called when an overwhelming number of patients are expected to arrive at a hospital due to a significant incident such as a natural disaster, pandemic, or mass casualty event. During a Code Triage, healthcare providers are expected to work quickly and collaboratively to provide the best possible care to a large number of victims, often under challenging and chaotic conditions. Every life depended on the hospital staff's expertise and dedication to saving lives.

Bonnie flew into automatic mode, quickly grabbing the bed census report and attending a brief huddle at the main desk with eight other nurses and three physicians. They promptly reviewed what ICU patients could safely be transferred from their area to make room for much more critical patients. Then, Bonnie headed to the Emergency Department with two physicians.

CHASE COULD NOT BELIEVE his stroke of good luck. Quickly, he entered Annella's room and pulled the syringe from his pocket. Uncapping the needle, Chase gave Annella a vicious glare before pulling up her gown to expose her thigh muscle. He quickly studied the site. *Good, no bruising from my injections. God, I'm so good*, he said to himself. *No one will be wiser.*

Annella helplessly watched as he shoved the needle into her thigh and delivered the contents of the syringe with a brutally fast push of the plunger.

Then, he stood back and smiled, hoping it was the last time she looked at him.

Annella sat still, watching Chase, waiting for whatever he'd given her to take effect. It was different this time. She wasn't getting sleepy. Relief flowed through her. She wondered how long Bonnie would be gone. What else might Chase, with his smug look of satisfaction, have in store for her? Time felt immeasurable. She couldn't take her eyes off him.

Tony entered with the coffee and croissant.

"Let's go home now," Chase said. "She's breathing well. Aren't you, baby? I'm returning to the hotel to nap," Chase commented before walking off. "Let's go. So, I can make those phone calls you told me about."

Annella watched them leave and waited, patiently observing for any new symptoms. Ten minutes later, nothing had changed. She closed her eyes in relief. *What did he give me?* Annella kept a close eye on the clock.

After thirty minutes, she felt much calmer. Whatever Chase had given her wasn't that strong, or it simply just didn't work. She felt the same. Things, however, slowly began to change as a heavy feeling developed in her chest, and her lungs wouldn't suck in the air. She could barely hold her head upright. Annella commanded her chest to rise and breathe. It had worked before. But not now. What was happening? The slow onset was ominous as her breaths became tiny. Ineffective. Then, the muscles of her chest were, once again, paralyzed. Annella's eyes even failed to move. She watched the ceiling spin in and out before it faded to black like a closing hole.

ACROSS THE HALL, Glenn reacted to The Code Triage call with a surge of adrenalin. As an E.R. physician, he longed to jump out of bed and run to the E.R. True disasters rarely happened. He knew it wasn't a drill because he would have been notified long ago, as drills were well-planned. His mind went crazy imagining what it might be.

Glenn struggled to increase the television volume as Breaking News came through. The newscaster appeared anxious and excited in front of a large empty field. "*We're reporting live from the scene of a major chemical spill. As you can see behind me, the yellow cloud resulting from a train derailment and subsequent release of the highly toxic chemical chloride extends far beyond the collision site involving a dump truck. The spill has prompted a widespread evacuation, and I'm told that authorities are rapidly expanding the evacuation area to ensure residents' safety."*

Glenn couldn't take his attention away from the news as the reporting camera panned over to the wreckage site. He could visualize the chaotic but controlled response taking place down in the

E.R. Technicians were moving stable patients not yet seen by a doctor—back to the waiting room. ICU nurses were moving critical patients upstairs. Floor nurses were taking over the non-critical patients. The E.R. nurses and doctors were preparing for incoming patients. Glenn recognized the yellow cloud immediately and knew the culprit was chlorine.

"*The chlorine spill has led to mandatory evacuations for thousands of people who live or work nearby the train derailment,*" the journalist reported, her voice urgent. "*Over forty victims have been transported to the hospital, many with life-threatening injuries. At least thirty fire trucks, ambulances, and Hazmat Response Units are on site at this deadly catastrophe. So far, there have been fourteen confirmed deaths from the poisonous gas, with more expected.*"

In his mind's eye, Glenn could see the emergency response unfolding. His inability to help left him feeling utterly useless. He was highly trained for this situation, and his heart burned at the colossal loss he felt. Glenn let the tears freely fall for the first time since he'd been shot. Watching the disaster on television—of all places—clearly painted his future. His physician days were gone. He laid his head back on the bed and turned the tv off, suddenly realizing he would rather be dead than live a hollow, empty life, unable to speak.

Glenn looked over at his other loss. Annella. He'd lost her as well despite all the hours he'd stared at her focusing on their recovery.

In that moment, Glenn's finely tuned ears, trained to hear every different kind of medical alarm—picked up the loud sound of a steady ominous drone of a monitor—warning a heart had stopped. He strained to get a closer look at Annella. She wasn't breathing. Her body was slumped over. It was her alarm blaring out for help.

Physician instinct kicked in, and Glenn struggled and finally got out of bed. Straining, he only made it a few steps before collapsing to the floor, hitting his head hard on the corner of the sink as he went down. "Heeeeellllp! Heeeeeellllp!" He called, his voice raspy and weak.

He helplessly watched as nurses rushed to Annella's bedside from every direction. Quickly, the nurses transferred Annella from the chair to the bed just as the crash cart was moved into place. Glenn listened to the calm voices.

"Intubation supplies are ready at the head of the bed," the nurse noted. "Where's Respiratory?"

"Here. The vent is ready to go."

"Get the intubation drugs ready," a doctor ordered.

Glenn watched. They were doing all the right things. They would keep her alive. He looked up to see his beloved Annella before everything went blurry and he passed out.

Chapter 24

The Kidnapper

The howling wind outside Willow's window became so loud at times it sounded like an animal in mourning, making her quite uneasy, like she was living in a Halloween movie with evil shirking all around. She counted on her fingers, trying to figure out how long she'd been captive. Had it been five days? Or six? Maybe more. It had been too many.

Willow was just as frightened as the day she arrived. Even though she had never met her kidnapper face to face or even been threatened with harm—she still felt afraid. Every minute of every single day.

She got her meals twice daily; if she was lucky, Willow got three. It didn't seem like anyone was living in the house with her. The same person came and went at the time of her meals. The only odd event was when they took her E.R. scrubs and hospital identification badge.

Over the days, Willow completed reading the entire nursing book. But now her eyes were dry, as was her nose, probably from the dry heat coming through the pipes. And her coloring book was a quarter of the way finished. It had given her joy and comfort. Coloring Mandalas took time, which she had plenty of, and she greatly needed the busy work to keep her mind occupied.

It had snowed twice since her arrival, and today, the rain beat hard against the window, the drops sounding icy, like fingernails tapping against glass.

Willow stared at the television, longing to watch it. She hadn't turned it on yet, because she wanted to make sure she heard every sound in the house. It had taken her a good three days to strum up the courage to shower; afraid her abductor might come in, find her naked, and rape her.

Despite washing her hair several times, she could still smell traces of gasoline. It was probably her imagination. Hopefully, soon, someone would find her.

Willow quietly tiptoed across the room, turned the tv on, turned the volume down so no one could hear it, then turned on *closed captioning* just in time for the local NBC news broadcast. According to the television, it was four fifty-five p.m. Willow leaned back against the end of the bed, crossed her legs, and covered herself with a blanket.

The biggest news story was about another robbery with a shootout in Charlotte where a police officer was killed. The lengthy funeral procession through Charlotte brought tears to her eyes. Willow knew the downed officer from his visits to the E.R. The memorial of flowers that mourners had placed in front of police headquarters in honor of the fallen officer looked as if it were now knee-deep—a sad but beautiful sight to behold.

Ten minutes into the news, Willow saw her face appear on the screen. The newscaster reported the nurse kidnapped from the hospital over a week ago was still missing, and clues leading to her whereabouts had all but dried up, according to the police department. Willow began to shudder as she watched her story unravel on the screen. It felt surreal. The woman reporter asked for the public's help finding Willow and posted the telephone number for people to call with any information. The hospital was offering a fifteen-thousand-dollar reward for information leading to her recovery. "*God love them for that,*" she whispered to herself.

Willow let out a sigh of sadness and felt a fatalistic mood come over her as she turned off the television and crawled back into bed. How would she ever get free? Her thoughts turned to Dorrie, and Willow prayed Dorrie was okay. Then she thought of Benny. Surely, he was looking after Dorrie and hopefully, Maggie was helping too. Willow recalled her brief glance at Maggie and the man holding the barrel of the gun to her head. The terror on Maggie's face was palpable. A look Willow would never forget. The robber was wicked, having already fired his weapon twice without remorse. It wouldn't surprise Willow if he shot Maggie, too.

The following morning, Willow woke with solid determination to attempt an escape and decided her colored pencils and the heel of her shoe might do the job of removing the door hinges. After breakfast came and her abductor left, Willow began working ceaselessly on the door all day. Using the end of her coloring pencils, she pushed relentlessly on the door hinge, tapping the pencil with her shoe. She had successfully removed the top pin when lunch was served. Again, her abductor left.

As she continued working on her escape plan, Willow's thoughts turned to Dorrie. Sweet little Dorrie had experienced too much violence in her young life. Jack, Willow's ex-husband, had beaten Willow severely, many times, in front of Dorrie. He'd even beaten Dorrie with a belt while Willow was at work. And if it hadn't been for Maggie intervening during Dorrie's E.R. visit, who knows what would have happened to Dorrie and Willow? Granted, Maggie's actions led to Dorrie being taken away by Child Protective Services, but it gave Willow time and resources to get her life straight, get free from Jack, establish a stable home for Dorrie and fall in love and marry Benny. Up until Maggie's intervention, every attempt Willow had made to escape Jack's wrath had failed. One time when Willow had fled with Dorrie, Jack found them, kidnapped Dorrie from school, and took her out of state. Willow was forced to return to Jack. Once again.

But thankfully, Maggie came to her rescue. Maggie was nouveau rich back then, after inheriting a million dollars from the death of her late husband, Kale. Maggie used some of her money to stop Jack's brutality. She hired an expensive lawyer, and Willow and Dorrie were freed from the horrid life.

Jack hadn't always been evil. They'd been happy for several years in the beginning, and he'd been good to both her and Dorrie. But things changed after Jack met new friends. Out of the blue one night, he came home late and demanded Willow get up and cook him a hot meal at one in the morning when she had to be at the hospital at six-thirty.

And then, she watched him harden, showing up with racist tattoos and carrying a belligerent rooster-husband attitude, demanding this, and demanding that. His love and respect for Willow evaporated as his brainwashing increased. Willow only brought up once how his friends were changing him. Her comment was greeted with a backhand. And over time, Jack became a monster. Or was the monster always there inside him, waiting to emerge?

She became afraid of him when Jack came home with blood on his clothes. His slaps became pushes, then fists. And life became a living hell. Willow started putting Dorrie to bed early and when the days became long ones, she made sure Dorrie had lots of activities to do in her room. And Willow—well, she just tried to stay away from the brute and desperately sought plans for how she and Dorrie might escape. With each failed escape, the beatings got worse.

Willow's hammering on the door hinges became more intense—each hit filled with increasing anger. Jack had disappeared after the Judge issued a restraining order. The restraining order was still in effect, meaning he rightfully should stay away from Willow, but there was no order in effect for Dorrie. Jack had taken the proper classes and was allowed limited, unsupervised visitation with Dorrie. But the visits never happened. He left. Dorrie told Willow she was glad because she was still afraid of him.

Willow couldn't stop her tears. Her desperation to get free felt impossible, with no way out. Poor little Dorrie. She prayed Jack hadn't heard about Willow's kidnapping, or else he might go get Dorrie and take her far away.

Chapter 25

Franklin

The following morning, everyone gathered in the break room. The television blasted the local news. Benny clipped his medical instruments to his waist and shut his locker door as Maggie entered and walked up to him. "Meet me in the chapel in five," she demanded. "It's urgent."

The chapel always comforted Maggie. It was always warm and welcoming, offering comfort with the dim lighting. The pulpit had lights shining on the image of Christ hanging on the cross. A statue of Mother Mary was at the side of the podium. Maggie often came to sit there, if only for two or three minutes, to destress after major events in the E.R. It helped her dump scary feelings and rejuvenate herself for another round. It was not unusual for her friends to ask her to join them in the chapel for the same reason. To debrief.

Exactly five minutes after Maggie's arrival, Benny slid into the pew directly in front of her. "Your friend from Rosie's is dead in room one," Maggie whispered urgently. "Homicide is on the way. He was shot last night behind the bar. It apparently took place right after we left. I took a good look at him. It's his face and the same plaid flannel shirt. I'll need you to help me with the forensics."

Benny couldn't wait to check out the body. He got to the trauma room first and was grateful when Maggie entered the room and came over to be near him. She acted very business-like, holding her clipboard up while filling out forensic forms. She nodded to Benny, and he pulled the sheet back to reveal the face of the victim. Benny indicated with a tiny shake of his head that it was indeed the same man.

Maggie stared down at the man with red hair, trimmed short with a lot of grey mixed in with his short beard. He looked to be in his sixties and was six feet tall with a mildly protruding belly. Maggie surmised it probably was from drinking too much beer. His skin was clean, well-cared for and his nails were spotless, indicating to Maggie he didn't do skilled labor for his livelihood. Curious.

"Looks the same as Titus' injury. Probably the same weapon. Same killer. I'm getting out of here before homicide gets here. I don't want them asking me any questions," Benny said.

They spoke briefly at the desk. "It's him. No doubt about it," Benny said.

"He doesn't look like the type to hang out at Rosie's. I think we're possibly on to the wrong person as co-conspirator." Maggie said, writing on her report paper.

"I'm pulling his chart," Benny said. "It's still on paper. They have his old chart at the desk. I'll get the admission page too."

"Don't tell me anymore. The less I know the better it is for you."

MAGGIE WAS WORKING IN HER OFFICE when she got a phone call on her private cell phone. The call held a lot of static on the line. "Hello," a voice said, sounding reverberated, like it was coming from a hole or poor transmission.

"Hello," Maggie replied, ready to hang up thinking it was a telemarketer. "It's—Kerring—."

"Kerrington?" Maggie cried out her voice delighted. "Where are you?"

"I'm not sure," he said, the static temporarily clearing from the line. "Are you in the United States?"

"No. Ukraine."

"Why?"

"We're trapped. Bombs started coming—Bridge—Gone."

"Are you able to get out?"

"No. Hope—soon. Enemy—"

The called was disconnected. Maggie tried to call him back but there was no connection.

Maggie hung up the phone and cried. *He's alive. Thank God. He's alive.*

FIFTEEN MINUTES LATER, Benny charged into Maggie's office. "You are not gonna believe what I have to tell you," Benny said, taking a seat on the rolling stool. His voice was filled with excitement that registered the same type of look on his face. Quickly he rolled the chair backward and closed the door before rolling back towards Maggie. "You wanna know what I know about the dead man?"

"Of course, you know I want to know. Stop toying with me."

"Franklin Wilkes," Benny announced, sitting straight up, his arms folded across his chest. "Get this. He was the former head of the pharmacy for over twenty years. We're not dealing with thugs here. This is a big deal. He quit his job and moved to another hospital because he thought they were on to him for diverting narcotics. Yet, he kept his pension, and it was all kept nice and quiet. It was documented as a resignation. They didn't inform the police like they should have. Nor did they report him to the Pharmacy Board. Nothing was done about it. Nothing."

"Maybe they didn't really have anything on him," Maggie responded. "Maybe he just thought they did."

"We'll probably never know that. My cousin's cousin told me and swore me to secrecy for fear of losing his job. Franklin appeared to have friends in high places willing to cover for his bad deeds."

"Well, then, we can't tell anyone. What good does the information do for us?"

"That's what we have to work on. Look how far we've gotten?"

"Yeah," Maggie said, deep in thought. "We're at an impasse, Benny. Where now?"

"We keep digging. Somebody else has to be in on this, Benny whispered. There is no way two people pulled this off. And we're not getting anything but a zip from Hanes. He's a smart man who won't tell us anything. Lamar maybe. But not us. I have one mission in all this, Maggie. I am not dragging things out. Every cop in this city is chasing their tail, trying to keep up with all the shootings, killings, and homicides. There's no way they can keep up with things. We have to make things move—for Willow's sake. I feel it. Time is running out."

"So. What's the plan?"

"We have to find the link to Franklin or Titus, then maybe, just maybe, we'll find Willow. I'll worry about that when and if he arrests us. You catch my drift, Maggie?"

"I do. And I'm in. Like you. I think we're running out of time and I'm not fine with waiting."

Chapter 26

The Traveler

Chase was on alert for a call from the hospital to tell him Annella was dead. But when the call never came, he became edgy and restless, eager to discover what was happening.

The minute visiting hours came back around, Chase quickly made his way through the hospital, showing his identification and getting his sticker ID badge for the day.

When he entered Annella's room, he was disappointed to find Annella alive and well and back on the ventilator. The curare had done its job, but the doctors and nurses had saved her in time. He wanted to spit on the bed.

Chase was delighted to find that Bossy Bonnie was off. The relief nurse was a traveler from Wisconsin, and she recognized Chase immediately. From the instant his eyes locked with hers, he had her eating out of his hand. It was the opportunity of a lifetime. Her name was Lucy, and she was a young redhead who had lots of freckles. Cute but not beautiful.

Lucy let him stay longer, and when it came time for Annella to receive medications, Chase was allowed to stay—unlike Bonnie, who usually kicked him out every chance she got. To his great delight, he learned lots of secrets that most nurses keep tight to their chest. Being a movie star certainly gave him advantages at times. This was one of them.

It turned out dear sweet Annella had a handy little tube surgically implanted in her side for feeding. Lucy had called it endoscopic, and that was all he caught of her description because it sounded complicated. It was a surgical procedure. What he also learned was that it could be used for medications in addition to liquid feedings. Chase asked all about it and watched her like a hawk as she delivered a liquid drug. She told him what it was for, but he didn't get that either, not that it mattered. Lucy gave him another long narrative about which meds could be delivered through the tube and how it's done. She eagerly answered all his questions, and Chase devoured the knowledge like a hungry wolf might feast on fresh meat.

He finally leaned back in his chair, satisfied he'd gotten all the information he needed, and now his complicated problems were solved. Sedating Annella was a task in and of itself, having to sneak syringes into the room, not to mention the risk of injecting himself accidentally and getting caught. It looked so easy. He could slip right up to Annella's bedside and drop a little GHB and alcohol into her feeding tube. Nice, quick, no needle marks to pin on him as evidence. And the GHB concoction was perfect because it mimicked the symptoms she was having. Chase smiled and knew his smirk looked wicked because it was.

Chase took the traveling nurse opportunity to learn as much as he could. He discovered the name of Annella's medications and the schedule for all her procedures during the day. It was delightful. He picked 10:15 am. as the best time not to get caught. Bonnie's assignment was always the same. Two patients. Both critical. "It's a union hospital," the traveling nurse explained. "The nurse assigned to Annella goes on break at exactly ten fifteen am—not ten—or eleven., which I prefer. And my lunch break is at one pm. No, ifs, ands, or buts about it, they said. And I don't like eating until two."

Chase delivered another dose of Curare and went on his way.

ANNELLA DID NOT LIKE LUCY. First of all, not once did she introduce herself as Bonnie did. And not once did she treat her like a living human being. Lucy didn't wash Annella's face with a warm cloth, instead it was cold and unwelcoming, and her bed bath water had not been warm enough. Her hands were not gentle like Bonnie's, they were brisk and harsh—and last but not least, she didn't like her because she fell for Chase's nonsense. He was up to something, Annella didn't know what, but she knew him well enough to know it wasn't about the girl. Yes. Chase was a lady's man for many years, and Lucy was not his style. So, what was he up to?

LATE THAT AFTERNOON, Maggie visited Annella and found her deep asleep, so she stepped over to Glenn's room before leaving. She was shocked at her findings. The entire right side of Glenn's beautiful, handsome face was one big, massive black, blue, and red discoloration. His orbit was so swollen she couldn't see his eyelid. At first, Maggie was alarmed but became less so when she saw him lift his hand to say hello. Her visit frustrated him as he looked like he was trying to tell her something and couldn't. She wanted to get him to write but noticed the swelling of his hand. He could barely hold the pencil. So, she spent the next few minutes trying to calm him down and succeeded. When she turned to leave, she promised him she would return to visit him soon and walked towards the door.

"Maaaag. Maah." Glenn barely muttered, trying to get her attention.

Maggie froze and spun around; her eyes broadened with surprise. "Was that you?" Glenn nodded proudly.

"You can talk! Oh my God, Glenn, this is a miracle." Glenn smiled and nodded his head.

Maggie called Bonnie into the room, and they jumped up and down with joy as they loudly celebrated his milestone victory.

"We should get him up in a chair and take him over to Annie's to visit as soon as he looks presentable. A little make-up and he'll look better. Let some of his good luck rub off on her."

"Bonnie! That's a marvelous idea."

"It's like a fairytale," Bonnie said with a delightful look on her face. "Sleeping Beauty wakes up to see her Prince Charming. Well, let's get you cleaned up there, Doctor Glenn. We can't have you being late for your princess. And we certainly want to beat Chase to the room."

"Yeah," Maggie said, smiling at Glenn. She was delighted to see him looking so happy. "I'll check in on you two later in my shift."

Chapter 27

Until Death Do Us Part

Willow sat on the bed braiding her black hair when she heard the front door close, the car engine starting, and tires crunching against gravel before slowly fading away. She hadn't received breakfast or lunch today, so she made her way to the door and listened closely, her ear flat against the door, waiting for any sign of movement in the house. But it was silent. Her stomach gave off a grumbling growl. Were they not going to feed her anymore? Her captor didn't even enter the house. The hair on her arms stood on end. Had they abandoned her? Left her to starve to death? The thought was horrifying.

Willow headed to the bathroom, where she cupped her hands under the water faucet and slurped several gulps before returning to bed, where she unsuccessfully tried to nap. Her emotions flew chaotically all over the place as she took in the reality of her situation. Good thoughts barely came anymore these days; all Willow did was worry. Her stomach burned from the stress almost constantly. When she allowed herself to think about Benny lying next to her, holding her in his arms, kissing her, and loving up against her—or Dorrie's sweet little hugs that made her heart feel like it was bursting into tiny chards caught up in a cyclone—it broke her heart. She closed her eyes and finally drifted off, a smile covering her face.

THE DISTANT SOUND OF a motorcycle became louder until it stopped outside the cabin. The noise of an approaching car sounded like it stopped in the same place as the motorcycle. Willow jumped out of bed and crossed to the window. She could barely hear the men's voices. Hiding behind the curtain, she strained to make out what they were saying but couldn't make out their words. Their voices got louder as they approached the side of the window. She kept low as she leaned in closer to listen. The car engine started up again, and then, in shocked disbelief, Willow watched as it went off the ledge and rolled down into the small ravine below, slowly coming to a stop in a crevice about one hundred yards away from a small shed where it looked like hay was stored.

"Jack!" A man's voice called out. The voice called again, not as loud this time. "Jack. Come here."

Willow pushed her face to the edge of the cold window straining to watch as the two men climbed down the ledge and began covering the green Chevy with bales of hay, attempting to hide it from any prying eyes that might come along. The shorter man turned and looked her way, but it was too late for her to hide. Willow stared at him in horror. It was Jack. He'd seen her and smiled. Willow trembled all over as the realization hit her. **Jack**, her ex-husband, was her kidnapper. If it was him, he'd been involved in the robbery and murder of an innocent friend of hers.

Willow felt like she'd been kicked in the chest. A fresh flood of unpleasant memories washed through her. Terrifying flashes of Jack beating her. Her attempts to escape his brutality. Dorrie's screams. Jack lunging at her as a belt cut against her skin. Her broken jaw.

Every muscle vibrated violently throughout her body as fear marched its way through her. Willow sank to the bed and leaned forward, elbows on her knees. The game was over. And it had most likely been a fun game for him. In his eyes, Willow had seen a flash of victory and delight when Jack shot her a quick look, acknowledging he was back in control. And she had no way out. His relationship with her had always been about power, not love. Because Jack, as she'd learned in counseling, wasn't capable of love. It made him feel powerful when he controlled her. He'd held his thumb over her, controlling her money, threatening to take Dorrie away, not giving her use of the car but making her take the bus, divvying out tokens one at a time. He even tried to manipulate her thoughts.

Petrified, she crawled under the bed to hide and waited for death to arrive. Jack had no reason whatsoever to spare her life. Up until now, her kidnapping had gone smoothly—but not anymore. Jack was a demon, and he had her in his possession again. This time—he would most likely kill her once and for all.

Rain poured from the sky; she could hear it rushing beside the house down to the ravine below. Willow shivered under the bed, too afraid to come out. Her mind raced for how she might escape. Nothing came to mind. She'd tried them all anyway. The window was solidly closed. Willow was unable to budge it. And the door lock—she hadn't been able to pick no matter how many times she tried with her hairpin. And the pencil on the door jams didn't look like it would work either. The end of the pencil was shredded.

It was over. Willow knew she would never see Benny or Dorrie again.

AFTER DARK, JACK ENTERED the house and opened Willow's door. After a quick search, he reached under the bed and dragged Willow out by her arm, scraping the skin from her elbow as it slid across the floor. When she got up, he waved his arm towards the rest of the house, indicating she could leave her room.

"I've missed you, babe. Let's have dinner," Jack said, pushing her gently towards the door. "Things went a little bumpy in our life together for a while—but now you're back where you belong—and that's a good thing. We're going to Mexico. You've never been there. You'll like it."

Willow wanted to tell him Benny had taken her there on their honeymoon. Jack was right in the sense she loved it there. But that was because of Benny. She was so shocked by his plans she didn't know what to say. He'd done this before, forcing her to be with him, thinking the love in their relationship was all fine and good. He never got it. And it was clear he didn't get it now. She should carefully tread as she wondered if his violent streak was still a part of him. After all, Willow hadn't heard from him in over two years.

"Aren't you happy, baby? I'm gonna go get Dorrie, and we're all moving to a new life together. Out of this Godforsaken country where people will leave us alone."

"I'm married, Jack," Willow said quietly.

"I know all about that, but we can undo that in a snap."

"But I don't want to go to Mexico, Jack."

"See what Maggie does?" Jack stood up—his happy mood flipping to hot anger like lightning skipped over the ground to strike a new spot. "She tore us apart and brainwashed you against me. We would still be together if it weren't for that witch. I'm sick of her getting all up in our business where she doesn't belong, how she ruins everything. But I know you love me, Willow. I know it. Till death do us part. That's what you said. I'll be so good to you," Jack said, his voice gentle and kind again. "I promise you, baby. I'm a changed man. As you said, I went to the classes and learned a lot. I've learned to calm myself and my anger. You'll see."

Willow thought to herself. *It is true, all right. Until death do us part. If I hadn't left, you'd have killed me.* Willow headed to the kitchen, searched for food, pulled a Stouffer lasagna out of the freezer, and preheated the oven. The cabin was cute with its polished pine interior. And it, too, was as clean as her bedroom had been when she arrived. Despite the howling winds, it was warm inside. The front door was solid; sadly, it had a deadbolt lock, and the key was gone.

Jack turned on the television, and she opened a beer and took it to him. It was a maneuver for peace to keep friction under control. Willow felt like she was walking on giant eggshells that might crack any moment and pierce her feet.

The meal was quiet, with only the sounds of the television and their eating utensils hitting their plates. The tension was so thick that Willow felt she could sever the air into two pieces if only she had a blade.

The news was the same, two shootings, an armed robbery, and a couple of stolen cars. Carolina Place Mall was closed due to an undisclosed reason. The broadcaster gave an update on the deadly shooting at a local hospital and made another plea to the public for information. The reporter reminded everyone that the deceased medical secretary had been a grandmother. "We are also seeking any information related to the kidnapping of a nurse." Willow swallowed hard when a big picture of her appeared on the screen for everyone to see. She made herself busy by clearing the table. Jack abruptly stood up from the chair and turned off the television.

"You're going to get caught, Jack. They won't stop looking for you. Or me," Willow said, making a significant effort to make her voice sound concerned about him.

"I'm not gonna get caught, honey. We were careful."

"You murdered someone, Jack. You were there. And what happens to me when you get caught, and I'm locked up here with hardly any food in the house and no way out? I don't have a phone and can't get help."

"Don't go making mountains out of molehills, Willow. I got this. We're okay. We're leaving for Mexico as soon as I get Dorrie."

Chapter 28

Suspicions Build

Maggie and Benny quietly entered Annella's ICU room early the next morning before the day shift started. She was in a deep sleep and looked comfortable. Bonnie stepped in to hang an I.V. and reported Annella had been stable all night.

Maggie, filled with angst and fury, blurted out. "Something's not right here. It doesn't make sense, Bonnie. None of it. It's like neurologically, she gets better, gets worse, gets better, moves, doesn't move, breathes, stops breathing, codes, and now we're back where we started. She can't even blink an eye."

"That's exactly what Dr. Richardson said. None of it makes sense."

"Especially Chase," Maggie spouted, sending Bonnie a suspicious look. "I know deep down in my soul their marriage is a scam. Kerrington planned to have it all checked out legally, but then he disappeared."

"And why is Chase here three times a day?" Benny asked. "Trust me. That kind of man is not a devoted man to anybody but himself. Yet here he is. Rain or shine."

"Did we ever figure out what happened to Annella's toe?" Maggie asked.

"Actually. No," Bonnie replied, pausing, hesitating. Maggie could tell Bonnie's mind was racing as if the decision to say more might get her in trouble. Finally, she spoke, nodding towards Maggie. "Let me show you something new," Bonnie whispered, stepping over to Annella's bedside and gently lifting the sheet. "Take a look at this, guys."

Benny craned his neck to look over Maggie's shoulder. Then, he shrugged and bent in to get a closer look. "That looks like a needle mark to me."

“A new one,” Bonnie whispered, looking at Maggie. “I’ve poured over all the documentation by the traveling nurse and the Code Blue team. There’s nothing to indicate that an I.M. injection was ordered or given. She does get Heparin. But it’s subcutaneous, not intramuscular.”

“That wasn’t from an SQ injection. The needle was big, from the looks of it,” Maggie noted before taking a seat. “But why would he do it?”

“For her money,” Benny replied, his voice laced with anger. “For crying out loud, Maggie. He put a For Sale sign on your property. He’s not a normal person.”

“And then, there’s the GHB thing,” Maggie said thoughtfully before rising and heading for the door. “It’s time I paid someone a visit.”

LATER THAT AFTERNOON, Maggie and Sunday ended their tennis match at Quail Hollow Country Club. “You know, it wouldn’t hurt for once to let me win,” Maggie pouted, sitting down at the table in the dining area.

“Why would I do that? I’m a competitive woman,” Sunday replied, grinning at her friend. “Did you order?”

“I did. Just before you got here.”

After their usual small talk and interruptions by the waiter delivering their food, Maggie finally dropped the bomb she’d been anxious to release. “Something’s not right about Annella’s clinical picture.”

“I agree. It’s been a roller coaster ride taking care of Annella. By now, she should be stable and slowly improving to whatever level she’s capable of—but stable. At the very least.”

“What if she’s being poisoned?”

“That’s absurd. We’re dealing with respectable Hollywood stars. But—then again—how often have we caught family members or friends poisoning patients right under our noses?” Sunday asked.

“Too many,” Maggie replied. “I mean, to our credit, eventually, we caught them.”

“Yes, we did.”

“Did you know that Glenn Sloan and Annella planned to marry? He confirmed their romance with me before he was shot.”

“Our Glenn Sloan?” Sunday asked, shocked.

“Our precious and sweet Doctor Sloan. And get this. Annella said Chase was a terrible kisser. Who in their right mind would marry a terrible kisser? Does that not blow your mind?”

Sunday's eyes widened as she screwed up her face and gasped. "Now that adds credibility to your claim. That's disgusting, Maggie."

"As I said," Maggie spilled all her worries as Sunday leaned in, listening intently. "Annie wrote in her diary on Christmas Eve that she planned to stop making films. She wanted to marry Glenn and have his babies. I read it with my own eyes. So, why would she marry Chase the next day and show up in our E.R. with GHB in her system and a severe head injury? She wanted to have a baby—not go on a head trip with drugs. She would not have married him, Sunday."

"That doesn't mean he's poisoning her."

"C'mon. Think about it. Annella shows up married along with all these official documents she suddenly signed, giving Chase her power of attorney—putting him in charge of her assets and everything else. Who does that on their wedding day? Really. Under the influence of GHB, no less. Her levels on arrival were still quite elevated, indicating that he possibly drugged her and forced her to marry him to take her money and property. And now that he's got it, I think he might kill her. Did you know he's planning on taking her home with a private duty nurse?"

"What?" Sunday replied. Her voice filled with shock. "But he's rich himself. Why does he need her money?"

"We heard he's broke. Gambling. Drugs. And the studio won't rehire him as per his private secretary, Tony."

"Okay. So, we ban Chase from visiting," Richardson suggested, sipping on her tea.

"Tried and failed. Chase takes his complaints to the higher-ups in the Ivory Tower and threatens to notify the media. Besides, if we ban him—we can't catch him. And we have plans."

"What plans?"

"It's best you don't know."

"Yeah," Sunday agreed, looking around to see if anyone could overhear them. "So, how do I fit in? I assume you asked me here for a reason, not just a storytelling session."

"I want you to retest Annella for drugs. Every kind of drug on the planet," Maggie said, all but begging Sunday for her help.

"You're serious?"

"I am," Maggie confirmed. "Annella has another needle mark on her thigh. She coded. Something's not right. I feel it in my bones."

"I have to have a reason to order such an elaborate panel."

"Sunday, you're a doctor. Just do it because you want to. You're smart enough to come up with a reason. Chase may very well be drugging or poisoning her as we speak. If the test returns negative, just say oops, I didn't mean to order that. If it comes back positive, you'll be the hero! Get Bonnie to draw the specimens. She'll never let Chase find out, and she'll do anything to save her movie hero Ursula."

"It's a deal," Sunday finally said. "And it's a good one. You've got me convinced."

"I'm so relieved."

"Good. And while I have your attention—where do you stand with getting your license as a Nurse Practitioner?" Sunday asked.

"I'm done. I have to take the boards," Maggie said with delight.

"Good luck. I want to hire you. If you're interested."

Maggie shot her a quizzical look. "What happened to your NP?"

"He's moving to Boston in four months. Going to medical school. I'm asking ahead because the job takes considerable training. I'd like to have you with me in the O.R."

Maggie took a bite of her potato chip and digested the information, unsure about how she felt about the O.R. "Don't some of your cases go on and on, like forever and a day?"

"Sometimes. Not often. You may have to wear diapers. Takes getting used to," Sunday said with a funny laugh. "Well. Let me know. Gotta go."

Maggie stayed behind, enjoying her iced tea, her mind still spinning with the news of the offer and laughing to herself about the diapers. It had drawbacks. She didn't like leaving her friends behind—specifically Benny. The upside had incentives. She'd always secretly longed to work in the O.R. Besides, she could always book overtime in the E.R. if she missed it too much. Kerrington wouldn't be happy about the hours, but it was part of their agreement. She was a nurse, and that required lengthy and unusual hours sometimes. He'd agreed to live with it just like she'd agreed to live with his constant international travel. Maggie had to admit, she was intrigued by the thought.

Maggie spent the rest of her day off studying for her Nurse Practitioner boards. She thought about Benny and wondered if he'd be interested in the O.R. It would be nice to have a friend accompany her to her new life.

Chapter 29

Three Strikes, You're Out

While watching Annella's room closely, Bonnie pushed the button on the pneumatic tube system to send Annella Wryn's blood specimens to the lab for drug testing.

When Bonnie saw Chase enter Annella's room, she secretly positioned herself to watch his every move. Chase stood for several moments at the foot of Annella's bed, looking into his phone. Then he looked about suspiciously before making his way around to the head of the bed and leaning in towards Annella, who was asleep.

Bonnie made her move and bolted into the room. "What are you doing?"

"Saying hello."

"Three strikes, you're out!" Bonnie admonished. "Why do you always put me in this place of having to be an unpleasant person? First, your mask is below your nose. I've taught you how to properly fit it to your face several times to protect Annella—your wife. You've broken the six- foot distance rule three times, even though I've told you several times that she is in the High-Risk category and Covid could easily harm her. That makes you dangerous to my patient."

"Covid is on its way out," Chase argued.

"Not yet. The rules haven't changed. All hospitals mandate masks because we take care of the sick. Besides, common decency dictates you should put your wife's needs first. If you don't like wearing a mask properly, you should not be visiting. When I caught you the first time, when Covid was powerful, I gave you the benefit of the doubt, Mr. Hayworth. I assumed your behavior was not willful and therefore supplied you with the education you needed to be successful at keeping your wife safe from infection. The second time I caught you, I issued you a warning—and by the way, it's all documented in the system. Yet you require a third—and final warning—which tells me your behavior is defiant and disrespectful with a willful violation of the visitation rules. Your visitation rights are therefore suspended. To restore them you'll have to meet with the nursing supervisor. So, you need to leave. I have work to do. And it's going to take me a long time."

"You're being quite rude."

"I'm not being rude at all. You are putting my patient at risk. Now, that is rude. Annella needs me. I'm busy now, and she needs her privacy. She won't be having visitors today. We'll see you tomorrow. And if you break the rule again, the hospital will permanently bar you from visiting—husband or not. Read the poster on the wall on your way out. It's on every floor, and it clearly states the rules." Bonnie gave him a fake smile and closed the curtain in his face.

Chase stood stunned, staring at the curtain before finally stomping off, fists clenched. Smiling, Bonnie picked up her phone and dialed the Nursing Supervisors office. "Hey, Greta. How ya doin'? It's Bonnie Lulu. You'll have a steaming mad, obnoxious movie star trotting into your office any minute now. He broke the six-foot rule again. I told you about the other two times. Don't be swayed by the fact that he's famous and beautiful. I'm sure you've heard that—but in real life, he's actually quite an ass. Could you back me up on this? Sure. Great. Thanks, buddy." Bonnie smiled. She wasn't sure what was happening with this Hollywood couple, but she was determined to find out.

LATE THAT EVENING, Annella, having missed medication from Chase, noticed how bright the world was outside the window. Her bed was tilted towards the river view, allowing her to see the trees and birds jumping back and forth through the branches. Was it her imagination she moved her head while sleeping? She tried to recall how Bonnie had positioned her before leaving for the night. Her head had been positioned straight forward. Now, it was turned right. Had she moved it? She strained to make it move the other way. And did it without hardly any effort at all. She wanted to cry out with delight but couldn't because the breathing tube still in her throat pressed against her vocal cords.

Annella told her finger to move—and discovered she could move the entire hand! She struggled to get the call bell to call for help. Her heart sang inside. She was recovering—and definitely not paralyzed. She hesitated to push the call button to reach Bonnie. *Should she keep her progress a secret?* Indeed, if Chase found out about her recovery, he might kill her. Her mind swirled with what his motive or plan might be. She'd thought of nothing else since her first injection and the news that the world thought they were married. The biggest question now was, what should her next move be? *Practice moving every minute you get the chance. The night shift would be a suitable time. In the meantime, pretend to be in a coma.*

Out of the corner of her eye, Annella saw Chase enter her room. His movement was rapid when he saw her hand on the nurse call button. "No. Hell no, we don't," Chase called out, grabbing the call bell. "We can't have you pulling this crap behind my back." With a rapid movement, he lifted her gown, leaned over her, and injected medicine into her feeding tube. She grabbed his hand but was still too weak to control him. She couldn't see what he was doing but suddenly felt the immediate haze take hold of her body. Within minutes Annella was no longer able to move. Her body felt like it was no longer hers to control. Tears spilled from her eyes just before she felt them closing.

WHEN DOCTOR RICHARDSON finished her examination, Annella noticed her pause as a furrow built between her eyebrows. She was concentrating hard, like thoughts ran a million miles an hour through her mind. The doctor repeated the reflex exam with her hammer. Then, she stood silent with one hand wrapped over her waist and her elbow propped up on her wrist. Doctor Richardson's eyes locked hard with hers. The doctor's gaze held many unspoken words and thoughts as she looked deep into Annella's eyes. "Can you blink for me?"

Annella tried but couldn't, the effects of the recent medication still lingering heavily in her body. The doctor quietly said, "I get it."

"What do you get, doctor? I didn't say anything," Bonnie said.

"Oh. Nothing. I was talking to myself. I do that a good bit." Sunday said, looking away from Annella.

"I get it," Bonnie laughed. "I've heard you say that so many times."

"I just thought of a procedure I might change," the doctor answered, writing notes in her Gucci notebook. She looked at Annella and gave her a solid wink. "Looks like there is no change in our patient's condition. You can tell the husband that information for me, if you don't mind. No improvement. Let's move along with rounds. Call me when the drug tests return."

SEVERAL HOURS LATER, Chase entered Annella's room and sat in the chair at the end of the bed. Bonnie entered and reported that the doctor said Annella wasn't improving. Tony arrived just in time to hear the news. He responded. "Not at all?"

"She wasn't talking to you," Chase admonished.

"Oh, yes, I was. The doctor said her examination was the same, meaning she's not improving," Bonnie replied, pointedly ignoring Chase's presence.

"That's sad to hear," Tony replied, genuine sadness buried in his voice. "How are you today?"

"It's a busy one. Thank you for asking."

Chase abruptly stood up. "If you two want to continue your idle chit-chat, please leave the room. I mean, really. You're obnoxious."

Tony rolled his eyes and shot Bonnie a knowing smile. "Shall we? Do you have time?"

Bonnie looked at Chase with a get-even look. "For you, Tony. I'll make time."

Chase sat back down, irritated, and pulled a magazine clipping of a house from his pocket. It was the perfect answer. He had to get Annella out from under their prying eyes, or he would have a nervous breakdown sitting in this gawd awful room day after day.

He stared at Annella—hating her. How happy he'd be when she was dead. Annella had been one snotty little bitch towards him before her head injury. She'd been born with a silver spoon in her mouth, and her *Trust* made her hundreds of millions of dollars annually without breaking a sweat. The whole family would be getting a shocking surprise soon. He'd already sent quite a bit of her fortune to foreign bank accounts in his name only. Chase wanted to be careful not to alert anyone by registering too many transactions, but slowly he was draining her financial accounts. How convenient her brother Kerrington was out of the country. Uninformed about her finances. Soon, Chase's work would be finished, and he'd be out of Dodge.

If he had it his way, he'd much rather shoot her in the head and watch her die fast than do things this drawn-out way. His impatience was impacting his nerves. And Annella was eating into his drug supply. With Tony on his back, he had no way of getting more.

Chase jumped, caught by surprise when Tony re-entered the room. "I wanted to update you before I went to get us coffee. I called about the house, you know, the one you wanted to lease, and I gave them the info they needed. They just called me back, and um—how should I say this—they declined your offer due to your poor credit score."

Chase slammed his hands down on his chair and let out a litany of foul profanity that made Tony leave in a desperate search for the coffee. Chase jerked his mask down, feeling he might smother if he kept it up one more minute. The house was the next crucial step. He needed privacy and wanted to get Annella out of here with a private duty nurse who didn't launch missiles at him every time he entered the room.

Chase put his mask back up, stepped out into the corridor to see if anyone was around, and saw the empty hallway. He hurriedly stepped over to Annella's bedside and injected the drugs into Annella's feeding tube. Then he stormed out of the room and removed his jacket. Sweat was popping out all over him. He felt trapped and didn't know how much more of the situation he could handle.

Chapter 30

The Gilded Bar

Benny was studying for his final nursing exams in his room when he saw Hanes pull up in the driveway. Hurriedly, he made his way to the edge of the stairwell in time to hear Lamar greet him. "I thought I'd treat you to drinks tonight. Come on. Let me show you the bar."

As the two men made their way to the far side of the first floor, Benny followed, careful not to be seen. He pulled his phone from his pocket and tried to call Maggie, but she didn't answer. Benny knew she was home and that, undoubtedly, she would want to be a part of his spying. He texted her to join him in the bar and not to make any noise. Benny also told her not to call him. Then he turned his phone off.

The bar was huge, like every room in the house. According to Kerrington, it remained untouched since it was built during Kerrington's great-great-grandfather's age. It reeked of old wealth dating back to the Gilded Age, as most of the mansion did. Thick, lush draperies and gold-framed oil paintings of Fifth Avenue in New York City embraced the bold polished mahogany walls. Benny hid behind one of the statues to listen.

Lamar poured the expensive liquor, clinking the bottle again the heavy glass. "So, what's the latest?"

"What's not the latest, man? The city's gone nuts, frankly. The Feds have sent in men to help with the shooting investigations and a team to try to reduce crime, but it's like people lost their freaking minds during the Covid lockdown. Everybody is back out trying to re-establish the territory they lost during the shutdown—fighting and killing each other to gain control, racing their cars in the street, and closing down traffic. People are scared. Cops are burnt out and not well- liked. No matter what we do, it seems everybody is out to get cops, especially when we're out doing the homicide investigation in the street. It's downright bizarre, Lamar. It's not just Charlotte. The whole country has gone bananas."

"So, I hear," Lamar replied. "It's a tough business. However, I have something that might brighten your day—but we have to make a deal. You scratch my back, and I scratch yours."

"I have so little to give you. I hope you can do better than me," Hanes replied.

"I have empty drug vials from the robbery," Lamar announced, with a sly look on his face. "Holy crap, dude!" Hanes's voice dripped with excitement.

"There's a hitch."

"What now? Why do you always have to make things a bargain?"

"That's how it's always worked, pal," Lamar replied dryly. "That's how we always operated from the start. Before I turn over the goods, you make a promise. When I found the drugs, I brought them here and asked Maggie and Benny to help me see if they might be from the robbery—since they worked for the hospital. Their fingerprints are on some of the items."

"Come on, Lamar," Hanes shot back, perturbed. "That's a bunch of hogwash, and you know it. There's a lot more you're not telling me. For instance, how did you just happen to stumble upon the dope," Hanes shot back, his voice carrying an elevated level of tension which was highly unusual for him. Lamar tried to go with it, remembering the pressure the job bought with it sometimes, which seemed like most of the time now.

"That's what I'll say on the stand if they call me. I'm just telling you how it is. So, what do you have for me? I need to find the girl."

"We're making progress in the robbery and related homicide. But we've got nil on the missing girl."

"So, what do you have?"

"Well. We have a speck of dirt. A piece of fabric. A black hair. And a boot print from a pair of Timberland PRO work boots. Made in 2010. Well-worn grooves."

"That's all?"

"We're still analyzing the evidence further. The dirt is believed to have come from Alabama or Louisiana and was contaminated with oil, possibly from a gas station, auto repair place, or an oil rig. We're analyzing it further. And the piece of fabric is from a pair of well-worn, faded, and dated Levi's. The processing of the black hair is still in the works. It appears female according to the growth rate, hair texture, and thickness. It may have come from a female staff member who possibly didn't tuck the hair properly under the O.R. cap. Plus, the hair DNA search came up empty. So where does that leave us? Whoever owns the boots and jeans is probably one of the perpetrators, but they are not our shooter."

"What about the tip line?"

"We've got plenty of tips. All dead end, sucking up a lot of our time. One tried using voice alteration, bad alteration—I might add, easy to track, and he's a frequent caller. We visited him, and I venture to say it'll be his last fake call," Hanes said, stopping to take a drink.

"Well, it sounds like Maggie, Benny, and Willow are not the peeps you're looking for, after all."

"You're jumping the gun, dude. I understand you have friends at stake in this, and you're in a big hurry to find the girl—but remember, so are we. We're still gathering evidence. As of right now, we have no idea who the hell did what. My detectives are working overtime. Now, do I get the drugs?"

"Gladly. I'll be happy to get the hot stuff off my hands."

"Where'd you get them?"

"Not saying. Not yet at least. You investigate the evidence and get all the information you need. Then—I'll tell you what I know when the time is right. In the meantime, I want the drugs off our property."

Benny watched as the two men walked out to the lanai at the back of the property. Lamar pulled the bag out of the wooded area and turned the drugs over to Hanes, and they turned back towards the house.

Unsure whether he should be terrified or delighted that the drugs were officially turned over, Benny hid behind some trees in the back of the solarium until he knew it was clear.

Benny raced out of the room, hot on Lamar's trail. "Why did you tell him?" Benny demanded. "Why did you give him the drugs? My God. Maggie and I will go to jail. Damn, bro!"

Maggie came out of her room just in time to hear the confrontation. "What's happening, Benny?"

"Let's go to my office," Lamar suggested, turning to leave.

"Let's do it!" Benny declared. "I hope you have some good way to explain your actions."

"What did he do?" Maggie asked, walking fast to keep up with the two men.

"He gave the drugs to Hanes. The drugs with our fingerprints on them. You dog."

"Calm down, Benny," Maggie spouted quietly. "Stop. Let's hear what he has to say."

Lamar closed the door behind them and began to explain. "Yes, Maggie—I gave them the drugs. He won't use the DNA against you in exchange for information and a promise. I made it look like I found them and asked you two to help me identify them as hospital property. So, settle down."

"What did you get in exchange?" Maggie asked.

Lamar shared all the details Hanes had given him. "It looks like the evidence he has may free you of suspicion. The boots sure don't belong to either of you. They were size 13. And the black hair came from a female—also locking you out. So, we have to focus on keeping our noses clean now. More than likely, Hanes will apply more pressure on you two to find evidence to clear you. I've worked with him for a long time, and I know his ways. Instinct tells me he knows you didn't do it, but he has to be able to dispute what evidence he has on you two."

Benny signed with relief. "Sorry about my attitude," Benny said as he offered his hand for a shake.

Chapter 31

Got A Bad Feeling

Maggie was working in her office when her mind wandered to Kerrington. Again, she tried to call him, but all she got was static. She wondered if his phone had been damaged. Her mind wandered to heavier thoughts of him. When she began to wonder about the *what-ifs*, she stopped before letting herself go too far with worry. Recently, she'd done too much of it.

Instead, she focused on the good memories of the two of them lying on the beach in perfect weather on their honeymoon. Kerrington, with his rock-solid, well-cared-for body leaning back on his chair, reading a science journal as she read her medical articles. Both studiously enjoyed their time together. Their elegant seaside dinner was breathtaking that night, and she could still see his tanned, handsome face with his striking features and bright blue eyes highlighted by the romantic flickering candles. They sat in the moonlight, drinking wine and talking about the world. Their lovemaking was delightfully sweet, gentle, and filled with flaming fiery passion. Her skin tingled at the memory of his naked body against hers, skin to skin. Just the thought of being in his arms made her long for him. She tapped her pencil against the phone, staring at it. *When will he call? He's alive. I feel him. At least, I think I do.*

LATER IN THE AFTERNOON, Maggie was alone in the E.R. Nursing Supervisor's office when Benny entered, seemingly troubled. "I've been thinking about this Chase thing and how we might be able to catch him in the act. Otherwise, even if drug tests come back positive it's merely a **he said— she said** thing. We have to pin it on him, Maggie, or else he gets away with it."

"Right. I've spent day and night worrying about how to help Annella."

"Well. Here is my latest idea. I've given it a lot of thought and planning. Don't throw it out the window. I want to plant a nanny cam in her room so we can watch what's going on."

"Benny—It's illegal."

"Illegal Schmegal, who cares Maggie? I've got a bad feeling he's going to kill her."

Maggie paused, turned, and frowned. "Annella is certainly worth losing my job over. Plus, I have the money to hire great lawyers," she sighed. "Well, I did have—until Chase took it all for the house. But why not? Money has never mattered to me. I'll take out a loan." Her voice picked up excitement. "We need to get the camera."

"I already got it—locked up tight in my locker. I've read all the directions and tried it out a few times in the hospital parking garage. By the way, do you know how many employees slip out to their cars to make out? It would shock you. Anyway, let's plant it. Now. Come on, while you got the time—and you're not scheduled out on the unit."

They left and promptly headed up to the ICU. Maggie noted a lilt in Benny's walk. He was filled with excitement for the first time in a long time.

THE ICU HAD A CODE GOING ON in one of the rooms, which made the timing perfect for their surreptitiously planned escapade in Annella's room. Maggie stood as the lookout beside the door as Benny planted the camera and tested it—giving the signal all was well. Then, they both fled the ICU.

WHEN MAGGIE'S PRIVATE PHONE RANG, it was Dorrie. Her voice grabbed Maggie's immediate attention. Dorrie sounded like she was crying and calling from a bathroom stall or a closet, her voice was filled with panic.

"My dad, Jack—he called me at school, Maggie. They paged me to the office. I didn't know what to do. He said he was picking me up after school today. I told him he couldn't—because the Au Pair drives me home, and he needed to talk to you first. I don't think he understands what an Au

Pair is. Then, he yelled at me, saying he is my father and has full parental rights to pick me up whenever it suited him. Is it true, Maggie? Please tell me it's not true." Maggie could hear Dorrie sobbing, and it broke her heart that she wasn't with her to comfort her and make her feel safe. She also didn't know how to answer her. "He's coming, Maggie. And I'm so scared. What do I do? I don't want to go. He's mean, Maggie. Real mean."

Maggie took a deep breath as her mind raced through alternatives. "Where are you?"

"In the bathroom. The one we go to when you have lunch with me."

"Stay there. Inside a cubicle with the door locked. The last stall on the end around the corner. I'm coming to get you."

"You're so far away. Hurry, Maggie. Please."

"I will, baby. Don't worry."

Maggie turned the supervisor's phone and pager over to Cora and said she and Benny were leaving for the day. She promised to come back if she could. Cora told her not to worry, so Maggie grabbed Benny and ran to her car.

While running, she called Lamar. He promised to be at the school in no time with the chopper and two security guards. Maggie told him to advise the attorney about what was happening.

Maggie called the school and told the secretary she would pick up Dorrie so they wouldn't have to go through all the paperwork. She also advised them that Jack could not pick her up because he didn't have official authority.

"That was a stretch," Benny said, with dots of sweat decorating his forehead.

"It is. But we're not taking a chance with Dorrie's safety. We can work it out on the backend with lawyers, and I'll simply say it was a misunderstanding on my part. For now, it buys us time. Trust me. Once we get Dorrie home, we're barricading her for as long as possible," Maggie slammed her hand on the steering wheel and cried, "Dammit! Where the hell is Kerrington when I need him?"

The helicopter blades were still churning when they pulled up to the school. Lamar and one security person stood by the front entrance to the school. Maggie ran inside, got Dorrie, and waved at the secretary as they passed.

"What's with the helicopter, Maggie?" The secretary asked.

"Oh. That. I've got a flight to catch and I don't want to miss it," Maggie lied and waved again, exiting the door.

Jack screeched his tires to a stop just as Maggie and Dorrie exited the building running towards the helicopter. Bennie grabbed Dorrie's hand and rushed her to the chopper, helping her get safely strapped into her seat before he, himself, loaded in behind her just as Lamar lifted the helicopter high up into the air. Jack screamed profanities as he shot his fist in the air multiple times, declaring he would get even with Benny. The security guards escorted Maggie to her car as Jack followed, shouting, "I'm gonna get you for this, Maggie. I will make you pay, mightily."

BACK AT BLANCHARD HOUSE, in a meeting with security personnel, Lamar, Benny, and Maggie laid out the plan to keep Dorrie safe. Lamar assigned a full-time security officer to be with Dorrie at all times, even at school. Lamar ordered more drones. Two would keep the school under surveillance from a distance. If Jack ever showed up again, they would follow him.

The best thing that came out of the whole brouhaha was that Benny got the License tag number off of Jack's car.

Maggie had to work hard to calm Dorrie. They ended up playing Fortnight and buying a bunch of new character skins, which always lifted Dorrie's mood. Still, Maggie could tell Dorrie's mind got trapped in a dark place occasionally. It was apparent Dorrie needed to talk about the day, but getting pre-teens to voice their feelings was a complicated process at best. It took patience—but Maggie wasn't leaving her until they talked about what happened earlier in the day.

After they grew tired of the game, Dorrie turned off the television and Xbox. Maggie scooted closer to Dorrie, careful not to invade her bubble but close enough to convey that she was there for her. They sat quietly for what felt like a long time when Dorrie finally whispered, "He's a freak, Maggie." Her tears fell freely from her face as she finally broke into a heartbroken sob. "I need my Mommy."

"I know. But you're safe with me and Benny, Dorrie. I can promise you that."

"He beat me. You saw it that day in the E.R. It wasn't the first time. He even bit me," Dorrie said, sticking her hand up in the air and pointing to the old, scarred injury on her finger. "All because I ate the last of the peanut butter, and he wanted a sandwich."

Maggie put her arm around Dorrie and hugged her, unsure what to say, so she said nothing.

"I don't know why he wants me. I'm nothing to him unless he wants to use me to hurt Mama—and now she's gone. Sometimes, I don't want to live anymore; it hurts too much. All the time. The pain—it just won't go away."

Maggie flipped into nurse mode out of habit but chose her words carefully. She needed to find out how deep Dorrie's thoughts went regarding suicide. Softly, she asked, "Have you ever *tried* to hurt yourself?"

"No," Dorrie whispered, wiping her tears.

"Have you ever thought about how you might do it?"

"Sometimes. Maybe pills."

"So, what stopped you?"

Dorrie sat silent for a moment. "Hope," Dorrie replied, starting to cry again. "Hope—that Mama will come home. I wouldn't want her to come home and find me gone." Dorrie remained quiet before suddenly taking Maggie by surprise. Her curious pre-adolescent brown eyes tilted up to meet Maggie's. "Why don't you love your mother?"

Maggie held—speechless, not knowing how to answer the direct question. "I do love her. A lot. But she makes bad choices that sometimes hurt me."

"What do you mean by bad choices? Your mother looks like a nice woman to me. She seems to love you. But I can tell you don't love her back. It's like you're afraid."

"It's not like that. My mother has an illness."

"But you're a nurse. You need to help her."

"I tried to, but my mother has to fix herself. It's that kind of illness."

"Oh, I learned about that in school. They teach us about drugs and alcohol and that kind of stuff." Maggie noticed the sheer innocence buried in her eyes, her trusting look. Maggie felt a tug in her heart and didn't want to let Dorrie down when she clearly needed her guidance.

"Yeah. Well, that's what's happening, and I have to be firm. But that doesn't mean I don't love my mother."

They continued talking for almost two hours, and Maggie got Dorrie to agree to see a counselor tomorrow. She felt the two had made considerable progress in bonding and building trust. Still, Maggie knew her work was cut out for her and that Dorrie would require close monitoring. She made Dorrie promise to call her whenever she became overwhelmed by her thoughts. Dorrie agreed. Dorrie even shot up her little finger and offered Maggie a pinky swear.

Maggie tucked Dorrie in bed and said, “I love you.”

Dorrie smiled. “I love you too.”

Chapter 32

Sister Marquerite

Maggie held Dorrie by the hand as she led her down the reverent, quiet corridor that dated back to the beginning of Saint Vincent's Hospital. They were in the nun's wing, lined with wainscoting walls with small stained-glass windows. It was well maintained over the years.

They stopped at a curved wooden door, and Maggie knocked lightly. After a good two minutes passed, Maggie was about to leave. She hadn't called for an appointment but came anyway because she felt the need was urgent—for Dorrie.

The door finally opened with a light creaking noise. Sister Marguerite looked at her curiously before glancing at Dorrie. Without words, the sister knew Maggie's need was significant. She nodded at Maggie, indicating she would need a minute, so Maggie led Dorrie to the well-worn solid wooden bench where they sat and waited.

Maggie had chosen Sister Marguerite to help her because that was what she always did. Whenever she had a patient acting out and throwing things, Sister Marguerite was better than any medicine for calming people down. Sister Marguerite had an angelic way about her. Maggie was sure she saw a halo about her head on some days. First, the nun was elderly, and her eyes carried a look of great wisdom. Her habit was floor-length and solid white. The cincture, the rope around her waist, hung down to her knees and carried a plain brown cross at the end.

Maggie prayed she'd made the right decision by bringing Dorrie here. Sister Marguerite was licensed as a counselor, and many nurses and doctors sought her out when things became overwhelming. Maggie had visited her quite a few times over the years to help her deal with the overwhelming things she saw day after day. Sister Marguerite would help Maggie make sense of all the suffering in no time. So much so that Maggie rarely came anymore.

When the door opened, Maggie was shocked to see Benny exit. He didn't see her, and clearly, he'd been crying.

Sister Marguerite motioned for Maggie and Dorrie to enter. Dorrie stared at the Sister. Her eyes were filled with childlike innocence and a look of open seeking.

Maggie spent the next fifteen minutes explaining why she had brought Dorrie to see her and noticed that Dorrie did not once look away from Sister Marguerite. It made Maggie feel better.

Sister Marguerite asked Dorrie to tell her why she was there.

Dorrie's voice was quiet but calm and trusting. When Dorrie was finished talking, Sister Marguerite asked Maggie to wait outside while they talked. And so, she did. Over an hour later, Dorrie emerged from the Sister's office, smiling and relaxed. Maggie could tell she'd cried earlier during the session because her eyes were mildly puffed.

"I'll see you both tomorrow," Sister Marguerite said before nodding and closing the door. Dorrie chatted excitedly all the way home. For the first time since Willow's disappearance, Dorrie seemed to come to life.

SISTER MARGUERITE SLOWLY WALKED to her prayer bench where she kneeled in prayer and fervently beseeched God to surround Dorrie with His angels, protecting her from harm. Though she sensed a genuine goodness and Godliness when she held Dorrie's hands, troubling visions appeared and plagued her mind. She saw Dorrie trapped deep in the wilderness, encircled by a persuasive aura of wickedness and evil.

The visions, with their sinister implications, were intimately linked to the presence of a man. Sister Marguerite perceived him as the embodiment of dark wickedness, representing a malevolent force that threatened Dorrie's well-being. The man's influence or actions seemed to cast a dark shadow upon the child's path.

She sought God's intervention, beseeching Him to shield the child from the malevolence that loomed on her horizon. Through her unwavering faith, she sought to counteract the potential wickedness and evil that threatened to ensnare Dorrie's spirit.

Chapter 33

The Clean Slate

Hanes stood in the War Room holding a stale cup of coffee while pondering the evidence before him. The Murder Wall had all the photographic crime evidence of the murder of the medical secretary Betsy Lee.

Titus Wilkes, the hospital security worker with serious debt worries, was most likely involved in the robbery as his fingerprints were on one of the vials from the hospital. Then he was murdered in cold blood. Bank statements proved he spent a lot of money just before his death. The deposit was made in cash. He studied Titus's photograph hard and felt a lot of pity for him. Most hospital employees interviewed after his death spoke highly of him, claiming he was a good family man. Hanes moved on.

Franklin Wilkes was Titus' stepbrother. He was a handsome man. According to bank records, Franklin had come in to about the same amount of money and made a cash deposit on the same day. He, too, had worked for the hospital and was fired for stealing drugs. Lab analysis by the medical examiner showed his blood to be free of illegal substances. So, what the hell was up with him? It made him a likely candidate for the hospital robbery. But why? Was he a dealer? Hanes wrote a big question mark beside his picture. Then he followed the many arrows leading from Titus and Franklin to their family and acquaintances. There was a couple who stood out to Hanes.

The stepsister Sara Lee had a criminal past for cashing bad checks. Hanes put a big "X" over her name. He'd gotten a report earlier in the day confirming Lee was in jail at the time of the robbery.

And then there was Buddy Wilkes. He was reported to be a quiet kind of guy. But he had speeding tickets out of the yen yang while driving his souped-up red Mustang—meaning he took chances. Yet acquaintances called him a computer geek. Known as a big gaming fellow famous among friends for his high scores at playing Call of Duty, he befittingly worked high up in the **Information Services (IS) Department** of the hospital. He lived in a nice two-story home in Huntersville and had bragged recently to one of his friends about how he'd managed to hack into a video game and alter the scores.

Hanes couldn't quite connect the dots with Buddy's job at Saint Vincent's. He was pretty high up in Information Services, which handled patient information, electronic medical record management, and the newly popular telemedicine program that became mainstream during Covid. Buddy's background with IS didn't seem to be useful knowledge in helping to plan the heist. But, when Hanes visited him, he felt suspicious vibes crawling out of Buddy—through his body language. Especially when Hanes brought up Titus's and Franklin's names. Buddy was nervous and agitated—with shifting body movements. He held his head down and avoided eye contact with Hanes. It was hard to tell if that was his normal social behavior or if he deliberately avoided looking at Hanes. In a figurative sense, avoiding eye contact with homicide could indicate a reluctance to confront involvement—or an attempt to hide or admit their responsibility or actions during a crime. He studied Buddy's picture taken through a long lens. *Maybe it's time I put a tail on good ole Buddy.*

What didn't fit yet was Jack Webster—Willow's husband. Hanes couldn't wait to get the information on him which was due any day now. Jack worked at an Alabama oil rig, and the employees had to wear work boots. The speck of dirt found in the O.R. was believed to be connected to his workplace. Plus, he'd quit his job just before Christmas. Hanes knew he was in Charlotte because Lamar told him he'd tried to pick up Dorrie from school. Still, he could not connect the Wilkes boys and Jack.

Of one thing, he was sure. Maggie and Benny were innocent. So was her mother. Hanes turned off the light and exited the War Room. It was time he took care of things between himself and Maggie. And Benny. Hanes had always had a special relationship with them.

It was his new partner Jim Bowles that had pushed Hanes hard to nail Benny, Maggie, and her mother for the hospital murder, and it had given Hanes immense pleasure to tell Jim that he'd proven them innocent. Not a day passed that Hanes didn't wish Bowles would transfer because Hanes loved his job and wanted Bowles out of his life. Bowles was a young upstart know-it-all relatively new to homicide and thought he knew everything because he had a master's degree in criminology. Hanes had his masters too, but by the way Bowles talked and acted, one would think Bowles thought Hanes was incompetent and lowly. Bowles was still wet behind the ears and Hanes considered him dangerous because Bowles simply had no limits to his smart-ass attitude.

It had been difficult for Hanes to explain how he'd come across all the evidence Lamar had given him, but Hanes had managed to keep things together officially. He didn't know however, how long he could hold out on how exactly he'd come across the stolen drugs from the hospital. Maybe it was time to pressure Lamar into revealing his resources. But first, it was time to mend broken bridges.

IT WAS AN UNUSUALLY slow day in the E.R., allowing extra cleaning and organization of all the work areas. Maggie spotted Hanes the minute he walked through the door. Benny just happened to be beside her, and she shoved him gently with her elbow. When she saw Hanes heading their way, she turned her back and warned Benny.

"Holy cow," Benny whispered. "He looks like he means business. Think he's here to arrest us?"

Hanes stepped up close. "Is there somewhere we can talk? Away from the staff?"

"Sure," Maggie said, not feeling confident by a long shot. Her hands were sweating when she pushed the lever on the door leading to a large empty room far from the nursing station.

Maggie and Benny remained quiet, waiting to be arrested. Maggie saw that Benny looked as nervous as she did because he was chewing his bottom lip like he always did under pressure.

"I just wanted you to know you have a clean slate. Evidence gathered so far clearly points away from you. I'm sorry if the investigation caused you discomfort, and I know it did, but I was just doing my job."

Maggie and Benny stood speechless for a long uncomfortable moment. Until Benny finally spoke. "Thank you, Mark," Benny said, his voice suddenly firm and relaxed. "Can we call you that again? I mean, we <u>were</u> friends once upon a time."

"We've always been friends, guys. That never changed. I didn't want to look down the path I did, but I had a lot of external political pressure from inside the department. Some believed you were involved and guilty. My job was to clear you of the crime, as I always believed in your innocence."

"Thank you, Mark," Maggie said in a humbled tone that reflected her gratitude."

Hanes smiled in return, then lightly laughed. "Trust me. You two, along with Lamar—didn't make it easy on me with your forensic sleuthing on hot scenes leaving your trails of DNA all over the place. You made my job complicated." They all chuckled with amusement once allowed to see things through Hanes's lens.

"Hopefully, when all this is done and over, you'll tell me everything. Benny, I am so sorry about your wife missing and hope we'll find her soon."

"Me too, pal," Benny said, sticking out his hand, which Hanes firmly shook even though handshakes were considered a no-no until Covid cleared.

Hanes reached out and hugged Maggie hard. She couldn't help but become teary-eyed because his hug was genuine. He whispered in her ear. "The last thing you said to me was that we were not friends. But I want to make myself heard clearly. We <u>are</u> friends. And always will be."

They all smiled, and forgiveness was granted as they broke the barrier that had been built between them. Their long-term friendship began to heal as they all made a significant effort to chat like they always did. Maggie invited him over to the house to join them with Lamar for dinner and drinks, hoping Kerrington might get home in time to join them.

THAT VERY NIGHT Hanes came over, and all was back to normal again. Hanes even told them he wished he had more detectives in his department as bright as they were. "You two are naturals."

A lot of laughter circled the dining table that night as Maggie and Benny let loose all the details surrounding their escapades. The wine flowed freely, and Maggie was grateful to see Hanes happy again.

"I still have a question I need answered," Hanes said, looking around the table, catching each of them in the eye. "Where did the drugs come from. I mean, clearly, they came from the hospital robbery, but how did they get here?"

One could hear a pin drop as Maggie, Benny and Lamar looked at each other. Finally, Maggie spoke. "We found them at my house. The one on Park Road. Benny found them beside the garbage can just outside the back door."

"They were warm, like they'd just been placed there," Benny added. "We had nothing to do with it, I swear."

"I know you didn't. But it's odd. Why your house?" Hanes wondered aloud.

"I have no idea. It was like they wanted you to think I was part of the robbery. Someone was out to get me."

"They brought them to me, right away," Lamar added. "Which placed our household in a precarious position. That's when I turned them over to you." Lamar shifted in his seat, craving a cigarette.

"Do you know Willow's ex-husband, Jack?" Hanes asked, looking at Maggie. "Not really. I know he hates me," Maggie responded.

"Why?"

"Because he was a wife beater and I caught him at his game and stopped him. He had a long history of hurting Willow. She'd had many hospital admissions for serious injuries. I got Willow to leave him and hired a lawyer to get her a divorce and issue a restraining order."

"Did you see him the night of the robbery?" Hanes took a drink and studied Maggie just as hard as Benny did.

"I'm not sure. I've really only seen Jack once and that was in the waiting room the night we helped Willow escape from him."

"Okay. Sorry to bring it up, but I have to somehow account for where I got the drugs."

"Yikes," Benny replied. "I thought that was long over."

"It is. But my partner Bowles doesn't seem to want to let go. So far, I've held him at bay by distracting him with something new, but it's bound to come up again."

As the men talked, Maggie's mind wandered to the faces and bodies of the robbers. The man behind Willow wasn't Jack's size. But the man beside her was his size, although she'd only seen a glimpse of him in the glass reflection. Jack smoked. She'd once seen a pack of cigarettes rolled up in his tee shirt that night long ago in the waiting room. Her mind festered on visions of them as she sipped on her wine. The more she thought, the more, she was sure. She recalled Jack's voice as he screamed at security in the waiting room. The voice. She concentrated hard. Could the shooter have been Jack?

Chapter 34

The Monster Emerges

Jack slammed the door when he entered the house, letting out filthy curse words one after another, with each word surpassing the previous one in nastiness. Willow hunkered her back against the wall and covered herself with pillows, and the blanket rolled into a ball, knowing he'd be coming straight for her. His boots sounded harsh as he stomped across the floor and unlocked her door.

"Willow! Get in here!" Jack screamed, kicking her door open.

Willow timidly made her way to the doorway keeping her eyes steady on Jack—watching his every move. He was in her face the second she stepped over the doorstep, yelling and dramatically swinging his arms in the air—too close for comfort.

"You been talking bad about me in front of Dorrie? What did you say to make her afraid of me? Did you turn her against me? Huh?"

"I wouldn't do that, Jack."

"You're a liar!" Jack screamed, slapping her hard across the face. "I went to pick her up from school to go to Mexico, and the scummy brat made me feel like an ass. My own daughter called Maggie and Benny and refused to go with me. They got there before me and hauled her off in their high and mighty helicopter with security guards to boot. Dorrie did that to me—holding onto Benny like he was her father. Why do you suppose that is? Huh?" Jack inched closer to Willow's face and pinched her cheeks hard together with his hands, grinding her cheeks against her teeth.

"Are you trying to make Benny her daddy? Are you replacing me with another man? You've lost your mind is what you've gone and done. You've taken complete leave of your senses. But you need to get this! She is my baby, and she will always be my baby. No one will replace me. Ever! I won't let that happen. And I won't even think twice before killing you and Benny. Don't think for a minute that I won't."

Willow backed away until she was against the door jamb—breathing hard. Blood from the inside of her cheeks tasted thick—like there was a lot of it. She felt it trickling onto her lips. Willow swallowed hard and closed her eyes, unable to look at Jack's face any further, knowing what she would find. His eyes always held a malevolent darkness during these times. Evil. Pure evil.

Jack raged forward with pieces of spittle shooting from his mouth. "You bitch!" Jack shouted before slapping her hard again. Willow placed her hand against her stinging hot skin. "I've worked my ass off making enough money to provide us with a new home in a beautiful country, and this is how you pay me back, Willow? I can't believe you betrayed me. Again. You turned your back on me like we were nothing. When will you understand that you are my wife and the love of my life? I will die before I give you up. We're going to Mexico, so you might as well decide that you'll love it there."

Willow didn't argue. She knew better than to utter one word. It would set him off like a rocket. And he was close to that now. Real close.

Jack shoved her into the chair by the table and opened the refrigerator door, pulled out a beer, snapped it open, and took a long drink. He wiped his mouth with the back of his hand and sat across from her, glaring. "This is how it's gonna go. We're getting' Dorrie one way or another. And we're moving to our little hacienda where nobody will bother us again. We have plenty of money, and neither of us will have to work. But I'll tell you what—you need to get your shit together so we're on the same team. You're lucky you got a forgiving husband—ready to love you despite the fact you went whorin' off with another man. You're also lucky that I'm a changed man. I could be hittin' you more, ya know. But see how I'm controlling myself?"

Willow still didn't speak. He was the master of twisting her words when he was on a violent streak. Jack went back to the refrigerator and pulled out another beer. "Why don't you get up, be a good little wife and make your hubby some food? I'm hungry."

Willow got up and did as she was told, opening the cabinets and the refrigerator. Rice and beer were all she could find. She wasn't about to say to him that was all they had. It would set him off for sure. While boiling the water for the rice, she looked around and rechecked her surroundings, seeking an escape. She took a deep breath when she found a can of Cream of Chicken soup in the back of a cabinet. She heated it to serve on top of the rice.

"I fixed that bitch, Maggie," Jack continued with his raging temper. "She always thinks she's so smart. She won't think that anymore after they find the drugs in her backyard. I also planted some of your clothes in her house. That backfired on us. They now think you're involved with the robbery—and the killing. I forgot to tell you that. You couldn't go back home if you wanted to. They'll haul you off to jail. You and Maggie and Benny will spend the rest of your life there. Sorry babe."

"You did what?" Willow said, in astonishment as she placed Jack's plate in front of him. "How could you?"

"I had to get rid of the evidence. And Maggie deserved to have it found at her house. And it worked out perfectly. It turns out Mamma Darlene was sleeping in the house too. Now she's involved. And I'm off free and clear. And I'm going to Mexico with my family."

Jack picked up his fork to eat and stared at his plate. "This is my dinner?"

"It is. That's all we have."

Jack stood up and slammed his hands on the table. "I'm not eatin' this crap. You're always trying to make me look bad. Like, I forgot to do this, and I forgot to do that. I'm hungry! You didn't look hard enough! There's food in this house!" Jack went to the cabinets and opened and slammed cabinet doors, looking for food that wasn't there. Far from Willow's view, he found a can of spam on the top shelf. He turned and glared at her. "I bet you think this is funny. You think this is funny?"

Willow didn't move. Jack's rocket had launched. He threw the can of spam like a baseball, hitting her above the eye so hard it split her eyebrow tissue wide open. Blood flowed freely as she desperately looked around for a way out. There wasn't one.

"I can see it. You're laughing at me. Inside. I see it in your ugly eyes."

Willow quickly moved to the far side of the table, terrified. His anger management classes had done him no good at all. Jack moved faster than she expected, and she was in his grasp in no time. His fingers wrapped around her hair as his hand slammed against her face, stinging ferociously. The next to come was Jack's balled-up fist, violently stroking her upper jaw. Willow felt bones shift in her face as her head spun wildly. Blood dripped fast into her eyes, making it hard to see as he shoved her crashing into the table chairs to the floor.

"I hate you when you make me do this," Jack screamed, holding his head in his hands and waving his body sideways. "I hate you—you bitch!"

Willow searched desperately, trying to find words that would make him stop, but she knew there weren't any. Jack would only stop when he was done. He'd never been this violent.

Jack's foot cracked against her chest and then up against her head. Shooting stars popped into her vision with the next kick. Pain pierced her entire body when he jumped up in the air and came down crashing, landing on her with both feet, the total weight of his body on her abdomen and chest. She gasped in horror and pain as the breath was knocked from her chest. Unconsciousness rapidly followed.

Chapter 35

Information Services

The next day, Benny ran up the steps to the mansion and into the open front door, held open by Ronnie. He headed straight to the solarium, where he found Maggie reading a book.

"What happened? Did someone die? You look fit to be tied." Maggie commented.

"I took all my finals and aced them. Got out of school early—and—well, I couldn't stand it having all that free time on my hands, and it's like our investigation came to a lull. So—just on a hunch, I decided to visit an old friend in Human Resources and see if another Wilkes is working in the hospital. Bingo. Buddy Wilkes works for Information Services. Three guesses what I did."

"Good grief, Benny," Maggie said, annoyed for the umpteenth time by Benny's playful way of telling stories. She poured him some lemonade and handed him the glass. "Get on with it."

"Well. I slid into the offices of Information Services and saw my Aunt Pam gossiping away with a bunch of co-workers. So, I joined right in because I knew most of them, and Pam obviously did not want to leave the discussion. Then, I saw why. Behind the glass walls was none other than Hanes himself and his partner Bowles standing in two of the back senior management offices with their notepads drawn. There's something serious going down in that department today. I can tell you that."

"They're onto Buddy."

"He's the perfect third, Maggie. According to Pam, although Buddy works in Information Services, he works many overtime hours subbing in security. Guess where? The big secret security room where we get battery replacements for our pagers."

"Holy crap! Benny! That's huge," Maggie said, curling her legs beneath her and turning to face Benny. "This means Buddy knew every secret path, every door, every exit, and every camera posted throughout the hospital. With that knowledge, he knew how to zip through top-secret places with an easy ability to be unseen in no time. I mean, most of his job entails watching all the live hospital activity of people coming and going all over the place on the full wall of live video screens. Have you ever seen the Camera Wall? It's massive," Maggie said with excitement.

"No kidding," Benny replied, sitting on the steel arm of a lounge seat, and refilling his glass of lemonade. "Buddy was well-known on the I.S. street as a superior computer geek. He had access to all the hospital's cameras and electronic security control. Buddy often helped with snags in the video monitoring system when it went down for one reason or another. He reportedly knew how to bring it back up and shut it down. One security dude even openly complained that Buddy was given too much information about operations for a temporary fill-in employee. And homicide is all over him like flies on dog poop. Odd, he called in sick today, according to Pam, who knows everything about everything, and if she doesn't know it—she can get the information."

"He's the missing key, Benny," Maggie added. "He could easily have been responsible for the camera outage and possibly even blackout in the hospital's streets."

"There's more. Guess who is one of Buddy's oldest and dearest friends. None other than Jack Webster."

Maggie gasped. "Holy Mother of God, Benny. I was wondering if the shooter was possibly Jack. Wow. We know he's back in town. Maybe he didn't come back just to get Dorrie. Jeez. What if he <u>is</u> involved—maybe, he arranged for Willow to be kidnapped. He tried to get Dorrie to go home with him. And Titus probably knew Willow's schedule over the holiday, making it easy to plan the entire event."

"No kidding," Benny replied, his mind burrowing deep in thought about the possibilities Jack brought with his involvement. "He's a dangerous man, Maggie."

"I know," Maggie whispered back. They both slipped into visions of the injuries Jack had delivered to Willow in the past. "You think he has her?"

"I do," Benny said, his tone filled with worry.

As the two of them dealt with the reality of the situation with Willow, Dorrie entered, dressed in her private school uniform. She casually tossed her backpack on the chair beside Benny and poured a glass of lemonade. "So, what's up? You two look dramatic—like something serious is going on." Dorrie was happy, but then her mood dropped. "Is it Mommy? Is Mommy, okay?"

"As far as we know. Something just happened at work," Maggie lied.
"You know how that gets sometimes?" Benny said, rubbing his hand gently on Dorrie's head.

"Don't," she said playfully, moving out of Benny's reach. "You'll mess up my hair." Dorrie grabbed her bag and exited the room. "I'm going to get a snack and take a dip."

Maggie's breath caught in her chest. Dorric sounded just like Kerrington when he often said he was going for a dip. Maggie shook her head and repeated the words. "I'm going for a dip. You want to come?"

"Yeah," Benny replied, not very enthusiastically, as he got up and followed Maggie to the pool.

LATER THAT EVENING LAMAR caught Maggie, Benny, and Dorrie in the library. Maggie was eagerly studying a book on surgery, trying to memorize all the surgical instruments, excited over her possible new career. Benny was reading a novel by John Grisham. Dorrie was doing her homework.

Lamar started in, "The license plate number you got off Jack's car belongs to a dead woman who lived in the mountains. I got my guys tracing more information along with Hanes. We'll probably get the information before Hanes due to so many homicides over the weekend. And apparently, the missing person division is just as busy. A lot of people missing."

"I say we do a deep dive on this Buddy Wilkes, his best friend. Might come up with nil—but then again, we might strike gold," Lamar said.

Benny asked Lamar to order more drones. "Once we find out more about the dead woman, we can go up there with Sykes and search for Willow and the car. I'll see if Sykes is available."

After Lamar approved the order, they all went to bed, exhausted from the busy day.

"By the way, Benny. Now that Hanes has Jack on his radar—don't be surprised if they serve you with a search warrant on your house with Willow. I know how he operates—that's coming next. You might want to be prepared by searching it yourself before he does. After all, Jack did live there with Willow when they were married. It's possible; that's where Jack went as soon as he returned to Charlotte."

Chapter 36

Darlene

As a nursing leader within Saint Vincent's Hospital, it was an expectation for Maggie to volunteer her time for charitable services. She'd served over forty hours at the food kitchen and twelve hours for **Habitat for Humanity**. Today, Maggie worked at the **Salvation Army's Center of Hope**—a shelter for homeless women and children. The hospital provided lunch for the residents, and she served the food.

Maggie had a special place in her heart reserved for the women living at the homeless shelter. They were her passion. Life seemed to mean much more to her after she visited them and watched how they struggled and worried about life. The simple necessities that most took for granted—a bed, a roof, and food were a daily worry before they came to the Center of Hope.

The world always felt so much more humane when Maggie volunteered there. The stories were often sad, and they made her appreciate life. The children freely gave away hugs and smiles, and Maggie rewarded them with toys like play dough and coloring books. It was a God thing—a feeling she couldn't explain.

Maggie was smiling into the precious eyes of the various women's faces as she served the large wedges of **Subway** sandwiches. When she looked up, her heart fell. At a table in the distance sat her mother. Clean. Neatly dressed. And clearly, sober. For a moment, her heart stood still as her thoughts wondered about what she should do. Her mother was sober—and living in a homeless shelter.

Maggie excused herself and went into the backyard, leaned against a tree, and tried to calm her emotions. They were good, warm emotions that she hadn't felt since childhood, and her mother was normal. In a split second, she'd felt her dead father's presence as if he were still alive and they were all living a happy life before the crash. The god-awful crash that tore their life apart, killing her father and injuring her mother critically, breaking her pelvis, legs, and arms. The collision led to her mother's drug addiction.

Maggie worked hard to fix her mother to no avail. Oxycodone owned her soul. Lock, stock, and barrel until now—apparently.

She was sure her mother had seen her; it was her move now. Darlene wouldn't approach her. Not now. Not after all the hurtful things Maggie had laid painfully at her mother's feet. Maggie felt ashamed. Her mother had also been sober on the day she visited her house. She should show some grace and forgiveness, as Dorrie suggested. Was it finally time?

Maggie stood silent for a moment, taking it all in. Her options. The possible results. Could she handle her mother being back in her life after causing her so much pain? Should she dare trust her with her love again? At long last, the answer came. *Be the bigger person here, girl. Do the right thing.*

She returned to the kitchen and grabbed a turkey provolone sandwich, a bag of chips, and a soda. Maggie then cautiously approached her mother; grateful she was sitting at a table by herself at the far end of the dining area.

"Are you hungry?" Maggie asked, not knowing what else to say.

"I am," Darlene replied, looking up at her with eyes that looked older than her age.

Maggie sat and placed the food in front of her mother, who softly smiled her way. Maggie wanted to cry as she watched her mother's frail hands reach for her sandwich—hands that twitched with a feeble tremble. Her nails were painted a beautiful pink, meaning she cared about life and herself. An ache grew in Maggie's throat with a mixture of great happiness and sadness all blended together. Happiness from being with a sober mother. And sadness over all the lost years gone by.

"How long have you been here, Mom?"

"Mom. What a wonderful word to hear. Thank you for calling me that." Maggie wiped a small tear falling from her mother's eyes with a napkin. "I came here the day I left your old house. I'm in their drug program—and I am doing well so far. It's a daily battle, but I have the fight in me for the first time. Please pray for me, Maggie."

"Of course, I will. You know I will."

"Like I said. I want to make it right again—more than anything I ever wanted. I'm so sorry for all of it, the drugs, the lack of attention, the suffering I caused you. I can never make up for it, baby, but I will spend the rest of my life trying. Forgive me, Maggie."

"I do, Mama. I do. And I'm here to walk the road with you if you need me."

"Oh, honey. I do need you. I want you with me. More than you know."

"So, how do we do this?" Maggie asked. "How do we start?"

"How about with visits? I need to be here. I need to complete my program and get into a long- term treatment center. Can we do that? I can leave campus during the day. We could meet for lunch."

"I would love that. Do you have a phone?"

"I do. Would you like my telephone?"

Maggie grinned. "Yes. I'd love that. How late can I call?"

"Until nine p.m. Up at five a.m. Call me any time," Darlene looked at her watch. "It's time for class. I need to go." She reached her hand out and stroked Maggie's face. "I love you."

"I love you too, Mama," Maggie said before walking away. Although their conversation was stilted with short sentences, the communication was filled with wonder, filling Maggie with the most beautiful, heartwarming feeling of contentment. Finally. After all the years gone by. It had felt real. For the first time. Maggie cherished the word Mama, and since her mother loved it so much, she would use it frequently from now on. Maggie watched her mother walk away, loving the growing feeling in her heart. She hoped it never went away.

Chapter 37

Footprints

Maggie accompanied Benny to his and Willow's home on Tulip Bulb Lane. Maggie hadn't been there in six months and was surprised at the beautiful transformation. The gorgeous historic house had been falling apart when Maggie met Willow several years ago. As a wedding gift, Maggie had paid for the house's complete restoration from the funds she'd received from her ex-husband's life insurance.

The formerly rotten wood porch was now solid gray wood flooring. Faded, peeling, and water-stained wallpaper was now brand new and restored to its former glory. The house no longer smelled old but held the faint odor of clean and fresh paint. Willow had taken over the restoration project after she'd healed from her significant injuries from the serial killer that had terrorized the city two years ago. The project—along with marrying Benny—had helped bring a smile back to Willow's haunted face and lifted her torn down spirit. Her recovery due to a traumatic brain injury had been a challenging battle—but it seemed that the prettier the house looked, the more strength Willow regained.

Maggie's eyes briefly locked with the area on the floor where she'd almost bled to death. Her blood stains were gone. So were those of the maniacal serial killer who had tried so hard to kill her. She looked up at the second-floor handrail. It was repaired and showed no sign of Maggie having fallen through it, shattering it to pieces. Maggie shuddered and reminded herself it was all in the past. She tore her eyes away, not wanting to remember more about the Shadow Man—the killer.

After searching the entire house and finding nothing helpful the police would be interested in, they entered the attic. Maggie looked around at the too-familiar space, and her eyes automatically flew to the empty shelf where the green box had been stored. The same container that almost got her killed. Again, she removed her eyes from the painful memory. They landed on an item that was new to the room. Maggie gasped and pointed to the shiny polished shotgun tucked haphazardly in the far corner.

"The gun. It wasn't here before."

They moved to retrieve it when Benny suddenly shouted, "Stop."

They stood side by side when Benny pointed to the wooden floor. "Look at the heavy dust on the floor and the tracks leading up to the gun. Note the lack of dust on the weapon," he added dramatically, pulling out his phone and photographing the site.

"Are those boot prints?"

"They sure are. And I'd bet all I have that gun is the same weapon used to kill Titus. You fire that thing at a human, and it makes a big hole. Just like the wounds Titus and Franklin had."

"And here it is in your house. Want to bet Jack has been here?" Maggie replied. "I'm saying yes. And we have to get out of here."

"We can't just leave the gun here, Benny. What if he comes back to get it? The evidence will be gone." Maggie gasped. "Oh, my God. Here we go again. Our DNA is all over the place."

"Don't freak, Maggie," Benny said, putting his hands up. "We have a right for our DNA to be here. It's my house, and you've been here a lot."

"It's been six months at least. Explain my fresh footprints in the dust, would you?"

"Hanes said we've been cleared. So, stop ruminating and worrying. Now, about the gun," Benny said, staring at it. "We have to take it, Maggie. We can't leave it in my house. It's a murder weapon. And we're not leaving it here for Jack to come to get it and use it again."

"What do we do with it then?" Maggie asked, then paused, her eyes shooting sideways at Benny. "Don't tell me you want to take it to Lamar. Of course. To my house."

THE SUN WAS SETTING when they returned to Blanchard House, carrying the weapon in a blanket. Benny laid it on a balcony table and guarded it as Maggie went to get Lamar.

Benny opened the blanket to reveal the gun as Lamar approached the table. "We think Jack used it to kill Titus and Franklin."

"You've got to be shitting me," Lamar said, walking around the table and staring at the weapon. "The murder weapon?"

"Possibly. We're fairly sure. Remember the entrance wound on Titus? This weapon can certainly replicate that damage." Benny touted, using his big words again.

"You have got to stop putting me in these situations, Maggie. It needs to stop," Lamar said, his voice elevated with annoyance.

"Did you, or did you not—tell us we needed to search the house? Well. That's exactly what we did. And this is the outcome. I've been in that attic, and this gun was not there before. Jack lived in the house when he was married to Willow. He knew it was empty and chose to hide it there," Maggie touted, looking to Benny for support.

"I can verify that gun was not there for sure two weeks ago," Benny said. "And we took forensic-type pictures of everything—which we are both certified to perform. And it will stand up in court. And it includes the date and time stamped on it. Of even more fun—are the boot footprints in the dust. Take a look."

"Are you kidding me? Why didn't you just call the police?"

In sync, they rolled their eyes and tilted their head as if to say. *Really?*

"Okay. Okay," Lamar replied, waving his hand in the air. "Take me out there."

So that's what they did. Lamar did a walk-through at the house, ensuring he planted his DNA everywhere.

Chapter 38

Fool Us Once

Tony sat in the private lavish dining room at the hotel, waiting on Chase. As always, their table was out of public view, and Tony was grateful for that, especially tonight. Not that he didn't enjoy the luxury. He planned to order a big fancy meal and put the tab on Chase's room—a tip for all the pain he'd caused Tony. Chase hadn't answered his phone today, making Tony's plans feel more manageable and much deserved.

Tony's thoughts wandered to his future. He'd worked and sacrificed his personal life for his job for too long. He'd built a formidable reputation in the film industry and was known to be THE handler to call when you had a complicated pain-in-the-ass actor. And Chase fit that description. His job paid lots of money because usually, when they called on him, the studio was in a tight spot. Generally, the production was well underway, and the studio had already poured big bucks down the toilet each day the actor didn't show up or reliably perform. And time was money. When actors caused delays in filming due to problem behavior, the studio's need for a handler was urgent. When the studio called Tony to handle Chase, he initially refused because Chase's bad-boy reputation had preceded Tony's offer—but Tony eventually signed when they upped the ante, as they always did when they were desperate. Chase had become an insurance liability. Tony's fee would be peanuts if the insurance company refused to cover the actor. The contract required that Tony keep Chase off and away from drugs and alcohol and make sure Chase showed up to the set prepared to work.

During active filming, Tony had spent every moment with Chase, living on-site with him twenty-four hours a day until the film wrapped. But now things had become complicated. With Annella near death's door, the studio wanted her protected from publicity. Could Chase be relied upon to stay sober and keep up his end of the PR campaign? No. Tony suspected he would begin drinking or using drugs behind closed doors. At least Tony was no longer required to stay with Chase twenty-four hours a day. The agreement required Tony to be nearby whenever Chase was in public places. So far, Chase had attempted to violate the agreement at every twist in the road. But Tony was well-versed in handling problematic people—and everything had gone without incident so far. The studio was happy.

In the beginning, Chase met with Tony in front of a studio executive, and the contract rules were explained. Tony officially blocked a list of Chase's troublesome friends that held notorious reputations for partying and using drugs or alcohol to excess. And most importantly, the studio banned Chase from attending all parties unless they were studio-required. His presence at any event was limited to three hours—and no contact with any guest who might slip him a substance. Tony was to be by his side until bedtime, but their rooms adjoined each other. Tony ensured their suite was on a high floor to keep Chase from sneaking out, and when they retired for the evening, two bodyguards were assigned. One was assigned to stand outside the suite, and the other stood guard at the elevator.

As expected, Chase's reaction was like all the rest of Tony's clients—when it came time to separate. Chase threw a dramatic fit, whined, and complained about the ridiculousness of it all but eventually gave in and signed the contract. "It doesn't mean I have to be nice about it."

"Yes, you do," the executive producer had replied, firmly taking his pen back from Chase and waving him out of the room. "You," he said, pointing the pen at Tony. "I want an update from you about this clown every two days. We've lost enough money on his behalf. One more wrong move by him, and he'll be facing a lawsuit." Tony gave him a thumbs up and exited past a line of people waiting for attention.

Tony then pulled out his phone and opened his secret file of studio contacts, including an extensive list of psychiatrists, doctors, E.R. charge nurse numbers—and other significant people who understood his urgency when calling. They knew he was a handler. And they knew his calls were always troublesome. One psychiatrist specifically treated patients with addictions. Another one dealt with anger management problems. Tony had a unique capacity to get actors secretly treated—all at the drop of a hat and without the star being seen. Easy in. Easy out. Back on set. Little money was lost in downtime. Tony added the executive producer's hotline number to his phone, hoping he wouldn't have to call him with unwelcome news.

Chase was by far the most unpredictable client he'd ever had the misfortune to work with. Tony sighed. He was past the point of tolerance for babysitting the brat—and Tony couldn't wait to deliver his surprise. The filming was over, and Tony had a new assignment.

Chase delivered an insincere apologetic smile when he finally showed up. Tony updated Chase on the latest business, which was still quite hyped with the over-the-top media frenzy over Chase's love story with Annella. Reportedly, they still couldn't get enough.

"Tonight, at midnight, my contract terminates. Today is my last day working for you," Tony said, enormously enjoying the feeling of dropping the bomb.

"Thank God for that!" Tony retorted, unable to hide his shock.

"The studio tried calling you to let you know they re-assigned me. They said they'd tried all week, and you didn't answer their calls."

"They can wait for now," he quibbled before calmly taking a sip of water. "Besides, I make my own decisions, not them."

"You also haven't answered your agent's calls, I might add. I suggest you follow up with him. Soon. You can't ignore his calls, Chase."

Chase gave Tony a long, hostile glare. "He isn't sending me scripts! Do you not think I've been through enough lately? He'll understand. Trust me."

"No, Chase, he won't understand. He'll drop you like a hot potato if you keep up with your childish behavior. Pick up the phone and make the calls before your career is completely destroyed. I'm not making them for you. Not this time." Tony stood up and pushed his chair into place.

"Damn you, Tony," Chase yelled, slamming his hand so hard on the table it made the silverware clatter. "I don't need you anyway. I'm getting sick of you pushing me around."

Tony paused, looked back, and dryly replied. "Good. The feeling is mutual."

MAGGIE STOOD WITH BONNIE talking in the corridor outside Annella's room when they both turned and stared in wonder as Tony strolled into the unit dressed in a suit and tie, looking all Hollywood. His charismatic smile was easy to read despite the face mask. His eyes were full of smiles, and it made it easy not to scold him for being in the building after visiting hours.

"And you're here for?" Bonnie asked, smiling back. Maggie noticed a little flirt going on in her voice.

"I'm Annella's new private security detail hired by the studio to protect her twenty-four hours a day. The media attention is out of control, reporting untrue facts that could damage her career. I believe they're being fed lies by someone we all know."

"I'm not surprised," Bonnie replied. "That man is not normal, I tell you."

"My contract starts tonight at midnight. The hospital has approved me. My papers are filed appropriately with the legal department. Annella had a longstanding clause in her contract to be protected during hospitalizations or other such things. Until now, the studio has been going back and forth with the lawyers, and the hospital gave in, admitting that the security issues surrounding Annella are unique. Turns out, she's still under contract until the latest movie leaves the big screen."

"And what does Chase think of that?" Maggie asked.

"The studio lawyer is chatting with him, probably right about now. I don't expect this to play out well. He has an attitude problem. And the studio is having—should I say—issues with him."

"So, what is your plan?"

"If Chase is present. I will be present. I'll live in the VIP part of the room, so I can always be at Annella's bedside when Chase is there. Otherwise, I will be invisible. And I will step out to the hall when it's requested by the medical staff for privacy. That's my plan. If it's okay with you, Nurse Bonnie, I'd like to settle in."

"Well, sure, Tony. By all means," Bonnie responded in her charming southern voice dripping with niceness. "Make yourself at home. Can I get you a cup of coffee or a snack?"

"Thank you, Bonnie. I'm good. I brought things to eat and drink since I'm vegetarian. I'll set them up in the cabinet if you don't mind."

"Oh, not at all. Call me if you need me. For anything."

Maggie laughed and rolled her eyes at Bonnie as Tony walked away. "Can you make yourself more obvious?"

"I'm only being nice, Maggie. Nothing more than just being friendly and helpful."

"If you could just see yourself," Maggie said, laughing again. "You were very obvious. And he caught it too."

"Really? That's a good thing, right?"

Maggie smiled at the simplicity of Bonnie. She'd be willing to bet Bonnie had never been on an actual date. Briefly, Maggie wondered if Tony was the guy for her. Not likely, she thought as she looked over to catch the night Nursing Supervisor trotting down the hall, just a little too late with the official news of the unusual visitor. The supervisor handed Bonnie the official paperwork authorizing Tony's presence.

On that note, Maggie bid Bonnie goodnight.

Chapter 39

Annella

Doctor Richardson started in as soon as they were alone. "I've noticed some improvement in your physical exam that I don't quite understand, Annella."

Annella wanted to respond but was incapable because the drugs Chase had given her had not worn off. Sunday looked at Maggie quizzically and then looked back at Annella. "Blink once if you can hear me."

Annella didn't blink.

Bonnie rushed into the room. "It's back. The drug screen. Guess what it's positive for. GHB!"

The doctor stood speechless for a moment as she digested the information. "He has to be using her feeding tube. Okay. First thing, Bonnie. I want you to make the feeding tube difficult to access. You know how you nurses love to use tape so we doctors can't get to what we want to see sometimes? Now is the time."

"You got it. I'll be right back with dressing supplies."

"Tell me about this guy, Tony."

Maggie updated Sunday about the studio agreement with the hospital.

"Good. I want to catch Chase in the act. That's crucial. We have to keep her safe at all times. And let's post a security guard outside the room as an added precaution."

Benny burst into the room. "Maggie. You won't believe what I have right here in my golden hands. A video of Chase. We caught him. Take a look," he said, passing his phone to Maggie.

In turn, Maggie passed the video to Sunday. "He's guilty. We have him right where we want him. We just have to catch him actively in the act.

The video will most likely be thrown out of court because of how we obtained it."

So, they carefully plotted and planned their next move. Tony, Maggie, and Benny would hide behind the patient privacy curtain dividing the room, wait for Chase, and try to catch him in the act.

When it was time, they huddled together in the bathroom, so Chase wouldn't find them when he searched behind the curtain for security.

Like clockwork, Chase entered Annella's room and checked behind the curtain. Confident he was alone, he sat at the end of the bed. Benny held his phone up so all could see what was happening over the hidden camera.

After fifteen minutes, Chase got up and checked the hallway. Satisfied he was clear, Chase stepped over to Annella's bed, pulled the syringe from his pocket, and lifted her gown. "What the hell?" Chase spat, seeing the vast, complicated-looking surgical dressing Bonnie had left for him. Chase ripped at it desperately, hurrying to get his task done.

"What's up, pal?" Tony asked, pulling open the curtain. "What are you doing?"

"I'm…" Chase stumbled on his words as Tony, Benny, and Maggie moved in, pulling Chase out of the room and onto the floor. Chase fought Tony hard, kicking and fighting with him before the security officer posted outside the door moved in to help. Benny called the police as Chase was pulled into the corridor and turned on his belly, where they secured him to await police.

Over the next several hours, the crime scene was photographed, and evidence was secured as detectives carried out their investigation.

Bonnie saw that the portable privacy screens were placed at the end of the hall to keep employees and visitors out of view, although the action came a little too late.

During the commotion with Chase, a visitor captured a video of Chase in the hall, kicking and screaming, handcuffed on the floor, with several police officers in attendance. The video went viral spreading like a wildfire caught in a windstorm.

Bonnie walked over to Chase and stood staring at him before finally declaring, "Fool us once or twice, but not for long. We always catch on. And we always catch people like you that try to poison people in our house." She stood grinning as police dragged Chase away.

"Nice dressing," Doctor Richardson noted.

Bonnie smiled, satisfied. "It's not as complicated as it looks. I didn't use much tape at all.

You can actually remove the whole thing with one hand if you know how. Easy peasy."

"You're a great nurse, Bonnie."

"Yeah? Well, you're an awesome surgeon."

Tony came up from behind and put his arm around Bonnie's shoulder. "Thanks for your help.

You helped save her life."

LATE THAT EVENING, Maggie was sitting in the movie room watching the latest episode of **Stranger Things** with Dorrie when Benny entered and asked if he could interrupt.

"I need to talk to Maggie, baby," he said to Dorrie. "And it has to be private. Do you mind pausing the show and going upstairs for about thirty minutes?"

"No, sir, I don't mind," Dorrie said, feeling the seriousness of the moment. Dorrie quickly grabbed her popcorn and left the room.

"You might want to turn on the local news," Benny suggested somberly.

"What happened?" Maggie asked, flipping the television to the news station. A picture of Chase covered the screen. Then, there was a clip of Annella. It was followed by a video of her with Chase at the Oscars, having their picture taken as they posed for news photographers, looking like the perfect couple. The broadcast was mid-story.

Benny sat opposite Maggie on the plush sofa and listened intently to the reporter.

"*Fans are shocked tonight. Hollywood actor Chase Hayworth was booked on charges of attempted murder. He is accused of poisoning his newly wedded wife Annella Wryn, a film legend, as she lay helpless in a hospital bed. She is recovering at Saint Vincent's Medical Center, where she has been critically ill since being transferred to Charlotte for treatment for a fall.*"

The news cut to a video of Chase being handcuffed and led out of the hospital. *"The famous star then posted bail of what was reported to be half a million dollars,"* the female newscaster continued. *"As you can see in this next video, the actor calmly drove to the airport, boarded a private plane and fled to an unknown destination. Airport officials declined to provide information although an anonymous source said he was staying within Mecklenburg County. Another source claims he broke his bond and left the United States. We have been unable to verify the facts. So, who knows when he will be seen again? If ever."*

Maggie and Benny watched in wide-eyed shock as Chase boarded the plane, stepped back out, smiled at the camera, and waved goodbye to his fans lined along the fence.

"Wow," they both said in concert. Maggie covered her mouth, stunned. "So, what's next?"

Chapter 40

Gun

Hanes sat at his desk working while eating his favorite meal: a juicy chicken sandwich stacked high with lettuce, tomatoes, fries, and a giant-sized soda from Burger King. When his phone rang, he groaned when he saw Lamar's number on the caller ID.

"Yeah," Hanes answered.

"Lamar here. Want to come out to the house for drinks?"

"You got something for me?"

"Indeed, I do. And you'll want it."

"Be there in five," Hanes replied reluctantly, looking at his food. He put it back in the bag to eat on the way. Hanes did not like eating in his car. First, it would bother him all day if he got anything on his clothes. And second, seeing a crumb in his car would make him cringe. But, judging by the tone in Lamar's voice, the meeting couldn't wait. And Lamar wouldn't call him unless what he had was related to the case. Hanes chuckled. He hoped Maggie and Benny had been up to something because things in the investigation were going too slow for him, and the hospital was breathing down his neck non-stop.

The drive over to Blanchard House took a lot longer than Hanes expected. Sharon Road was in gridlock, dragging cars down to a creeping pace, but it allowed him to finish his long-anticipated meal. When his phone rang again, Hanes all but yelled into it. "Yeah. Hanes here."

It was the Bowles. "I got the warrant to search the kidnapped girl's house."

"Book it for first thing in the morning," Hanes ordered, hanging up with a massive grin. *Got you,* he said to himself as he pulled into the drive. At this point, he was unraveling Willow's life layer by layer, looking for any evidence she could be involved in the robbery.

Hanes was eager for his five o'clock cocktail when he entered Blanchard House. And what a fine cocktail that would be. Expensive. Smooth. Whiskey. He was beginning to get used to cocktails with his old buddy Lamar and especially enjoyed spending time in the grand house.

LYING ON A SHEET, on top of the bar, was a Remington 870 slug gun. Hanes' eyes widened with surprise. "Damn."

"You'll need a good stiff drink before I fill you in," Lamar announced excitedly. Hanes knew the look well and missed it after his buddy left the department.

As they sipped their drinks, Hanes said, "Don't you ever think about returning? You have a knack for detective work. I wish I had your talent."

"Ya'll can't afford me, boy. But—if we don't find the girl soon, I might be looking to return. Private detective work is not my cup of tea. Way too boring. Good money. But boring."

"Well, think about it. In the meantime, stop playing with me and tell me about this beauty." Hanes pointed to the gun as he raised his glass to take a sip.

"Not sure. But I suspect it might have been used to murder Titus. It's the right size. It fits. And suspiciously, it was found at Willow's house, where she lived with her ex-husband Jack before she remarried. I know he's in town. And I believe he dropped the speck of dirt in the O.R."

"Why is the gun here, of all places?"

"Maggie and Benny swept his house, thinking you might be ready to issue a search warrant."

"Did you tip them off?"

"I figured it was your next move."

"You scuzzy rat."

They both laughed.

"The two forensic sleuth investigators also took date and time-stamped pictures for you. They'll possibly do you good in court."

"I need you—pal—to tell them to STOP pilfering with evidence. No more! It doesn't matter what they find—tell them to leave things where they are and stop snooping and removing evidence from the scene. They are cleared of the crime. And my partner is a nut job. He could easily start looking at them again, and I can't take any more of his bullshit. All they're doing is making my job harder. They're driving me nuts. **You're** driving me nuts."

"They're afraid, Mark. That's why they brought it to me. I'm in charge of Maggie's security."

"Well, tell them not to be afraid—unless they do this again. The next time they do, so help me; I'm bringing them in and giving them a good scare. You get my message here?"

"Loud and clear."

"Make sure they get it," Hanes warned.

"We did, loud and clear. Just like you wanted," Maggie said with a big welcoming smile.

Benny trailed right behind her.

Lamar chuckled and reached for two glasses, holding the whiskey bottle up as an offer.

"No thanks," Maggie said, holding up her hand. "Too stiff for me. I told Dorrie I'd help her with homework."

"Me included. I'm going swimming."

"Seriously, Mark," Maggie exclaimed, laughing. "You're going to haul us down to headquarters and make us afraid? Oh—we're soooo scared."

They all laughed, and Maggie and Benny promised to stay out of his way.

Chapter 41

The Building

Sykes arrived just in time for breakfast. Maggie and Benny were well prepared for the meeting, having read the entire drone operating manual the night before. Sykes had taken care of all the licensing and registration. In addition, he had registered all the drones with the local aviation departments throughout North Carolina.

After breakfast, they went to a part of the estate's backyard, which was all green grass. Still green and lush because it was fescue, the type that stays green in winter. They learned how to do a pre-flight check at a large stone table to ensure the drone was in proper order for flying. Next, they checked their batteries to make sure all were fully charged. Maggie and Benny were given small drones to start with and later were allowed to fly Sykes's drone.

Maggie easily got frustrated on the first launch. She had great difficulty getting the drone off the ground, and on her third run, she lost track of it, and on her final flight, she crash-landed the drone into a building on the back of the property—a building she'd never noticed before as it was grown over with ivy. "Y'all can count me out. I do not have the skill or talent to fly a drone. Especially the big ones. I don't dare," she yelled back at Sykes as she gathered the pieces of the crashed drone, which were all over the place.

Then, Maggie spotted a building on the property she'd never seen. It was well hidden amongst the natural overgrowth. A small path traced around it to a back entrance. The stone building was solid and in keeping with the house's exterior architecture, except the building was one story.

There didn't seem to be a door. She was still staring at it when Lamar came running across the yard, calling her name.

Maggie climbed over the overgrowth and greeted him at the grassy area. "Is there something wrong, Lamar? You look distressed."

"No. No. I was coming to help."

Maggie scrutinized him and simply said, "Liar. You're lying to me."

"No, I'm not."

"What's with the building, then? It's peculiar looking. And odd, in the sense you can't see it unless you literally fall upon it. And you chased me out here. You don't want me near the building—isn't that correct?"

Lamar held for a moment. "It's an old icehouse."

"With no door? How do you get into it?"

"Only authorized persons have that knowledge."

"That's a peculiar choice of words—for an old icehouse."

"Mr. Blanchard wouldn't want you involved."

"That's an even messier statement. May I remind you that I am in charge until Mister Mystery Man shows his face again?"

"I can't help you, Maggie. I'm doing my job. Let me do it."

"Whatever!" Maggie replied, annoyed, before walking back to the group.

"What's up with you? You look pissed!" Benny said.

"I am. But I don't want to talk about it."

"Gotcha."

They resumed their flight drone lessons without further ado, but Benny couldn't help but keep his eye on Maggie. She never kept secrets from him. And the other way around. He looked back at the place where Maggie had crashed her drone. That had changed her mood. And whatever she'd said to Lamar had made him afraid.

Chapter 42

Revenge

Maggie and Benny were standing in the Resuscitation Room waiting for the Medical Resuscitation patient with CPR in progress to arrive. The medic was kneeling on the stretcher delivering cardiac compressions on arrival. Maggie spotted the white feet and knew it was over before they rolled into the room.

Benny delivered compressions as the medic delivered the report. "Found down under the bridge. Bystanders claim she'd been drinking and using GHB. CPR was initiated without response to ACLS protocol."

The usual hectic interventions proved useless and the physician pronounced the patient dead. When the activity settled, Maggie got her first look at the patient. It was the woman who had walked out of the NSICU after a GHB overdose. Maggie's stomach fell. Instantly, she regretted not having chased the girl down the hall herself to warn her again about the dangers of the drug. Possibly—she could have prevented her death. Maggie wished she had fought harder on the girl's behalf.

Maggie chewed her lip as she filled out the death paperwork, her anger growing hotter by the minute. She'd lost all care for her job as a supervisor. It was time to put her foot down. After all, she'd just gotten her license as a Nurse Practitioner and was seriously considering the job offer from Doctor Richardson. The E.R. was pounding her to a pulp. She loved being a nurse and there had never been a moment where she questioned her devotion to the practice. It was the supervisor bit that was far from satisfying. She was the middleman, always getting beat up by those above and below. Nurse-friends had warned her not to take the job and poked fun at her at times when she was under intense stress. Now, she wished she'd stayed at the bedside where her actions and caring actually benefited the patient.

Her fuming turned to resolve as she methodically made copies of the death paperwork. Her hard breathing eased, and her hands stopped trembling. Should she eventually decide to leave the E.R., it would be with a lot of noise. And on her call. And with respect.

Evans, her boss, had been relentless in his harassment of her since her write-up. He'd made life much more complicated than it should be by making her feel constantly scrutinized. His frequent E.R. visits were deliberately designed to threaten and intimidate her. Evans was an office-type man and had rarely ever walked through the department before her write-up. Maggie made three copies. One for the report she would file to make her voice heard loud and clear. The other ones she would deliver in person.

Maggie passed her pager and responsibilities over to Nurse Cora and made her way down the long hall to the back elevator. She pushed the button to the eighth floor and entered the Neurosurgical Intensive Care Unit. Walking her path through the endless corridors that wound around the unit, she finally saw her prize.

"Doctor Lockhart?"

The resident turned to face Maggie. His face scowled at seeing her. "Here to apologize? I hear you got a write-up for ineffective Customer Service."

"That's not exactly the reason for my visit," Maggie said, delivering a honey-sweet smile before slapping the papers on the counter in front of him. "I thought you'd want to read this before I file a report of misconduct—kind of a payback—but more because of what you did that led to a young girl's death. Your inappropriate behavior."

Maggie watched Doctor Lockhart read the death paperwork—gripping his cheap pen harder and harder—until it snapped.

"You had five minutes, doctor, to chase that young girl down the hall and save her life with responsible education regarding GHB. But your pride stopped you from doing the right thing. And you might want to fully evaluate the level of niceness in my voice as I share this message with you—using perfect customer service." Maggie smiled as she walked off—but she felt ashamed—not satisfied. Her smile faded.

In the corridor, Maggie instantly regretted her actions and did a U-turn, re-entering the unit, vowing she would not allow herself to become a person that tore people down. She would not become Evans.

"I apologize, Lockhart. I over-reacted to my patient's death, and I've not been myself lately."

"I heard about the robbery and shooting," Lockhart said. "That had to be a nightmare. I wouldn't be myself either, and I'm sorry you had to go through that. It was so—tragic. We've all talked about it a lot, and everyone sympathizes with you. We all fear it happening to us. You just ended up being the unlucky one."

"Thank you. For understanding," Maggie replied, feeling great satisfaction over her actions. "I need all the support I can get right now. It's been a rough road trying to get back to normal if such a thing is possible after what I saw," Maggie replied. It felt good to share her feelings and talk about the shooting openly. "I am sorry. And I'm not filing anything with anyone about misconduct—because I respect you work exceptionally long hours and still deliver great care no matter how exhausted you are. You are very dedicated to your patients, and we all say things in this environment that are sometimes less than perfect. It comes with the job. You are a good doctor. Thank you for what you do every day."

Maggie watched as Doctor Lockhart's face lit up with surprise. "Thank you, Maggie. I needed to hear that. Thank you for having the courage to think about me. And you're a great nurse. I was mad when I wrote the report on you. And tired. And I knew what I'd done was wrong, but it was too late to undo. I did try to contact the girl. Many times. I want you to know that. I couldn't reach her."

Maggie smiled his way before leaving.

"Hey. You can call me Chuck," he called after her.

Maggie waved goodbye as she walked out the door, happy she'd turned around and made things right.

MAGGIE'S NEXT VISIT WAS to her boss. She was determined to deliver her message with excellent customer service using a respectful but business-like tone. She couldn't be friends because their relationship had extended in the opposite direction and was far beyond the possibility of friendship—but she would not be harsh like she wanted.

Benny caught up with her in the hall on his way back from the lab. "What are you up to? I heard you turned the unit over to Cora."

"I'm getting ready to take care of some unfinished business."

"You look nervous."

"I do?"

"Yeah. It's written all over your face. Don't tell me you're on your way to see Evans." Maggie sighed. "Yeah, I am."

"I'm going with you for encouragement."

"You can't."

"I can and I will. I'll sit on the bench outside the door, and you leave the door open. If it gets nasty, I'll interrupt. Would it help if I told you Evans turned in his resignation about an hour ago?"

"For sure? That's awesome! But, I'm still meeting with him."

"Then, enter with courage and face that evil man with the knowledge that all the staff, including the doctors, are laughing their butts off and taking bets as to whether he was fired or forced to resign. The majority are in favor of him having been asked to leave."

When she entered his office, Maggie was nervous and spoke far faster than she intended. "I'll be brief, Evans. Homicide has cleared me of all suspicion in the robbery and shooting. And I'm expecting my NP license soon, so I'll be leaving the E.R., but my goal is to have a squeaky-clean record before I do. I can't have future employers reading nonsense on my employment record." Maggie noticed she was swaying—her arms folded defensively to her chest. She unfolded her arms. Maggie didn't want him to read fear in her body language. She forced herself to relax as she continued.

"As for the Sentinel Event follow-up regarding the elopement of my mother on Christmas night, I'm happy to report she's clean and sober and has been cleared of any involvement concerning the robbery. The Sentinel Event Committee did not find fault in my work regarding her elopement. So, you can dismiss that, too. The e-mail is sitting in your mailbox. I forwarded it to you, although I know you received the notification long before I did."

Maggie's voice felt edgy like it was giving in to her nervousness. She swallowed hard and moved forward with more confidence. "I'm officially contesting my Final Written Warning. I am asking for its complete extraction from my record. You can quietly do it or force me to file official papers with HR to contest it and ask for a full hearing. I will do whatever it takes."

Maggie placed the death report in front of him. “This is the death notice for the patient I defended against the physician who complained about my poor customer service. I don’t think you will find Doctor Lockhart helpful in backing up your claim, as the two of us have resolved our differences in a good and productive way. I consider it a good hit for our team since we all want the same thing—quality patient care. Have a good day now, and please notice the niceness I used to deliver my message.”

Benny was waiting on the bench outside Evan’s office. Further down the hall and out of Evens sight, they popped their pals together in the air and said simultaneously.

"Score!"

Then, they hurried back to the E.R. to respond to several Trauma Codes arriving at the same time.

Chapter 43

Buddy

Willow lay in bed listening to Jack cleaning his gun outside her door. She'd know that sound anywhere. Jack had made a point to clean his weapon in front of her, to make her afraid, get her attention, intimidate her, or just scare her—she didn't know what his motive was except that it made him feel powerful. He seemed to get a kick out of it. Willow couldn't help but wonder if that was his intention now. It certainly had gotten her attention.

When Jack was done, it got quiet on the other side of the door, and she wondered again what he would do to her for the hundredth time since being held in captivity. She couldn't take another beating and survive. He'd hurt her significantly this time. Willow rubbed her painful belly at the memory of him beating her. It hurt to breathe. Jack's hot anger, when it blew, knew no boundaries.

To say she was afraid when there came a knock at the door was an understatement. She jerked alive at the sound and started violently shivering until she realized the knocking was on the outer door of the cabin.

Willow struggled to get out of bed and sat in the chair by the door, eavesdropping.

"Hey, Buddy! Come on in," she heard Jack call out. Footsteps, that sounded like boots walked the short distance to the table. "Want a beer?"

"Does a frog bump its butt on the ground when it jumps? Hell yeah, I do. I bought us some burgers and fries," Buddy said, his voice happy, sounding like he'd had a couple of beers on his way over.

"Thanks, man. I was just gettin' ready to go out and get some grub."

The smell of the still-hot burgers and French fries drifting through the house made Willow hungry despite her aching belly. She strained to listen as the voices got to normal.

"Yeah—well," Buddy started in, talking with a mouth full of food and taking chugs of his beer. "Two police detectives paid me a visit. Scared the shit outta me when I saw them pull up in the drive. They were nosey, man—walked around my house looking at everything like they owned the place. One of the dudes poked in my shrubbery before the main guy pounded on my door. I tried to be calm. I didn't let on or anything."

"What did they want?" Jack asked. Willow could hear the tension and worry in Jack's voice.

Buddy had undoubtedly taken him by surprise.

"Some big shot detective, Hanes, wants to see me at the station. He has some questions for me. I told them I'd come on down in about an hour. Then, they left. Surprised the crap out of me. Damn. I thought they would put me in the back of the car and haul me off. I'm not going down to that place, not on your life. I heard that once they get you in the questioning room, they don't stop. I heard horror stories about those investigators. They wear you down. Get ya to confess even if you didn't do anything. No siree. I'm out of here."

"Did you talk? Tell them anything?"

"Hell no. Do you think I'm crazy? Did you? Did they talk to you yet?"

"What do you mean, yet?" Jack demanded.

"They're looking for whoever killed Titus and Franklin. Titus' fingerprints were on the drugs stolen from the hospital."

"How'd you know that?"

"They told me,"

"I thought you didn't talk to them. You said all they said was they wanted you to go down to the station. They baited you, dummy. What else did they say?"

"They asked if I'd seen you. I said, no. Not in a long time."

"You stupid son of a bitch. You lied. Then, got in your car and drove right to me. You're an idiot. Did it ever occur to you that you might be followed?"

Willow heard Jack get up and go to the door. He looked out the window and returned to the table and sat back down. Willow was relieved. She'd expected Jack to start beating up on Buddy, who she didn't know until today. Willow got to her knees and peeked through the door lock. She could see the side of Jack sitting at the table. He held a gun under the table. Willow felt her breathing hasten.

"Did you kill Titus?" Buddy asked, his voice shaking along with his fingers. He gripped his beer can to control his trembling movements.

"No one else had the guts," Jack replied, his voice even and icy. "Especially you. Titus spent all his money and couldn't go to Mexico. The dumb-ass deposited it into the bank—of all places. We had an agreement. We don't spend our money until we get to Mexico. We didn't want people to notice we came into a lot of cash. It's a good thing I did kill him. If they found his fingerprints, he would've talked."

"We also agreed nobody gets hurt," Buddy said, sweat popping out on his forehead. "And, then you go all wacky and kill people. What in the hell were you thinking, Jack? Titus was my family! My friend," Buddy's voice took on a squirrelly kind of fear, cracking. "What about my cousin, Frankie? Did you kill him too?"

"Hanes was suspicious of him. I saw him talking to Franklin out in the yard at his house. Frankie looked all nervous and ready to spill his guts everywhere. I couldn't take chances."

Buddy squeezed his beer can so hard it crumbled in his fist. "You got the pure devil in you man. You are not my friend. Not anymore. I didn't kill anybody so I'm sure as hell not taking the blame. And I'm certainly NOT going to the death chamber for your stupid shit behavior. I'm out of here—tonight."

"You're threatening me?"

"I'm just telling you like it is. If I get caught, I'm spillin' the beans and it's going straight on your doorstep where it belongs. You chose to kill them, Jack. They didn't have to die. And that makes you evil." Buddy slammed his fists on the table so hard it shook the tableware. He stood, walked to the door, opened it and turned back for one last look at Jack. "Who do you think you are? God?"

In horror, Willow watched Jack raise his gun and shoot Buddy between the eyes. Buddy's body blasted out the door to the ground.

"Maybe I am God," Jack said before leaving.

Willow heard Jack drag Buddy's body and put it in his car. She watched out her window as he pushed Buddy's car down into the ravine. Then, Jack's tires squealed off into the night.

She jumped into bed and pulled the covers over her head. Willow's thoughts whirled around like a spinning globe. She tried to think like Jack. *What would he do? What would he do? Her face wrinkled with pain as she cried out, "Noooooo."*

Chapter 44

Dorrie

After a long leisurely breakfast, Dorrie asked if Maggie could take her shopping so she could get some new clothes. She whispered, "I need some training bras. And soccer shoes. I want yellow ones, so you can tell who I am on the field," Dorrie said with a grin.

"A security officer will have to go with us." Maggie replied.

"I'm gonna have to buy bras in front of a man?" Dorrie exclaimed.

"We'll see if they have a female on duty. If not, I'll have the male wait nearby while you grab the bras. But they'll have to be everywhere else we go. You know, like, in the shops near us. Just ignore them like they're not there. It comes with the shopping experience."

"You have to do this every time you shop?"

"Not anymore. Kerrington wants me to, but I can't give up that much of my privacy. You, on the other hand, come with risks. Kerrington demanded it."

"Because of Mommy?"

"Yes." When Maggie stopped talking, Dorrie changed the subject as Maggie had hoped she would.

"Can I also get a soccer ball?"

"You can get whatever you want, Sweetie. It'll be fun. We need to get out of the house. We'll have lunch and get pizza. That suit you?"

"Yes!" Dorrie exclaimed, clapping her hands together as she headed upstairs to get ready.

The chilly breeze blew gently across Maggie's face, rustling her hair in the wind as they walked to the car. The air smelled heavenly. Maggie smiled at the tiny yellow daffodils peeking out from the ground. The large trees bore evidence of an early spring—tiny buds, ready to burst into leaves. It left Maggie with great contentment.

The shopping trip took less than two hours when they stopped briefly and got pizza, where Dorrie enthusiastically dug through all her shopping bags. It had been a beautiful, delightful, fun-filled day. Maggie purchased everything Dorrie wanted, which totaled almost five hundred dollars and included the new soccer shoes they purchased from the sporting goods store. Dorrie insisted on wearing the shoes home. She was one happy girl, running ahead of Maggie and heading to the parking lot. Being a typical enthusiastic child, Dorrie called back to Maggie to hurry. Maggie grinned, happy at how Dorrie had made her day so happy. Feeling Dorrie's youth, Maggie took off after her but was unable to keep up because she was carrying all the bags.

It happened just that quickly; the security guard stood on the sidewalk waiting for Dorrie to reach her—just as a car pulled up to the curb, and Jack got out holding a gun. He aimed straight at the officer. Maggie's heart felt like it might stop.

"Dorrie!" Jack shouted. "Get over here. Now."

"Daddy. What are you doing? Put the gun down. Please. Don't." Maggie watched the look on Dorrie's innocent face turn to one of pure living terror. The split-second Jack got close enough, he jerked Dorrie by the arm. The security guard raised her pistol, and Jack fired his gun, hitting the guard in the leg.

"You move again, and you're dead," Jack shouted as he backed up toward the car pulling Dorrie with him.

Wild chaos erupted as shoppers ran screaming in all directions to find cover as the security officer called for help on her radio. "**Active Shooter. Active Shooter**." Maggie ran after Dorrie as people dived for cover, yelling.

"Dorrie is my child," Jack yelled. "I will not hurt her, and you have no right to stop me. Get in the car, Dorrie. Now. Or I'll shoot Maggie."

Dorrie ran around to the other side of the car and got in as Jack entered the driver's side and sped off. Dorrie looked back to see the security officer trying to stand up. Maggie stood against the curb, crying, talking excitedly on her cell phone.

Several police cars pulled up and surrounded the mall exit as dozens ran, bumping into each other, trying to get into the safety of the mall.

Additional mall security arrived just as several police officers took off in hot pursuit of their vehicle. Dorrie turned and studied her father's face, noting it held an all too familiar expression he used when he would hurt her mother. The brakes squealed as Jack steered the car rapidly into a car wash at a gas station.

"Here's what we're doing, and so help me, Dorrie, if you make one wrong move, you will never see your mother again. When the rinse cycle clears your door—get out and run to that black car right there," he demonstrated, pointing at the vehicle. And that's what they did. They both got soaking wet during the escape but made it safely to the car. Jack roared the engine and took off, exiting the back of the station and merging into city traffic, which was easy because it wasn't even close to rush hour. In no time, they were on Interstate 77 headed out of town.

The speeding car terrified Dorrie as Jack swerved around cars, increasing his speed. Secretly, Dorrie prayed the police would catch them and save her. Dorrie was too frightened to speak—yet desperately wanted to ask him what he meant about not seeing her mother again. It almost sounded like Jack knew the whereabouts of her mother. She prayed he did. Instinctively, she touched the back pocket of her jeans and felt her phone, relieved; Maggie had put a family tracking app on it to track Dorrie in case something like this ever happened.

Dorrie shivered from fear of what her father might do. If Jack knew where her mother was, he must have been involved in the hospital robbery and the murder. That made him an evil man, far worse than she'd ever imagined—and that meant his list of criminal deeds was long. She began to shake hard at the thought.

Her father didn't offer conversation, which made Dorrie feel awkward and uncomfortable. After drinking so much soda at lunch, she needed to go to the bathroom but was afraid to ask Jack to stop.

After about forty-five minutes, when Dorrie spotted an old country diner, she finally got the courage to ask to go to the bathroom. Jack groaned and pulled over. "Make it fast." Dorrie was relieved. Finally, she could call for help when she closed the bathroom door.

"No funny stuff," her father ordered. "Remember what I said about your mother." Just before Dorrie got out of the car, her phone vibrated.

"What's that sound?" Jack demanded, shouting, getting out of the car, and stomping her way. "Get out of the car. Do you have a phone on you?" It vibrated again. "Give it up! Give it to me, now!"

Slowly Dorrie pulled it from her pocket and handed it to Jack.

"An **I-phone**. Figures," Jack said, throwing the phone far into the thick brush beside the road. "Those people have spoiled you rotten. What else have you got? Is that an **Apple** watch? Can you send messages with it?"

Dorrie shook her head affirmatively.

"Did you send any?" Jack asked, getting in Dorrie's face. Vigorously, Dorrie shook her head negatively, too afraid to speak. "Give it to me and empty your pockets."

Dorrie did what she was told and almost wet her pants before she got to the toilet. She hated Jack. Maggie had given her the watch and phone as a present. Dorrie was so proud to own them.

Jack stood directly outside the door waiting and pushed her to get going the minute she exited the bathroom. Dorrie hurried and returned to the car as quickly as possible to control her father's temper—if such a thing could be done.

By the time they turned onto I-40, Dorrie had imagined everything horrible that could happen to her. She also imagined every feasible way she might escape. But she needed to get more creative because none of the options she came up with seemed plausible.

Jack took the back roads, turning to the right, then another right, and left. It became so complicated Dorrie gave up trying to track where they were. It was getting dark, and she feared riding on the back roads, especially with her father. He'd hit a deer one time and totaled the car. Her body had hurt for days, especially her neck. She could hardly move it for a long time. Dorrie watched the sides of the road for signs of deer, ready to call out, but they were lucky. She was also grateful there wasn't much traffic on the country road that seemed to wind around in large curves. Dorrie figured they were in the back woods of a mountainous area.

Jack brought the car to a stop in front of a one-story log cabin home. It was well-weathered but pretty and clean. There was something familiar about it from a long time ago. Finally, it came to Dorrie. Her father used to bring her here when she was little—when he babysat her. It was her grandmother's house. Dread shot through her. Her grandmother was a mean woman and didn't like children. She also drank too much and smoked one cigarette after another until the house stunk so awful that Dorrie could barely breathe.

Jack went to the front door, opened it, and stepped inside. "You want to see your mother?" Dorrie ran to the door but stopped short of entering.

Her mother was standing in the kitchen, her face beaten black and blue. Severely swollen.

"Mama?" Dorrie called, her face wrinkling up to cry.

Dorrie saw the ***secret warning.*** *Two finger wipes. One swipe over her mother's top eye lid and one under the bottom.* It took Dorrie's breath away. They had practiced it many times. *The furtive eye signal was her mother's message to run away. Hard and fast. Do not hesitate.*

She felt like she saw things in slow-motion as she turned, looked at the woods, looked back at her mother, and followed her warning instructions. Dorrie ran fast—like she did on the soccer field, twisting and turning around trees and bushes like a rabbit—before heading down a deep ravine that she knew well from her childhood.

Dorrie was glad she'd chosen to wear her new soccer shoes out of the store because they helped cushion her feet and grip the ground with intention. She was also grateful she'd chosen to wear a warm jacket instead of a light one. It had been a toss-up due to the forecast for the day. Maggie led her to choose the heavy one because a cold front was coming. Dorrie knew she could outrun Jack without a sweat, so she changed her plan and decided to run uphill to make it harder for Jack to catch up to her. And Dorrie planned to run until she dropped from exhaustion. She would not let him win. He'd changed a lot lately. More wicked. More malevolent. Dorrie greatly feared him now more than ever.

She was a long way from where she started when a sharp pain stabbed her side, forcing her to stop and breathe. Dorrie looked around, not knowing where to go but up—however that prospect didn't look promising.

Dorrie smiled at the memory of Maggie. It was one of her favorite sayings when faced with a choice. *The choices were usually promising—or they were not.* Briefly, she wondered what Maggie would choose. Going straight up would put her so far in the woods where the brush was thick and scary. Sideways looked promising and would work better for timing. It would give her an edge over Jack. One thing she knew for sure—she was good and lost, deep in the woods.

At first, she'd known the land from her previous explorations as a child long ago when visiting her grandmother. But now, she was way off track. And she felt hunger pains and a dry mouth. Dorrie sat momentarily on a large rock—seeing in her mind's eye the images of her mother's battered face. She shot off a short prayer to God—to keep her mother safe from her monster of a father. She also prayed for herself.

It would soon be dark. Dorrie warned herself—she needed to make as much distance as possible before she'd have to hunker down for the night. Dorrie heard trickling water and headed towards the sound, following it, step by step, listening closely. Her search paid off when the water became more than a trickling sound. The creek was small but sparkled in the shaded light with the freshest-looking water she'd seen in a long time. And it was bitterly cold and refreshing. Eagerly Dorrie cupped her hands and drank water as if she might not find it again. Exhausted, she leaned against a tree and thought about her mother. She smiled. At least she was alive. Thank God for that. And she was positive, without a doubt, that help was on the way. Maggie and Benny would find her. They would never give up. She knew that for sure. Someday they would find her and take her home again. Dorrie wrapped her jacket tightly around her body, tucked herself under heavy branches for protection and warmth, and fell sound asleep.

JACK LOOKED ABOUT, STRAINING to see through the bushes—looking for any sign of Dorrie. He turned around and searched again. It was getting hard to see as evening shadows gave birth to fading light. Jack could only hear night sounds against the gentle wind rustling through the trees. A grassy rustle beside Jack startled him until he realized it was only a baby deer. Jack sat on a stump to rest and wondered where he could find food. He briefly played with the idea of returning to the cabin to gather some grub—then realized he didn't even know which direction to go.

How did things go so wrong—so fast? Jack wondered. Everything had been so tightly coordinated and rehearsed. Jack had come home from Alabama at least a dozen times to meet with Titus, Franklin, and Buddy to help plan the heist. It had been Franklin's idea because he knew the pharmacy system and the times of the day it was restocked with narcotics. He'd gotten Titus interested, but the key person was Buddy, who brought it all together with his ability to cut off all hospital security systems. Jack's job was to cover the critical area and make sure no one pressed the *panic button* in the E.R.

Jack rubbed his face with his hands. He hadn't meant to kill the secretary—he'd meant to scare her. Then, the doc headed for the second *panic button.* Jack shot him without thinking; after all, he'd already committed murder. He simply wanted the money and Willow. They'd go to Mexico and never be seen again. It was his way of getting even with Benny for stealing his wife and making him look like less of a man.

Jack had kept his eyes glued to Willow as she went to the different drug areas and emptied the storage system of all narcotics that had street value. When he was sure Willow was out the door and securely his, he'd pushed Maggie to the floor with satisfaction. He was sick of the bitch always getting into his business with Willow. Jack recalled the split second he'd paused to think as he'd held his gun tightly with his finger trembling on the trigger—aimed at Maggie's head. He'd almost pulled the trigger, but for some unexplainable reason, he'd backed out.

Post robbery, they gathered in the woods, wearing gloves to hide fingerprints. Following Franklin's instructions, they transferred the drugs from their hospital containers because they had serial numbers on them that were traceable to Saint Vincent's. Franklin put them in simple labeled vials to deliver to the street seller. Things quickly unraveled the minute Franklin delivered the drugs.

Titus became enraged when he discovered one of his gloves had a tear, and possibly, he'd left a fingerprint behind. He'd frantically gone through the garbage bag and wiped as many of the vials clean before Jack took the bag, insisting they were out of time and had to go.

Then, despite the agreement, Titus, and Franklin both deposited their money, leaving official records tying them to the heist—and leaving Jack with no choice but to kill them—along with Buddy. Jack reflected back on the moments of each murder. Regret was nowhere to be found in his soul. Buddy was right. He'd lost his soul to the devil. He would have to pay mightily for his sins, which was something he was not up for doing. Jack wasn't willing to be caged up like a dog for the rest of his life. He wanted freedom. And he would have it.

What to do with Dorrie was his problem. She'd turned against him along with her mother. He had a good mind to leave Dorrie behind—but Willow would never forgive him. He couldn't have one without the other. They were his family, and no one was going to take them away.

"Where are you, brat?" Jack called out, his temper getting the best of him. *Don't do that again*, he cautioned himself. *They'll find you. Your job is to find Dorrie and make your way to Mexico. Home sweet home.*

Chapter 45

The Drones

Blanchard House was abuzz with lots of police activity. Even Hanes was present. Lamar was busy talking with the family lawyers over by the sofa. Maggie sat in the wing-back chair in the living room beside Benny, talking with a female detective from the missing persons unit. Maggie stared at Hanes and couldn't help but wonder why he was there. She wiped her swollen eyes and nose, soggy with tears.

Thirty minutes later, Maggie still had her eyes on Hanes—cautiously following his every move around the room, thinking to herself. *What does he want? What is he looking for? It's not a homicide.* Her curiosity was piqued even higher when she saw him pull Lamar aside. Hanes looked at her as if to say, mind your own business.

Hanes turned his back on her and spoke with Lamar for a lengthy time. She turned her attention to Benny, who thumbed rapidly through Maggie's phone with his elbows propped up on his knees. He leaned over to Maggie and whispered.

"Here it is," he whispered, motioning with his eyes to Lamar, indicating to him to join them. "Per the Goggle location mapping system." Benny pointed, "This is where her phone is. It's idle, meaning she's there. Let's go outside," he whispered. The three of them excused themselves temporarily and made their way out to the back lanai.

Dover trotted across the lawn and joined them as if invited to the meeting, wagging his tail and looking about from face to face. Maggie rubbed his neck, fluffing his fur, which always calmed him. He finally settled at Maggie's feet, cuddling up against them.

"Here's my take on what's going on. Our window of opportunity closes the longer we sit here, letting these people tie up our time with their gabfest.

I can't live with sitting here and not acting on our own. We have extensive resources with a limited amount of time. Lamar, can we take the drones, get Sykes on the phone and let's find her. We know where her phone is. Someone has to have seen her."

"I want to go too," Maggie jumped in. "Lamar, call Sykes. We may need more drones. I read that to use them for missing persons, we may need more of the heat-sensing ones."

"Let's go. Right now."

"Hold it, Benny," Lamar ordered. "Hanes said the cops are all over it. They're at the scene, and Dorrie is nowhere to be found."

"What are you doing getting all buddy, buddy with Hanes? What were you two talking about?"

"Can't tell you."

"You will," Maggie retorted. "Or you will have to answer to Kerrington. I'm serious, Lamar. We're talking about Dorrie. And she's family! I'm sick of your secrets."

"Hanes said he wonders if Willow had Dorrie taken. He feels the possibility of Willow being involved can't be overlooked."

"Jack took her. Willow would not help him do anything."

"And she is definitely not involved with Jack."

"You don't know that, Benny. That's what all betrayed husbands say."

"May the Lord have mercy on your soul, Lamar," Benny replied, his brown eyes watering with sadness. "You are rotten to the core if you believe Willow would turn her back on me. You know her. She is the kindest, sweetest soul on the planet."

"I didn't say I agreed with Hanes. He's being a cop, trying to unravel this crazy mystery."

"We're going to look for Dorrie. Nothing is stopping us," Maggie exclaimed. "Tell the cook to pack some goodies while we grab an overnight bag. Then call Sykes and see if he can meet us there. It'll be faster if he can meet us. And don't you dare tell Hanes."

Benny stood up and clapped his hands together to move things along. "Let's go."

Maggie and Benny jumped into Kerrington's Land Rover, and Lamar followed them in a Hummer. It was almost sundown when they arrived at Black Mountain, where the police found Dorrie's phone. She was nowhere to be found. Sykes joined them at a local diner. They re-grouped before a large map and plotted their move for the next day. Lamar called and booked them all a night at a local Airbnb, and they agreed to meet back at the diner in the morning.

Benny left the table and walked to the diner parking lot to the bushes where Dorrie's phone was dropped. Maggie followed him.

"Why here? What's around here that's so special?"

They stood speechless, taking it all in—the beauty of the Blue Ridge mountains draping the distant landscape with a bright orange sun barely peeking over the ridge. Benny kept shaking his head. "I don't understand. Where was he taking her?"

Despite the mild winter, a harsh chill built in the air. Maggie shivered, ready to go to bed and prepare for tomorrow's journey. "Let's pack it in, Benny. We have to rise early."

THE AIRBNB WAS TWO STORIES and was comfortable enough to fit each in a private suite, all with working fireplaces. Maggie cuddled in a sizeable cushy chair and curled her legs underneath. Her thoughts returned to Dorrie and her happy face as she rummaged through her new things in the shopping bag. Maggie realized, at that moment, how she'd come to love Dorrie as if she were her own child. Even the slightest thought of losing Dorrie was dreadful and filled her with a deep pain of emptiness.

Maggie missed Willow terribly and wanted her to come home. But at the same time, she was jealous. *What if she suddenly appeared? Am I living in a wonderland of happiness that Willow could rip away? After all, she could return home and move her family back to her house. Where would that leave me? Stop it! You're being selfish. Jack is right. She's not your child. You're a strong girl. Deal with it and do the right thing.*

IN THE MORNING, BRIGHT AND EARLY, they quickly ate the food the chef had packed before heading out for the large parking lot behind the diner. It was near the forest, and Sykes and Lamar picked it as the best place to start. They all climbed onto the back of his massive black Lifted Chevy 4500 Duramax diesel truck which had ample space to fit them all.

An hour later, they came up empty without a single spotting of a human being. So, they methodically moved down the road to the next spot they'd picked out on the map.

"A little girl in a neon green jacket should stick out, I'd think," Lamar said. "We haven't missed her."

When they pulled into the new spot, Sykes gave instructions. "This area will be a little more difficult to search. Since I'm used to doing this, I'll take fifty percent of the territory behind us. Maggie, you take the left quarter, and Benny, you take the right. Go as far as the drone allows." Sykes instructed.

And so, the next stretch of the search for Dorrie started. Lamar drove. And the day began to repeat itself, with each new spot coming up empty-handed. Maggie felt Benny's growing frustration as she began to feel like they were on a safari with no animals around to see. So far, they had found only one person, a teenage boy out hunting.

THE SUN BEGAN ITS DECENT around 4 pm, casting long shadows through the dense woods. Sykes's sharp eyes caught a figure sprinting through trees. Maggie's heart sank as she took in the image on the screen, her voice trapped in her throat. In that chilling moment, she identified the image. "It's Jack!" Maggie declared; her voice raspy. "He's wearing the same weathered jacket and blood-red hat he wore when he took Dorrie."

Adrenaline charged through their veins as they leapt into the truck and took off, careening deeper into the foreboding wilderness, the rugged terrain beneath them challenging their every move. All were strapped tightly to the bed of his truck and wrestled with their drones, struggling to keep pace with the elusive Jack. Maggie's intuition whispered caution. She knew how dangerous Jack could be.

"Stop the truck," Sykes called out. In an abrupt and speedy motion, Sykes unlocked his strap, abandoned the truck, tore open the passenger door, and plunged his hand into the glove compartment, retrieving his trusted gun. "We're covered, just in case he's armed," Sykes declared, his voice filled with a hardened resolve. They were ready to face the monster in the shadows.

With bated breath, they observed Jack, their eyes scanning the surroundings, searching for any sign of Dorrie, when, in an instant, Jack vanished deep into the sinister depths of the forest. The silence exploded under the weight of Dorrie's frightening screams, piercing the air with a desperate cry. "Stop. Stop. Please stop, Daddy. Please."

Jack desperately dragged Dorrie by her hair, forcing her through the darkening woods. Maggie and Benny's collective fear transformed into a palpable urgency. They jumped from the truck, their feet pounding the unforgiving ground as they raced to rescue her. Maggie veered to the right; her steps cautiously concealing herself from Jack. Benny and Sykes froze in their tracks, paralyzed by Jack's sinister gaze—haunting, like a gateway to hell. Jack held his gun, aimed directly at Benny's chest.

Maggie's martial arts training took over as she moved at lightning speed, her legs scaling the tree beside Jack in a whirlwind of fury, landing on his shoulders. She clamped them around around Jack's neck as she grabbed his chin in a tightening grip.

Lamar seized the gun from Jack and Benny swiftly freed Dorrie from the clutches of the maniac. Sykes, with trembling fingers, dialed 911, desperately summoning help.

"Let go of me," Jack spat, his voice raging with venom, his mind consumed with delusions that defied reason. "You have no right to stop me."

"You murdered my baby boy!" Maggie screamed, her voice screeching like that of a mad woman, piercing and cutting through the chaos. Her fingernails digging deep slices up his face. "You <u>will</u> pay for that. You will not get away."

Sirens wailed in the distance, growing louder, their harsh symphony announcing the arrival of help. Jack deliberately collapsed his body to the ground, his weight toppling over Maggie, who unleashed a torrent of kicks. Maggie desperately clutched at the fringes of his pants, halting his frantic flight. Jack delivered a solid whack to Benny's head that split his eyebrow open. Then he grabbed a wad of dirt and threw it in Maggie's eyes. She lost her grip.

Jack bolted, ran into the thick forest, and seemingly disappeared into thin air as local police officers emerged from the woods from behind, their guns drawn. They formed a united front with Maggie as they traced Jack's movement through the woods—until the woods disappeared into nothing.

They peered over the precipice that Jack failed to see coming in his path. Down below, on the paved road, Jack lay sprawled in a huge pool of flowing blood, motionless, the remnants of his life extinguished.

Maggie stopped Dorrie from approaching, grabbing her tightly in her arms, shielding her from the grotesque scene. “Don't look. Do as I ask,” she whispered into Dorrie's ear, her words a lifeline of reassurance for the terrified child.

Hand in hand, they sprinted towards Benny, who stood at the edge of the woods with Sykes. The first aid kit lay open as Sykes applied large **Steri-Strips** to Benny’s brow. A bloody tee shirt on the ground revealed Benny had bled a lot from his wound.

Benny pulled away from Sykes as Maggie yelled, “We have to find Willow.”

They all ran to the truck as the police secured the scene. Benny hugged Dorrie hard, and they jumped into the back of the pickup truck.

“Mommy's in a cabin where my grandma used to live,” Dorrie said. “And she’s hurt bad. Real bad. It can’t be more than a couple of miles from here. Maybe three.”

Maggie, Benny, and Dorrie got into the truck with Sykes and rode off to continue their search before the police got a chance to stop them for questioning. Lamar stayed behind.

"I'll take care of them. We'll meet up with them later. Go. Go."

They stopped two miles down the road because Dorrie declared it looked familiar. Sykes and Benny raised the drones in the air once more and began their final hunt for the day as the sun would be setting soon.

After about twenty minutes, Benny yelled. “I found the car. The green one. And a red Mustang. Not much further ahead.”

All of them got back into the truck and pushed forward. Sykes guided the way, having taken over Benny’s drone.

IT WAS ALL WILLOW COULD DO to crawl out of the house; she could only move a bit at a time. Her heart was racing, and she felt weak. As a nurse, Willow knew she desperately needed blood. Gratefully, in his haste to run after Dorrie, Jack had left the door open. The pain in her abdomen was now severe, and her belly felt swollen and hard. She was bleeding inside and running out of time.

Jack had finally delivered what might be her fatal injury. Willow had no idea which direction to go and opted to get as close to the road as possible so someone driving by might spot her. Her breathing became rapid from the exertion, and her increasing dizziness made it hard to focus. It would be dark soon, and animals would quickly come out of hiding. Bears specifically. She'd seen them from her window.

Willow could no longer hold her head up when she heard a truck pull up on the gravel road near her. "Please don't let it be, Jack. Please," she whispered, barely able to speak. She heard footsteps running her way. More than one. She heard her name.

"Willow. Willow!"

"Mommy. Mommy."

"I love you, Dorrie—Benny, you too—please take care of Dorrie," Willow whispered before her ability to speak faded away.

Benny kissed her cheek. She felt his warm tears dropping down onto her face.

Dorrie held her hand, kissing it over and over. Both cried out how much they loved her and to be strong. Willow could no longer open her eyes but was grateful to hear the sound of the helicopter because she knew life was leaving her body. She felt Maggie's and Benny's medical hands examining her body.

"Her pulse is thready," Benny called out. "Hypovolemic shock."

"Her abdomen is grossly distended. Hard," Maggie said in her calm voice, assessing the damage. "Several fractured ribs. She needs a chest tube." Many other voices joined in—talking medical terminology as they placed Willow on a stretcher. Willow's body felt numb and cold. She no longer experienced pain.

"Mommy. Mommy. It's Dorrie. I'm here." Dorrie's voice was the last thing Willow heard before she drifted unconscious.

THE HELICOPTER TEAM dropped Willow off in the E.R. for a pit stop to receive care from the trauma team, where they started a blood transfusion and whisked her immediately to the O.R.

Hours later, Maggie sat with Dorrie and watched Benny as he paced the waiting room floor.

Her heart broke for him. And Dorrie.

Lamar was across the room talking on the phone, holding his hand to his forehead as if he had a headache. Some nurses from the E.R. were huddled in a corner, waiting to provide support whenever it was needed, either by retrieving tissues, water, and coffee or giving out hugs. Covid rules went by the wayside.

"Why is it taking so long, Maggie?" Dorrie asked.

Maggie looked at Dorrie's face, filled with worry, eyes puffy from crying so much. Maggie was wondering the same thing but wasn't about to scare Dorrie with her secret, fearful thoughts. "Sometimes, surgery can take a long time. This is normal." Maggie pulled Dorrie into her arms. "Try not to worry."

"I can't stop," Dorrie cried.

"I know, honey. I know," Maggie whispered back, not knowing what to do but feeling like she had to do something. Anything to make things better for Dorrie. She looked over to the Au Pair and thought about Dorrie and how much emotional trauma she had experienced today. "Maybe we should send you home, Dorrie, let you get something to eat and rest. It may be a long night. Would you like that?"

"I can't leave, Maggie. I think Mommy is going to die." Maggie looked down into Dorrie's eyes. They were filled with resignation. "What will happen to me? If—you know—where will I go?"

"We're family. Remember? You'll always be with us. But let's not worry about that. Ever.

Let's pray Mommy lives."

"I don't feel her anymore, Maggie," Dorrie said as tears filled her eyes. "I don't. When she was missing, I could still feel her. But I can't anymore."

Maggie was at a loss for words. Gratefully, Sister Marguerite entered and spoke with everyone before guiding them in prayer. Maggie watched Benny's shoulders shake. Exhaustion wracked her body. The long wait and unending hours of searching for Willow had taken a toll on all of them. And now, so much hope was literally hanging by a thread, if at all, and Maggie feared the worst might happen.

Maggie took Dorrie's hand when the priest entered through the side door. Soon after, the surgeon entered with the chief nurse. Maggie had often entered a waiting room beside the physician and therefore, she knew what was coming as she could read their faces. The wording wouldn't be the same, but the outcome would be.

"I'm sorry," the surgeon said. "We did everything we could. Willow did not survive the surgery. Her injuries were too significant, and her delay in getting to the hospital was too long. She died."

Benny openly sobbed as Dorrie looked up at Maggie with eyes questioning whether it was real. Then she leaned her head against Maggie and wrapped her arms around her. Maggie held her tightly. Dorrie had cried all night, and there didn't seem to be any tears left.

"Take me home, Maggie. Please take me home." Maggie led Dorrie out the door, and Benny followed.

Sister Marguerite promised to take care of the details and said she would call if she needed any information.

Chapter 46

A Somber Day

Lamar brought in Kerrington's social organizers to help plan the funeral. A grief counselor from the hospital for children came to the house to help Dorrie deal with the loss of her mother. The chef prepared an ornate layout of food for those coming to pay their respects to Benny, Maggie, and Dorrie.

AT THE FUNERAL HOME, Willow looked exquisite in her casket, dressed in a crisp white, long- sleeved uniform that held her golden nursing pin. Maggie and Benny stood with Dorrie as they all shed tears together as a family. Maggie ached to have Kerrington present, and the event made her worry more about his absence.

Dorrie seemed to have grown up overnight, greeting Willow's friends with a mature handshake, perfect posture, and grace.

THE FUNERAL WAS DRAPED in somber hues that matched the weightiness of the sorrow that hung in the air. The hospital chapel, adorned with white flowers and a hushed ambiance, became a poignant backdrop for the final goodbye to Willow. Topping the white casket was Willow's nursing cap bathed in a stream of light that appeared ethereal and holy. The church resonated with Willow's spirit—as it was the place where she had knelt and prayed for her patients many times during her noble journey as a nurse.

Sister Marguerite, a figure of wisdom and compassion, stood before the gathering, her voice strong and compelling yet filled with bare emotion at times, which was rare for her to ever display publicly.

Sister Marguerite painted a vivid portrait of Willow's unwavering dedication to her profession. Willow's eulogy unfolded like a tapestry of memories that recounted the countless lives Willow had touched with her prayers, healing hands, comforting words, and her unwavering presence. Everyone listened, with hearts swelling with both grief and appreciation for the enormous impact Willow had made in the realm of nursing.

Maggie stepped forward, her hands trembling from fear she might not do as great a job of honoring Willow as Sister Marguerite had. Her voice did not betray her as it came forth with a mixture of mourning and a deep-seated love for her dearest friend. As Maggie spoke, she felt the mourners holding onto her every spoken word—captivated by the tender images she painted with her memories of Willow. With vivid detail, Maggie's voice wove a masterpiece of emotions, conjuring images from a night long ago.

"One cold, wintry night, we found ourselves standing atop the hospital's parking garage," Maggie began. "Willow was excited and captivated by the formidable sight of our massive, illuminated hospital which she had never seen from above. Together, we marveled at the sight of one of our helicopters ascending from the rooftop. It hovered, suspended momentarily in the air before it flew into the distance on a life-saving mission. As our eyes traced its vanishing trail, Willow surprised me with a sudden unwavering declaration—a decision that would shape her destiny. With a radiant gleam in her eyes, she shared her resolute news: she was going to become a nurse.

At that very moment, Willow's eyes sparked with an infectious passion. The flame of the **Nightingale Lamp**, that everlasting emblem of nursing, had been kindled within her. It shimmered brightly, embodying the essence of compassion, resilience, and selfless dedication—the sacred qualities inherent to the noble profession she was about to embrace. Willow possessed a rare and true gift for healing, a genuine calling that I was privileged to witness as it bloomed before me.

Willow's decision stirred gratitude within me, for I knew that the world would be forever touched by her presence and her unwavering desire to forever serve the ill and injured. And I felt honored to bear witness to the birth of her true calling."

Maggie's voice softened, caving into the weight of grief. She spoke of the immense void that would be left in the halls of the hospital.

"The profession that Willow wholeheartedly embraced will mourn the loss of an outstanding nurse. Her flame may have been extinguished too early, but its enduring legacy will forever burn within the hearts of those she touched. And I was one of those hearts."

As the mourners quietly filed out, their steps laden with grief, they joined a yard filled with nurses dressed both in formal white and a mixture of scrubs. All held a single flaming candle to show their commitment to the spirit of Willow's dedication to nursing.

Willow's funeral birthed a profound healing amongst a multitude of nurses whose flames had been snuffed and almost extinguished by the relentless grip of the Covid pandemic. Covid had brought too much suffering and death. Willow's memory became a guiding light, helping healthcare workers re-discover their dedication and purpose.

A WEEK LATER, Maggie returned home from her martial arts class amazed at how the winter was like a roller coaster. Two days ago, it was thirty degrees. Today it was in the seventies. And it felt good.

Maggie felt like she needed the infusion of vitamin D that came with sunshine. It would help with her depression and improve her mood, which she needed. So, she lay in the sun for two hours. Later, she found Benny in the solarium and brought him a glass of iced tea.

He'd been solemn since Willow's death—and they'd had heavy talks. The fact that Willow had been missing for such a length of time was helpful to both Benny and Dorrie because both of them had dealt with her absence on many levels, getting used to life without her. But the reality was still there, left to be dealt with.

Benny didn't say anything, and neither did Maggie. They were wrapped in their thoughts, comforted by the falling water and the soft nature music in the background. They lay that way for over an hour until it was time for Dorrie to come home. They put on happy faces and made sure to be at the door to greet her.

Maggie chose activities to keep the household busy so they could move on. They went out to dinner instead of staying home. Maggie put on delightful movies at home. Fun movies. No violence. Soon Dorrie laughed, and when she laughed, Benny laughed.

After the funeral, Maggie insisted they return to their regular routines. And soon, the household got back to normal.

Chapter 47

The Hidden Lab

Days later, Maggie waited until Lamar went out to drink with Hanes to make her move. She slipped out of the house and went to the far back part of the estate, where she sat down on a stone bench and ensured the hedges hid her well. The drones were no longer present. They always disappeared when Lamar went out or when Sykes wasn't on the property. Everyone felt a lot freer to roam about since Lamar had declared the property safe.

The sky was golden with colorful layers of white clouds with purple light filtering through. Her time was limited before the sun went down and it became dark. With a bolt, Maggie lowered herself into a crouching stoop and raced to the back of the building. There she ran her hands over the cool stone wall that felt ancient—with subtle imperfections, tiny breaks, chips, and irregularities that developed over time. The roughness evoked feelings in Maggie of a long ago past, a bygone era of a sacred time in history. She felt peculiar waves of oddness, as if she might be traveling in time. She could almost imagine the hands that carved the magnificent stone. As her fingers carefully explored the wall for a doorway, all she found were splits between the stones—evidence the building hadn't been cared for as carefully as the mansion. She finally discovered cracks that actually formed a door, but there was no key access.

"What are you doing?" Maggie jumped at Benny's voice, startled. She braced her back against the chilly wall.

"Nothing. Just—looking at the stone." Maggie was taken aback by Benny's surprise visit but tried to feign innocence. "Um. What are **you** doing?"

"Watching you," Benny replied. "I saw you sneaking out back here and hiding for a minute. You can see everything from my room. It's so high up, you know. So, are you going to tell me? Or are you going to lie to me?" Benny said, smiling, his grin holding a look of challenge.

"I can't."

"What do you mean I can't," Benny repeated.

"I'm really not doing anything!"

Silence hung between them.

"After all we've been through. No secrets. No holds barred type of friendship… and you're lying to me?"

"Okay. It's nothing. Really. It's a strange building I found the other day. And I was curious. I'd never seen it before. It's so old. And get this—it doesn't have a door. What kind of building doesn't have a door?"

"A building that doesn't want anyone entering."

"I knew it!" Maggie whispered. "What's he hiding?"

"Who?"

"Kerrington. It's his property."

Benny's eyes reflected the color of sundown as he looked at her—staring. "We're really gonna do this?"

"I have to."

Benny ran his hands over the stone. "Press them all. One might move."

"That's what I was doing," Maggie retorted, as her hand suddenly gave in to her pressing.

Maggie jumped in surprise at the slow grinding sound of incredibly old stone-on-stone grating against each other. The door slowly opened. Maggie stood still in amazement. "That's weird, Benny. I was expected an old musty odor, but the scent is quite different."

"It smells oddly… like a hospital. That is weird," Benny said as he sniffed the air.

Maggie went first, descending the giant stone steps that went down at least one story or more.

Benny came right behind her, hopping down the stairs as if it were an ordinary place.

Bright lights automatically came on as soon as their bodies entered the space. They looked like hospital operating theatre lights. The tall hidden chamber was huge and at least equivalent to the size of an oversized basketball court.

"Oh, my Heavens to Jesus, "Benny exclaimed softly, his eyes going everywhere around the room, taking it all in. Maggie's jaw dropped as she, too, looked around.

The entire area was stark white, modern, and sleek in design with clean lines and held a minimalistic aesthetic look. Polished stainless-steel tables were everywhere and included expansive cabinets with glass doors filled with laboratory supplies. Vast refrigerators, ovens and warmers lined one side of the wall. The tabletops were covered with microscopes, pipettes, test tubes, Petri dishes, centrifuges, and other science lab equipment familiar to Benny and Maggie, including specialized air vents and a ventilation system that was humming overtime due to the fact they had left the door wide open.

Maggie and Benny looked in awe as they walked through, each buried in their own deep thoughts of amazement. Maggie gently ran her fingers over several high-resolution microscopes and DNA sequencers. The centrifuges were advanced, nothing like she'd ever seen.

"Holy Toledo," Benny exclaimed, pecking the keypad on his phone. "It's a **CRISPR-Cas9**. According to Google it's a gene editing tool. Scientists use it to make highly specific changes to DNA sequence of an organism. Maggie, we're talking about big stuff here."

"That's a sophisticated piece of equipment," Maggie mumbled as she made her way deeper into the lab. The rest of the equipment was staggering, beyond Maggie's understanding.

Against the far wall were safety goggles, lab coats, gloves, and full decontamination suits. Far ahead of them was a heavily sealed room with thick glass walls. Maggie walked over to it and turned to face Benny. She felt as stunned as her face surely was. "It's a bio-hazardous lab."

"It gets worse," Maggie declared suddenly turning left and pointing to the far corner that was not visible from the entrance. "It's an elevator. There's more."

The two of them stood fixated in place, staring at the elevator. "Do we?" Benny asked, his voice low, with a hint of fear.

"I say yes," Maggie said pushing the button. "I want to see all three floors."

And so, they did. There were two more floors, which served as support areas, such as tissue culture rooms and a storage area for biological samples and reagents. The other floor held empty animal cages.

"And this is all out in the backyard, Maggie? It staggers my mind to think of how much money is invested in this place and yet it sits empty. It has to be millions and millions. We need to get out of here. Like now."

Benny said, pushing the elevator button adamantly, acting like pressing the button ten times would make it work faster.

Maggie took her time, looking around, taking in each item and its meaning. Finally, she made her way back to the elevator and up to the main floor, where Benny ran up the stairs two at a time, rushing out the entrance. Maggie followed and pushed the door closed behind her and stood leaning against it, staring at Benny who was in an equally deep state of shock. The weight of what they'd found brought acid to her throat and a feeling of panic and dread.

Benny took off for the outdoor lanai, where he poured them both a stiff screwdriver, making them both half vodka, half orange juice.

It was the most prolonged time Maggie and Benny had ever gone without talking. Maggie took a final gulp from her drink and placed her glass on the table with a heavy thud. She leaned over and buried her hands in her palms. "I wish I could go back and undo what we did. What have I done? Oh, God. What have I done?" Maggie sobbed openly, knowing she could never return to not knowing what she now knew.

"I won't say anything. Ever. I swear my life to you, Maggie. I swear," Benny said.

Maggie didn't even answer him. All she could think about was her betrayal of Kerrington's confidence. He had never spoken of the lab or its existence, even. This moment could never be fixed, and she would have to deal with her sneaky deeds. She didn't want to know Kerrington's answers were to her questions. And yet, she knew she had to ask them.

Chapter 48

Unexpected Guests

When Lamar joined Maggie, Benny, and Dorrie at the morning breakfast table, Lamar brought a foul mood and a frigid chill that radiated into the air from every pore of his skin. Lamar sat and unfolded his napkin with a flip in the air that made a crackle. He was peeved far beyond anything Maggie had ever experienced. It was her first time seeing the former homicide cop part of him. Neither of them dared look him in the eye.

Maggie and Benny eyed each other from across the table, sending each other a clear signal to prepare. Lamar knew. The question was how much?

When Dorrie finished eating, she grabbed her backpack and went out the door with the Au Pair, pecking Benny and Maggie on the cheek before leaving and saying. "Love you," to both.

After he finished eating, Lamar pushed his plate forward and spoke. "To say I am disappointed in both of you is an understatement. Maggie, I asked you to stay away from the building."

"**After** you lied to me about it, Lamar. That was equally disheartening—and I might add that it only piqued my curiosity more. So, with that being said, I'm…" Maggie stood up to go.

Lamar slammed his hands on the table so hard it rattled the dinnerware. "You are not going anywhere. You will sit down right now and listen. It's not a child's game."

Maggie slowly took her seat, feeling the flame rushing over her cheeks. She caught Benny fighting a grin and wanted to smack him.

"You think this is funny, young man? Huh?"

"No, sir. No. Not at all." It was Benny's turn to be embarrassed, and Maggie saw it written all over his face.

"What you came across last night is classified information. The lab is no childish boy's prank. All authorities and governing bodies since the 1900s have properly licensed it, and there is a five hundred-million-dollar contract with our government that's gone on for generations. Why do you think he hired me to live on the property? Not because I was a private detective. He knew I would get the job done. Did you ever stop and wonder why we have all the security officers here? Are you blind? Why do you think he was in Ukraine? Only him. A corporate billionaire. Get your head out of the clouds, Maggie. Both of you need to zip your lips—or you'll simply suffer the circumstances."

Their meeting was interrupted by the sound of three loud knocks on the large double-sized front doors. The door knocker echoed harshly through the entire entranceway and into the dining room. It even caught Lamar's attention, making him stop talking. Ronnie entered the room looking terrified. "There are gentlemen at the door, sir,"

"They don't have an appointment. Have them return in an hour, please, Ronnie,"

"I don't think they're a waiting type, sir," Ronnie replied, his voice anxious.

Lamar looked shocked, and Maggie felt alarmed. She stood and followed him as did Benny. Maggie thought her heart would stop when she spotted two silver-haired men dressed in official dark-colored suits. They held a no-nonsense look about their firm faces, and both had their hands firmly clasped. "We're from the FBI," one said as both held up official badges.

Maggie felt Benny's breath on the back of her neck as he gasped loudly and hid behind her. "Don't go anywhere, sir. Move where we can see you."

Benny stepped out from behind Maggie and stood beside her, the edges of his sleeve trembling against his arm.

"Is Kerrington Blanchard here?"

"No, sir."

"Do you know his whereabouts?"

"He's at the CDC in Atlanta. They have a committee meeting," Lamar replied as Maggie turned and dropped her jaw in astonishment. "Can I help you with something? I'm head of his security."

"An alarm went off last night. We're doing a follow-up. The persons entering the area were these two," they said, pointing at Maggie and Bennie. They're not authorized."

"This is his wife," Maggie Blanchard.

"And this is my co-worker, friend, Benny," Maggie quickly shot out. "He and his family live here. We didn't mean any harm. I'd never seen the building before and stumbled my way in there out of curiosity. It was nothing."

The lead man stared hard at Maggie. "It wasn't 'nothing,' Mrs. Blanchard. It's a classified area."

"We didn't touch anything, sir. Well, not much, that is. We pretty much just came, saw, and left," Maggie stuttered on her words.

"That's a problem."

"We'll write the report and do the appropriate follow-up. You are not ever to return or attempt to return to the area, nor will you discuss what you saw with anyone. It is classified. Do you understand what I'm telling you?"

"I do," Maggie piped up immediately. "Me, too," Benny repeated her words.

"As head of security, you'll have to do some paperwork. A lot of it, I'm afraid," The head man handed Lamar a large purple envelope marked boldly 'Confidential' on the cover. "Call us if you have any problems, sir," the man said, turning to leave.

"That's it?" Lamar asked, stunned.

"Yes, sir. Unless you have questions, we'll follow up if needed, but I believe Mr. Blanchard will keep his household in order. We understand he's been under unusual circumstances." The two men looked at Maggie and Benny directly, then smiled and exited.

All three let out a sigh of relief. As the door closed, Maggie turned on Lamar. "Kerrington is in Atlanta? And you never said a word?"

"I didn't know until this morning. Kerrington had just returned to the country, landing in Atlanta just in time for his scheduled meeting. He was in a hurry and wanted to talk to you, but you were in the shower. And don't worry. He knows."

"Oh. My. God," Maggie spat out the words giving emphasis on each one. "This is unbelievable. I would rather be at work than go through this."

MAGGIE AND BENNY were both off for the day and for the first time ever, avoided being around each other as they recovered from the stinging blow delivered earlier.

Several hours later, Maggie ran into Benny as she emerged from the sauna in the solarium and joined him on a lounge chair opposite a small table between them.

"I apologize, Benny, for dragging you into such a mess."

"You didn't drag me, Maggie. I was equally guilty. And, in a way, I egged you on. I wanted in just as much as you did."

"All the tragic stuff since the robbery—it's taken a toll on me and changed me, not in a good way," Maggie said, speaking in a faint voice, worried Lamar might be spying on them. "Our digging and searching for the truth—after a while, I got to feel like it was our right to go anywhere we wanted and open any door. And I know we didn't have a choice back then. But that was then, and now it's a different situation. Because it was Kerrington's private space."

"I don't know what to say, Maggie. When I think about what Kerrington will think of me, it tears my heart out."

"What about me? Kerrington will be devastated by my dastardly behavior. He loves me and trusts me. How could I do such a thing?"

"Maggie. You had no idea what you were doing. It's not like you said, 'Oh, Kerrington is hiding something from me—let me beat him at his game.' You somewhat had a right to be curious. Seriously—I'd be curious if I came across that building on my property, especially when a hidden door opens. Hell, it was like calling us."

Maggie tilted her head and looked sideways at him. "And that's what I'm supposed to tell him—that it was calling me. He's my husband, Benny. What was I thinking? Okay. I admit I was angry with him for leaving me at a time when I needed him more than anything. I was afraid. Terrified. God, I'm so ashamed." Maggie got up and left.

"Where are you going?"

"To work. I have to get out of here."

"Wait. I'm coming."

Chapter 49

Kerrington

When Maggie and Benny got home, they went through the usual doffing of their medical gear, which had become Maggie's workday ritual since she started working in the E.R. with all the germs and blood. When Benny moved in—the maid made a space for him. They stopped in the giant washroom and stepped into a basin filled with an inch of sanitized water, where they slipped out of their shoes to allow them to soak overnight. After putting on slippers, they stepped into separate changing rooms, removed their scrubs, and put on new ones. Then they tossed the soiled scrubs in the washer and turned it on. Looking like two robots in motion, they sanitized their hands and quietly left the room. Silence prevailed as neither of them knew what to say.

Maggie went to her home office and turned on her computer. She entered Amazon and typed in textbooks and entered the word genetics. And there it was **CRISPR-Cas**. She placed the order and paused. Next, she changed the delivery address to her old house. After searching more, Maggie ordered the **Biotech Primer for Non-Scientists** textbook plus four more textbooks on Biotechnology. The order would be sent in two days and delivered to the privacy of her little blue house on Park Road. She had a lot of studying to do in order to understand what was going on in the backyard lab. Maggie recognized that what she would be studying might be over her head, but it had always been her experience that if you studied a subject long enough and intensely, it would eventually breakthrough and make sense. Besides, she needed a new experience to keep her mind off things.

MAGGIE ENTERED HER BEDROOM and lay on the bed, turning to her right side and tucking her arm under her pillow. It was her favorite position to get ready for sleep. She was exhausted from the day and worried about Kerrington and what he might think of her dishonesty. When the bed moved, Maggie expected Dover to jump on her and deliver wet licks to her face. But he didn't. The smell of Kerrington caught her heart. Tears gathered. She closed her eyes and waited for his reaction, praying he wouldn't be angry with her.

Kerrington's gentle hand slipped over her face and turned her to face him. He wiped her tears and placed his lips on hers before moving on top of her. "I missed you."

"I missed you too."

"So, I heard," he said, smiling. "You got yourself into some trouble."

"I did." Maggie gazed into his brilliant, soft blue eyes and asked, her voice but just a quivering whisper. "Please forgive me."

"What's there to forgive? You were just being Maggie."

Kerrington got out of bed, took Maggie by the hand, and led her to their private bathing chamber, where the maid had prepared a bubble bath in the giant garden tub. Maggie giggled and kissed him—they both quickly stripped off their clothes and got into the tub.

They let out all their built-up passion as they frolicked in the bath, stroking each other's skin. It was a thrilling, happy night as they delighted in each other in the soothing water. Later, they returned to bed and made mad passionate love before drifting off to sleep. It was Maggie's first night of sound sleep since he'd been gone. She was no longer afraid or worried about anything.

OVER BREAKFAST THE FOLLOWING DAY, Maggie hesitated to ruin Kerrington's homecoming with all the awful news but realized he needed to know as soon as possible so he could take what action he needed. She started with the tragic news about Willow's death and that Dorrie was living with them and getting counseling. Then, she updated him about the hospital robbery and shooting, including her escapades with Benny regarding Titus, Rosie's Bar, Franklin, the gun, the narcotics, the search warrant, Dorrie, Jack, the drones, and Willow.

"My God. I wish I had been here. Are you okay?"

"I am. I'm cleared of any charges, and so is Benny. But there's more—much more important news. You might want to sit down." Maggie urged.

Maggie told Kerrington about Annella, the poisoning, how they caught Chase in the act, and how he fled from the country. "She's okay now. And she's recovering nicely."

Kerrington looked like he was fit to be tied. She'd never seen such anger on his face. "He tried to kill her?" Kerrington asked, his face holding a look of disbelief.

Maggie shook her head affirmatively.

"We'll find him. And when we do—Chase will never get out of jail."

"There's more," Maggie added. She almost wanted to laugh at the ridiculousness of it all and also with relief that it was finally over. "Chase put half the house up for sale. And threatened us with the news that he had an undisclosed buyer. He demanded five million dollars in cash. I pretty much emptied my account and purchased it." Maggie filled him in on Annella's hospitalization and how they finally caught Chase.

Kerrington sat staring ahead. Maggie could tell his mind was whirling with thoughts of Annella. "I'm going to the hospital. Do you want to come?"

"Of course, I do."

THE VISIT TO THE HOSPITAL was brief because Kerrington said he had a lot to catch up on. Tony stepped out of Annella's ICU suite—as did Maggie—to allow Kerrington privacy with his sister. Maggie watched them. The two were so beautiful together, so alike one might think they were twins. Eventually, Kerrington took Annella's hand and kissed it. She could tell he was crying with relief. And so was Annella. They warmed her heart.

They didn't talk long because the physical therapist came to give Annella her therapy for the day. But when Kerrington left the room, he was smiling with his eyes. A big smile. All was well.

THEY MADE A PIT STOP BY Glenn's room so Kerrington could say hello and wish him well. Glenn was in an upbeat mood because he was learning to speak with the assistance of a speech therapist.

KERRINGTON WORKED from his home office and was busy on the phone all morning. His mood was foul when he emerged to join her for lunch on the balcony. Since Maggie had seldom seen the temperamental side of Kerrington, she didn't know how to start a conversation with him. She didn't have to worry about that for long.

"I spoke with the bank, and they transferred money from my account to yours to repay you for the house."

"You didn't have to do that," Maggie said, her brow wrinkling with concern. "I don't spend money, so I don't need it. My salary covers all my needs."

"Maggie." Kerrington's voice was agitated. "You will take it. Annella and I will settle this between us. I want her to get her inheritance back."

"Okay," Maggie said, feeling a bit out of place—and unsure of herself.

"I'm sorry, Maggie, for snapping. It's not you. Chase emptied Annella's bank account, put it all in a joint account, and then transferred it to an overseas account. That's why he wanted her in a coma and not dead. Chase probably would have eventually killed her, but not until he got all her assets. He was actively trying to access her trust fund—but failed and stopped because he got caught poisoning her."

"Now, I understand it all."

"There may be more that I just simply haven't uncovered yet—but I have people working on it," Kerrington added. "Plus, Lamar found some international private investigators to search for Chase's whereabouts. Supposedly they're top-notch at what they do. Maybe we'll recover her money before she comes home. So, tell me what going on with you at the hospital."

"I finished my master's degree. And I took my Nurse Practitioner boards. And I got offered a job in surgery."

"Congratulations," he said, kissing her on the cheek. "How about let's celebrate with a special dinner tonight?"

Maggie agreed, and then he returned to work.

KERRINGTON WAS INVOLVED in intense back-to-back meetings starting early in the morning and ending at six pm. They left the house by private car at six p.m. and headed off for their romantic dinner at the top of Kerrington's fancy hotel uptown. Maggie picked out the prettiest, sexiest black dress from her elaborate wardrobe—that had significantly grown since she'd married Kerrington. There was always somewhere fancy to go for his business obligations. Maggie's stomach was nervous and filled with jitters. She figured Kerrington would bring up the lab at some point—and didn't want to talk about it. Yet, she was curious to hear his explanation of why the lab was on their property.

They dined in a large private dining area near the back part of the restaurant, where their conversation couldn't be overheard. The rooms were far apart as an aftermath of Covid pandemic rules. Thankfully, the rules seemed to be relaxing all over the country. Neither of them wore a mask tonight.

The rose and lily bouquets provided a romantic ambiance that went well with the dim lighting of amber hues—providing a cozy and intimate dining area. The gentle, soft piano melodies in the background brought instant relaxation. Maggie felt it was a wonderfully romantic place to dine.

Kerrington and Maggie ordered the house favorite, consisting of a ten-course meal with foie gras, caviar, lobster, and wagyu beef with a specially chosen wine. She'd pretty much starved herself all day, hoping she'd be able to finish the meal. Maggie also made a point to have foie gras eliminated from her order due to the mistreatment of animals. She'd recently read that the duck or goose liver comes from the animals being fed by gavage method, in other words, they are force fed which turned Maggie off. However, it was Kerrington's favorite part of the meal, and she especially wanted to please him tonight, so she simply explained the foie gras was too filling and she wanted to leave room for desert.

As was his habit, Kerrington made small talk until his meal was complete. Maggie suspected his formal eating habits came from his long-standing heritage of wealth. Annella was the same way. Kerrington situated his silverware in a proper position on his plate to indicate he was through eating. Unable to eat anymore, Maggie followed suit. And soon, they were alone. As she suspected, he started right in on the lab. They were, after all, in a private place without maids or other people listening.

"So, knowing you, Maggie, you're curious about the building."

"The lab," she corrected, smiling devilishly. "I can't wait to hear what you have to say."

Kerrington smiled and took a sip of wine. "Actually, I don't have much to say, Maggie. I have an ongoing contract with our government, and my company is working on a project nearing completion. The end stage of the process ends in our private lab, and I use incredibly talented scientists to complete the process. I prefer to have a hands-on approach at every level of development. That's what I was doing in Ukraine. I brought the specimens here. First, to protect them, and secondly, to get them ready for clinical testing. The products were in Ukraine because I closed the lab on our property when you got pregnant."

Maggie took a deep sigh at the memory of her baby. "Specimens? There's more than one? Did you close it because it was dangerous?" Maggie whispered. "Am I in danger here? Or is Benny or Dorrie? Or you, even?"

"Heavens, no."

"The building is like Fort Knox. I laughed rather hard at the thought of you actually figuring out how to get inside. And yes, there is more than one. The second one, as it turns out, was completed just before my arrival—so **that** potential loss was recovered, thankfully."

"Are they bioweapons?"

"You and your imagination," Kerrington said, laughing softly. "Not necessarily. I can't tell you what they are because I'm not allowed to. That's in my contractual agreement."

"Ah—since you didn't directly say no—I'm left to assume they've got to have something to do with biological weapons. That's wonderful," Maggie exclaimed, sitting back in her chair.

"When we start up development, I'll take you inside the lab. We'll get you and Benny clearance to go inside. But I cannot tell you about the project."

"I think that would be a wonderful idea because I will literally die of curiosity until I know the whole deal. You will tell me in time. I'm sure."

"Maggie," Kerrington said, his voice patient but firm. "There are some parts of my life I must keep to myself. I know you are my wife, and I respect that, but business is business. Just like you can't tell me about your patients, I can't tell you anything that's classified and confidential in my business world. That's the best way to explain it."

"But—Lamar…"

Kerrington cut her off. "There are no buts. Lamar doesn't know anything more than you do. I've told you that you aren't in danger, and you have to trust me and accept that fact."

"The FBI came to our door."

"Good. The FBI should. They're doing their job. The lab is connected to the CDC by special wiring. There's a sensor on the bottom step of the lab entrance that triggers both the lights and a facial recognition ID scan. The FBI is notified to do a follow-up any time anyone enters without a registered facial recognition ID."

Maggie took a deep breath and gave in for now. She recalled being in the same type of room at the hospital. A secret room that very few knew about—that was wired directly to the CDC. She was given access only because she was certified as a CBRNE disaster response expert by the Center for Domestic Preparedness and FEMA. She held many more disaster certifications, but that was the one that got her access to the unique code to enter the room. It contained all the drugs necessary to treat a Chemical, Biological, Radiological, Nuclear, or Explosive attack.

"Would you like dessert?"

"If you do," which was always her answer. Her mind remained glued to the lab.

They ate their desserts in silence. Kerrington smiled after finishing. "I've made a decision. I will empty the lab and shut it down. Obviously, it makes you uncomfortable, Maggie. You come first. Therefore, I will move the lab to other premises. It will take a little time because people and contracts are involved—but it's my property—and that should give me a say about what goes on."

Chapter 50

Recovery

The day was perfect for celebration. Annella and Glenn came home by private car. All the house staff and family stood on the stairs awaiting their arrival. Annella had wholly recovered all of her neurological functions and Glenn was speaking again. Once inside, Annella looked about the grand entrance with joy—and tears formed in her eyes as she entered the dining room beautifully set for an elaborate family dinner. "Home— finally. I don't know that I'll ever leave again."

"Sure, you will. With me," Glenn said, smiling.

"No, darling. You're coming with me. Will you?"

"I'll do anything you want, Annella. Anything."

Other guests arrived in a steady flow. Tony came with Bonnie. He was still working for Annella, taking care of thank you notes for the cards, gifts, and flowers from her fans. She had a lot of other pressing business issues that had gone by the wayside during her illness. Tony had retired forever from handling actors—having made a fortune for all his pain. He didn't have to work another day in his life but chose to stay with Annella because she was extraordinary, and Bonnie loved her. Maggie watched them both with loving eyes as Bonnie flashed her big diamond for all to see. Happiness glowed all over her face.

Maggie greeted Sunday and her husband next, and Hanes was right behind. Benny and Kerrington entered the room with Lamar. Dorrie was beside Benny, who was holding her hand.

Dorrie looked timid to be in such a large crowd, but she was with the right person—as Benny always blended right in—no matter the environment.

Annella, with her dramatic flair, had renamed the sit-down meal ***The Healing Dinner***.

After everyone arrived and walked about chatting, Maggie made her way to the balcony, where she felt drawn and compelled to look at the ivy-covered stone building. Her imagination went into overdrive as she tried to picture the size of the underground laboratory, trying to estimate how far the lab extended into the grassy area. She figured it went as far as the hidden helicopter landing pad obscured by groomed, luscious green shrubbery. It ended most likely under the far side of the fountain.

Benny watched Maggie from across the room—and sensing she was obsessing—decided to join her. "Let it go, Maggie," he warned.

"I can't. I don't know why, but I can't. There's a freakin' lab in our backyard."

"Not really, Maggie. You don't have a normal backyard. Yours is at least three football field lengths in size, probably more. Think back. It came with the house. It goes back generations. It's not your business."

Maggie turned to look at Benny. "Funny. That's what Kerrington says. He compared it to me being a nurse and having to keep secrets about my patients from him. And his business requires secrets be withheld from me. His wife. But there it is," Maggie said, holding up her hand, palm to the ceiling in the direction of the stone building. "I live here Benny."

"I do too, Maggie. And you don't see me going off my rocket about it. It is what it is. Let it go and stop ruminating about it."

Maggie's shoulders sagged as she let out a sigh of resolve—and the two of them rejoined the group. Her spirit lifted with the jovial conversations. She was so happy to see Annella and Glenn alive and recovering. They held hands and shared loving glances between them. Maggie was jealous. She wanted that kind of love back in her life. Her eyes went to Kerrington. She loved him passionately. He was good to her. And she resolved in that moment she would not ruin it over a building that meant nothing weeks earlier. Technically, all she could see of the building from the house was a big batch of ivy and heavy, beautiful trees. She would let it go.

LATER THAT NIGHT, Kerrington asked Maggie and Benny to meet with him privately in the back of the bar. The chef had made lovely delicate puffs of crab and shrimp and had their favorite cocktails waiting at a table surrounded by soft, leather booth-type seating. Maggie couldn't help but wonder what Kerrington was up to. He'd certainly not given her any warning.

Kerrington got straight to the point. "I love Dorrie. As I know, both of you do. She is hurting. What I'm asking is special for all of us that are involved in her life."

Maggie looked at Benny. He looked stunned—blindsided and hurt, even. *Did Benny think Kerrington would ask him to leave the mansion?* She hoped he wouldn't. But realistically, she didn't know what Kerrington was thinking anymore.

"If you recall, Maggie, I spoke with you about Dorrie before I left for Ukraine. If Willow's absence became a long-term situation, I would like for us to adopt Dorrie, officially making her our child."

Benny gasped. "I can't lose her too. I can't."

"It won't be like that, Benny. If you agree, you can live here forever with her and act as a co-father. If you get married and want to, you can bring your new wife to live here. You're like family, Benny. And the house—it's plenty big for you to even have your own children here."

Maggie smiled, loving the idea. She just hoped Benny did.

They all sipped their drinks and ate shrimp and crab treats. Finally, Benny spoke.

"I want to do right by Dorrie," Benny explained. "I want her to have a good life and go to a nice college someday where she can blossom into whatever her dream is. I can't give her that. Not yet. Not until I get my NP. And by law, she's not mine to even make this decision. I want what she wants. And if she sets her heart on it, let's give it to her. And, oh my, I would love to continue living here. I love it. I'd be crazy not to want to stay."

"Then, it's settled. We'll talk to Dorrie first thing in the morning and see what she wants."

"I know what she wants. She wants us all to live here as a family."

THE FOLLOWING DAY over breakfast, before Annella and Glenn came downstairs, Kerrington gently probed the adoption issue with Dorrie. Her first reaction was to look at Benny.

"You won't be mad at me, would you?" she asked, her brown eyes questioning.

"Of course not, baby. This is your decision. If you go with it, I'll continue to live here as well, and we'll continue on. However, if you want to go live with your aunt JoJo, you can do that too. She's opened her door to you."

"I don't want to go there," Dorrie said, wrinkling up her face like she was disgusted by the thought. "I want to be here. But I want you to adopt me too. Can all three of you be my adopted parents? Will the law let that happen? Can I?"

"I'm sure we can work that out. Benny?"

"Sure. I'd love it."

They all rejoiced when Dorrie jumped up and down, clapping her hands.

LATER THAT EVENING, while it was still light outside, Kerrington took Maggie and Benny on a lab tour. It was empty. All the equipment was gone.

"You did it!" Maggie exclaimed. "I'm so relieved."

"Me too," Kerrington said, taking her hand and holding it gently— showing in his touch— how much she meant to him.

"Thank you," Maggie said as she reached up and pecked him on the cheek.

Chapter 51

The Betrayal

Two months later, on a perfect spring day, guests gathered in the vast garden for the grand celebration. Finally, Maggie felt relaxed, rejuvenated, and at peace with the world. Annella had planned the entire event. And everything went exactly as planned.

Glenn's speech had returned to almost normal, and he was back in the hospital working at his desk, running the E.R. but wasn't seeing patients yet. His healing was considered a true miracle. Doctor Richardson advised him not to move too fast when returning to complete duties—thus, she insisted Glenn not treat patients for another six weeks.

Maggie couldn't help but smile, genuinely happy to see Glenn near full recovery after such a severe injury. It was indeed a miracle.

Annella and Glenn walked to the altar surrounded by hundreds of friends. Doctors. Nurses. Actors. Producers. Annella looked gorgeous and perfect—as if she's never been sick a day in her life dressed in her **Vera Wang Peacock Feather** wedding gown, chosen by a designer friend at a cost of one and a half million dollars.

Next to follow were Bonnie and Tony. Bonnie cried as she said her vows and looked like an angel in her wedding dress because, of course, she was an angel in her heart. Tony looked smashing in his tux, and it was clear how much he loved Bonnie by the way he was always looking at her.

Maggie and Kerrington, with Dorrie in between, walked the aisle to the sounds of a multitude of birds singing in the trees. Benny trailed immediately behind them. At the altar, they said vows of adoption—where Maggie, Kerrington, and Benny took Dorrie as their child.

The reception was held in the ballroom. Guests freely roamed downstairs as it was tradition to showcase the mansion during social events.

A five-piece orchestra played until sundown—and then a DJ turned the house lively with dancing and laughing and love.

Lamar pulled Kerrington and Maggie aside and updated them on the latest events. Chase had been captured and was landing in Charlotte—where he would be returned to Mecklenburg County jail. The Private Investigators had also tracked down Annella's money, and the banks were making the transfers, giving the required extensive documentation that Kerrington had approved.

When Annella and Glenn returned from their Honeymoon, they would move into Annella's suites on her floor, making the family complete.

IT WAS ALMOST MIDNIGHT. Maggie sat on the balcony, enjoying the warm night air and the gentle breeze. Benny joined her and brought Maggie a glass of red wine.

"In celebration," Benny said, tapping his glass against hers.

"Thanks. I don't know how I'll like the O.R.," Maggie replied, taking the glass. "But I accepted the job. Our former boss cleaned up my employee record, and I gave two weeks' notice. What about you?"

"I got an offer from the O.R. as well," Benny said, his voice bragging. "I'm planning on accepting in the morning. Got a nice bump in pay. And you'll be happy to know I put in my notice. Wouldn't you know it? Covid has all but faded—and the hospital officially lifts mandatory masking—and we're transferring to a place where we'll be back to wearing masks again. Go figure." Benny laughed at the irony of it. Maggie joined in.

Maggie took in the delicate beauty of the perfect night, her slender fingers cradling the crystal wine glass. It was as if the air itself was filled with a hint of mystery as the sliver of moon cast a soft glow upon the massive, perfectly landscaped estate grounds.

A shooting star carved a luminous path across the vast midnight-black sky as other stars tried to compete with its beauty—shimmering radiantly—each one seeming to possess a unique twinkle that whispered tales of distant galaxies. In that fleeting moment, a smile flickered over Maggie's face as her eyes widened in awe and wonder. It was as if the universe itself had conspired to captivate her with its enchantment.

As Maggie took another sip of her wine, a bittersweet melancholy washed over her. She missed Kerrington. This night, so perfect, would be so romantic if he were here to share it with her. It reminded her of her first date with him.

By sheer coincidence, Maggie just happened to be looking in the right place, or else she wouldn't have seen the fast flickering of a bright flashlight cascading over the ivy on the side of the lab building in the back. Her heart skipped a beat at the meaning.

"So, when is Kerrington coming back from New York?" Benny asked. "Tomorrow night," Maggie answered, "One of his business partners died and they have an emergency meeting tonight."

Maggie stared transfixed at where she'd seen the light movement. Kerrington said he'd halted all lab testing and moved the laboratory elsewhere. He'd even taken her and Benny to the lab and shown her evidence that the space was empty. Maggie saw another flicker.

"What the hell is that?" Benny asked. "Are those beams from a flashlight? I thought the lab was closed."

"Yep. That's what I was led to believe. You too. We saw it was empty. Nothing but bare walls and floors."

"That's a curious thing. Who would be there? How come security isn't all over that?" Benny asked.

"They got rid of the extra security when Kerrington closed the lab. Want to check it out?"

"I do."

They tiptoed down the stairs and made their way around the shrubbery to the lab. Maggie peeked around the corner into the dark area. Finding it empty, she stepped up to the door lock stone and pushed it.

Benny followed her down the stairs. Their movement along the stairs would typically trigger the lights to come on. But the bright lights were already on. And the sounds of monkeys chattering filtered their way up to them.

Maggie hesitated at the entryway to take it all in. The two silently crossed the lab, taking in the monkey-filled cages lining the wall and the steel lab tables topped with equipment that had not been there two weeks earlier.

Maggie stopped and put her hands to her face in disbelief. Two women dressed head to toe in full bio-hazard gear actively performing lab experiments behind the heavy glass wall.

A shiver shot up Maggie's arms as goosebumps broke out all over. She licked her dry lips and quietly turned and exited.

"Maggie?" Benny called her name, following her.

Maggie turned, tears stinging her eyes. She was barely able to talk above a whisper. "Don't, Benny. Please don't say anything. They know we've been here because of the facial recognition scanner, but we'll act as if nothing is wrong because there isn't. They have a permit. We'll never speak of this again. I mean, it's obvious. Kerrington lied to us about closing the lab—but that's a discussion for later when he gets back from New York."

"Don't get me caught in between the two of you," Benny warned sternly. "I don't belong in marital discussions—especially of this nature. It could turn ugly. Uh-uh. Count me out."

MAGGIE SAT FOR HOURS, dwelling on her betrayal. Kerrington had taken her and Benny to the lab to prove to her it was closed. Then he moved it back. **What a liar!** She didn't know what to do, but one thing was sure: there would be no baby with this building on the land. Birth control pills would be started first thing tomorrow as soon as she got the refill in her hands.

And as for forgiveness—she was wandering in a whirlpool of doubts. The new evidence launched a small war inside of her—uncontrollable emotions attacked Maggie's sense of well-being. Profound sadness. Heartbreak. A yearning to return to her love with Kerrington before she had invaded his privacy. The lab and her uncontrollable curiosity had been her undoing. *How can a man love you and lie to you?* Maggie was filled with rage towards herself for destroying her relationship with Kerrington—something so precious to her. She wondered if they could they ever recover?

THE NEXT DAY MAGGIE WENT TO her house to retrieve her ordered books. She sat alone for hours studying the complex genetic information buried within the pages of the textbooks. Maggie left, feeling like she understood a lot, but the more she studied, the more she realized how much more she had to learn.

Kerrington was home when Maggie got home. Her stomach swirled with nausea, wondering how their encounter would go. There had to be a confrontation. There was no way out of it.

Ronald met her at the door and steered her to the library, where Kerrington sat in a wing chair.

Benny was beside him; all worked up.

Two FBI agents stood at attention; hands folded intensely in front of them. Maggie wanted to run and get as far away from the meeting as she could. This was undoubtedly an official response to Maggie and Benny entering the lab, which they had been clearly warned not to do. What she was caught up in was more than marital discord. She'd violated government laws, which she hadn't thought about after seeing the bright flashing lights. All she'd cared about at that moment was investigating the source of the light. She hadn't informed Lamar. She'd simply done her thing. Maggie felt a wave of shame run through her; certain her face was bright red with embarrassment.

"It is a problem, sir," the taller agent said.

"You bet it's a problem," Kerrington replied. "I did not give permission to re-activate the lab on my property. They had no right! It's my property. I officially indicated we would move the lab to another facility, which I found. And the lab was moved. What the hell is going on? I demand an answer." Maggie watched Kerrington with new eyes. She'd never seen him so livid.

"The government didn't agree with you, sir. According to the Congressman who sits on the committee, the new site you chose doesn't meet security standards—or privacy that we enjoy here—and you are bound by the contract. We restored operations back to how they were."

"We'll see about that," Kerrington replied. "You're dismissed. I'll take things from here."

"We have more business, sir—that of your wife and Mr. Maxwell."

"I said… you are dismissed. I will deal with the Congressman and the CDC—and with my wife and Mr. Maxwell." Kerrington stood, placed papers in a purple folder, and handed them to Lamar. "We'll complete your required paperwork as requested. Good day, sirs."

Ronald escorted the FBI and Lamar to the door to complete the discussions regarding the mandated forms completion. Maggie collapsed into a wing chair and didn't speak as Kerrington resumed his seat in the chair. Silence owned the room, and Maggie knew it was deliberate on Kerrington's part. He'd once spoken about how his silence commanded a room to give him a chance to think. It was obvious he'd been caught by surprise by the FBI.

"Benny, you can leave."

"Leave the property, sir? Like, move?" Benny replied, his face filled with a painful shock.

"Heavens no. I can tell by the look on your face you have clearly learned a lesson here. Don't repeat it. And don't talk about it."

"Thank you, Kerrington. I won't. I promise."

Benny promptly left the room, closing the door behind himself.

Maggie festered in misery, wondering what was to come. "I'm sorry, Kerrington. I violated your trust." Her speech rambled on, fast and unplanned. "I saw the bright lights late at night and went to see what it was."

"That was your first mistake, Maggie. That's why we have security."

"They didn't respond," Maggie replied.

"Then, you call Lamar! What if it had been something dangerous, like burglars? I don't ever want you to take risks like that again. You know what is below the ground."

"I do. Speaking of which, you said you moved the lab—and I trusted you."

Kerrington leaped from his chair, his face painted with fury as he walked to the window and looked out. Maggie thought she saw a look of uncertainty cross his face. "I did move the lab, Maggie. Did you not hear the conversation? Did you not see the lab empty?" Kerrington was outraged, to say the least.

"I did."

"I've been betrayed. That's noticeably clear." Kerrington said softly, pain evident in his voice. Maggie's heart sank. Here it came. He was talking about her. She knew at that moment she didn't want it to end. She treasured their marriage and their life together. She knew she would never get over it if he divorced her. His rejection would tear her to pieces. "I understand," she whispered.

"No, you don't, Maggie." Kerrington turned to face her. "I've been wanting the lab off my property since I inherited it, but I was too young and inexperienced to tackle it. Annella doesn't even know, and I feel like I have deceived her too. I knew this day would come. I knew it."

Kerrington walked over to Maggie and lifted her from the chair, placing his hands on her face in an intimate gesture to make peace. "I'm glad you went back to the lab. Otherwise, I wouldn't have known they'd moved it back here. I thought it was gone, and I was so relieved."

"So, you love me?" Maggie asked, her eyes searching his.

"Of course I do." Kerrington kissed her sweetly before pulling away. "We have a genuine problem, Maggie. I still have possession of the samples from Ukraine, so that's not what they are working on. Don't go back down there again until we know. I've lost control of the lab, and the consequences could be disastrous," Kerrington warned. "I've got a big battle on my hands. A battle I have to fight secretly without ruining my name and reputation."

"No wonder you were so upset," Maggie said. "I had no idea."

"Neither did I. Please forgive me, Maggie."

"There's nothing to forgive, Kerrington. You haven't done anything wrong."

Maggie's heart sang as they held each other. Their magic was back. She would help him in any way she could. They would fight this together. That would be their future. Their love was strong. Healed. The battle facing them, however, would test them in a mighty way.

THE END

Dedication

This book is dedicated to all the survivors or those who died as a victim of Domestic Violence.

If you or a loved one suffer from domestic violence call **1-800-799-SAFE**. The hotline is available 24 hours a day

Warning signs of abuse:

- Telling you that you never do anything right.
- Showing extreme jealousy of your friends or time spent away from them.
- Preventing or discouraging you from spending time with others, particularly friends, family members, or peers.
- Insulting, demeaning, or shaming you, especially in front of other people.
- Preventing you from making your own decisions, including about working or attending school.
- Controlling finances in the household without discussion, such as taking your money or refusing to provide money for necessary expenses.
- Pressuring you to have sex or perform sexual acts you're not comfortable with. Pressuring you to use drugs or alcohol.
- Intimidating you through threatening looks or actions.
- Insulting your parenting or threatening to harm or take away your children or pets. Intimidating you with weapons like guns, knives, bats, or mace.
- Destroying your belongings or your home.

About the Author

Marilyn Benner Sowyak is the author of *Crematorium*, a psychological thriller. *Locked Inside* is her second book. Her storytelling has delighted readers, who have left wonderful reviews regarding her work.

Benner's storytelling ability is derived from her lengthy career as one of the entertainment industry's most in-demand medical advisors. Her credits span twenty-five years and include Emmy winners: *As the World Turns, One Life to Live, Guiding Light,* and *Another World.* Benner was the Medical Technical Advisor for *Law & Order* and the Medical Coordinator for over twenty major feature films, including *Godfather III, The Fisher King, Bonfire of the Vanities, and Home Alone – Lost In New York.*

During her time spent in the entertainment industry, Benner was also hired from time-to-time to serve as a Handler. *"That, was a complicated job."*

Marilyn Benner Sowyak is a Registered Nurse who has worked in the Emergency Departments of New York City's Bellevue Hospital, Mount Sinai Medical Center, New York Hospital Cornell, Saint Vincent's Hospital, Orlando Regional Medical Center, and Carolinas Medical Center Main in Charlotte, North Carolina.

Many of her stories come from events she witnessed as a nurse.

From the Author

Annella's story came from a true story I witnessed long ago. Some of the facts were altered slightly to make the story work within the time frame. It's not unusual for patients to present to the hospital due to poisoning. At times, family members or friends will attempt to continue poisoning the patient while they are still in the hospital. In today's times, we are faster at recognizing that poisoning is taking place. The patient did survive because we caught the person delivering the poison on the night shift.

The storyline of the hospital robbery is also a true story fictionalized for the purpose of storytelling.

It was quite hard for me to write Willow's story and be true to the story. I originally constructed her story be a happy ever after one but when I got to the final scene, I knew I couldn't cheat the story. I had to treat it with the truth and respect it deserved. As a nurse, I have lost so many women due to domestic violence and some of their stories will haunt me forever. I couldn't do wrong by them by not telling their side. I had to be their voice.

Acknowledgements

Thank you to Kenny Maxwell who allowed me to use his image as a muse for the character Benny Maxwell. I worked with Kenny in the E.R. and when I needed a medical character to carry the story forward – he was perfect. So perfect, he became a central character. Thank you, Kenny, my friend forever.

Thank you also to my husband, Michael Sowyak, who has been my mentor. He's been so generous with his time, and he edits what I write. Thank you for keeping me on the straight path. Here's a big shout out for my daughter Sunday Richardson who say, "I want to be in your book. Make me a doctor." So, I did. She also was the perfect muse for Annella's story. Thank you also to her husband Jason, my grandchildren Anna, Ella, and Wryn, and my brothers and sisters, Sidney, Pam, Sheri, Greg, and Kathy, who cheered me forward and patiently listened as I talked about my book.

I also owe a debt of gratitude to Brandon Pope, who gave me the idea for using drones in my book. He served as a resource for the character Landon Sykes. Thank you, Brandon, for inspiring me and helping me make the drones an interesting event. Brandon owns BPope Productions in Hickory, N.C.

Beta readers are the spine that holds up my book. My deep thanks go out to Maggie Jackson and Tony Jackson for their in-depth editing and advice. Thank you, Tony, for allowing me to use your name as a character. Also, I'm sending a shout-out to other beta readers Anna Richardson, Pam Morris, and Kenny Maxwell.

And finally, I would never have authored a book had it not been for Gwen Hunter, an author who inspired me - no, made me – write my first chapter of Crematorium. At the time, I only knew scriptwriting and did not believe I had the talent to write a book. Thank you, Gwen, for believing in me and pushing me forward.

I also thank the following authors for enjoying the passion of writing together. Craig Farris, Faith Hunter, David Pearson, and Paul McDonald, who have supported my passion.

Ingram Content Group UK Ltd.
Milton Keynes UK
UKHW010633200723
425492UK00004B/359